LALINE PAULL was [...]
English at Oxford, s[...]
married with childre[...]

@LalinePaull
www.lalinepaull.com

Praise for *The Ice*:

'No other recent novel I've read has such fully realised female characters, even ones who shout their feminist credentials from the rooftops ... Its sparkling descriptions of ice and snow will certainly chill you out on a hot day at the beach. And thanks to just the right amount of aspirational scene-setting and more holiday porn than a year's worth of *Condé Nast Traveller*, this memorable eco-chiller allows you to dream about luxury wood cabins while cursing the evils of capitalism'   *The Times*

'A gripping, brilliantly textured climate thriller. Its timeliness is chilling. A stunning read'   LIZ JENSEN, author of *The Rapture*

'Convincingly researched, Paull's thriller pushes her colourful characters into extremis, and as her anti-hero discovers, facing the truth hurts. *The Ice* is a rallying cry that we still have time; that we can and must protect the Arctic – all wrapped up in a deceptively entertaining read'   JOHN SAUVEN, director of Greenpeace, *Ecologist Magazine*

'It is a rare treat to find oneself reading a new book with real delight, admiring the prose style and getting caught up in the story. I experienced all of this while reading this fascinating novel set in the near future ... what makes *The Ice* unforgettable is Laline Paull's well-informed description of the setting and, above all, her outstandingly good writing'   *Literary Review*

'A chilling tale for our times ... Fascinating. The chilly environment adds a strange, magical quality – and it will not be lost on readers that, a[...] [...]ing and urgent argum[...]   *The National*

Praise for *The Bees*:

'[A] gripping Cinderella/Arthurian tale with lush Keatsian adjectives'
                                                        MARGARET ATWOOD

'Beautifully written and unusual … a brave and original story that highlights our modern environmental crimes'
                                                        LUCY ATKINS, *Sunday Times*

'Ambitious and bold … told with such rapturously attentive imagination … few novels create such a singular reading experience. The buzz you will hear surrounding this book and its astonishing author is utterly deserved'
                                                        New York Times

'One wild ride. A sensual, visceral mini-epic about timeless rituals and modern environmental disaster. Paull's heart-pounding novel wrenches us into a new world'
                                                        EMMA DONOGHUE

'A rich, strange book, utterly convincing in its portrayal of the mindset of a bee and a hive. I finished it feeling I knew exactly how bees think and live. This is what sets us humans apart from other animals, that our imagination can allow us to create a complete, believable world so different from our own'
                                                        TRACY CHEVALIER

'An astonishing achievement'
                                                        MARTIN CRUZ SMITH

'An extraordinary feat of imagination, conjuring the life of a beehive in gripping, passionate and brilliant detail'
                                                        MADELINE MILLER, author of *The Song of Achilles*

'[An] unusual and cunningly imagined thriller … thought-provoking'
                                                        ANGUS CLARKE, *The Times*

'Violent and full of terror, but there are moments of luscious beauty, too'
                                                        Telegraph

'There's sex, violence, war, catastrophe, terror, secrets and suspense. A clever and imaginative work'
                                                        Independent on Sunday

LALINE PAULL

THE
ICE

4th ESTATE • London

4th Estate
An imprint of HarperCollins*Publishers*
1 London Bridge Street
London SE1 9GF
www.4thEstate.co.uk

First published in Great Britain in 2017 by 4th Estate
This 4th Estate paperback edition published in 2018

1

A catalogue record for this book is available from the British Library

ISBN 978-0-00-755777-6

With grateful thanks to the following for their permission to reproduce copyright material:
Extracts from *Arctic Adventure* by Peter Freuchen by permission of Echo Point Books.
Extracts from *Farthest North* by Fridtjof Nansen by permission of Skyhorse Publishing, Inc.
Extracts from *Lost in the Arctic* by Ejnar Mikkelsen, published by William Heinemann. Reprinted by
permission of The Random House Group Ltd. © Ejnar Mikkelsen 1913. Extract from *Polar Bears* by
Nikita Ovsyanikov by permission of Quarto Publishing Group. Quote from Judge Rüdiger Wolfrum
courtesy of the International Tribunal for the Law of the Sea. Extract from 'Century of the Wind' from
The Wayfinders: Why Ancient Wisdom Matters in the Modern World, copyright © 2009 by Wade Davis
and the Canadian Broadcasting Corporation. Reprinted by permission of House of Anansi Press,
Toronto, www.houseofanansi.com, and the University of Western Australia Press. Extract from *Northern Lights;
The Official Account Of The British Arctic Air-Route Expedition* by F. Spencer Chapman, published by
Chatto & Windus. Reprinted by permission of The Random House Group Limited.

While every effort has been made to trace the owners of copyright material reproduced herein,
the publishers would like to apologise for any omissions and would be pleased to incorporate
missing acknowledgements in future editions.

Printed and bound in Great Britain by
CPI Group (UK) Ltd, Croydon CR0 4YY

MIX
Paper from
responsible sources
FSC
www.fsc.org   FSC® C007454

This book is produced from independently certified FSC paper
to ensure responsible forest management

For more information visit: www.harpercollins.co.uk/green

For my brothers
Geoff and Gordon
with love

Among dogs are found characters almost as various as among men. Some dogs do not give a damn what they eat; some will eat their own mothers, as I have often witnessed, and others will starve to death before touching the bodies of their team-mates. Again, some refuse to eat the meat while it is still warm, but perhaps after it is cold they forget what it is and devour it greedily.

Arctic Adventure: My Life in the Frozen North (1936)
Peter Freuchen

1

They were rich, they were ready, they were ravenous for bear. Nine days into their fourteen-day voyage on the *Vanir*, the most expensive cruise ship in the Arctic, the passengers' initial excitement had turned to patience, then frustration, and now, a creeping sense of defeat. As sophisticated travellers they knew money didn't guarantee polar bear sightings – but they still believed in the natural law that wealth meant entitlement. *Ursus maritimus* sightings very much included.

'Realm of the Ice King' stated the brochure, featuring competition-winning photographs of sparkling ice and polar bears with cubs and kills, taken by recent passengers on this very route. But now instead of high blue heavens, the skies were overcast. Instead of a crisp and exhilarating minus three or even ten degrees (they were eager to test their new clothing), they suffered a vile gusty swelter that turned the Arctic dank as an English summer, and for which no combination of clothing was right. Plus the endless daylight was oppressive – medication schedules went awry and watches became meaningless.

There were several lawyers among the passengers. They invited the tour leader to the bar to look at the brochure and hear their formal complaint. The voyage was misrepresented. They had been mis-sold. Enough with the beach landings to stare at derelict huts and piles of whaling junk. Enough birds too, that didn't fob them off. What they'd all paid for were sightings of live ice-obligate mammals. That was the primary focus of the text and image of the brochure, a sales document with a legal duty to accuracy. No icebergs either, just some dirty glaciers. They were considering a class action for compensation.

The passengers repaired to the salon and put on the compilation film that had become their envious obsession. With the blinds down to keep out the bullying daylight, they stared avidly at the on-screen polar bears; the one standing on a crimson mat of ice ripping flesh from a red rack of seal carcass, then the mother and her yearling swimming between the floes. Best of all was the large male standing on his hind legs, staring into the camera, his muzzle bright red. *That* was what they wanted.

The tour leader ran to the bridge to confer with the captain and the ice-pilot, who by law they were still required to employ, even though the summer sea ice was two years gone. They stared out at the grey chop of the Barents Sea. All knew, though they would not say for fear of their jobs, that the animals had all but vanished and the footage in the salon was several years old. There was one solution, prohibited, but every tour company knew it as a last resort. Send up a drone and find a bear.

Two miles away around the coast, down a deep M-shaped fjord, a large silvery wood cabin blended with the dark cobble of its beach. Modern extensions at its rear and sides were made of the very rock of the mountain that rose up behind it, and a close look would reveal several windows that reflected sea, sky and rock. But no one did look, in that intrusive unwelcome way, because this was Midgard Lodge in Midgardfjorden, and by direct intervention of Oslo, to the Sysselmann's office in Svalbard, special rules applied.

Most outraging to those who knew of it, was the one which flouted a major conservation regulation and allowed Midgard Lodge helicopter flights between Longyearbyen airport and the tiny beach in front of the Lodge, which was just large enough to land a twelve-person Dauphin.

The second was that no cruise ship penetrate the Wijdefjorden system past a certain point, thereby closing the spectacular rock stratification of Midgardfjord and its peculiar forked glacier Midgardbreen, one side blue, one white, off to tourism.

The third, which caused the autocratic Sysselmann the most disquiet, was that these diktats were verified at the highest level but relayed verbally, via a female assistant defence minister. She refused to confirm them in writing and though the Sysselmann had not heard of her, she was rather too well informed about him. He duly made sure Mrs Larssen's requests were observed, and in consequence, Midgard Lodge was not.

Except for today, when general manager Danny Long, on duty in the cabin office looking down the fjord, felt his instinct tweak him to take another look at the AIS radar screen. He had just checked it at mid-scale, taking in the little coloured arrowheads that showed, variously, pink and purple for fishing and sailing vessels, green for cargo, and god forbid, red for tankers coming in too close. He looked at the screen more closely. Something was off.

He clicked on the green arrows and saw what he expected – Asian cargo ships on the new TransPolar route. He clicked a couple at random: the *Hao Puren*: Rotterdam to Shanghai. The *Zheng He*, going the other way, Dalian to Algiers. A couple of others – everything moving smoothly.

Then he studied the dotted blue arrows of the cruise ships. Now the ice-free and liquid North Pole was just another bit of sea and offered no photo opportunities, Svalbard's stunning coastline was clogged in the summer. All captains tried to stagger their route to minimise bottlenecks, but because of the rarity of animal sightings, the tour operators had an agreement to share the information with each other on Channel 16 – despite this leading to what amounted to a cruise ship race to be second at the kill. The coastguard policed what it could, and was glad of Midgard Lodge's ability to offer search and rescue – but both knew that would be a last resort.

There: he saw it. The tiny blue cursor which had crossed into Midgard's unofficially restricted area. He clicked. Passenger cruise ship *Vanir*, he knew it. High staff-to-passenger ratio, regular circuit – except today. Probably after a bear. There was a huge male passing through, he'd seen it standing in silhouette on the fjord's bone.

He would report the ship's transgression later, but for now the protocol was to ensure front-of-house was neat and clean, everything quiet. Keeping an eye on the *Vanir*'s position, he hit a speed-dial on the iridium phone never far from his hand. A moment later, the phone flashed back at him. Message received, they would stay out until further notice. Then Long called down to reception and was pleased to hear everything was in hand. He returned to the screen, watching the little blue cursor slowly blinking around the headland, coming closer.

When the bear was young and the snow fell clean and white, his fur showed creamy, even pale yellow at times. Now the snow had a greyish tinge, causing him to shine even brighter against it. He had grown long yellow guard hairs on his massive forelegs, increasing his appearance of power, and when the sun shone through them it gave him a gold aura. He was following the scented track of a female in oestrus who had passed by, but paused to watch the ship heaving into the narrow mouth of the fjord, its engine thundering the water, its fuel stinking the air.

The deck was crowded with people, bare-skinned faces with shiny black insect eyes turned towards him. Their human body smells mingled with the smell of food from the ship, and metal, and fuel. The engine sound died down and the vibrations slowed then stopped. The voices faded.

The black walls of the fjord held the Arctic silence, until the bear lifted his white anvil of a head, black nostrils flaring for more information. His every move drew clicks and whirrs from the ship, becoming a frenzy as a curl of wind tickled him with a clue, and he lay down and rolled in the female's trail.

On the bridge with the captain, the tour leader looked down at the entranced passengers, and relaxed. The bear was massive by any standards and on the most photogenic blue side of the Midgardbreen glacier, where the ice terminus formed a cliff above the water. On the other side of the black bone of rock, the glacier was younger white ice and debouched in a relatively gentle slope down to the cobbled beach. With a start, the tour operator noticed the silver-grey wood cabin, extending back into the mountain.

'Is this the British guy's place? I heard it'd been sold – what goes on here?' Neither the Norwegian captain nor ice-pilot replied. They had crossed a line to find her passengers their bear. Svalbard had many enigmatic structures. No comment.

*

4

Crowded at the rail, excited as schoolchildren and all thoughts of class actions gone from their minds, the passengers of the *Vanir* were busy changing lenses and exclaiming in wonder. The bear was as huge and charismatic a celebrity as they could dream of, they guessed him at eleven or twelve feet, nearly a ton, maybe more. Through powerful telephoto lenses they saw his duelling scars, and the way he stood up on his hind legs, the edge of his pelt shining gold around him. He stared straight back with knowing black eyes, and they felt a euphoric jolt of fear. He could kill them.

Without warning the white god dropped to all fours and changed into a frightened animal, running for the edge of the glacier. In consternation the passengers watched him stagger and clamber into the shadows, where he vanished. They groaned in disappointment, they scanned around for what had scared their bear, but though their hi-mag lenses probed the darkness of the lower crags and pored across the bright rock striations, nothing moved. They stared at the layers of colour and tried to appreciate the earth's history laid bare. But they felt angry and tiny.

Someone shouted out: there! that puff of snow higher up the glacier – surely too far and they had not seen him run – but they focused in hope. They gasped in wonder as a hundred hidden chimneys below the surface puffed out more sparkling ice-smoke. The air clenched and the sea sighed. The *Vanir* lifted as a great pressure wave passed through the water.

And then it started. First a distant boom, a detonation deep inside the glacier. Nothing, for a few long seconds, then a huge tearing, cracking sound that shook the air, before time stretched and the blue snout of the glacier, sliding belly down from the ice cap, moaned and pushed out over the water – and then with thunderous bangs like car-crashes it exploded all along its front, hurling shards of ice into the air and seismic bursts into the water so that the reinforced steel hull of the *Vanir* vibrated with the charge.

Wraiths of glittering ice-dust drifted over the sea. The passengers gripped each other as the *Vanir* lifted and fell again, and the shards of ice so small as they splashed, rolled out into the fjord as icebergs tall as the ship.

And then, as they watched, something happened that made no sense at all.

In front of the still-shuddering glacier, an invisible hand pinched a fold of sea like cloth then pulled it high into the air in a fistful of waterfalls. Out of the dazzling torrent emerged a great sapphire castle with turrets and minarets, throwing sparkling foam and mist as it cleared the water for one long stupendous second.

The passengers on the *Vanir* screamed and shouted as their eyes brimmed with wonders – some saw the streak of gold glowing deep within the frozen blue, some the detail of the minarets, some saw gargoyles' faces in the ice – but their voices were lost in the roaring sound as the vision leaned and fell, making a great bowl of the sea in which it twisted and rolled over, completely inverting itself.

All they saw now was a dark blue ice floe the size of an ice-rink, its pinnacles and spires forever hidden. Like a sentient thing, it glided towards the *Vanir*, a peculiar ridge of water pushing the ship aside as if to clear its way. Unearthly and real, the great floe followed the other icebergs out towards the mouth of Midgardfjorden, and the open sea beyond.

The passengers of the *Vanir* had no more words, but one, a woman, was making a convulsive, almost sexual sound. Oh, she kept whispering, still filming everything, the calving ongoing within her. Her lens followed the newborn icebergs, the whirling eddies in the water, and back to the glacier face. She filmed the water slapping and rocking at its base, and the cave of deepening blue ice where the water surged and circled. Something swirled at its centre, making the current waver. Something that had not been there a moment ago.

Without taking her eye from the viewfinder, she reached out a hand for her husband. She pulled him towards her and gave him the camera, still recording. She pointed to the red shape rocking just below the surface.

'My god,' she said softly, 'is that a body?'

There is one place on the coast of which they stood in some dread –
the great glacier of Puisortok. Travelling in early summer in their
umiaks, they necessarily hug the coast, and utilize the narrow leads
that exist between the pack-ice and the glacier. The literal meaning
of the name is "the thing that comes up", as this peculiar glacier
often calves by huge pieces breaking off underwater, which come to
the top and shoot like breaching whales into the air. Instant
destruction is the penalty for misjudgement or mere bad luck.

I remember an old hunter saying: "Do not speak, do not eat, until
Puisortok is passed."

Northern Lights: The Official Account of the British Arctic Air-Route
    Expedition 1930–31 (1932)
Frederick Spencer Chapman

2

The calving of the Midgard glacier was a tiny stitch in a larger pattern. While the male corpse it disgorged was already in Tromsø and under autopsy, all around the Arctic Circle scientists were recording calving events of unprecedented magnitude. This apparently synchronised new behaviour of the ice was strongly active for about seventy hours in Greenland, Nunavut Arctic Canada, Alaska and Russia, before stopping as abruptly as it started.

Twenty-seven degrees south in London, the Saharan dust storm that had blown over Europe for the last three days also ceased, leaving a fine red film over the whole city and adding respiratory patients to overcrowded A&E departments and private surgeries alike. Entrepreneurial Londoners sold white paper masks by tube stations and only the reckless still went running.

Age fifty (but looking younger) and mindful of his mental state without hard exercise, Sean Cawson was one of them. Although his knees now protested and his thoughts clawed at him for the first two or three miles, afterwards he felt good, and that was rare. He left Martine sleeping, or pretending to, and slipped out of the apartment. Last night's conversation was only on pause. He would have to deal with it before long.

He jogged past the neighbour's door, smelling coffee and hearing their new baby crying. His daughter Rosie was almost grown up, and hated him. At the beginning, Martine had said she wasn't interested in

9

family life, and he'd been relieved: one conspicuous failure was enough. Now she'd changed her mind, and he felt betrayed.

He pulled the heavy black door shut and stood for a moment on the empty street while he chose his running music. It was early but muggy, the sky was grey and no birds flew. The white porch pillars of the houses were shaded with the ochre Saharan dust, which also gave an autumnal cast to the plane trees of the communal garden. As he chose a random mix and set off to the park, London looked and felt wrong.

The music matched it – harsh declamatory rap in African-inflected French that fitted the dislocated feel of the city. His feet caught the hard pounding rhythm and as he entered the park by the Kensington Palace gate he felt the spasms in his knees but ignored the pain. He was good at that. As if in reward, there ahead of him was one of his favourite sights, one of the privileges of early risers in certain parts of London: a troupe of army horses being exercised. Sometimes he'd pause to watch them cantering on the sand track that ran alongside Park Lane, a powerful river of satiny chestnut and bay muscle. The heavy rhythmic vibration of their hooves into the earth had risen through his feet into his body and connected him to some elusive feeling he could not name.

It was a crazy thought and the horses would easily outstrip him, but he wanted to run alongside them. He pushed himself harder. He could smell the fragrance of the animals as he cut across the grass, a wolf heading them off as they turned on the sand track for their canter – he would sprint and burn himself out until they left him behind—

His phone buzzed from his arm holster. There were only two people he set to bypass his Do Not Disturb – Rosie, who never called, and the other whose name now flashed on the screen, his mentor Joe Kingsmith.

'Joe!' he panted. 'I'll call you back.' The riders were gathering up their horses, the animals were stamping, knowing what was coming.

'Don't, Sean, stay: it's an emergency.'

Sean stopped short.

'I'm here.'

'Are you home?'

'I'm in the park – what's happened?'

'Sean boy, I'd have called you at home but no one has a landline any more. I want someone there with you.'

Sean stood still. 'Tell me.'

There was a silence, and by its quality, Sean guessed Kingsmith was airborne. He tried to slow his breathing. The kind tone frightened him.

'Sean, I am so, so sorry. I've just spoken with Danny at Midgard. Tom's body washed out of the Midgard glacier two days ago—'

'Tom's body?' Sean heard the words clearly, but his mind rejected them.

'They had the positive ID this morning. It's definitely him. I'm so sorry, Sean. I wanted to be the one to tell you.'

The park vanished. Sean's world contracted to Kingsmith's voice. 'Out of the glacier?' He felt stupid and slow.

'Shit. I knew I shouldn't have told you on the phone, but how else? I don't know that much. There was this huge calving almost in front of Midgard Lodge – that's when his body came out. Some cruise ship was down there and saw it all. Danny got sent away by the coastguard when he went to look, they were holding it as a crime scene—'

'A crime scene?' Sean came back into his body. 'There was no *crime*, everyone knows that!' He was shouting but he couldn't do anything about it.

'Sean boy, I'm trying to tell you, will you please listen? They call it that for protocol when they want to record everything. Of course there was no crime. Now I know you haven't been up there for a while, but Midgard is still a business and this could have a PR effect, so we need to handle it right.'

'They're sure it's Tom?'

'One hundred per cent. They had a good idea it could be and they matched DNA with a family member, apparently.'

'No one told me. No one's rung. They've known for two days?'

'I guess you haven't been in touch so much lately. We knew he was dead but ... this is still a big shock.'

Sean walked away from the people coming towards him, out onto the great grassy plain of the park, the horses forgotten. He sank to his knees on the dry ground.

He felt the fingers in his right hand start to burn, as if they still had frostbite. He stuffed them into his left armpit and felt his chest trembling.

'Danny should have called me.'

'I wanted to be the one. I only know because I had to call him about something.'

'What thing?'

'Look: I completely get why you haven't been up there. But you've got a lot of catching up to do, and now isn't the right time. I'm glad you're interested again, but you've got an awesome team taking care of things so don't even worry.'

'I should be helping bring him back, I should be there.'

'You can't do anything: it's all in progress. You weren't next of kin, but I guess they'll be in touch with you, they'll be able to have a funeral at last. And an inquest, but that's separate.'

'An *inquest*?' The word was so ugly. 'But we know what happened, I've said it all, we've been through it.'

'I know, but it's what happens when someone's brought home. Same in the States as in the UK – just a formality. I'll be there to support you, I promise … Sean, can you hear me?'

'Yes.' The grey sky pulsed above him.

'You get yourself home, get back to Martine. She's got a good head on her shoulders, she'll know what to do. Sean, say something.'

'What were you talking to Danny about?'

He heard Kingsmith's bark of a laugh.

'Boy, are you persistent! But I've always liked that. OK, mea culpa, I put in a retreat, very small and last minute, a favour for a pal. I saw a void in the schedule and he's paying top dollar. But this is hardly the time—'

'I'm still the CEO. Everything goes through me.'

'And if you are thinking like that at a time like this, you are the right man for the job. Point taken. Sean? You're breaking up but I hope you can still hear me: you need to speak to your friend in Oslo, about keeping traffic away from Midgard – it's important—'

The phone connection dropped out – Kingsmith's signature goodbye. Sean stood alone on the dusty red plain of Hyde Park, barely able to breathe.

He started to run.

*

Martine was in the wet-room shower when he came in, sweat-soaked like it was raining. Still in his clothes, he walked into the torrent and held her. She smiled, her eyes closed – and then she looked and saw his stricken face.

'Oh my god, what's happened?'

Sean hit his forehead against the streaming wall. 'They've found Tom.'

'Stop! Come here.' She held him to her, keeping them under the streaming hot water, undressing him until he was naked. She kicked the clothes away from the drain and held him until he stopped shaking, then she turned off the water and helped him out and into a robe. As she put on her own, he went into the kitchen. She followed, watching while he took a bottle of vodka from the freezer and poured a big slug into a tumbler.

'Don't,' she said. 'Handle it without that. You don't need it.'

He knocked it back. Then he told her, in the barest detail, about Kingsmith's call, and the facts he knew, including the fact of the inquest. Martine nodded slowly.

'I'm so sorry, my darling. But Joe's absolutely right: this is closure at last, and if there's an inquest we'll get through it. I need to plan how we handle it. First thing is I'll work on a statement on your behalf, and then we've got a bit of time.'

Sean listened to her as she walked around their dressing room preparing for work, thinking aloud. Joe was right, she had a good head on her well-set shoulders, working out which journalists could be trusted, how she would cancel certain invitations so they were not seen out enjoying themselves for a while …

He wished she had burst into tears. He wished she cared more about Tom, and less about damage control. Her voice went on as he stared at the rails of his clothes. Abruptly she was beside him.

'I'm staying with you.'

'No,' he said, getting up. 'Go to work. I'll be OK.' He pulled open a deep drawer and took out his Arctic travelling clothes, alien with lack of use. 'I'm going to Midgard.'

Martine held his arm. 'That's crazy. You're in shock. Look at yourself.'

He did. The mirror showed him a beautiful young woman standing there half-dressed, her dark hair wet, beside an older man

13

who stared back at him, eyes haunted and dangerous. Sean turned away.

'Joe put in a retreat. Without telling me.'

Martine frowned. 'Really? He shouldn't do that.'

'It's because I haven't been there. I've dumped everything on the team.'

'No. You've delegated. You can't personally run every single one of your clubs, you pick right then you trust people.'

Sean threw some clothes into the bag and zipped it. 'I'm letting everyone down.'

Martine tried again, embracing him and pressing herself into him from behind.

'You're not! Forget about last night, forget all that. Just come back to bed and let me look after you.' She ran her hand down his chest and closed it over him. 'Be sad in my arms. I won't go in today.'

'No, go. I'll be OK.' He kissed her, to deflect the rejection. She stared at him in the mirror as he went out into the bedroom and found his car key. She followed.

'You can't drive, you've just had a huge vodka. And if you're on the afternoon flight you've got plenty of time – where are you going?'

Sean looked out into the square garden.

'It's bad to hear it on the phone.'

'Oh.' She moved away. 'I see.'

'Martine, please, you know how fragile she is.'

'Actually no, I don't think she is, not at all.'

'She loved Tom as well.'

'Fine. But I think she was prepared to pull any stunt to try to stop you leaving. I think she's manipulative and angry and she's turned your own daughter against you, and *me*, and it's totally a mistake to keep being sentimental about a marriage that was over long before I came along.' She sighed. 'I'm sorry. That sounded harsh. I just want to protect you from more pain at a time like this. You shouldn't go.'

'You're right.'

'Yes, I am. But if you don't want me to stay with you today, or to come with you to Midgard, if you want to just be alone with the bad feelings—'

'Yes! I'm a fucking mess, I told you I was a bad deal—'

'I never make bad deals.' Martine pulled back and looked in his eyes. 'But if you want healthy boundaries you'll have them, and if you want to put yourself through the wringer, you'll do that too.' She kissed him on the lips. 'So I really care that you're so sad, but as you won't let me help you, I am going to work. Let me know when you're back. I'll be here.'

He listened to her light step down the outer hall, then the click of the front door. He went back to the freezer, but stopped. Martine was right, of course. He was in no condition to drive.

The easiest way to learn, of course, was to inquire of an angakoq (wizard), and in the course of my long conversations with Igjugarjuk I learned many interesting things. His theories, however, were so simple and straightforward that they sound strikingly modern; his whole view of life may be summed up in his own words as follows:

'All true wisdom is only to be learned far from the dwellings of men, out in the great solitudes; and is only to be attained through suffering. Privation and suffering are the only things that can open the mind of man to those things which are hidden from others.'

Across Arctic America: Narrative of the Fifth Thule Expedition (1927)
Knud Rasmussen

3

Sean once knew the sequence of lights so well that he never got caught on red. Now the route had become as alien as his old home and he misjudged every stretch. To keep his mind away from thoughts of Tom, he focused on driving impeccably and not as if he had gulped three fingers of vodka in the last hour – but the morning rush-hour traffic was infuriatingly slow and he suddenly felt self-conscious in his car.

It was a beautiful Aston Martin Vanquish in a custom missile-bronze colour, and part of its appeal three years ago – the longest he had ever kept a car – were the looks he caught as he flashed past other drivers. But today, passing slowly made him uncomfortable. Perhaps he should change it for a Tesla to show what a good, upright, ecologically concerned citizen he was, as well as a flash bastard.

Perhaps the lights were stuck. The white van alongside him made little feints forward, and he glanced over. Two schoolboys in green uniforms clambered over each other like puppies, waving at him and pointing in admiration of his car. They tugged at their driver dad, a tough-looking young man with a shaven head, who stared straight ahead.

Red-and-amber – the white van surged ahead the very instant the lights changed to green, and Sean saw the boys cheering and goading their father faster.

He drew alongside then fell back a couple of times, pulling faces as if he were striving and failing to overtake, so that the boys screeched with joy and bounced up and down on the bench seat. As he saw the filter lane for his exit, Sean pretended he was giving up, and the boys pumped their fists in triumph as he let the white van surge past him. The tough young dad flashed him a grin and he felt a wave of good feeling. Then he indicated, tipped the wheel and the feeling frayed like a thread as he wound back on the roads of his old life.

He drove slowly for the last few miles, surprised to see it had rained heavily. There was no sign of the red dust of London and the fields were green. The track to the house was badly potholed and he felt irritated – it wasn't as if Gail couldn't afford to get it graded. The thought of the settlement still pricked him. He would have been generous had she let him, instead of taking out her anger against Martine in financial terms. He had not thought her capable of being so petty. But put that aside: he was here to deliver a terrible blow.

Gail, I've got some bad news. Gail—

Something on the track ground against the undercarriage and he cursed and slowed down. He would go out the other way. The grading of the lane was not his business and this would be the last time he would come here, so it didn't matter. But still, his eye ran over the orchards in some dismay. The fruit was retarded and the leaves too heavy. All the rain without the sun.

Instead of the old blue Saab in the garage, there was a new silver BMW four-wheel drive. Only now did he consider the possibility that Gail might not have been home, or not been alone. He pulled up, blocking the garage, the way that always made them look out. And there she was, coming to the kitchen window. To his surprise, she waved. He walked down the path, hoping she had not got the wrong idea. No flowers, no bottle, a bad time of day to visit. He brought bad tidings of great pain. *Gail, I've got some bad news …*

She opened the door before he knocked. One year younger than Sean, the glaze of youth had cracked into a filigree of lines around her eyes. Her face was softening and dropping and she wore her clothes sexlessly loose. But she was still wearing perfume.

'Sean, I'm so sorry,' she said. 'Are you OK?'

'You know?' He stared at his ex-wife. 'How? I only just found out.'

'Ruth called me.' She stood back to let him in. 'Crack of dawn.'

'They told her first?' Sean was assaulted by the smell of home. The old oak floors and stairs, the extortionate beeswax polish. He noticed a bowl of orange roses on the table. 'You cut the Whisky Macs.' They always left them blooming on the path, for visitors to enjoy their scent.

'Saves them from the rain. Someone called her from Svalbard: Tom named her next of kin, apparently. But you already knew that.'

Sean touched a rose and its petals dropped. 'I don't remember every single detail of that time.'

'I do ... But they saw each other, didn't they? That one last time.'

'Yes, but I didn't realise she was officially ... next of kin.'

Sean winced at the idea of Ruth Mott relating her version of that last night. But that was the only way Gail could know, because at the time they were in the final throes of *nisi* to *absolute*, and only their lawyers were speaking. He looked up the stairs. Someone else was in the house, he could feel it.

'Whose silver car is that out there?'

'The colour's called mineral white. And it's mine.'

'You said you wanted to keep the Saab forever.'

'Out with the old. Apparently this new one's attached to a satellite, so I'm tracked from space if I want and even if I don't, unless I sit down online for hours and work out how to switch it off. It's got this inbuilt—'

'I'm glad you've got yourself a good car.'

She'd moved the pictures around. There was a new light on a table. Tom was dead, that was why he'd come. So that Gail could express his grief. She wasn't doing that properly.

'You and Ruth have made up then.'

'I was unfair to her.'

'She shouldn't have meddled.'

'I should have listened.'

Alarmed by the tremble in her voice, he went into the kitchen. A muscle memory prompted him: dump the coat, dump the bag – he looked down at the settle. The newspapers and the big tabby cat that slept there were gone.

'Where's Harold?' He looked around, making the sound that called him.

'He died too. Last year. Tea? Coffee?' Gail filled the kettle, her back to him.

'You didn't tell me.' He couldn't help himself, he looked around. Each thing he recognised was like an accusation. 'Isn't this place too big for you now?'

Gail turned. 'Sean, why did you come? You could have phoned.'

'That's what Martine said.'

'Ah. She's so thoughtful.'

'You don't even seem upset about Tom. Aren't you upset? You could have called—' He stopped. It was obvious she was upset.

'Yes. I'm upset. But I don't call you any more, about anything, unless it's Rosie. I assumed you knew.' She did not cry. 'So, there'll be a funeral, what else? Your knighthood's finally arrived?'

'Not yet, but it will.' He felt bewildered. Gail wasn't like this. She was soft.

'Your services to British business. One in the eye for my father.'

'Here's hoping.' He felt the trembling ghosts of parties and dinners, the familiar plates he'd eaten off, the cupboards that held them. The bunches of herbs hanging up. 'The lane,' he said abruptly. 'It's in a shocking state, do you want me to make a call? You'll never get round to it and it'll just get worse. I don't mind.' He had not meant to say that.

'I know you're a master of the universe and all that—'

'Those are bankers, I've never been a banker—'

'—but in case you hadn't noticed, it's been raining solidly for a month.'

'It hasn't rained a drop in London.'

'I don't care what happens in London! You can't grade a flooded lane, you have to wait for it to drain. It's all organised. But thank you for pointing it out.'

'So you're OK then. Not – clinically depressed.'

'Sorry to tell you, I'm absolutely fine.' She wiped her eyes, her back to him.

'Is that Sean?' His daughter Rosie swerved round the kitchen door in a long T-shirt that said OCCUPY, and her honey brown hair ruined into dreadlocks. Her ears were multiply pierced, and to his dismay, he noticed another tribal tattoo on her upper arm.

'Rosie,' he groaned. 'What have you done to yourself?'

22

'Grown up without you? Why is Mum crying? Sean, why are you even here?' Rosie put her arm around her mother and glared at him.

'I'm fine,' said Gail, 'really. We're just talking.'

'And I don't like you calling me that,' he said. 'I'm still your father.' The way she looked at him broke his heart.

'Uh-uh, you sacked yourself. A father is someone you're supposed to be able to trust, who gives his word and keeps it, who doesn't cheat and lie again and again, when they've promised not to. Mum cries every day you know.'

'Oh for goodness sake, I do not—'

'My god! Why does *everybody lie* the whole time?'

'Some day, Rosie,' he said, 'you might understand that things are not always black and—'

'White,' she finished for him, 'I know. They're in the *grey*, and in the *grey*, Rosie, is where people like me make their money and tell their lies and generally screw up other people's lives. In the grey. I've got it. Sean.'

'She doesn't know,' Gail said quietly.

'Know what? Ugh: you're expecting a little bébé with *her*. Well it's never going to have anything to do with me.'

'No, that's not why I've come, and I didn't know you were here, I thought it was term time. I came to tell your mother that Tom's body has been found. And in person, Rosie, not to be insulted by you but to break it gently to her. Except she already knew.'

Rosie stared at her mother in shock.

'Ruth called me this morning.' Gail put her arm round her daughter. 'I'll tell you all about it.' She looked at Sean over Rosie's shoulder. 'Thank you for coming. I appreciate it.'

He stared at his crying daughter, and his stranger of an ex-wife. He was being dismissed from his own home. Ex-home. But still his child.

'Rosie,' he said gently, 'if you ever wanted to see me—'

'Why would I want to do that?' She didn't look at him.

'Because you're my daughter and I love you.'

'Don't hold your breath.' She ducked out from under her mother's arm and ran upstairs, her face crumpling.

*

The Vanquish blinked an electronic greeting. Sean drove carefully down the rutted, waterlogged private lane, then into the long single-lane road. The numbness was definitely gone, the encounter had left him raw with failure.

A short sharp blast of a horn ahead returned his attention to the narrow road, where a battered red Land Rover pulling a trailer was upon him. A man and a woman in matching jackets – James and Emma Goring. OK, he could do this. He'd only just gone by a passing place so he waved then reversed, shaking himself out of his funk, ready to greet them. The shattered bones of the past, knitting back together. He would tell them what had happened.

James and Emma – he couldn't remember their children's names – but over nearly a decade they had eaten at each other's houses, bought rounds at the Acorn, gone to firework parties, shared New Year – the stuff of life that slowly accretes into friendship. But they did not appear to recognise him. In fact, James raised a casual finger of thanks and was about to drive on, until Sean called out.

James did a double-take, and stopped. 'Sean!' he said. Emma lowered the phone she had been checking, and just that second also officially recognised him too, with a bright smile.

Engines running, they exchanged enthusiastic concerns about the weather and the state of the lanes, and Sean told them about the dust storm, which they'd seen on TV but only got a little of here, weren't they lucky with their microclimate? And then the awkward pause.

Sean knew they wanted to go. He felt angry, he kept them talking, anything, about all the new vineyards, the farm, while he absorbed the fact they hadn't wanted to stop. Pretending they hadn't recognised him. People got divorced, people moved on – he looked pointedly at their trailer, where big sound speakers were covered with a tarp.

'Of course!' he said. 'Your solstice party – here's hoping for sunshine!'

'Oh,' James said quickly, 'very small this year.'

'Big speakers, for a small party.'

'Not really.'

They looked at each other, their smiles fading. They were not going to invite him.

'I came down to tell Gail a dear friend of ours died.' Sean had to look up at them from his lower vehicle. 'We're still friends.'

'Best way,' said James. 'And sorry for your loss.'

'Absolutely,' Emma said. 'So sorry. Take care, Sean.'

James put the Land Rover in gear and the loaded trailer rattled dangerously close to the Aston as they passed, attention fixed on the lane ahead. Then they were gone.

Sean stared after them in the rear-view mirror, his heart pounding like he'd been in a fight. He'd thought of them as friends – he'd brought out his best wine and put up with their tedious company in the hope that they would surely reveal themselves at some point – he presumed it was just that English reserve—

No. They had never been friends; they had always been cold to him. It was Gail they'd liked, he knew they thought she'd married down. The loss of Tom burned through him again: Tom who had been a true friend and a gentleman, always showing the same kindness and self-respect whether he was talking to a tramp or a billionaire. Sean heard Kingsmith's voice in his head, from the old days, when he'd taken a business loss. *Learn, and don't look back*. He checked the time, and told the satnav Heathrow.

There is a power that we call Sila, which is not to be explained in simple words. A great spirit, supporting the world and the weather and all life on earth, a spirit so mighty that his utterance to mankind is not through common words, but by storm and snow and rain and the fury of the sea; all the forces of nature that men fear.

When all is well, Sila sends no message to mankind, but withdraws into his own endless nothingness, apart. So he remains as long as men do not abuse life, but act with reverence towards their daily food.

No one has seen Sila; his place of being is a mystery, in that he is at once among us and unspeakably far away.

Across Arctic America: Narrative of the Fifth Thule Expedition (1927)
Knud Rasmussen

4

Sitting in 1F, crammed against the plastic wall, the smell of his neighbour's duty-free aftershave in his nose, Sean remembered Tom's grim prediction that Svalbard would become the Ibiza of the north. The midnight sun, exotic locale, and public awareness of the fragility of the region had created the strongest driver for tourism the Arctic had ever seen. Now Longyearbyen even had its own club scene, a Mecca for outward-bound hen and stag parties and rich kids bored of skiing.

Sean watched the stewardess and her cart coming closer. The clink of ice made him swallow in anticipation. He must reframe the shock as closure. A stone – a literal heavy headstone, could be laid on Tom's recovered body in its grave, and on the hope he would return.

'Sir, any drinks or snacks?' the stewardess repeated, with an economy-class smile. She passed him his two miniature vodkas, tin of tonic and a plastic cup with a single ice cube and moved on quickly before he could ask for more. He didn't bother with the tonic, just poured in both vodkas and knocked it back. No matter what Kingsmith and Martine said, in his heart he knew this was anything but closure. He'd learned to live with the idea of Tom lost in pristine obscurity – that was how many Arctic heroes ended their story. His reappearance was unscripted, as if the glacier itself had moved against him.

Another shadow fell on his thoughts, provoked by Gail's reference to his still-imminent knighthood. The New Year and Birthday honours had come and gone three times, but there was always a good reason he had to wait – bit of a backlog, wheels within wheels, don't worry—

He guessed why it hadn't yet materialised: there were questions about the accident. All right then, let the inquest lance that boil of suspicion. He'd tell them whatever they wanted to know and as he publicly cleared his name, he would also remind the world that risk and danger were at the very heart of exploration and even to this day the fittest and best-prepared polar adventurers still sometimes died. Surviving was not a crime, nor was making a fine living from Midgard Lodge, where the beloved Tom Harding had died. An aggrieved journalist, turned down for membership at Sean's other clubs, had written about Midgard and called it 'Dirty Davos'. This was not entirely untrue. Sean Cawson's group of membership clubs around the world catered to a global elite, but Midgard Lodge was different. The northernmost hostelry in the world and converted from an old whaling station, it was inaccessible to all but its guests, and provided for those who valued discretion, whose reputations were not the holiest, but who wanted to improve their standing in the world as well as their profits. These were the people about whom the World Economic Forum felt squeamish, who would never be invited to actual Davos, but whose decisions were of great economic and political import. If they were excluded from the best business society – publicly, at least – they were welcome to meet, and talk, and explore different business models in the stunning environment of Midgard Lodge. Sean believed and Tom had agreed that it was pointless preaching to the converted; also that honey caught more flies than vinegar. A luxury retreat in a uniquely inspiring location, security assured, was part of the realpolitik of environmental progress.

The stewardess was at the rear of the plane. Sean felt anxiety coursing through him but he didn't want to arrive blunted by alcohol. A delicate thing, for a CEO to re-establish the chain of command after so long an absence – but Danny Long was slipping up as general manager if he was reporting to Kingsmith first. Kingsmith might have recommended him, but he was only Sean's sleeping partner in Midgard, not an official shareholder like Martine and her clean-tech investors, nor

Radiance Young and her friends in Hong Kong. Sean always smiled at the thought of Radiance and her bare-faced insistence she was investing all her own renminbis, not those of the People's Republic behind her. Fine, if that was what she needed to say. But she certainly brought the Party with her.

It would probably be a few days before details were released to the press and then the news cycle and the eulogising would start up again. 'Glacier gives up the ghost', or more soberly, 'Body of missing British environmentalist discovered'. As if Tom Harding were Franklin's lost expedition, the subject of national mourning for decades. And then, of course, there would be the pictures. Tom shaking hands with indigenous protestors at the line of jungle they had saved. Tom swimming with that bloody whale shark, as if he were the only person in the world ever to do that. Tom with actors draped on his shoulders, celebrity trading for rugged moral virtue.

The prospect of reliving the cult of Tom was as irritating now as it had been while he was alive, but the worst of it was, Tom had disliked it too. Sean couldn't even call him on his ego – or his looks, which were not his fault. Women adored him, men admired him, and this idolisation was a large part of why Sean had so doggedly courted him for Midgard, refusing to take no for an answer. But it wasn't the whole of it. Despite their years of distance, Sean knew that if Tom believed in Midgard, then he had truly created something of real value to this world. His old friend's approval had really mattered – and Kingsmith was right, he must get out in front of all this and use the drama positively.

'*Up in our country we are human!* And since we are human we help each other. We don't like to hear anybody say thanks for that. If I get something today, you may get it tomorrow. Some men never kill anything because they are seldom lucky or they may not be able to run or row as fast as others. Therefore they would feel unhappy to have to be thankful to their fellows all the time. And it would not be fun for the big hunter to feel that other men were constantly humbled by him. Then his pleasure would die. Up here we say that by gifts one makes slaves, and by whips one makes dogs.'

A hunter, to Peter Freuchen
Arctic Adventure: My Life in the Frozen North (1936)
Peter Freuchen

5

Fourteen nations signed the Svalbard Treaty of 1920, giving each of them the right to settle, purchase property and conduct business on the archipelago, provided that, in the words of the legislation, it was 'not for war-like purposes'. By the time Sean Cawson was writing draft after draft of his purchase proposal for the old whaling station, the Treaty had forty-three signatories and seven new-formed states seeking approval. But treaties and laws are as subject to ageing as the hands that wrote them and the times to which they applied.

Family firms likewise. The derelict structures he bought by consortium and rechristened Midgard Lodge were built and owned for two hundred years by a wealthy Norwegian family: the Pedersens.

The youngest generation rejected their elders' pride in their whaling past, instead feeling shame that their family fortune was built on the near-genocide of several cetacean and pinniped species. It was like inherited wealth from slavery – no bar to public office, as Great Britain proved, but something they felt a debt to repay. In karmic offset, they embraced diverse environmental causes to distance themselves from the documented accounts of their forebears, of the joyful slaughter of pregnant beluga whales in Midgardfjorden, and the flensing of live walruses on the beach they still owned. The surviving elders, who still used the candelabra made of narwhal horn on Sunday nights, mourned many aspects of the past under the safe code word: Tradition. The middle generation just wanted the money, and made discreet inquiries about the old lodge on the shores of Midgardfjorden. The price it might fetch, the complications.

In Svalbard, Oslo, Bergen and Tromsø, each realtor charged with this investigation broke into a sweat at the prospect of the kill: private property for sale in Svalbard, demesne to encompass landing beach, deepwater access, and a plot reaching right back to the mountain. Of course all land permanently belonged to the Crown of Norway – but the most demurely conservative estimate of the value was stratospheric.

For once the family agreed: it was time to let Midgard go. They chose a single agent, Mr Mogens Hadbold. Very discreetly, he dropped a hint of that possibility into international waters. The feeding frenzy was almost instantaneous. First came the Norwegian government itself, who brought much patriotic pressure to bear on the family agent, who duly passed it on – noting that two Russian oligarchs (bitter rivals) had more than doubled the government's best offer. Both were ready for a bidding war, but one was ruled out for his rapacious extractive activities in the Laptev Sea, albeit carried out by a Romanian proxy company. The other, a prominent Siberian land-owner, had airlifted every polar bear within three hundred square kilometres to create a private reservation close to Moscow 'for conservation' where he was reputedly breeding cubs for sale as pets. He too was ineligible.

The still-patriotic Pedersens paused to consider. The property was worth far more than the Norwegian government was willing to offer; why did they not understand? Their agent explained: if the govern-ment paid the premium the Midgard property commanded, they might then find themselves hostage to any Norwegian landowner north of 66 degrees, keen to leverage large amounts of cash. This truth caused the Pedersens' patriotism to somewhat fade.

But other bidders – from the US, Canada, Russia, China (the most) and India, were numerous. Seventy-five per cent were ruled out in the first round of investigations, but then the British-led consortium returned, demanding ('begging really,' said the family agent) to be reconsidered. This was because of the new involvement of one Tom Harding – a name that rang discordant bells (Greenpeace?) for the older Pedersens, but chimed most harmoniously (Greenpeace!) for the younger. He had led the charge to clear the Plastic Sargasso and driven the investigation into clinical trials corruption at more than one chemicals giant. The older generation, emotionally blackmailed by their children, allowed that the British consortium could re-submit its proposal – so long as they knew that the odds were against its success.

Long odds were what Sean Cawson had beaten all his life. The sale went through, Midgard Lodge was built and still running despite the terrible accident that had marred its birth – and three and a half years later, here he was disembarking into the sharp mineral air of Longyearbyen once more.

It was good to see Danny Long standing waiting on the tarmac. Behind him was the familiar yellow and blue Dauphin helicopter in which they would fly to Midgard, and standing by his general manager's side, a Longyearbyen airport official ready to conclude the briefest of passport formalities.

He and Danny greeted each other warmly. There was no difference in Long's appearance, or his comfortable quiet manner. He was everything you wanted in a pilot, and though Sean had intended to broach the difficult matters straight away – as they rose up over the slopes of the coal mine behind the airport then veered away from the town, he found he could not speak. Silently, he absorbed Svalbard's stark beauty. This time, there was none of the churning panic of his last visit, unwisely made too soon after the accident. He was here to put that failure behind him and lead with confidence again.

Not until they had left the black peaks and steely water of Adventfjord behind them, and were beating their way over the white-ness of the von Postbreen glacier, up to the razor-tipped ice plateau of King Olav's Land, did he clear his throat. He heard the tiny answering click and, to Sean's surprise, the pilot spoke first.

'I'm sorry I didn't call you, sir, about Mr Harding. But Mr Kingsmith called, so I told him – then he wanted to tell you himself.'

'Yes. He told me he'd put a retreat in. You know that—'

'Yes, sir. Everything to go through London, he set me straight on that earlier today. If you don't mind my saying, Mr Cawson, it's good to see you again.'

'And you, Danny. It's been far too long.'

The pilot looked straight ahead. 'I still feel very bad.'

'Not your fault, Danny.' Sean looked down at the ice.

'But if I'd been in there with you …'

'You were needed on watch. But thank you.'

He remembered how much he liked Danny Long. In his late forties, he was blunt-featured, of average height and stocky build, and his modest manner belied his high competence – but that was probably part of the protocol of close protection. Kingsmith had told him he had saved his life, but the details were private. Sean admired him for not turning it into a drinking anecdote.

He stared down at the ice cap, filling up on its peculiar charge of beauty and fear. Today it was glittering white velvet, strewn with lozenges of emerald and turquoise lakes. He did not remember so many of them, nor the line of five white radomes on a plateau of tundra. They had not been there the last time he was here.

'Indian,' said Danny Long, in answer to his unspoken question. 'In the last year. Over on Barentsoya there's another new construction going on. Telecom, or meteorology.' The pilot smiled. 'Improving our broadband.'

'Good broadband is a valuable asset.'

'Indeed, sir.'

Sean did not speak again until they were over Hinlopenstreten, where a convoy of cruise ships made white dashes on the dark water. He remembered Kingsmith's admonition about his friend in Oslo.

'Have there been many ships in Midgardfjorden? Before that one?'

Danny Long shook his head.

'Sometimes they stop at the mouth – for photographs, I believe. Then they go round the other way. But the *Vanir* came right down deep. When it all went off on the radio – not the calving, when they went out and confirmed it was a body – the coastguard were close across at Freyasundet, in that new fast boat of theirs.'

'Joe said they held it as a crime scene.' Sean kept his tone neutral.

'They did, sir, but they told me and Terry not to worry about the words, it was just so they could take all the phones and such from the passengers. Then we were ordered to stand down – return to the Lodge – by the coastguard. So that's what we did.' He paused. 'We had Mr Kingsmith's guests to look after.'

'And what did you tell them?'

'Facts, sir: a body had been recovered from the water. They didn't know anything until they came down for breakfast. The coastguard had gone by then.'

'How were they? The coastguard.'

'Very polite, sir, as always. It was Inspector Brovang, he was out on their new boat, that's why he was in the area.'

Sean imagined the heavy medevac cradle swinging in the air, trails of water falling behind. Tom's dead body netted and trussed beneath a helicopter, as high as he was now. Less than forty-eight hours ago.

He put his right hand under his left armpit and pressed down on it. The tingling had come back. Nothing physically wrong with his hand, no nerve damage. Brovang had saved it, with his own body heat. He had taken Sean's statement as he recovered in the Sickehaus in Longyearbyen, but they had not spoken since that time. Nor had he taken up the standing invitation to either visit Midgard Lodge with guests, or any of Sean Cawson's other clubs around the world, though he had declined courteously. Sean cancelled out the obscure bad feeling that gave him, with a large annual donation to the children's charity which Brovang supported and mentioned on his Facebook page. Brovang had never accepted his Friend request.

'Well, at least he had all the details. He didn't want to speak to the visitors?'

'No, he was keen to get going.'

'Who exactly are they?'

'Excuse me, sir, I'm not good at names, especially foreign ones. Faces, I never forget. But you can meet them, they're still at the Lodge.' He banked the Dauphin over the great crumpled blue-white sweep of a glacier – that stopped short of where Sean's eye expected it to turn.

He must have misremembered the glacier, it could not have retreated so far in a year and a half. Everything seemed different. 'Danny,' he said, 'remember something: Midgard Lodge is my company and I am your CEO. Not Joe. You report to me.'

'Yes, sir. I know. I made a mistake. I should have informed you first.'

'Good, then we're sorted. How's everything else?'

'All good, sir. I was in town a week before the Tata-Tesla retreat, and there were some Russian boys from the new place.'

'The Pyramiden hotel? Or the one in Barentsburg?'

'Oh those are long finished, and two more as well. This new one's called the Arktik Dacha. They were joking with us about it, but in a friendly way. I reckon they've had a look at us.'

'How would they do that?' Sean's stomach lurched as they suddenly rose up over the last peaks that pierced the ice cap.

Danny Long grinned. 'Same way we don't, at them.'

Although I had joined the Royal Geographical Society some years earlier, under the misapprehension that by so doing I would obtain Sunday tickets for the Zoo, I had only the haziest idea as to what a glacier was. I did not know at what temperature water froze. I had no head for heights, was not used to handling large, fierce dogs, could not row or ski or splice, and knew nothing of the working of an internal-combustion engine, or even a Primus stove.

But none of these considerations sobered my high spirits. I had enlisted for Adventure, and that was all I asked for. I had no responsibilities or misgivings and was as carefree as a kitten.

Sledge: The British Trans-Greenland Expedition 1934 (1935)
Martin Lindsay

6

They landed on the narrow strip of cobbled beach. The boathouse doors were ajar but all was quiet. The Lodge itself looked better than Sean remembered, the wood more weathered, the structure even more camouflaged. He waited for the bear all-clear signal then went in to greet the mystery guests. The discretion of Midgard Lodge did not extend to its founder and CEO, and absent or not, he had a right to know who he was hosting.

Two men were waiting in the lobby and jumped up to greet him. The first of Kingsmith's pals was Benoit, from the Central African Republic. He was tall and broad with a winning open smile, and he pumped Sean's hand warmly.

'You don't remember me? I came to all your parties on Spring Street!' He looked to his companion, a young elegantly dressed Asian man, also smiling politely. 'Jiaq, our host gave the best parties in Manhattan, didn't you?'

'You're very kind.' Sean smiled over his confusion. He had no memory of Benoit, but he had indeed lived in a loft on Spring Street in New York, owned by Kingsmith, in his first year after graduation. Kingsmith had him running errands and apprenticing for him, while he learned what he called 'housekeeping'. Spring Street marked Sean's first experience of making real money through his mentor's generous guidance, and he had never looked back.

Jiaq complimented Sean on Midgard Lodge and apologised for not personally knowing Miss Radiance Young, though he had certainly heard of her.

'Your facilities are a credit to you,' Benoit smiled. 'We feel very safe!'

'Excellent. I'm glad it's all going well for you.'

Benoit apologised for their unscheduled visit – the result of a chance call to Joe, who suggested that if they were in the neighbourhood …

'The neighbourhood?'

'Of Iceland.' They broke into peals of laughter. They explained they had been showing off their new ice-class yachts to each other, comparing anti-pirate protocols. Now the Arctic was open for business it was good to be prepared, like boy scouts!

Their high spirits grated. Sean said he was very pleased to have them there, and excused himself.

He pulled on waterproofs and went back down to the beach. The Dauphin rested at one end, facing down the fjord in readiness for their return. At the other, Danny Long had pulled one of the smallest Zodiacs from the boathouse, alongside the single kayak Sean had requested. This was his manager's mute comment on the safety infraction of Sean's stated intention to go out alone. A breeze glittered the water of the fjord – and carried the faint beat of rock music. He looked around. It came from the building beside the boathouse.

Sean looked at Danny Long in question, then walked towards it. His manager came with him.

'I'll tell them to keep it down, sir. But now might be a good time for them to meet you, if you're happy with that?' He hurried alongside as Sean pushed through the vestibule doors.

Twenty men jumped to attention off their bunks, their eyes down. Sean stared in surprise. No one said anything. He had never seen any of them before, and did not remember there being so many of them on his last trip. But everything about that visit was confused. He would check when he got back.

'The new detail, Mr Cawson – they've only been in a week, but they're all good.' Danny Long's voice changed as he addressed the men. 'This is your CEO, Mr Cawson.'

The men looked at Sean and saluted. They wore dark clothing and looked very fit.

'At ease.' Sean had no military training, but apparently it worked because the men sat back down and resumed looking at their screens, or lying on their bunks. Danny Long seemed to be waiting for him to say something.

'Good,' he said, to cover his surprise. He went out into the open air. A retreat was in place he knew nothing about and a new detail of men – he had forgotten that part of the arrangement – were gathered in that dark cavernous room.

'All good, sir.' Danny Long was watching him.

'Right then.' Sean took out his own binoculars and stood back to back with his manager, sweeping the rocks and peaks of the bay with hi-mag scrutiny. He could not – would not – ask Danny Long questions that would reveal his ignorance and completely undermine the authority he was there to resume.

The manager's radio crackled. From the upper lookout in the Lodge, his second in command Terry Bjornsen was also scanning for bears. All clear.

'Waiting,' Long said into his collar, as he completed his own slow survey. He raised his arm to the Lodge. 'All clear below.'

Sean lowered his kayak into the water, climbed down the steel ladder and slid into the seat. He took the paddle from Long, coiled the red tethering rope into the cockpit and pushed off with a long slow glide. There was no wind. Midgardfjorden was a black mirror, the only movement was the undulating wake behind Sean's kayak, and the slow rise and fall of his paddle, hissing softly as it cut the water.

He skimmed out towards the centre, the rising shimmer of light around him showing that the sky was drying as the sun burned through. His consciousness fused with the subtle motion of the kayak and the long ripples of sunlight. He kept his eye on the jutting inner point of the M. He knew the current that circled the inlets and made a little area of turbulence close to the shore that could capsize the unwary – but here it was now, all the way out in the centre.

Dipping his blade, he felt the pull from the water, the tug all the way up into his arm, as if it had caught on something. The current swirled like a water snake but Sean had good upper body strength and kept his head. He judged its velocity and angle, then twisted his paddle blade into its force. He felt the energy from deep in the water travel up his paddle, his hand, his arm, into his shoulder, neck, and face. He held the strain – and the hook of the current released him in the right direction. Only five or six seconds – but long enough to go in if he'd panicked. But he hadn't – and in that instant of instinctive reaction, in that correct response, his feeling of power came flooding back – and he was embracing that beautiful and terrifying lover once again: the Arctic.

His heart pounding with joy, he glanced back. Danny Long stood on the jetty, a tiny figure beneath the rearing mountain, his rifle above his shoulder like a tribesman's spear. Sean rounded the point and moved out of sight.

From the air the glacier was one thing, but approached in humility by kayak, she revealed another nature. Sean lifted his paddle and slowed, poised in the water. The towering blue and white face of the ice filled his vision, the Arctic silence his ears and mind. Sometimes it was so intense it almost formed into a sound; sometimes he had heard the bumping and scraping of the pack ice form abstract fragments like music.

The silence gathered around him so that he could almost hear the squeeze and suck of his heart in his chest. He felt his sweat blot his base layer, and the bracing of his tendons far away inside the kayak shell. Below him the dark depth of the water; above, a thread of breeze that dried the molecules of sweat. His vision filled with the deep blue strata of the most ancient compressed ice, forty thousand years old.

When Sean was eleven and in the care home while his mother was recovering from yet another attempt, he saw a huge oil painting of icebergs on one of the off-limits staff landings. It was so beautiful he started using this longer route, despite the punishment when he was caught, just to gaze at the space and the colours of this pristine frozen world. While he stood before it, he forgot his distress, and threw his consciousness into the ice.

There was a mast from a shipwreck in the foreground, and he imagined himself the sole survivor. Everyone else was dead but he must find a way to keep going. As he gazed at it one day it came to him like a truth – his father was on that ship, or one like it – he had gone exploring and been shipwrecked, that was why he'd never known him, why his mother wanted to die. The ice had taken his family and he must go there to get them back.

The iceberg painting grew in his imagination, even when his mother returned from the hospital and reclaimed him to the ugly council house where she struggled on in depression and drinking. Sean fixated on his lost explorer father, and everything to do with the Arctic, and he had bolstered his fantasy with such authentic details, backed up with angry fists for doubters, that it became fact.

His fighting was a problem until a social worker intervened. Sean was in danger of serious delinquency but clearly bright, and the social worker goaded him into agreeing to sit the scholarship exam for The Abbott's School.

This was the grand, grey-stone public school where Sean had often joined the townie gang in attacking boys who wore the strange uniform – but now he was to be one of them. He'd listened outside the door after his interview – 'Oh, the poor boy, think of what he's gone through, yes, yes let's extend a helping hand.'

So Sean Cawson received the academic scholarship and the sports bursary and the charity award that topped up the rest and meant he could go for free. By the age of fifteen, he had become a chameleon at Abbott's, sloughing off the misfits who would have been his natural friends and gravitating instead to the leaders of the pack, in sport and academic excellence. There he worked out the answer to the question he'd always pondered, about fairness and beauty and ugliness and justice. It was wealth.

Sean blinked. Not eleven in the care home, not in the dorm at Abbott's. In the kayak, frozen. The current had taken him closer to the ice face – how long had he been zoned out, thinking of the past? A few seconds – a couple of minutes? The temperature had dropped and the light was that milky veil that can suddenly appear in Arctic air like a spell, blanking out contours, hiding crevasses, wiping out direction.

His heart slammed. In the few seconds he had mentally drifted, the current had taken him directly in front of the mouth of the cave into the glacier from which Tom's body emerged. It was deep; the ice was the darkest blue he had ever seen, and as he paddled backwards, he could hear the echo of his blade striking the water. His ears blocked as if he were airborne and his mouth was dry. The new cave was the source of the pull in the water, it had changed the current pattern of the fjord.

He felt a terrible urge to go in, but he knew that was crazy, like standing on a high cliff and thinking of jumping. Of course he would not do it. He braced his feet and bladed back, admiring the cobalt twists in the ice, the darkest sapphire catching flashes from the water. There was nothing more beautiful than Arctic ice.

Something touched him. Not physically – but he felt it in the prickling of his scalp – something was there, around him or under him. He stared into the cave but saw nothing; he looked down and the water was grey-green translucent. Then he looked up.

Standing on the lip of the glacier, staring down from directly above him, was an enormous male polar bear. It was close enough for Sean to see the duelling scar that twisted his black lip, giving the impression of a cynical smile. It must have stalked him while he was years away, and now they had come together.

Sean dug his paddle to move away from the cave but caught another current that pushed him closer to the ice face. The bear watched with interest and slowly walked along the edge above him, keeping pace.

Sean knew not to take his eyes from it. He felt it most distinctly – the bear was pondering leaping in now, or waiting a little longer. If he came closer, if he lost control and capsized, it would take the chance and jump. Bears had been known to go for kayakers before, but always from the shore.

This glacier was high – but the bear was enormous and highly intelligent; it knew the currents – it was standing waiting for him. When he met its gaze, he felt it willing him to panic and make a mistake. He stared back with equal force and ignored the jolt of fear down both legs.

The current was a muscle of water writhing around his paddle, tugging it under the kayak. The light glittered and the mountains reared up black and strobing around him, locking him in. The bear lowered its head, looking for where to jump. He wanted a knife – why had he not brought a knife with him? He might have done something with a knife …

As the bear gathered itself, a sharp growl bounced against the granite walls of the fjord, and it looked up in irritation. The vibration of the Zodiac engine came through the water. Sean did not take his eyes away – the bear would still strike, even now. Man and animal felt each other's stare. Advantage animal – but man was lucky. The bear turned and loped away up the glacier and out of sight.

Danny Long slowed the Zodiac as he approached, his rifle on his back. Benoit, Jiaq, and two young blonde women were his passengers, all wearing bright orange survival suits and busy photographing the scenery. They had not seen it.

'Excuse me, sir: the guests wished to come out.'

Sean reached down into himself for human speech again.

'Of course.'

Long carefully circled the Zodiac around behind Sean, giving him the benefit of the wake to help him out of the current. 'How is it, in the kayak?'

'Great,' Sean said over his shoulder. 'But no one else out alone. The current.' He scanned the slopes. The bear had vanished and he was glad.

'Yes, sir. It's changed, I noticed as well.'

Sean left Kingsmith's guests exclaiming over the colour of the glacier and paddled back. Only as he boarded the plane that evening did he realise he had not thought about Tom for a moment out there. He had gone to see where he'd died, and mourn, but instead the confrontation with the bear had made him feel truly alive, and even joyful. Sitting on the plane coming back, he missed Tom with a fierce longing for that friendship, and for everything else he had lost.

This snowless ice-plain is like a life without love – nothing to soften it. The marks of all the battles and pressures of the ice stand forth just as when they were made, rugged and difficult to move among. Love is life's snow. It falls deepest and softest into the gashes left by the fight – whiter and purer than snow itself. What is life without love? It is like this ice – a cold, bare, rugged mass, the wind driving it and rending it and then forcing it together again, nothing to cover open rifts, nothing to break the violence of the collisions, nothing to round away the sharp corners of the broken floes – nothing, nothing but bare, rugged drift-ice.

Friday, 15 December 1893
Farthest North: The Norwegian Polar Expedition 1893–1896 (1897)
Fridtjof Nansen

7

London, four years earlier

Sean had found out about the Midgard sale, put together the proposal and finance, and fought to stay in negotiations. He was at the decisive final round of talks when it looked like Tom's puritanical ego would destroy the whole venture.

'I don't want to do this.' Tom hadn't even waited for the meeting to officially start. The Pedersen family agent, Mogens Hadbold, their lawyer and their accountant, stared at Sean in confusion.

'Wait.' Sean felt like he was in a bad dream. 'Tom, what is this?' They were in a penthouse suite at Claridge's, and Tom was holding up Sean's bid proposal in its embossed leather cover.

'I do not want the Pedersen family to sell their property,' he said, 'because it's in such an environmentally sensitive location. The Arctic ecosystem is already massively stressed by warming seas. There *is* no more summer ice. Politicians pay lip-service to bringing the temperature down while quietly drawing dividends from their fossil fuel investments. We've got government ministers on the boards of oil companies. I don't want that either, but that's reality.'

Sean consciously relaxed his hands so they did not make fists. What an absolute fucker, telling him one thing and waiting until now—

'But,' Tom continued, 'we're here because someone is going to be chosen as the new owner. Someone is going to become responsible for that corner of the Arctic, at a most critical moment for its safety. I'm here to tell you that, if this sale is going to happen, I stand with this man to buy it. We're here because the numbers are right.'

'Certainly in the correct area,' confirmed the family agent. 'But above a particular threshold that Mr Cawson has passed, the family are even more concerned to select the correct buyer.'

'I led Greenpeace for two years,' Tom said. 'I've been involved in environmental issues my whole life and I will continue to be. I've known Sean since we were at college together. I've learned a lot from him, and as I'm now in this room, I hope it's become a two-way street. I used to turn my nose up at people whose main interest was money, because they didn't seem to care how they made it. Now I'm less naïve. The only way the world will change for the better is if it is precisely those people who start thinking differently about profit.' He looked at each of them in turn.

'Last year's coup in the Maldives cost every hotel group there untold sums as well as several lives. Many people saw it coming, the hotels were warned, they absolutely knew what was going on, but profit blinded them. Climate change means the poorest people suffer first – people who don't buy organic or vote for liberal democracy. The Maldives is happening all over the world, in every poor country where the sea level is rising and the land is flooding.'

'Mr Harding,' Mogens Hadbold smiled patiently, 'we all care—'

'Caring is meaningless without action. We must stop the economic apartheid that is killing this planet.'

'Tom, for pity's sake!' Sean was on his feet too. It was appalling, Tom was like a mad man, he hadn't seen him like this before.

'Sit down, Sean. You wanted me here, you wanted me on board, so let me continue. I'm nearly finished. Look at the world – a great big band of drought or flood that just happens to coincide with mineral resources, with political instability and then with foreign intervention by the very powers that benefit from the extractive rights. Powers that do not give a shit about the cost, human or natural, of that resource exploitation. What we're looking at is a global environmental *sacrifice zone* – and the Arctic is just the latest part of it.'

Sean sat there, his face burning. Tom's ego was out of control. How could he not have seen it? What was he doing now, with the mineral water? Holding it up to the big mirror on the mantelpiece. He looked mad, speaking to the flowers.

'Bottled at source in the Alps. Where the shrinking snowline means only the highest resorts still exist, and their prices make even the rich feel poor. And if *they're* starting to think about climate change, you know we're in the last-chance saloon.' He turned and came back to them. 'When that chunk of Venice collapsed into the lagoon, the dead included guests at the Cipriani, as well as refugees.'

He drank again.

'So if you're not worried, you're not paying attention. And if you are, then it is your moral and civic and patriotic duty to either keep your property and be vigilant stewards of the Arctic, or, ensure that you only sell to a buyer who will use it to be a vigilant pain in the arse to any and everyone who is trying to make a killing up there. I don't know, you might be those people yourselves. I don't know you, but I do know this man.' He pointed to Sean.

'Arctic obsession started our friendship. We've gone our separate ways, but that's still our bond. He might have become a capitalist pig – but he'll never do anything to destroy the Arctic, in any way. I know that. He's clever or crazy enough to invite me to be a board member, and if there's one thing I've learned it's that people hear you better if you're in the room, not yelling through a loudhailer from the street. That's why I'm in with Sean: he knows the very people I want to reach, the brokers between governments and mining companies, the shipping people, the people who make things happen, or make things disappear. I'll be in the room with them on this.'

He laid down the bid proposal on the table. 'How can people say what they really think at places like Davos? It's about being seen to do good, and someone with a vested interest in the outcome is always playing the host. Sean's plan takes that layer away. A luxurious private retreat in Arctic grandeur – who doesn't want to go there?'

Sean had to admire him. He was such a showman. No – that wasn't fair. Protecting the environment was Tom's life's work, he had the broken bones, scars and jail time to show for it – as well as the adulation of thousands of people. He'd put all his money into it too, though his family had tried to stop him; Sean remembered hearing that.

'Enough with the bleeding-heart liberals crying over the polar bears. I want the greediest, ugliest-thinking, most short-sighted, ego-crazed politicians and plutocrats we can find to stay in the place Sean will build on the shore of Midgardfjorden. There's a reason men have risked their lives again and again for the Arctic; it shows you your soul, even if you think you don't have one.

'I'm naïve: I still believe you can reach people through their hearts. But I'm battle-scarred: profit speaks louder. Sean's plan combines both those things. So that's why I say that my first position is still no more development in the Arctic. But as it *is* happening, from all sides, as the summer ice has gone – twenty years ahead of government projections, and as it *is* a free-for-all, no matter what people say, then let us be there, let us try to guide development to do the minimum harm, and protect the life of this fragile, sublime, vulnerable environment. You can only lose it once.'

Tom walked round behind Sean and put his hands on his shoulders. 'I know my friend and I trust him.' He took his seat again.

No one spoke for a long moment. The atmosphere had shifted. The lawyer and the accountant were staring at Tom with that star-struck look Sean had seen on people's faces before. Mogens Hadbold's laptop pinged, two, three, four times, breaking the spell. Hadbold looked across to the mantelpiece and waved. Only then did Sean spot the tiny camera in the flower arrangement.

'Yes,' said Mogens Hadbold. 'I'm sorry that I did not tell you the meeting was streaming live. They wanted to be present, but discreetly.'

He turned his laptop to face Sean and Tom, and the quartered screen showed different Pedersens on Skype.

'That was very impressive,' a female voice said, out of the screen. 'We will let you know. *Tak*, Mogens.'

He replied in a rapid burst of Norwegian, and closed the laptop.

'Mr Harding is something of a hero to the younger generation, you know this. They are the ones making all the big noise about the right buyer. The older ones – well, you know how we are as we get old. We like security. And money! But the young have the power.' He stood up, as did the lawyer and accountant. 'Thank you very much for returning.' The meeting was over. Sean stood too.

'You don't want to ask me anything?' He looked from one to the other. Mogens Hadbold shook his head. 'We have looked into your partners, Miss Martine Delaroche and Miss Radiance Young. We are satisfied of your financial commitment. And of course we know Mr

Harding's environmental work. And you know Midgardfjorden, so there is no more to say on that. Everyone is clear what is on the table.'

They were both silent in the lift going down. Only when they were out on the street did Sean explode.

'You knew there was a camera!'

'Yep. Want a drink?' Tom grinned. 'I'm gasping.'

They went into the first place that smelled of beer. It was the middle of the afternoon, a strange time to be in a pub, but everything was strange. Sean had taken Tom to the presentation as his mascot; Tom had taken control. Sean had said almost nothing. Tom put his arm round his shoulder.

'I wasn't so bad, was I?'

'You were an utter, utter bastard. They loved you.'

'Didn't overdo it?'

'You chewed the furniture – I wanted to throttle you.'

'You're very welcome.' Tom ordered two pints without asking what Sean wanted. Sean wasn't a pubbish sort any more, certainly not any old boozer on a midweek afternoon. Not that he was in any state to do business – he was fizzing with energy and outrage at Tom's hijacking of his event.

'You are the most egotistical fucker I have ever met, Tom, you know that?'

'If I'd gone in there all mealy-mouthed, you'd be dead in the water.' Their pints came. They clinked.

'Bastard.'

'Bastard.'

They drank hard and talked lightly of current affairs, excluding the one with Martine. Tom thanked Sean for the picture. They discussed the latest closure of the Suez Canal, the skinhead revival, and remembered a mutual friend from college, recently killed reporting from Ukraine.

'We underestimated him,' Tom agreed. 'A hero in our midst.'

'Like you,' Sean said. 'You're a hero. I mean it. Your life counts.'

Tom drained his pint. 'Sean, so does yours. You can move mountains. You've pulled yourself up by your bootstraps.'

Sean felt a glow that was more than the beer, and the afternoon sun coming in through the sand-etched windows. Putting the world to rights with Tom, boozing an afternoon away. What a rare pleasure. He was about to tell him that; he might even have been about to tell him how much he'd missed him, after ordering another pair of pints, when the door opened and a beautiful girl walked in.

She was about twenty-five, fresh-faced, casually dressed. Without realising, Sean pulled in his belly and sat up straighter. She looked across and walked over. Her smile was lovely. Perhaps she'd been in one of his clubs, and recognised him. He prepared himself. Tom put his arm round her. They kissed.

'I'm ready,' he said.

'Then hello and goodbye.' She smiled at Sean, playful and polite.

'Christ,' he said. 'Tom, she's the image of Ruth.'

'Rubbish.'

'Is that a good thing?' The girl looked from face to face. 'Who is Ruth?'

'Mutual friend,' Tom said. 'A brilliant woman.'

The girl's smile lit her up. 'Then I don't mind at all.'

Sean gazed at her until Tom punched him lightly on the shoulder.

'Let me know how much they hated me.'

Sean watched them disappear out onto the street, and into their shared afternoon. He found himself alone, quite drunk and acutely bereft.

The lovely girl was young enough to be Tom's daughter, if he'd had one. This brought the image of his own sharply to Sean's mind. Rosie, the angry sad child who could not understand how her father needed to feel like a man more than a husband. How her mother had changed into a woman who saw him as he really was, instead of the hero he wanted to be.

Sean knew he was drunk, but maybe that was the best way to tell Rosie how he felt. He wanted to say sorry, for so much. There at the bar he took out his phone. The call went straight through to her voicemail. At least it didn't ring several times, as often happened, before going dead. That meant she knew it was him, and didn't want to talk. This time, she was just busy. Then he called Martine, and the same thing happened.

Why did they not pick up? Sean left his pint unfinished. Only sad old men drank pints on their own in daylight. Tom had done this to him.

A bright burst of laughter seemed aimed at him and he turned. Two girls sat at a corner table, they looked away when he caught their eye – but not before flashing him a quick smile. He did not know what to do with himself; it was that awkward time when the pub was just filling up with the early after-work crowd, the low earners who couldn't wait to get away. One minute he was enjoying a liberating freedom with Tom, drinking pints in an unfashionable pub at the hour they felt like doing it – and the next he was beached on the shores of other people's lives – like some loser.

The girls sent arcs of laughter up through the air, they were lassoing him and drawing him over, they wanted to play. He looked in the mirror behind the bar, where he could see them angling their thighs towards him, rearranging their shiny hanks of hair.

Before he left, he spoke to the barman and bought a bottle of champagne to be sent over when he'd gone. Their faces fell as he went out, and he felt a grim satisfaction that he had not fallen for it, drunk as he was. He could have gone over and within a couple of drinks – maybe not even that – adjourned to somewhere more comfortable. A hotel. *An* hotel. He had learned to always use that weirdness, to demonstrate his adherence to the right set of rules. Inviting people for 'a kitchen supper', never 'dinner'. Repeating 'how do you do,' instead of ever answering the question. In English society, nobody cared – that was something he learned too – and they would be horrified if you told them. But they always cared that you were rich.

Standing outside, Sean watched the girls receive the champagne. They were suitably over-excited and he drew back as they scanned the pub for him. What a strange thing to have done. It gave him no pleasure, he was just acting out the anxiety of waiting, of being compared and judged after the presentation. He should have just said that to Tom, but he'd been too busy struggling with the feeling of inadequacy because of how brilliant Tom had been. If they'd only had longer, and more to drink, he would have blurted it all out, they could have talked again like they used to – he could have told him about how it had gone wrong with Gail. Tom was kind, he was always kind, he would have known what to say. Instead, he'd gone off with that girl, who *did* look like a young Ruth. Tom had fucked things up too. Sean wasn't the only one.

He slammed into the wall of the pub, drunker than he'd thought. When he and Tom had been drinking together, he'd been happy in a way he had forgotten, relaxing into that long-lost feeling of comradeship and solidarity. Only now did he realise he'd been looking forward to talking about their Greenland trip again, to indulging in a full-blown nostalgia fest, to drinking more, to calling Martine drunkenly to say he was having dinner – supper – with Tom, that it didn't fucking matter what happened with the Midgard deal, at least they'd reconnected.

He peered through the pub window. To feel so disappointed was pathetic. Nostalgia was for people whose lives were over. Tom had a date, and those girls in there had been joined by two meaty-looking boyfriends. Sean watched some animated talk about the bottle and the boys jerked their necks and squared their shoulders in ritual male display for the rich sod who'd undercut them.

Aimlessly drunk, emotionally disorderly, he decided to clear his head and walk back to Devon Square through Hyde Park and Kensington Gardens, in the hope of seeing the cavalry.

But it was too late in the day for the horses, and Sean sat on a bench with a coffee from one of the kiosks, trying to sober up. Vodka he could skilfully calibrate, but pints of beer somehow sidestepped that control and made him too emotional. From deciding as he walked away from the pub that he would park the whole Greenland nostalgia trip, he was now flooding with memories of it. He'd been there on three separate expeditions, the first with Tom, on the Lost Explorers' Expedition when they were twenty. They had been racing partners on the ten-dog sled, and both had imagined that reading about it was tantamount to expertise. They had made complete fools of themselves and had never had a better time. The next couple of times had been for Kingsmith, investigating some mining tender that came to nothing; he had spent time in the capital Nuuk – but it had still been Greenland, still the Arctic.

The first time was the best, despite their incompetence. Because of it, perhaps. He and Tom sweating and stumbling about in the snow, desperately trying to wrestle ten dogs into their harnesses, the air snapping and flashing with the frenzy of excited barking, the dogs fully aware they had novices to deal with. One by one they got them in, resorting to both of them grabbing one dog and managing at last to work out which leg went through which bit of harness – exhausted before they even set off, but the dogs howling and leaping with the thrill of it, as if they'd never done it before either.

It was a shock when his phone rang, in Hyde Park. It was Mogens Hadbold, and he had good news.

One is often asked what is the attraction and what are the joys of Polar exploration. The answer is – Adventure – going where man has never gone before. Achievement – discovering something of value to mankind, such as the whale-fishery of South Georgia; or ramming your way through ice or any difficulties under steam or sail. The wonderful pure beauty of these regions, the healthy invigorating life; and last but not least – comradeship – the comradeship of men. Men who fight alongside you, toil with you, laugh with you, and chaff you. Pals who rack their brains for abuse and epithets to hurl at each other, and who fight for their absent chums. Pals who stand by each other through thick and thin; who share trials, hardships, joys, dangers and food, and are determined, at all hazards, to 'see it through' together. For such men you feel a great affection, and the results are teamwork and loyalty of the finest, highest quality, with joy of memory that never fades away.

Under Sail in the Frozen North: The Log of the 1926 British Arctic
    Expedition (1927)
Frank Arthur Worsley

8

From his park bench, Sean sent emails to Kingsmith, Radiance and Tom. He phoned Martine and said he would be over soon, then he called Gail, to say he wouldn't. He told her the news and first she congratulated him then asked for a divorce. She knew that Martine was part of the consortium and not one of his silly little girls, and she understood that now his relationship with her would become paramount. Gail wanted the dignity of immediate separation. She told him her lawyer's name and hung up. Sean was shocked that she was so prepared.

When he arrived at Martine's apartment she had a spare key and a bottle of chilled Krug waiting. This was the moment they had imagined, and though he enjoyed seeing her blaze with their triumph, he felt oddly detached. Perhaps this was a sign of success; when vintage Krug became a fizzy drink. Not a noble pint in a fuggy all-comers pub, with a mate who kept you level.

Martine slid down onto her knees in front of him and smiled, in the way he understood. He closed his eyes. The effort was over, success was his. The strain of living a lie with Gail was also gone. And Tom had come in and done exactly what Sean had brought him in to do: make him the winner. But he did not feel happy. After a while Martine looked up, concerned. He wound her hair in his hands and tried to surrender to her skill. He tried harder, thinking of the two girls in the pub, of recent porn – an appetite no woman would ever

65

wean him from. Still nothing. Gently he lifted her back up to him. He held her.

'Why am I not happy?'

'You got what you wanted. Now you feel empty.'

He nodded. It was true, and her insight made him feel tender. He stroked her hair, in silent consolation for their first erotic non-event. Later they watched television together, also for the first time.

'A decent man's content with profit,' Kingsmith used to say to him, in the early days. 'Only fools want more – and fools are tools but never partners.' And Sean, or *Sean boy* as Kingsmith called him, had laughed and watched the money rolling in, and worked seven days a week if necessary, as it often was, learning his mentor's particular ways, travelling with him, growing familiar with the Russian dolls of his financial habits, and Kingsmith's migratory routes: the Caymans to Panama, Monaco to Jersey, to Zurich – to thin air. Very often a scrap of a percentage point of profit fell under the table to Sean, sometimes as a cash bonus, but more often as a last-minute allocation of some IPO, some hitherto obscure company Kingsmith had carefully cultivated up to its stock market debut, usually but not always connected with mining, one of his major interests. Sean proved himself an excellent steward of his financial good fortune, using part of his profit to grow his property portfolio, and always reinvesting in something else Kingsmith recommended.

Both knew Sean would never be in the same league, but he was a quick study and had become personally wealthy beyond the dreams of his twelve-year-old, or even twenty-year-old self. Wealthy enough to acknowledge that money was not enough. What he'd always dreamed of was his name on the map. Literally. Like Barentsz or Bering or – well, OK, not like Cecil Rhodes – but to be a man of daring and discovery and honour, whose explorations could name mountains and seas.

Now, after the Pedersen deal, that secret glory-seeking part of him rejoiced like never before. He, Sean Cawson, owned a tiny piece of the Arctic. The ice was receding and the TransPolar sea route was busier every day, moving global markets from supermarket checkouts to construction contracts as the price of goods went down. Untold mineral wealth was newly within reach. There was something magical in the air; it *was* a new golden age of trade and opportunity, and he was a very modern buccaneer, in it for positive influence, not plunder. Surely that was worthy of some sort of recognition?

Midgard was Sean's biggest coup, but somewhere deep inside he had always known he would succeed. Several months ago, and in the face of the heavy odds against him winning the bid, he had placed a large retainer on the services of his chosen Norwegian architect, in order to capitalise on the narrow time window for the work. The morning after the Pedersen decision, and after Martine had left for work, he made that call from her apartment, and the sound of jubilation in the Oslo office buoyed him in happiness all the way across Kensington Gardens.

He was walking towards Selfridges, to kill a bit of time before meeting Joe Kingsmith for lunch. As yet he did not know the venue or the hour – but that was typical. Sean hadn't even known he was in London but found the email when he woke, saying he'd be at the Wallace Collection, then they could grab a bite. He liked to look at the old weapons collection, Sean remembered. It was the older man's indulgence to himself, and usually meant things were going well.

The sky was an empty blue and it was so hot for February that although the trees were bare the joggers were dressed for summer. Sean walked across the park, repressing a feeling of irritation at how his mentor, affectionately though he felt towards him, still seemed to think of him as the callow and grateful undergraduate, willing to dance attendance on his whims. That was a lifetime ago, but if Kingsmith still treated him like a kid, then that was the price of access to his capital. One hundred and fifty million dollars in this case, which, along with Tom's participation, had got him Midgard Lodge. Once Sean had referred to him as 'the old man' and people had thought Kingsmith was his actual father. He had not corrected them; he felt much more Kingsmith's son than his own unknown father's. And though wild horses wouldn't have dragged it out of him, in Sean's heart he was sure the old man had some paternal affection for him too. So fine, he would kill some time in the Watch Room at Selfridges, and wait for his call.

This was a place long soothing to Sean's spirit, and he had visited it many times before he could afford the things he wanted. It was always the same, the dawdling wealthy shoppers, sparkling vitrines and his own enhanced reflection in the tall apricot-lit mirrors.

He should commemorate his journey from staring at the painting of the icebergs on the care-home staff landing, to standing here, the legal owner of a piece of the Arctic, with a watch. A new time in his life, something that fitted his new role of merchant prince and environmental champion. Nothing vulgar. Sean had no idea what that would be. It amused him that as he went from case to case, the glittering dials, exotic straps and satin-draped plinths jostling for his attention, he gathered sales assistants like iron filings to a magnet. There was a new display since he had last come in, 'The Hall of Fame' case. And in it, a platinum Rolex Cosmograph Daytona, with its ice-blue dial the colour of a glacier. He tried it on and looked at his reflection. He didn't want to take it off so he bought it and slipped his Patek Philippe into his pocket. Collecting beautiful watches went with his self-image; even if the price made him slightly nauseous.

Perhaps he should buy a watch for Martine too. No more philandering. Marriage to Gail had not worked, but he still wanted a mate – not to be like Kingsmith, who for all his wealth and rosters of willing beauties around the world, seemed to lack the centre of gravity that a relationship gave. He had no children, no regular partner, but a different gorgeous woman was always available, wherever he was. Once Sean had thought this highly desirable, but now it seemed increasingly sad, though that was one emotion he'd never seen Kingsmith display.

Sean browsed the women's watches. He wanted to buy something for Rosie, but the idea of calling her and asking what she liked, and the possibility of her being vile to him on this day of triumph – he shrank from the pain of that. What about Radiance Young then? This was also her triumph. She had brought China to the table and he wanted to show his appreciation – but she was so eccentric. Who knew what sort of inappropriate behaviour a gift from him might trigger? She kept her Facebook page frequently updated and either referred to herself as 'Bi-Polar Babe' due to her extraordinary feats of endurance at both Poles, or, 'Simple Girl Looking For Love'. Sean had yet to meet another thirty-four-year-old single Chinese woman with hundreds of millions of dollars at her disposal. Or a chain of specifically Chinese-friendly hotels in hitherto untapped markets (most of Europe), a portfolio of interests in several African countries, and her own shipping line, a wharf in the port of Dalian included. Radiance was bumptious, exuberant in her appetites, driven, tactless and generous: but simple she was not.

'That's so pretty, would you like to see?'

A smiling sales consultant was already unlocking the case before him, and lifting out a black ceramic watch with a diamond bevel. Sean took it from her.

'Is it waterproof?' He imagined it dripping on Martine's wrist when she wore a black bikini. He knew she wanted to be invited onto Kingsmith's beloved yacht *Brisingamen*, the nearest place he had to a home. He would ask him about it over lunch. As if by telepathy, his phone trembled in his pocket and he grabbed it at once – Joe never let it ring more than three times before hanging up.

The name Rupert Parch flashed on the screen. Sean knew him vaguely, he was not quite sure how, but apparently he had given him his number.

'Rupert.'

'Is that the famous polar explorer?' said an enthusiastic voice. 'I said I'd get you. I'm testing this amazeballs app from the MoD, locates your contacts. Asymmetric intel, heard it here first. Probably not though, you're well clued up. DQM, though.' Which in Parch-speak meant: don't quote me. 'That's a nice watch, by the way, you should get it.'

Sean spun round. Parch's voice was in his ear, and also coming up behind him in person, a big smile on his beaming face, his hand out-thrust. Sean took it and Parch pumped enthusiastically.

'You – are – the coming man! Massive congrats!' He looked around conspiratorially. 'Ah, but maybe you're still keeping the schtum-powder on it? Shouldn't bother, everyone's talking about you. Sean Cawson has never been so sexy. True dat.'

Somewhere in his early forties, Parch still looked like a naughty schoolboy, with bright colourless eyes that sparkled, pale brown hair he wore to one side, a slim frame and a rapid, confident delivery. Sean was never quite sure what Parch actually did; he seemed to move around a lot, like some kind of cleaning fish, his exuberance commensurate with the status of his current host. Large, by his manner.

'Have you just traced me, illegally?'

'Illegally? As if! I just happened to be in the area. Although sadly not dropping sixty grand on man-candy like the plutocrat I'll never be, hashtag sighs. No, definitely not illegally. But you have correctly sussed that Parch has gone up in the world. And my master is terribly impressed with your latest news.'

'What news?'

'Don't freeze me out.' Parch looked even more innocent. 'Anyway, he desires me fetch you to him for a spot of luncheon, were you available at such short notice.'

'And your master is?'

'Philip Stowe. I'm his new private secretary. Proud to say I've already outlasted my predecessor. Very talented man.'

Sean had heard many other things too. Stowe had seized the post of Defence Secretary after a vicious and decimating Westminster rumble of his own creation. Sean waited for his payment to be processed. Stowe had sent for him? He felt Parch's eyes on his back and smelled his soapy cologne.

'Might you be free? Offers like this don't tend to repeat. Unlike my master, but I shall never mention that. By the way, there's a car waiting outside, on a double yellow. Only if you had no other plans. I'll run along if you do.'

Sean's phone buzzed again, this time Kingsmith. He had never before dropped his call. But the money was banked, the deal done, and Midgard Lodge was his. The buzzing stopped, and Parch turned from the display case over which he'd busied himself.

'Nothing vital?'

'I'm free.'

'Good man! Hope Indian's OK? One of those pop-ups, all the rage. And if you don't mind my saying, you look like you could kill a Cobra.'

Inouarfigssouak, Grand Massacre Bay

Grand Massacre? Kratoutsiak explained it in a few words. The story, though old, is worth telling. It remains in all memories.

Two boys were fighting on the shore of an island – the island where we were. A little brutally perhaps, like most children. One of them fell over. He shouted. The other, to keep him quiet, pummelled him with feet and fist. By chance, the grandfather of the fallen boy saw him. He ran up and joined them as he ought. There was a battle. Full of anger he hit so hard that one of the boys fell dead upon the rock. The other grandfather was furious and intervened. So did fathers, shrieking mothers, mothers-in-law, uncles, aunts, cousins, nephews and nieces. The whole camp was fighting. Injuries, invectives, horrors. All were in a state of unspeakable fury. They threw stones and bones at one another's heads. Someone pursued a woman with a bloodstained harpoon. They destroyed themselves. Of the whole village only one person was left.

The story does not say how the survivor died.

The Last Kings of Thule (1956)
Jean Malaurie

9

As the ministerial car with darkened windows headed south, Sean assumed he was meeting Stowe at Westminster, and all this cloak-and-dagger stuff was Parch's misplaced sense of drama, intended to impress Sean with his own command of perks. But they skirted Parliament Square and sped east along the Thames, and Parch begged Sean's forgiveness in not saying more.

By the time they were passing the Tower of London, Sean guessed they were en route to Docklands, and by Canning Town and the highly visible police presence on the streets, he remembered seeing some protest on the news about the bi-annual arms fair, held at ExCel Centre. Parch rolled his eyes.

'Word to the wise: we say Defence Expo.' They looked out. A dense crowd of respectable-looking businessmen, and a few women, waited at the main entrance. Many had flight cases. 'The British Government would not dream of sponsoring something as mercenary as an arms fair. Oops, don't say that either.'

'What, mercenary?' Sean enjoyed his temporary Whitehall gravitas, reflected in the faces of the armed police waving their car through security. 'Or Arms Fair?'

'I'm serious. I can't tell you why you're here because all I know is that Stowe's keen to meet you, so I crow-barred some daylight in his diary then chased you down, like the good dog I am. I'm guessing it's a one-shot opportunity, but who for I don't know. DQM, or poor Parch will be thrown off the gravy train.'

The car passed through tall steel gates and into the shadow of a line of battleships, moored outside the conference centre. As they got out they paused with a small crowd, watching a black-clad commando team demonstrate how they would take a ship, from a rigid inflatable boat several storeys below on the brown water of the Thames. Six men in balaclavas shot lines that attached to the freeboard of the ship, which they then scaled with extraordinary strength and dexterity. Sean felt soft and inadequate.

'Here' – Parch slipped a lanyard over his head – 'you're an MoD consultant for the day. Anyone asks if you're a journalist, leave them in no doubt. One weaselled in yesterday under false pretences, then refused to leave. Started shouting about freedom of information. Like he'd know what to do with it. Come on, I'm starving.'

Parch's 'super-cool pop-up' was in the Officers' Mess of the Indian naval destroyer *Kali*. At the top of the gangplank a phalanx of dazzlingly starched officers waited to welcome them and Parch was as airy in his greetings as if he were the British Defence Secretary himself. He led Sean through to the source of the delicious aromas – a buffet hidden behind a wall of tall and broad khaki, navy and black backs, gold braid abundant on their shoulders. There was no getting through for a while, so he and Parch accepted samosas and bottled Cobra beer from passing waiters. Parch looked wistful.

'We did one on ours, yesterday. A lunch. Friends, allies and countrymen, poached salmon and Coronation effing chicken, who thought of that? I wouldn't say the tumbleweed blew, but it was nothing like this. Waft a bit of curry around, et voilà! Prey and predator at the watering hole. Spend on the catering, that's the motto.' He dropped his voice. 'Problem with old Team GB is, their tastes were formed at public school. No gristle in the custard, they send it back.'

Sean tried not to stare. The mess looked like a fancy-dress party before people had had enough to drink. The bristling moustaches did not look real, and the braid and ribbons were comically bright. Out of a porthole he could see a golf-buggy full of men in Arab robes stopping at the bottom of the gangplank. One had a large hooded bird on his wrist.

At that moment, a volley of laughter burst from a nearby group and Sean saw the face of the British Defence Secretary, animated at its centre. The Indian commodores and generals around him were vastly amused.

'Probably just mentioned Coronation Chicken,' Parch murmured, smiling deferentially at his boss. Stowe nodded to Sean and held up his finger. Like Kingsmith, he thought. Sit, stay, up for a biscuit. But … good biscuits.

'Before I go,' Parch said in a low voice, 'he's very pro your price. For what you've pulled off, everyone thinks you deserve it.'

Sean took a slow pull at his Cobra.

'My price?'

'Come on.' Parch looked at him sideways. 'A Special K. You said you wanted one.'

'Wasn't that some kind of old nightclub drug?' Sean knew exactly what it was, slang for a knighthood. But how on earth did Parch know he wanted that?

'I believe it might have been. Didn't you mention it at that brilliant party after Wimbledon last year? Or was it Royal Ascot? Land of Hope and Glory ring any bells?'

'Not really.' Sean looked at his new watch. He remembered all too well. It was at a post-racing party in Berkshire held on the Last Night of the Proms. Things had been very bad with Gail – or rather, he had behaved extremely badly yet again and only a massive bender could anaesthetise his shame.

It had all culminated at this party. At first all was well – the beautiful horses in their stables and the Union Jack bunting, the strangers who shared their coke, the cocktails – and then out of nowhere he was talking about his marriage, any marriage, surely everyone knew marriage was hard, surely everyone needed help?

The coke grabbed him by the lapels and announced through his drunken mouth that he didn't mean to be such a shit, he was going to fix that just like he'd fixed himself his whole life, he wasn't finished yet, and one day it was his ambition – he was up on a table by this stage – his ambition to serve his country and do something that mattered. He would show the world that he was a man of honour and the proof would be that he, Sean Cawson from nowhere, would win a fucking knighthood. For his country. He loved his country even if it didn't love him. People had clapped, someone had helped him down. No. He had fallen. He shuddered at the memory.

'I was totally fucked up too,' Parch confided, '*much* worse than you, don't even worry. I only remember it because it was such a rousing speech. You were like Russell Crowe in *Gladiator* when he's going to kill the one with the twisty face. I thought, aha now, there's a man to watch. And wasn't I right? By the way, I even heard you mentioned at Chatham House the other day, in the same breath as the words: paradigm shift. *Before* you won the bid. Certain people have been watching you very closely. Obviously I can't reveal who.'

'Obviously.' Sean went to drink his beer and found it empty. While Parch wittered on, name-dropping the latest world leaders and giving the impression he was almost on sleepover terms, Sean kept an eye on Philip Stowe. The new Defence Secretary paid smiling and intent attention to each of the Indians in the circle. Sean could not decide which way the interview was going – or if it were a circle of wolves deciding whether they would eat the creature in the middle. As he looked at his watch, Stowe disengaged from the group and came over.

'Go away, Parch.' Philip Stowe had a pleasant voice and twinkly eyes, which he kept on Sean. He offered his hand. 'Good of you to come.'

'And you to ask.' Sean shook with equal brevity and firmness. Stowe had asked for the date, let him lead.

'How'd you do it?' Stowe didn't mess around. 'Midgardfjorden. Not the biggest, not the prettiest, ruled out weeks ago – but suddenly you've got the ring on your finger.'

'Charm?' Sean picked up his beer again. Parch was already on the far side of the mess, hooting with laughter at someone's joke. Stowe didn't smile.

'Well done. However you did it. Wanted to congratulate you in person, not bloody email.' His smile flashed. 'So, the Midgard Consortium—'

'Trust. It's a trust.'

Stowe's eyes flickered at his misinformation.

'A trust. Registered in Tortola, administrated through Jersey?'

Stowe was guessing. He had no legal power to compel Sean to shed more light, and was himself known for many obscure directorships. He knew all the routes. Sean smiled. Stowe looked irritated for a second.

'So that's your management company for the consortium. Private British equity with some foreign partners, correct?'

'Correct, sir.' Sean intuitively added the sir, not from respect but because he'd sized up Stowe as not nearly as rich as he was grand – and therefore likely to resent the far greater wealth of the self-made man. Whatever deal was on the table, Sean wanted him to feel superior. That was when people revealed themselves.

Stowe's eyes were also recording Sean. 'You got, what? Forty, forty-five per cent majority?'

'Fifty-one.' That much Stowe could discover; he would save him the trouble. 'The balance shared between my foreign partners, one of whom has dual Swiss-American citizenship. But in both law and cultural perception, Midgard Lodge will be a British enterprise.'

'You're the CEO. Buck stops with you.'

'One hundred per cent. The work has begun and should be completed next year. The season is very short.'

'So soon?'

'I commissioned the plans when I made the proposal to the vendors. I've had the architect and contractors on retainer.'

Stowe raised an eyebrow and Sean knew what he was thinking. How expensive. But instead the Defence Secretary looked thoughtful.

'Midgard. Norse mythology. The world of men.'

'That's the name of the fjord, since whaling days. Maybe because the mountains are in the shape of—'

'Fascinating political environment, Svalbard.' Stowe looked up as the Middle Eastern golf-buggy passengers with the hawk entered. He paused to catch their eye and raise his hand, before turning back to Sean.

'Our Norwegian friends are relieved it was bought by a British citizen.'

'Rather than …?'

Stowe twitched a smile. 'The Russians still believe Svalbard is theirs. Svalbard and a large part of the Arctic up to and including the North Pole.'

'Because of the Lomonosov Ridge.'

'Exactly. We'd do exactly the same if we could. Shetland doesn't quite cut it.'

'But don't Norway and Russia have an amicable relationship on Svalbard?'

'Amicable is a word that only ever implies tension.'

Sean thought of the email from Gail's lawyer, waiting in his inbox first thing that morning. The word 'amicable' had been used. The Arab group were moving closer, the bird now unhooded and staring around with fierce golden eyes. A nervous waiter came up with a saucer of raw meat. The bird turned away.

'Don't worry about them,' Stowe didn't look. 'They're early. Bringing the falcon's a good sign. We've got too many pigeons. Tell me the real reason they chose you.'

'Tell me why I'm here.'

'You're attracted to power. You're curious.'

Sean decided he liked Stowe after all.

'OK: the money was right, but we're small, British, environmentally committed – we're not a threat.'

Stowe leaned forward.

'Bullseye. No flags on the seabed, no subs turning up unannounced with two hundred men for an unscheduled sleepover, no new settlements under construction. You're a legitimate British business with an environmental champion at your helm, a clean tech hedge fund filling in, and a Chinese partner bringing stability and responsible investment to Guinea Bissau and the DRC.' The eyes twinkled again. 'Or do I mean the Central African Republic?'

'Both.' Sean didn't smile. 'It's like you've read the confidential bid proposal. It's like you can see my emails.'

Stowe waved that away. 'You'll offer different security details for each retreat?'

'I'm anticipating we'll have VIPs, I hope political as well as corporate.'

'Bit of a faff, isn't it? All that bureaucracy with the Sysselmann's office each time, all those different permits?'

'We'll manage.'

'And you trust all your partners.'

'Of course.'

'Even though you know Greenpeace does more to ruin brand GB than—'

'That's contentious. Anyway, Tom left Greenpeace over five years ago. I trust him with my life and his participation is the reason we closed the deal.'

'And in so doing, created a unique opportunity to serve your country.'

Time slowed for Sean. The great door was opening at last – to what, he didn't know. But the Defence Secretary of Great Britain was definitely offering him something.

'To serve would be the highest honour, sir.' This time the sir was unforced.

Stowe held his eyes.

'And an honour, your fitting reward.' Stowe's tone became casual again. 'Lot of interesting stuff at the fair, especially the Scandinavian pavilion. Care to take a look?'

Sean felt the impatience of the Arab contingent, waiting close behind. 'Don't you—'

'Oh no, not with me. Completely under your own steam.' And with a nod, Stowe pivoted into his next meeting.

As Sean came down the bright gangplank, his sense of surreality was heightened by the sight of fighter jets and Chinooks parked as close as space permitted outside the vast hangar of the ExCel. The little boy and kit fetishist in him very much wanted to go and have a look, but he understood Stowe had given a cryptic instruction, and he went directly in search of the Scandinavian pavilion.

At least, he intended to – but there was simply too much to look at. Each of the four sections of the conference centre was designated a compass direction, and each was the size of a sports stadium. Presentation arenas were cordoned off for military speakers of distinction, and military men and associated suits were crammed in, standing-room only.

The sound in the halls had a curious booming underwater quality, and the ambience evoked something of a cross between Selfridges and a souk of death, with all the bright display cases holding bullets, pistols, rifles, RPG launchers and missiles. If Sean looked too long at the carpeted seating areas, the huddles of men would pause in their discussion and look up with undisguised hostility. But the vendors avoided his eye. He was not their customer, they would not waste time.

Like all trade shows, the best pitches were bought by the big companies, and the independents who could afford it, lined the edges. Sean avoided the village-hall-style cheap tables featuring 'non-lethal crowd control' utilities and rubber bullets, and gravitated towards the massive gleaming rocket launchers at the centre. Here was space to breathe, amidst pleasingly designed and spotless military hardware. Some looked familiar from news broadcasts in war zones, others were of exotically futurist design.

Sean picked up a programme and located the Scandinavian pavilions – on the far side. He paused to take a complimentary orange juice from the stand of an upright British company whose earth-moving equipment was unremarkable on any building site – except here, where large mounted photographs featured it demolishing settlements on what looked like the West Bank. Sean pocketed an exact miniature of a digger from the give-away bowl and moved on into the crush.

The crowd looked either military or business, and seemed to consist of small groups that flowed around a dominant individual who carried nothing. Sean continued through the tanks of the Land Arena, where he was barged aside by meaty men in tight-fitting uniforms and contemptuously sidestepped by brisk-paced officers of the upper echelons. Only the unhealthy middle-management types lugging flight-cases scanned him with cold eyes and he instinctively disliked them. He should have been at the Scandinavian pavilion by now, but he must have taken a wrong turn, because he found himself in the Medical Arena. He stopped short.

Under a big sign that read 'Follow the Care Path!' a young soldier lay on the ground, his bleeding shattered legs stretched out in front of him. Sean could not look away from the obscene sight of the bloody white cartilage and spikes of bone, and the dark clotted gore between them. Then a nurse with a tool box sat down on a stool by his side, and began reapplying the gore. She pulled at a bone shard to make it more prominent. Sean felt faint.

'Lovely,' the soldier said admiringly. He looked up at Sean. 'Just like it was, you can see it over there.' Sean looked where he directed, and saw a body on an operating table. A theatre nurse in a Union Jack mouth-and-nose mask went through the motions of the field-hospital operation, footage of what he assumed to be the real event, playing on a large HD screen to one side.

'There I am,' the soldier on the ground called out. 'Lucky or what? That's me on the table too, up close and personal, and this is me here on the ground – still waiting for my Equity card. Job for life – travel the world, legless!' He looked very pleased with himself. 'What's it with you then, PTSD? No shame, mate – all in it together, aren't we? Sometimes you find yourself right where you need to be. Just admit it. You'll feel better.'

'I don't,' Sean said. 'I don't have PTSD.'

A large man in a white coat loomed up beside him, his smile deep and cold.

'Can we offer you support? It can be hard to accept. Denial is the first stage.'

'Nah, you muppet,' called the legless soldier. 'It's the bloody injury!'

'I'm looking for the Scandinavian pavilion.' His mouth was dry.

'I can show you.'

Sean turned at the friendly female voice, with its faint Norwegian accent. A tall blonde woman, her beauty plain as new bread, smiled at him with white teeth and pink gums.

He followed her past the disappointed pastor of the Medical Arena, and into the frenzy of the Scandinavian pavilion, where thrash metal deafened from the Finnish stand. This was inadequate to contain the colossal green-and-black tank jutting out into the walkway, which also starred in its own wall-mounted music video.

Sean and his new friend paused to watch for a moment, as, to the apocalyptic soundtrack, the tank crashed through a pine forest, breaking trees like matchsticks, before the film cut to an urban setting where it rumbled down a deserted city street, raising clouds of white dust. It pivoted with amazing dexterity before ploughing into, then over, a row of shops. The crowd roared approval.

The woman smiled wryly. 'Finland is not in fact in Scandinavia, but is a Nordic country. I am surprised the Expo did not differentiate.'

'Me too.' Sean said it knowledgeably, though this was also news to him. He walked on with her and they entered a serene and spacious area marked Dronningsberg, the centrepiece of which was a snowy missile launcher whose base was the size of a large tractor, and whose barrel protruded so high over the surrounding stands, that Sean had seen it from halfway down the huge hall, but assumed it was part of the building. The name Dronningsberg rang a bell – yes, it was in his architect's plans – they were the provider of broadband on Svalbard. They also did missiles.

The woman indicated a couple of chairs. As Sean sat, an aide drew a screen across, concealing them from the rest of the stand. She poured them both some water, drank deeply, then offered her hand.

'Mrs Skadi Larssen, Assistant Defence Minister of the Kingdom of Norway. I am so pleased to congratulate you, Mr Cawson, on your success at Midgardfjorden in Svalbard. We are extremely happy to welcome you as our newest neighbour, and this is a wonderful chance to say hello, and take the opportunity to discuss your plans!' She looked at him with great warmth. 'If you have five minutes?'

Sean had as long as Mrs Larssen needed.

'In Svalbard we have something of an open house, as you know.' He nodded, absorbing her provocative combination of size, strength, and femininity. 'A lot of friends,' she went on, 'can mean a lot of different values. It is very enriching – but sometimes, like now, we feel somewhat anxious about one of our neighbours.' She looked at him directly. 'Sometimes we feel quite threatened, but to discuss such things might make us seem weak, and maybe even encourage a lack of respect. And increasing our home security would almost certainly be seen as antagonistic. Then maybe our neighbour would want to do the same.'

'And you would feel even more threatened.'

He heard the strain in her laugh. 'How can I help?'

She leaned forward. 'It would be very good to think we had a new friend in Svalbard, who would understand our concerns and keep an eye out for us. Who would be there for us, in an emergency.' She paused, and they both listened to the rowdy shouts passing nearby, hidden by the partitions. Sean didn't know the language.

'Is that Russian?'

'Danish. The bear next door has been too boisterous to be invited this year.' Her clear blue eyes met his. Sean felt she wanted him to say something.

'Ah. In Ukraine.'

'In quite a few places.' She held him in her gaze, silently prompting him.

'I try to be well informed, Mrs Larssen, but most of us only know what we're told by the news, don't we?'

'Mr Cawson, Philip tells me you are an explorer, and you have a deep and longstanding love of the Arctic.'

'That's true.' Sean felt incredibly gratified that Stowe had passed this on, that he had even known it in the first place.

'Our two nations share historic loyalty and friendship.'

'Now you don't come raiding any more.' Sean's attempt to lighten the mood fell flat.

'Those were the Danes.' Mrs Larssen paused. 'Now. Do we trust each other?'

Philip Stowe, Defence Secretary of Great Britain, thought of him as a noble explorer. Sean unconsciously added in that word to the compliment.

'Yes, we do.'

'I think so too.' Mrs Larssen leaned forward, and Sean kept his eyes above the glimpse of lace under her jacket. 'Mr Cawson, it would be wonderful to be able to count on your friendship in Svalbard. In return, we will do all we can to assist you in establishing Midgard Lodge. Philip tells me you will be hosting a variety of security details for your guests? I hope you don't mind that I know this; the security of Svalbard is my business.'

'How can I help? I'm all yours.' He wasn't sure of that, but it sounded right to say it, and he wanted to see where Mrs Larssen was taking him.

'I would very much like to think so.' And she explained her idea. Midgard Lodge would host a private standing security detail, which could also be an emergency resource of the Sysselmann's department – mainly for Search and Rescue – if required. Very unlikely it ever would be. But so comforting for her to think of it. And Midgard Lodge must benefit too, in ways they would devise.

Sean thought for a while. 'Mrs Larssen, I'd love to help, but Midgard Lodge is necessarily small and discreet. We couldn't make a difference in terms of strength.'

'But knowledge is power.' She smiled. 'Observing the beauties of Svalbard, the ever-changing conditions.'

'As in, spying?'

'Such an old-fashioned word! But romantic.' She stood up; the

LALINE PAULL

meeting was evidently over. She seemed to be offering her cheek, so Sean kissed it. She laughed.

'A charming gesture!'

'Sorry – I didn't mean – I didn't mean to offend you.'

'I am not offended if you find me attractive. Thank you so much for your visit, Mr Cawson, and once again on behalf of the Kingdom of Norway, welcome to Svalbard. Looking after Midgard Lodge will be my pleasure.'

90 N LAT., NORTH POLE
April 6, 1909

I have to-day hoisted the national ensign of the United States of America at this place, which my observations indicate to be the North Polar Axis of the earth, and I have formally taken possession of the entire region, and adjacent, for and in the name of the President of the United States of America.

I leave this record and United States flag in possession.

The North Pole (1910)
Robert E. Peary

3 May 2007: Vladimir Putin makes a speech on a nuclear icebreaker *urging greater efforts to secure Russia's 'strategic, economic, scientific and defence interests' in the Arctic.*

2 August 2007: Russian expedition Arktika 2007, *led by Artur Chilingarov and employing MIR submersibles, descended to the seabed at the North Pole, where they planted the Russian flag. They took water and soil samples for analysis, continuing a mission to provide additional evidence related to the Russian claim to the mineral riches of the Arctic. Several other countries wish to extend their rights over sections of the Arctic Ocean floor. Both Norway and Denmark are carrying out surveys to this end.*

10

Martine was in Paris for the night, and Sean was glad of a night alone, to absorb the tumult of the week. In particular, today's visit to the Defence Expo (not arms fair) where he had been tapped to provide a standing security detail (not mercenaries) by not one, but two actual defence ministers. And mentioned, if Parch was to be believed, in glowing terms at Chatham House.

Life was certainly getting very interesting. Sean felt as though some brake had been removed, and this time it had happened through his own individual striving rather than a hint or handout from Kingsmith. He tried to think if they'd actually had a plan to meet for lunch, or if it were just contingent on Kingsmith's last-minute availability – the usual dynamic. He worked his way through the last few numbers he had for him, none of which took messages, then rang the Carrington and asked to be put through. They apologised; they could only take a message. Sean smiled – he must point out to Joe that for someone who valued discretion so highly, his favourite hotel always gave the game away when he was staying. He left word he'd be there for breakfast.

It felt good, setting the agenda for once. A healthy levelling of their relationship, long overdue. He owed so much to Joe – he always would – but now they were operating together as equals, not squire and lord. With nothing urgent to deal with on the clubs, and only one missed call from Parch – no doubt for a chummy debrief – Sean disconnected from the outside world.

Bell ringers were practising from some nearby church as he opened a half-bottle of claret and looked for something to eat. The fridge held mysterious bottles and vials of things he didn't understand, and suspected were skincare. He left them alone and made himself spaghetti with parmesan and olive oil, then sat down on one of the elegant white leather sofas to watch the news.

More coastal towns uninhabitable after the floods. Record deaths this month both sides of the Schengen Fences. The riot belt still burning in the US, Japan finally ceding the Kuril islands to Russia, bewailing its lack of international support. Then the usual footage of interchangeable street battles somewhere in the Middle East, a Kevlar-vested reporter shouting to camera as behind her young men ran for cover. Compared to what he'd seen earlier today, the weapons looked stone-age. With a bizarre sense of decorum he waited until a big explosion had finished, then switched off.

Without Martine's animating presence, the apartment was passive as a hotel suite. His minimal possessions were all neatly berthed where she had made space for him, but it never felt like home. He wondered what Tom was doing and picked up the phone – then hesitated. To call him at this hour on a Friday night would be strange, and over-emotional. He'd have plans, probably with the pretty Ruth-alike girl. Perhaps they were in his tiny Richmond flat, its 'river view' only visible while standing at the kitchen sink. The last time he'd been there was for Tom's flat-warming party, when he was still with the original Ruth, and Gail was pregnant. When a magnum of champagne was still a rare excitement, and fatherhood was a great new adventure.

He put the phone down. Two of his own clubs were a short cab ride away. He would be greeted and feted and surrounded by people, but it wasn't just the possibility of Tom being with the girl. It was that, even if he weren't, Sean didn't want to say what he'd done today. Tom could be very narrow-minded.

With great will-power, he avoided going online, just to fill up his anxiety at being alone. He wanted a real pint in a real place with a real friend, or for Martine to come back so he could lose himself in sex. Instead he took a sleeping pill and went to bed alone, intending to enjoy the travesty of thinking of Mrs Larssen and her pink and white smile, but he was asleep before he could summon her to play.

*

In his grey joggers and hoodie, Joe Kingsmith looked like a conscientiously fit American retiree, braced by some early morning exercise in the Royal Park, and now tucking into eggs Benedict in his regular suite at the Carrington. He waved away Sean's apologies about yesterday's lunch plan, also his opening gambit of laying out the schedule of works for Midgard Lodge.

'I'll leave all the details to you, Sean boy,' he said. 'Complete confidence. Coffee?' He picked up the silver pot to pour but it was empty.

'I'm good thanks.'

'I'm not.' Kingsmith looked around. 'There. They don't stick properly.' He retrieved a large silver button from the carpet, clicked it and dropped it on the breakfast cart. 'You want to ask me something big, but you're nervous. Spit it out.'

'I've been asked to host a permanent security detail at Midgard.'

'Have you indeed.'

Ignoring Kingsmith's slightly irritating look of amusement at this revelation, Sean had just begun explaining Mrs Larssen's suggestion when the door buzzer sounded.

Kingsmith went to the door and looked through the spyhole before opening it. Followed by a butler bearing a tray with another silver pot, he came back to the table. 'Go on. Don't mind him.'

The butler laid down the new coffee. 'Will there be anything else, sir?'

Kingsmith pointed at Sean.

'A dinky private army for my friend. Very discreet.'

'Not quite like that.' Sean pushed down his irritation. At what point was Joe going to take him seriously? And revealing it in front of just anyone—

'Our only army is of butlers, sir.'

'Then we're good.'

Sean waited until the door had closed behind him. Kingsmith was watching him.

'You're frowning. You didn't like my little joke.'

'How did he know you wanted coffee?'

'Oh, that button thing. I'm not sure I like it.' Kingsmith's smile faded. 'So who's this anxious pal of yours, and what does he want? Boots on the ground, eyes in the sky?'

'She's a woman. And she specifically doesn't want it to look like that. She – thank you' – Sean accepted a coffee he did not want – 'she wants us to offer top-level security to our guests that is flexible and vigilant on Norway's behalf.' Kingsmith drank his almost scalding. He chuckled.

'A private military on Svalbard, with a fluffy green eco-front.'

'You're mocking me.' Sean tried to say it lightly.

'OK, maybe I am, but you are so deadly serious, and this is not the big deal you think it is. But go on.'

Sean lounged back, mirroring Kingsmith. 'It's important to her it's genuinely our own in-house security. We were going to let clients bring theirs in, with all the bureaucratic hassle that rotating in and out meant – surely this is better.' Sean watched Kingsmith absorb this. 'Everything's more streamlined, it makes our life easier and it adds value to what we offer. Plus we can offer twenty-four seven emergency response and search and rescue.'

Kingsmith chuckled.

'She's worried about the Russians.'

'She calls them the bear next door. Have you ever worked there?'

'I have pals there, sure. Pals everywhere. But you know me, I like to do things my own way. I'm happy with my patch.' Kingsmith rubbed his hand over his bald head, gleaming and smooth. It was his only tell that Sean had ever noticed. So Kingsmith had history with Russia. 'What are they offering you?'

'Offering?'

'We don't spend our own money.'

'Oh. Flight permits, for a start. Cuts the transport time, makes it much more practical to attend for a day or two. And naturally I build it all into the retreat costs so that everyone saves. From landing at Longyearbyen, all the way through, to airborne en route to wherever next. Midgard handles every detail.'

Kingsmith held a pot of marmalade up to the light.

'A bitter jelly full of twigs. It's perverse.'

Sean knew what this was about – Kingsmith wanted him to plead. And if he refused, then later changed his mind, it would mean locating him wherever else he was in the world and doing the whole dance all over again.

'Joe,' he said, 'one of the first things I learned with you is that you can't work from a place of insecurity. I know it's not one size fits all; every private military company is different.'

'Sean boy, that's not the side of things you've ever been interested in. You're on the sunny side of the street. Stay there.'

'I'm not a kid, Joe. I've been asked to do something very important. Yes it's a stretch, but not for you. This is what you do, you make places safe. You did it for the *New York Times* in Basra, you do it for telecom companies in Africa – it's how the world does business now.'

'If they can afford it. So, what sort of size are we talking about? What sort of anxieties does your pal have? Maybe she could get in touch—'

'No. Please don't take this the wrong way, but it specifically has to come through me, as the British CEO of Midgard Lodge. That's crucial.'

'Crucial. I see. But why does your special friend, or friends, trust that you know a single thing about private contracting in the Arctic environment?'

'I won the bid, I'm having breakfast with you. I'm qualified.'

'Hah! Are you taking some kind of supplement I should know about? I've never seen you like this.'

'Carpe diem.' As Sean said it, he knew it was true. 'Midgard Lodge is my great opportunity. A home in the Arctic whenever I want. I can help protect it, *and* make money. From the time we met—'

'I know. Obsessed with the ice. But, just to be quite clear: you're offering me more risk and more work, for nothing?'

'For the stake you already have, in Midgard. And for honour. To do something worthwhile in this world.'

'Tell me what they've dangled at you. It must be something special.'

Sean said it as casually as he could. 'A knighthood. I think.'

'A what? I hope it comes with a side of real estate. Come on, I thought you hated all that inherited privilege crap.'

'I do. But you know where I come from. I've worked, I'm talented, I pay my taxes and create jobs and wealth – and I want my place at the table. Money's not enough in this country. Money alone doesn't get you respect.'

'You think a bit of ribbon will?' Kingsmith shook his head. 'Sean boy, let me tell you something. When I was last in Dallas, I went to that art museum and I saw your painting. *The Icebergs*, Frederic Church. Saw it with my own eyes, stood in front of it, and imagined you looking at it as a kid. How old?'

'Twelve.' Sean felt choked at the thought of Kingsmith doing that.

'I asked if I could buy it, so I could give it to you.' Kingsmith looked at him. 'But it is literally priceless – they wouldn't sell, at any figure. Come on now, don't get emotional, you know I can't cope.'

'Of course I'm not.'

'Good. My favourite people come from nothing and you're one of them. You're a rich man. But if that's not enough, if you want to bust a gut for a bit of ribbon – OK, to you it's more than that.'

'I want to protect the Arctic. This is the way.'

'Fine. Each man has his demons or grail or whatever. So if you say you want my help on this, but the rest is all on you, then you've got it. OK?'

'Thank you, Joe. Thank you very much.'

'Told Tom about this little detail?'

'Not yet.' Sean said it easily, but he did not want to meet Kingsmith's eyes. He hadn't told him yet; he could do it later.

'Here's what I'll do.' Kingsmith was looking at his phone. 'I'll hook you up with Danny Long. Countryman of yours, but really a global citizen. A very safe pair of hands. Tell him I recommended him.'

Sean's phone buzzed with the contact. The mention of Tom made him uncomfortable. He would have to find the right moment to explain things to him, but first, he must get things moving.

In 1867, the United States paid the Russian Empire $7.2 million for Alaska (US$123.5 million in 2016), officially ending Russia's reign over the area. Of this sum, a reputed US$165,000 was supposedly used to bribe senators opposing the purchase, to vote for it regardless. The purchase, made by Secretary of State William H. Seward, was initially ridiculed as 'Seward's Folly', but in 1880 gold was discovered, and in 1890, oil.

11

The plane trees of London form a scattered forest. Pollutant-resistant, their tall deep trunks shed scales of gold, green and grey. Normally they came into leaf in May, but later that February evening as Sean hurried along the South Bank to meet Martine, they were already tipping green. They were attending a private screening of the 1927 documentary *Nanuq of the North*, hosted by the Canadian Embassy. He'd seen it a long time ago, when the Lost Explorers' Society had screened it as a backdrop to a party – but been so drunk he couldn't remember a thing. Tonight it was the official main event, before the real one of Arctic networking at the post-show reception.

The audience was seated and the house lights dimmed as Sean apologised and bumped his way along to his seat with Martine. She squeezed his thigh in greeting and kissed him. Parch craned round from a seat three rows ahead, and waved to Sean. He mimed a drinking gesture then pointed at his watch. He'd come for gossip from the arms fair.

A woman and three men came on stage. Tanya Tagaq introduced her band, then the big screen flared with sepia light, and the Arctic of 1927 came back to life. Sean jumped as the woman began to sing – if that was what her unearthly keening and grunting sounds could be called.

The Inuit people on the big screen moved in quick jerky movements, familiar in Charlie Chaplin films but disconcerting in an anthropology documentary. Wearing clothes of skin and fur, they bent down to the camera and waved out at the twenty-first century. Sean couldn't concentrate, because of the noise the singer was making. He vaguely remembered on the invitation that it was with live musical accompaniment, and had expected something worthy in the orchestra pit – not this twisting fury in a long bronze dress clinging to her like fish skin, and whose bizarre sounds agitated him to his core.

The band followed every swoop and dive of her voice. Sean focused on their sound instead of hers – it was human at least, even if its abstraction and runs of sound were not what he would call music, exactly. But the woman's voice had him pinned back in his seat like an Arctic gale, her body now in spasms so violent he was sure her dress would split any second. One moment she sounded like a bird wheeling in the air, the next, some underwater devil gurgling obscenities.

Her vitality seized his full attention, it was the only way to bear the experience and sit through the film that she prevented him from watching. Sean gave up and stared at her – her strong female shape, her pale flesh gleaming in the stage lights. Her face was broad, her eyes slanted above high round cheekbones. Her long dark hair, which began pinned up, was now coming loose and her performance was more a case of public possession with an audience.

As he stared at her and surrendered to her sound, the singer and the band disappeared, and Sean was with Nanuq the hunter, smelling the mineral scent of snow, narrowing his eyes against the needling wind. His body stayed in its deep leather seat in the Queen Elizabeth Hall, but he was on the great walrus hunt.

Her voice hovered in pent-up excitement with the hunters as they spied the great prey hauled out and resting on the ice, and the drums sizzled their restraint. Tanya Tagaq slid inside her dress as her voice dropped down, coming in to ambush the walrus, closer and closer as the camera inched forward to where the walrus families rest unwitting.

One beast, a big male, is singled out. Nanuq's spear is pure hunger as he crawls towards the animal, the rest of the hunt behind, crafty and low on many bellies towards the walrus, still blissful on the ice.

A couple of animals raise their heads on lookout, but the hunters freeze faster – and the walrus return to their grooming and nuzzling and rolling together. Sean does not know how tense he is, leaning forward as Nanuq the brave edges forward with his spear, kneels up and in one fluent move buries his harpoon deep into the creature's flank. It bellows in pain.

On stage, Tanya Tagaq channels the terror and panic of the walrus herd as they stampede into the water for safety, but once there they do not abandon their stricken fellow. He tries to plunge in after them, but the tearing barb in his flesh holds him back, and the hunters come out like wolves. Mindful of his tusks and strength, they too hurl their harpoons into his body – a big bull walrus full of meat and warm blood. They close in on him as he struggles to reach the water, his big eyes rolling in terror. They haul on their lines to drag him away, back from the sea where the herd have all turned and are bellowing to him and watching in horror.

The sweat shines on the singer's white flesh as she roars the walrus bull's agony, the drums thunder the passion of the kill as the hunters twist the lines of the harpoons around an axe head buried in the hard ice and four, five, six, seven men strain to pull him in as he roars and struggles for his life. Their numbers bring him down and they drag him back towards the edge of the floe to finish him off. But in the water one cow walrus comes in closer than the rest, at risk of her own life, her eyes wild and riveted on the stricken bull, and Tanya Tagaq channels her too, as the merciless camera goes closer on her face as she watches her mate butchered on the ice floe.

The audience stayed stunned in their seats until *Nanuq of the North* had finished. Then they found themselves on their feet, roaring in praise and relief, stricken and thrilled by their part in the kill. When it was over, they rushed for the reception, and the drinks.

News of Sean's Midgard victory had spread. The Canadians greeted him warmly, and Sean inquired after the health of their new ice-breakers. Then as a group of Chinese businessmen approached, the cultural attaché took Martine's arm and they segued away to greet them. Rupert Parch materialised in her place.

'Obvs one doesn't actually *enjoy* something like that, but dear me, you know you've been out. Enjoy the curry, the other day?'

'Delicious, thank you,' said Sean.

'Must have been, as I'm told rather gracelessly to keep my nose out of it now.'

'So you're stalking me?'

'Oh, you know me, I go to as many openings, closings, commemorations, launches, memorials, bar and/or bat mitzvahs, Diwalis, festivals of Eid, Speed – you name it. Protracted throat-singing combined with a very long silent documentary is just another top night out. Look around – this is a Who's Who of the new Arctic! Listen to that buzz: it's the sound of money.'

Sean saw Tanya Tagaq come in with her band. She was still in the bronze dress, but had wiped off most of her stage makeup. She was immediately surrounded by admirers. He jumped as Martine slipped her arm through his.

'She's so intense. But come with me now, and meet my new friends.'

They were as useful as Martine hinted, they knew and admired Radiance, they had been to the Yellow River research base in Ny-Ålesund, they invited Sean and Martine to visit them in China. They had more feeling for Iceland than Norway and more still for the opportunities of Africa – the Arctic was busy and crowded – but they were very keen to be among the first retreatees at Midgard Lodge. In fact, they had bid for it themselves. And then all conversations foundered, because of what was going on in the night sky beyond the glass wall of their reception room.

Three days earlier and ninety-three million miles away, an eruption through the surface of the sun caused a colossal cloud of magnetically charged plasma to burst into the solar system, travelling at a million miles an hour. The cloud spread out into many charged particle streams. Around the time Tanya Tagaq's shell-shocked audience began colliding with alcohol, one of those cosmic currents discovered the atoms of the earth's atmosphere.

The smokers outside on the terrace of the Queen Elizabeth Hall shouted out to attract the attention of guests inside, urging them to hurry out. In London's night sky huge veils of Auroral light rippled green and violet over the city. Cries of delight in several languages went up as a curtain of gold fluttered through the heavens, over the UK and unprecedentedly low latitudes of Europe. The news reported it lasting just over eleven minutes; its like had not been seen since the Carrington Event of 1859. Meteorologists cautioned it was not cause for celebration, but Sean took it as a most auspicious blessing on his new venture.

Why did you take this voyage? ... Could I do otherwise? Can the river arrest its course and run up hill? My plan has come to nothing. That palace of theory, which I reared in pride and self-confidence, high above all silly objections, has fallen like a house of cards at the first breath of wind. Build up the most ingenious theories, and you may be sure of one thing – that fact will defy them all. Was I so very sure? Yes, at times; but that was self-deception, intoxication. A secret doubt lurked behind all the reasoning. It seemed as though the longer I defended my theory, the nearer I came to doubting it. But no, there is no getting over the evidence of that Siberian drift-wood.

Sunday, 5 November 1893
Farthest North: The Norwegian Polar Expedition 1893–1896 (1897)
Fridtjof Nansen

12

Four years later, in Kent, the parish church in the village of Wickton was hosting Tom's funeral. It was a tiny Saxon structure with an already overflowing graveyard that had taken over a neighbouring field. The car park was on the other side of a fence, and as Sean got out he saw the raw earth pit waiting. *Tom's grave*, he forced himself to think, though the words seemed ludicrous. He hurried in to beat the undertakers unloading the coffin, which also seemed completely unconnected with Tom. At least it was proper solid-looking wood, not some frail, terrible wicker thing.

The cold church smelled of stone and tuberose and dusty kneelers. He had come without Martine, glad to plead its small capacity. There were Gail and Rosie at the front, and without thinking, he went up to join them. They looked at him in surprise as the entrance hymn began, and made room. He saw they had both been crying and wished he had too.

On the other side of the aisle, across from him, were Tom's family – Angela his mother, Granny Ruby, and he presumed, some other relatives, weeping unashamedly as the coffin was brought in and placed on the stand in front of the altar. They did not appear to notice as he came in, and his mind tumbled with how to speak to them afterwards.

I'm sorry I didn't visit more – I thought it would make it worse to see me – when the truth was that it was unbearable to see them. After the accident, he had gone back to Wickton once, and endured an agonising tea with Angela and her mother-in-law, Granny Ruby, reminiscing about his student days with Tom, Greenland ... They had taken out photographs, they had wept – their raw grief ripped at his mind and heart so that all he wanted to do was escape the pain. That was survival.

Sean stared at the coffin, gleaming and dark and conventional with its brass handles. *Tom's body is in there.* He repeated it to himself, hoping he would be overcome with emotion. *Behind that wood, under that lid. Is it screwed down? It must be, by now.* The priest was speaking; he couldn't focus on a single word but he could feel the frigid two inches Gail was keeping between them and hear someone sobbing. He needed to see Tom's body for proof, and now it was impossible.

The priest was small and business-like, Sean doubted he had a clue what Tom was like. He had been agnostic, which hurt his devout mother, he'd said that once. Surely he'd rather have had a Viking burial on a burning ship, out in Midgardfjorden. Or remain lost in the depths of the glacier, as pure a burial as anyone could wish for.

The service went on, dreamlike, a lot of standing and sitting, the coffin filling his vision until he could see every screw in the plates of its handles, the grain of the wood, the details of the corners. Sean let the green clothbound covers of the hymnal fall open, because he could not open his mouth, let alone read or sing. He felt a tap on his arm – Gail – and he realised everyone had sat down. Quickly he did too, and as he did, looked directly into the eyes of Ruth Mott, getting up out of the pew and walking to the front to make a speech. Even in her funeral black, she looked vaguely hippyish. To his horror, she didn't go up to the altar, but stood beside the coffin, resting her hand on it.

'Tom, our truly beloved Tom' – and she stopped for a moment – 'is not really inside this box.' Sean stared. Her eyes hurled him back as if by force.

'Tom is still alive, in everyone's heart who ever loved him, in the passion he communicated to us all about how to look after our world. He won't die, while we continue his work. And I'm sorry, but this building is no closer to god than the Arctic that he loved. The natural world was his true cathedral, it's mine and it's everyone's, it's where we can all feel something sacred.' She looked at the priest. 'But what's also true is that Tom's family take great comfort in the Church, so I think he'd be happy to know they took comfort – in this ceremony.'

Ruth Mott gathered herself for a moment, and in the silence, Sean heard Gail make a sound, her eyes fixed on Ruth, as if urging her to be strong. Ruth met her eyes and nodded.

I loved him too, Sean thought. *And I wasn't even asked to speak.* He kept his eyes on Ruth Mott's hand, its bitten nails, its firm contact with the coffin. She said Angela and the family would be organising a bigger memorial in London later this year, for all those who wanted to come today but could not. People could put their details in the book at the back of the church. Then she made her way to her seat, and her hand left an aura of moisture on the wood.

Sean sensed Gail weeping silently beside him. He felt paralysed. If she turned to him, he would have to put his arm round her, but she didn't. The service finished, and the bearers took up the coffin. He allowed Gail and Rosie out ahead. They walked arm in arm, and though both were civil to him – Rosie managing a tearful hello but keeping her distance – he let them go on. Tom's family went out, comforting each other, Ruth Mott with them. It was like he did not exist.

Outside in the fresh air and sunshine after the tomb-like church, the birdsong burst like jazz and the mourners became human beings wearing black, revived to conversation and mutual consolation. Sean watched them hugging each other, but he remained alone. No one took his arm or spoke to him.

It hit him: they all thought he was the reason Tom had died. His venture, that he had called Tom into. His fault. He wanted to laugh in sheer tension at how awful it all was – he wanted to shout at them to turn around, all of them, and acknowledge that he was Tom's friend, he loved him too, Tom knew the risks, he took the money gladly, he was just as excited …

He caught up with the group and positioned himself closer to Angela and the family. They didn't seem to notice him. He began to pulse with self-consciousness. He heard someone mention the wake – to which he had not been invited. The email from the funeral director only mentioned details of the service, and he had just presumed – he wished he'd let Martine come with him, as she'd first wanted. If this was how they were going to treat him, what did it matter what anyone thought?

The coffin was lowered into the pit. He stood in his black linen suit, a force-field of repulsion around him. The mourners processed past, those who wanted to throwing handfuls of earth, flowers, messages on pieces of paper.

He walked away from the terrible sound of the mud on the coffin. Ruth Mott was comforting Angela Harding. He went over.

'Angela,' he said, 'Ruth. I'm so, so sorry.'

Angela Harding took his hand. Ruth Mott looked like she would shatter if someone touched her.

'You mentioned a memorial,' he said, 'later in the year. If you haven't already planned it, perhaps I could help? At our annual fund-raising dinner, we could make a new award in his name, we could come up with something together.' He wanted to say he loved Tom, that he was sorry, but it didn't come out. Instead he started talking about hosting it at the Carrington, in the ballroom.

'Sean, thank you,' said Angela. 'We've missed you. Haven't we?' She turned to the small white-haired woman whose hand Ruth Mott was now holding.

'Granny Ruby,' Sean said. He was going to kiss her, but she held herself back. Her old blue eyes were wet, but she was no longer crying.

'Sean,' she said. 'You've been a stranger.'

'I thought I gave you more pain to see me.'

'It's as if you were hiding.' The old lady turned away. 'Excuse me.'

She went with her daughter to the embrace of other mourners. Sean and Ruth Mott stood stranded together. The thuds of earth on the casket fell slow and hard.

'How's Midgard?' she asked. 'Making you a fortune?'

'Please, Ruth,' he said. 'Not now.'

'Do you even know what's happening in the Arctic any more?'

Even here, at Tom's funeral, he thought, she's ready for a fight. Especially here. Unless it was the way she coped with pain, like an animal.

'It's changing, we all know—'

'Some of us know more than others though.' Her eyes were very bright.

No, he thought, right the first time. She's ready for a fight.

'What are you talking about?'

She shook her head. 'I'll say more at the inquest.'

'Don't wait. Say it to my face.'

'All right, I will: Tom was the love of my life and you took him from me.'

Sean recoiled as if she'd physically hit him.

'I didn't. It was an accident.'

'Then I wish it had been you instead of him.'

'So do I!' He didn't realise he shouted it until he saw all the horrified faces turned towards him. Gail was coming to them, for a moment he thought to help him, but she went to Ruth and took her away, quieting her in the soft voice he remembered.

He was in his car before he knew it, driving the blind green bends of the country lanes without really seeing anything, until the broad grey monotony of the M20 clicked into focus at ninety miles an hour. He slowed down. He did not remember leaving the funeral, but he was glad he had. The last hymn went round in his head like static.

All things bright and beau-ti-ful, all crea-tures great and sma-all …

It could only have been Angela's choice. Tom would have gone for something like Joni Mitchell. They paved paradise blah blah. A cliché, but it would work at the Carrington fund-raiser, if he could persuade Angela to agree. It was the least he could do. And Martine would goad and seduce the business community into embracing its corporate social responsibility – they only ever scheduled those meetings at 5 p.m. on Fridays, they bloody knew it wasn't enough. He felt a bit better, planning it out.

All things wise and won-der-ful …

He switched on the radio, anything to rid his brain of the plodding infantile rhythm. Old Kylie, *Newsbeat*, Shostakovich, Gordon Busbridge Furniture will enhance your home – he clicked through the stations searching for anything with a decent signal. A scratchy white noise disrupted all of them.

It must be all the pylons. Wickton was a forgotten pocket of rural beauty in Kent, no longer en route to anywhere but itself, saved by its uselessness, but here on the M20, a swathe of industrial developments were broken by a few thistled fields, on which grazed scatterings of doomed sheep and occasionally, a few raw-boned shaggy horses. The miles of desolate development below either side of the sweeping motorway gave Sean an idea for the speech he would make at the benefit.

All around us is evidence. Greedy piecemeal interests. Now all anyone wants is investment in the US-Russian Arctic Agreement …

Sean put his foot down. Now was not the time to compose a speech. The radio hissed white noise from every station and he slammed the wheel in irritation. The CD player had broken too, the magazine whirring but refusing to load. And now the day which had been so bright and blue was whitely overcast. It looked like smoke from somewhere, drifting thick across the four lanes of traffic, forcing everything to a crawl. Probably from one of the industrial estates – Sean opened the window a crack to sniff for chemicals.

To his surprise, the air was freezing cold and damp, like sea fog. A hard wind whirled around the cabin and he pressed the button to close the window – but the electrics jammed and it stuck open an inch from the top. When he pressed the button again he heard a whining sound inside the door, and then a crack as if something broke. He switched on the seat heater and all the cabin heating, so that warm air whirled out from several ports. Then that too cut out.

Sean stared out, into what was now a mere fifteen feet of visibility. He could just make out the double red glows ahead of him as the traffic moved on into the fog. It was July – this was freezing fog. Shivering in his lightweight black suit he remembered the travel blanket in the boot, unused and still in its leather bands – but he couldn't see to pull over.

The fog lights shone cones of swirling whiteness. Tiny pale specks formed on the windscreen – snow, or ash from some volcanic cloud? The lights ahead melted into the milky gloom and disappeared. Sean stared out into the pale shape-shifting glow, his muscles clenched in the cold. Some primal part of his brain took over. Pull over. Get the blanket. Get information. Something must have happened – maybe a factory accident at one of those massive complexes a couple of miles back. A fast-moving front from the North Sea.

He indicated and moved cautiously across what he judged to be one, two, three lanes. There was nothing to gauge where he was, no bumps in the road he could feel – but no collision either. Instead, he had a sense of vast space around him. Perhaps this part of the motorway had been newly widened, and he didn't notice on the way down because he was so fixated on getting there in time. Perhaps he had strayed into a marked-off area. Perhaps there was a great drop he couldn't see, and he was at the edge. He had that sense.

He stopped where he was, his heart going fast. There was no sound coming from outside, only the swirling white. He already knew before he looked at his phone that there would be no signal.

As he opened the door the wind yanked it back so that the heavy panel almost banged against the chassis. The wind was freezing cold as he climbed out, and there was something in it that stung his eyes. He had to almost close them as he felt his way around to the boot of his car. Too late he felt ice underfoot and slipped – and found the ground around him soft with snow. He touched it in amazement. The blizzard whirled around him as he stood back up, reaching for the car to steady himself.

It was gone.

Not possible. He had just got out of it, not taken two steps from it.

But there was something in the whiteness, a familiar sound: the ting-ting of metal traces jingling – the sound of a dog team in harness. He shouted, but the wind took the sound. He could feel the vibration, the distant rhythm of the dogs' trot, too fast for a man to walk alongside, too slow for him to run. That funny pace you had to use – two steps run, one step walk. A big team, eight or ten pairs, coming closer – he tried to shout again but he couldn't make a sound. The traces sounded wrong, a metronomic clicking, or some harsh drum. The drum took over.

Sean jerked awake to the sight of a police officer's face outside his window. Blue lights flashed beyond the windscreen where two highway patrol cars were stopped. The repetitive clicking was the sound of his own hazard lights. The Vanquish was parked nose-first, inches from the concrete wall of the hard shoulder, at a crazed angle. His key was still in the ignition.

Sir, the officer was saying. Sir, please open the window.

Sean did. His head hurt, he felt pain in his chest and throat, where the seatbelt was tight against them. He looked around in dismay.

Sunshine, motorway traffic, though it slowed to see what was going on. The police officers stared in at him.

'I pulled over,' he said hoarsely. 'In the blizzard. Or whatever it was. Has there been an accident?'

'Sir, have you been drinking?'

Sean hauled his mind back down to walking pace.

'No,' he said emphatically, giving himself more time to think. 'Definitely not. I've been at a funeral, but I haven't been drinking.'

They breathalysed him anyway, and he waited in silence, stunned by the hallucination. Surreptitiously, carefully, he looked around. Everything was dry. There was no sign of snow. He wanted to kneel down and check the ground, but instinct told him not to.

'Mr Cawson,' said the first officer. 'You show no alcohol in your bloodstream, but could you tell us what happened? You mentioned a blizzard.'

Sean made himself stretch, so his watch came into view: 2.50 p.m., said the ice-blue face. The funeral was at 11 a.m., he must have left the churchyard by 1 p.m., and been on the M20 within half an hour. He put his fingers to his temples and massaged circles, thinking fast. Blizzard.

'That's the easiest way to describe how it feels,' he said. 'The migraines, they're like a white-out in the snow. I was at a funeral in Wickton and I hadn't eaten. Perfect storm: high stress, no food. I should have known. Usually I keep biscuits or something in the car, but—'

'Tom Harding's funeral?' The young female officer's face was ardent. 'I heard it was today, I knew he came from round here.' Her colleague gave her a disapproving look, but Sean seized his chance.

'Yes he did. We were old friends.'

'Oh, Mr Cawson, I'm so sorry for your loss,' she said. 'I read about it when it happened, and how you survived. He sounds such an amazing man.' Her sincerity struck at his heart.

'Yes,' said Sean, 'he was. Thank you. And I'm sorry to have caused you concern. I feel much better now, and I'll stop at the next opportunity and get some food and drink.'

'You're lucky you didn't have an accident,' she said. 'I mean, again.'

'Yes. I am.'

They diverted the traffic to let him out, and followed for a mile, where he signalled off to the petrol station. He got a Diet Coke and a packet of chocolate peanuts for instant energy, and checked all the electronics. Everything worked. He looked in the boot – the blanket, the hat and gloves, all still in their bag. He wanted it to be a migraine, very badly. But he knew it wasn't. Tom was dead and he had survived. The inquest was moving towards him like a great cargo ship on the horizon, and he was locked in its path.

Two thousand six hundred and sixty-four miles away, on the top of the world, the blue cursors moved slowly across Danny Long's screen as he looked in on what used to be the ice of the North Pole, now just water. It was getting busier, the cargo ships joined by tankers. He clicked on a few. Cosco was sending a lot over the top from Shanghai to Rotterdam, and Maersk went the other way. Some Russian vessels, minding their Ps and Qs. Nothing to report, just as he liked it. He fired off a quick email to his boss, to confirm it.

At supper this evening Peter told some of his remarkable Spitzbergen stories – about his comrade Andreas Bek. 'Well, you see, it was up about Dutchman's Island, or Amsterdam Island, that Andreas Bek and I were on shore and got in among all the graves. We thought we'd like to see what was in them, so we broke up some of the coffins, and there they lay. Some of them still had flesh on their jaws and noses, and some of them still had their caps on their heads. Andreas was a devil of a fellow, you see, and he broke up the coffins and got hold of the skulls, and rolled them about here and there. Some of them he set up for targets and shot at. Then he wanted to see if there was marrow left in their bones, so he took and broke a thigh-bone, and sure enough, there was marrow; he took and picked it out with a wooden pin.'

'How could he do a thing like that?'

'Oh, it was only a Dutchman, you know.'

Wednesday, 24 January 1894
Farthest North: The Norwegian Polar Expedition 1893–1896 (1897)
Fridtjof Nansen

13

A week later Sean encountered Parch at a summer party on the roof-garden of a bank in the Square Mile. Under a thunderous sky the crowd drank Pimm's and champagne cocktails and ate foie gras and oysters. Parch circled through the crowd until they could spontaneously bump into each other, and Sean remained where he was, to allow it.

'Forgive my ghoulish interest,' Parch said after the first salvo of pleasantries, 'but I've heard that the inquest date for poor Tom Harding has been set. A whole week – is there really that much to say? Yes, I'm a bad person, I saw it on a memo. All right, I peeked. No one likes being disintermediated – I introduced you, but now I'm not supposed to know anything.' He sighed. 'Hashtag bag-carrier.'

'Stowe knows about the inquest?'

'He takes a friendly interest in your well-being. And before you accuse me of stalking you and throw me over the parapet, here—' He gave Sean a business card, for a Nicholas Sawbridge, King's Counsel. Chambers in Lincoln's Inn, private office in Mayfair.

'Why?'

'Here's what I know about inquests,' Parch said. 'Everyone wants someone to blame. And if my master consults said important lawyer and puts a load of work his way, then he must be pretty good.'

Sean tucked the card away. 'And you're doing this because …?'

'Sharing is caring. No obligation.'
'None taken.'

Rather than his Lincoln's Inn chambers, Nicholas Sawbridge KC chose to meet Sean two days later at his private Mayfair office. After the grandeur of the foyer with its haughty receptionist and mantel-piece dripping marble grapes, it was a surprise when down the stair-case bounded a man much younger than Sean had expected.

In buoyant middle years with a good head of hair just greying at the temples and a lean tennis-player's body, Sawbridge had merry eyes behind retro tortoiseshell spectacles. Sean took in his wood-panelled office that was more of a club room, with its humidor in the corner and dark tartan carpet, comfort signals to a certain clientele. After offering Sean a drink and cigar of his choice, both of which Sean declined, and ascertaining he did not mind, Sawbridge re-lit his own from the big crystal ashtray on his desk, and they got down to business.

Sean told him how he learned of the reappearance of Tom's body—

'No.' Sawbridge looked over the top of his spectacles. 'You got the traumatic news by phone from Joe Kingston—'

'Kingsmith.'

'Kingsmith, I'm sorry, telling you that *Tom* had been *found*. Talk about his body "*reappearing*" and it might give the erroneous impres-sion that you'd seen it before.' Sawbridge pulled out a transparent file insert, in which Sean recognised his own *Sunday Times* interview from three years ago, part of its Polar Heroes feature.

'Marvellous interview, by the way, hit just the right note. Sorrow, courage, patriotism. And great god, what a feat of survival.' When Sean said nothing, Sawbridge put it down and continued. 'Well, I base my information on your account here, in which your old friend and valued business partner was very much alive the last time you saw him. Correct me if I'm wrong.'

'Tom was alive.' Sean had a sudden sense of claustrophobia. The smell of the cigar smoke, the fresh shoe polish on Sawbridge's brogues beneath the desk. The muffled traffic sound through the double-glazed mullioned windows onto Brook Street. He reached for his water glass and found it empty. Sawbridge replenished it.

'Jolly good thing you came to me,' he said. 'It's one thing to know on paper what you have to do, it's another to be in the room and feel all those eyes on you. It's not a business presentation, it's not an award ceremony. It's a very intense experience.'

'But it's not a trial.'

'Absolutely separate, purely a fact-finding inquiry. Much as the bereaved frequently want to apportion blame and guilt – which is only human nature, and who can blame them – that's not what the coroner's interested in. So I can promise you there won't be any sentencing or anything like that. We are going to present ourselves in a spirit of respectful cooperation, and assist our good coroner in creating a true account of what happened. Which is to say, it's going to be bloody awful and you need to be ready for that. Are you fit?'

'Fit? Yes.' Sean looked at the wood panelling behind Sawbridge's head. There was a knot, from which the grain swirled out. He looked away as it started to move.

'Ever seen Tom Harding's dead body?'

'What? No!'

Sawbridge clapped his hands together, as if breaking a spell.

'My dear chap! I'm giving you a taste of what it might be like. A sudden mischievous question out of the blue, like that. Excellent reaction, by the way. We want a clear round, no spooking or refusals – I've got a pony-mad daughter, I've picked up the terms – but to revert: this tragedy occurred three years ago. Now to the conscious mind that can be both a lifetime and, depending on any trauma, five minutes ago. The judge – or coroner, in this case – always says they make allowance for the passage of time, but in fact they tend to press rather hard on areas of uncertainty. Clarity makes their job easier, so we will give it to them. And everyone goes home not exactly happy, but at least with a sense of closure, which is the point of the event.'

Sean understood. He recounted the details of Joe Kingsmith's early morning call, and his own journey up to Svalbard the same day. He heard the change in his voice as he related those details. So did Sawbridge.

'Anything of note, this last time?'

Sean shook his head. The bear stared at him from the edge of the glacier, black light spilling from its knowing eyes, willing him closer.

'Nothing to do with Tom, anyway.'

'But anyway. Just in case.'

'I saw a bear. That's all.' Sean felt an odd sense of betrayal, saying it.

'A polar bear?' Sawbridge's face lit up. 'I really must see them before they're all gone. Reservations just aren't the same, though of course it's the only way to save them now. Was it doing anything?'

'Just standing.' Sean hadn't even told Martine.

'Wasn't there a bear involved in the accident in the first place? I seem to remember hearing something about that.'

'There was an incident with a bear earlier that day. Eclipse tourists. We were delayed in Longyearbyen because of them.'

'That's right! Attacked them, didn't it? Rather gory. But nothing to do with your group?'

'Nothing whatsoever. Except we were delayed overnight because all the helicopters were requisitioned for medevac, including the one we were going to use.'

'So the next day – the day of the accident – you all went up to Midgard Lodge. No bears involved there.'

Sean shook his head. Sawbridge made a tiny pencil note.

'I've been reading up on the Arctic, since knowing you were coming in. Utterly gripping. All those brave fellows. Can it really be peaceful there, like they say? Sounds rather terrifying.'

'It's both. It's sublime.'

'Now there's a word you don't hear very much. I really must go, while it's still there.' Sawbridge studied Sean. 'I do hope you'll trust me. The more you can tell me, the better I can steer our ship. That's how you must think of it: it's a voyage through this inquest, and there will certainly be some weather. And in my experience with my clients, when there's been a close relationship with the deceased, the worst weather comes from within. It's going to hit you again, make no mistake.' He laid down his cigar. 'Let's not pretend that this is not about death. And forgive me for bringing up something else that is painful but pertinent: your divorce.'

'What's that got to do with this? And how do you know?'

'I always research my clients, part of the job. The reason it matters is that, not only did you have the traumatic experience of the accident and the loss of your friend and business partner – one of them, anyway – but that was then followed by your divorce, in the following year.'

He paused, reading Sean's silence as permission to go on. 'For the purposes of context, was there overlap with your current relationship? You would be amazed what opposing counsel might think is relevant to mention, even in the supposedly non-adversarial environs of an inquest. Miss Delaroche?'

Sean looked at the carved nymphs either side of the fireplace, and their small nubile oak breasts.

'Yes, we were having an affair while I was still married. But by the time of the Midgard trip, the divorce proceedings were almost concluded. I'm now divorced and Martine is my partner in both business and life.'

Sawbridge's pleasant expression did not change as he made another tiny pencil note.

'So, whilst business has thrived, on a personal level it's been fairly turbulent. Following the accident, as documented in that marvellous article, you went straight on with business. Barely a week's recuperation.'

'There was a lot to do.'

'And entrepreneurs drive themselves ten times harder than everyone else. How's the sleeping?' Sawbridge peered at Sean. 'Sleep's vital.'

'Could be better.'

'Been bad how long?'

'I suppose … since the accident.'

Sawbridge steepled his fingers and tapped them on his lips.

'I have an idea, if you'll consider it, that might be very useful for us as we approach this process. I'd like you to consider the *possibility* that you *might* be suffering from PTSD. Post-traumatic—'

'I'm not.' Sean said it so fast they both laughed. 'Seriously.'

'No then, that's splendid. However, and I'm not speaking out of turn and she'd never name names, but there is a very fine therapist in London who helps top-level military clients. Going to see her could be an excellent investment before we enter the inquest.'

'PTSD is for people with no legs. Not businessmen who had a shock.'

'You'd be surprised. Jenny Flanders sees some extraordinary people in public life as well as the military. My job is to take all possible measures to prepare you for what is to come. Bereaved families need to complete their grieving process; that is not the aim but a very important by-product of an inquest. They have a hunger for all the details, and to identify the person or organisation responsible for the death of their loved one. This is natural. Going to see Jenny Flanders, a pre-eminent therapist in the treatment of PTSD, shows that you too have suffered, though you survived. It is a signal to the coroner, and it is a signal to the press, should they be there.'

'It's Tom. Of course they will.'

'Right. So expect mud to be thrown. Expect pain and raw grief in that room – and expect some of it to be yours. My job is to help you survive it. To that end, in all good conscience, I urge you to see Jenny Flanders.'

Sean thought of the blizzard on the M20.

'I'll see if I can fit it in.'

I sat in my kayak day after day waiting for the seals. The water was, as the natives say, 'merely oil'. The air was calm as an empty room and the sun like liquid fire on the glass of the sea. The hunter must not move, for the slightest shift of his body will disturb the small craft and frighten the seals away.

It is then that the mind begins to wander crazily. I dreamt without sleeping, resurrected forgotten episodes from my childhood. Suddenly great mysteries became for the moment plain to me. I realised I was in an abnormal, or supernormal, state and revelled in it. I cannot explain the feeling exactly, but it seemed that my soul, or spirit, or what you will, was released from my body, my life and obligations, and it soared impersonally, viewing everything as a whole.

I have often wondered if this was a touch of brain fever, or 'kayak disease' – or merely a state which everyone experiences at one time or another. I have never known, and no one seems willing to talk about it.

Arctic Adventure: My Life in the Frozen North (1936)
Peter Freuchen

14

Jenny Flanders worked from her home, a gracious house on the far side of Thurloe Square, facing the Victoria and Albert Museum.

She was a middle-aged woman with kind blue eyes, a blonde bob, and an all-beige attire that evoked a robustly sprung roll of cashmere. In an armchair against the tall bright window, she waited for him to reply. Sean studied the good furniture, the worn silk rugs.

Why *was* he embarrassed? He shrugged. He felt unbearably scrutinised.

'To be here, in the first place. Complaining about anything, when I've got all my limbs and faculties. I'm a very fortunate man, I know that. I live the life people dream of.' He adjusted to a more at-ease position on the sofa. 'Racing drivers don't look at the barriers, they look at the track.'

Jenny Flanders considered. 'Is that how you feel? Like a racing driver?'

He had told her about the drive back from the funeral, but briefly.

'I mean you don't focus on all the things that could go wrong, or have gone wrong. You look ahead at where you want to go.'

She didn't answer for a while. The room was silent, except for the second hand of a small clock he now became aware of. The ticks alternated in tone.

'What happened on the motorway sounded rather serious.' For a moment, Sean had the sensation of falling. He adjusted his position, so that he looked completely at ease.

'It could have been. But some survival instinct kicked in because I managed to park and put the hazards on. I thought it was a real snowstorm, but when I googled it, it was like a migraine checklist. Snowstorm effect, disorientation, strange noise in my ears like a howling wind. Triggered by stress. And what could be more stressful than Tom's funeral with my ex-wife there who hates me and my daughter who won't speak to me and Tom's ex-girlfriend – that's probably her permanent role in life now, as well as chief mourner – who wants to make trouble. It's not surprising that I had some sort of reaction.' He heard himself laughing it off. Jenny Flanders did not smile.

'Trouble?'

'She said some cruel things to me at the funeral.' He looked at his hands. 'She doesn't accept it was an accident. If something doesn't fit with her world view, she just denies it. It's why she lost her job – she was a field biologist up there – and she'd probably blame me for that as well, if she could. Sorry, but that clock is really distracting, could you move it out of the room? It's like you're trying to hypnotise me.'

'Clock?' Jenny Flanders looked around in concern.

'I can hear it – listen.' Sean looked around but could not see it. They both listened, as a motorcycle went past in the street. When that sound had faded away, so had the ticking clock. Anxiety moved around his body, settling in his hands. He folded them to keep them still. He felt the vibration under his fingers, faint and rhythmic. It was the second hand inside his watch. It couldn't have been that. That would be crazy. 'Weird. It's gone now.'

He stared at a bowl of tulips on a table by the window, almost prostrate with the weight of their striped ragged heads. The petals were white, splashed with red streaks.

'Everything's online,' he said. 'Everyone's bloody life and death laid out. My divorce, my work, pictures of me with women, skiing – pictures of me and Tom – a ton of pictures. It's like whatever's there becomes the truth.' He sat forward. 'Why didn't you prepare better to meet me?'

She didn't answer. To Sean's surprise, instead of jumping to his feet and walking out, he found himself extremely tired all of a sudden.

'You're giving me the silent treatment too, are you? You hope I'll burst, and spill my guts all over your old rug? It's a very nice rug. You must have had it a long time.' A small part of Sean's brain was fascinated by his own attitude. His entire career had been based on networking, on relating well to everyone. 'And people come to you for this once a week? They must be in a bad way.'

'You could come more often.' Jenny Flanders startled him. 'Twice weekly can be useful, at the start of a collaboration.'

'Collaboration? Sounds like Vichy France.'

'That's an interesting association.'

'No, it's not. Sometimes a cigar is just a cigar.'

They sat in silence, Sean determined to wait it out.

'I'm struck,' Jenny Flanders said after a while, 'by how you talk about Ruth Mott. As if she might have been the most difficult part of the funeral.'

So she had paid attention. And it was true.

'She's a very angry woman.'

'You've known her a long time?'

'From the time we were students. Me, Tom, her. And Gail.' He shrugged. The air stilled in the room. Jenny Flanders had somehow tricked him; he'd been about to walk out before. He saw her eyes move, and realised he was fiddling with his empty ring finger. He stopped.

'Sorry, but I thought I was here so you could give me some practical tools to manage the stress of the inquest. I'm not interested in trawling ancient history.'

Jenny Flanders continued to look at him with the same inscrutable expression, that still somehow held kindness. But not enough, Sean felt. Not actually on his side.

'I'll have to live through the whole thing again.' He was about to tell her about his fingers, the frostbite, how they were tingling again, when she looked at her watch.

'I'm afraid our time's up. Would you like to make another appointment?'

Yes, he thought, absolutely right. Fake kind, fake concerned.

'No I bloody wouldn't. And I'll see myself out.'

I had a visit from a man named Uvdloriasugsuk, who had come a day's journey to the north-west. He was a big, broad-shouldered fellow with a long black beard; a steady and reliable man, greatly esteemed by all who knew him. Nevertheless, he had shot his own brother the winter before. And it was in connection with this killing that he wished to see me. The brother, it appeared, was a man of unruly temper, who went berserk at times, and had killed one man and wounded others in his fits. His fellow villagers therefore decided that he must be killed, and Uvdloriasugsuk, as head of his village, was deputed to act as executioner. Much against his will, for he was fond of his brother, Uvdloriasugsuk nevertheless consented, regarding it as his duty. He therefore went in to his brother and having explained the position, asked him to choose his own manner of death; by steel, thong or bullet. Without protest or sign of fear, he chose the last, and Uvdloriasugsuk shot him on the spot. He seemed anxious now to hear what I thought about it. I could only assure him that where the safety of all was threatened and all had agreed upon the safety measures to be taken in defence, he could hardly have acted otherwise.

Across Arctic America: Narrative of the Fifth Thule Expedition (1927)
Knud Rasmussen

15

October

Sean decided to stay in Canterbury for the duration of the inquest. Early on the Monday of its commencement, he met Sawbridge in the breakfast room of the White Bear Inn, where they had both taken rooms. It was the highest-rated place to stay in the old city, and rather than ominous, Sean felt the name propitious.

His room was at the top of some crooked black wood stairs, and from the sloping window he had a view of medieval rooftops. A church bell, very loud and close, startled him – he had forgotten what proximity to the cathedral meant – but it was too late to change anything today. He wished Martine had come with him for the whole thing, instead of just arriving on Wednesday for her testimony. But the benefit was on Thursday and she didn't trust anyone but herself to oversee it. It was too important. The Tom Harding Bequest was £100,000, and although there was still an official shortlist, it was going to Imperial College for their newly patented biodegradable Fruit-Fly drones, nano-tiny and with unprecedented manoeuvrability.

In the sitting room of the White Bear, Sawbridge greeted Sean as if they were guests meeting for a wedding, rather than lawyer and client attending an inquest. He reassured him: everyone but Radiance Young had confirmed their attendance – even Joe Kingsmith. Sean's spirits rose at this last item; for his mentor to commit his time was uncharacteristically generous. It was indeed stressful, but it was also a formality that would soon be over, and then all suspicion would be blown away. Sawbridge made it sound as if they were off to see a top-reviewed West End play, and he had managed to get great seats.

Sean followed his lawyer's snugly pinstriped back through a short-cut into the cathedral precincts then out via a private gate in the city wall. As a King's School old boy, Sawbridge knew his way around, and cheerily hailed the flower of wealthy youth as they passed by in their uniform. Sean thought of his own alma mater. One drunken night he had revealed it to Tom, then felt ashamed and denied it as a bad joke. Tom had chivalrously agreed to believe him, and never again referred to it.

The coroner's court was a red-brick building beyond the old city wall, on the far side of six lanes of traffic. The main entrance was on a quiet side-street, with shallow brick steps leading up to the glass box of the reception area. The clerk handed over two copies of the running order for Court No. 1, and directed them to the private meeting room Sawbridge had booked for recesses.

He slapped the pages down on the table.

'I'd say we should be done by Wednesday. Coroner retires to consider for an hour or two if he needs, possibly overnight if he's truly dull – and then first thing Thursday morning delivers his Conclusion, and off we all can go.'

Sean looked through the list of names and time slots. Last night Parch, obviously with Philip Stowe's approval, had left a message of support 'from everyone', but this unexpected solicitude triggered more anxiety than reassurance.

To Sean's relief, Court No. 1 was half-empty. The capacity was maybe a hundred people, and the front three rows of chairs were clearly from some grander environment, high-backed oxblood leather with brass studs. The rest were a mix of serviceable office chairs, with here and there a brightly padded gilt chair commandeered from the Registrar's office down the hall.

It always surprised Sean how little people bothered about their environment, and how simple it was to improve it. As a way of distracting himself from the tension, he considered ways to do this. Clean the filthy sky lantern, for a start; get rid of the vile fluorescent strip lighting, rip out the carpet and put down sound-insulated wood for a sense of quality – find new chairs, all the same – emphasise the formality and get rid of the patched-together air of the room. An older couple in matching jackets sat to one side, and he wondered who they were. They were both tanned with silvery blond hair and the woman had an expensive handbag – and then Sean's attention went to the double doors opening, and his heart started pounding.

Tom's mother Angela Harding came in, his grandmother Ruby leaning on her arm. It struck at his heart to see they were dressed as if going to church, in neat floral dresses with jackets. Granny Ruby had a matching handbag, and they sat down in the second row on the left-hand side. A long trestle table had been set up down that same wall, at right angles to the rows of seats, where sat a very young journalist, tapping away at top speed on her laptop, pausing only to gulp from a paper cup. He stared at her sloppy clothes and flip-flops. He got up and went to her, and she looked up with a smile. Even younger than Rosie.

'Mr Cawson! I looked you up so I'd recognise you—'

'You cannot be here dressed like this.' Sean was appalled. 'A man has died. Show some respect.' He saw the alarm in her eyes. He took a deep breath. 'He wouldn't care, but I do. Appearances matter.'

'I'm really sorry. I'll change.' She looked mortified.

Sean shook his head. 'Sorry. I didn't mean to shout.' Then he steeled himself to talk to Angela and Granny Ruby.

'Sean.' Angela didn't move to embrace him, as she had at the funeral. 'You didn't come to the wake – I suppose you were busy.'

'I don't suppose Ruth invited him.' Granny Ruby's eyes held ancient light as she extended her papery old hand. Automatically, he took it. She tightened her grip and looked into his eyes. 'Tom admired you so much. I'm sure you would have saved him if you could have. Wouldn't you?'

Sean closed his other hand over hers, as much to stop her as comfort her. 'Yes, I would. And I'm glad to be here if I can offer your family support.' He went back to his seat, feeling like the old lady had knifed him. Sawbridge shifted as he sat.

'Best keep this side, for a bit.' He turned as the doors opened behind them. 'Aha. Mob-handed.' An older woman entered, followed by two young men. Each pulled a black document case. Sawbridge rose and bowed politely.

'Mrs Ursula Osman: tremendous to see you.'

The woman paused and blinked at Sawbridge. Everything about her looked slightly battered, from her face to her case to her dusty black suit.

'Nicholas. Good morning.' Even her voice had a rasp.

'Don't tell me you've given up criminal?'

'I give up nothing.'

'So true! Implacable honour your sword and shield. We salute you, madam, and are relieved this inquest is a mere Jamieson.' Sawbridge was as expansive as if he were hosting the entire proceedings.

'No inquest is ever mere,' she said drily.

'Touché!' Sawbridge straightened his creases as he sat. 'Fine KC,' he murmured after she had passed, 'but always looks in need of a good scrub. And my god she's aged. She looks appalling.'

Sean studied the woman who had provoked Sawbridge into such aggressive bonhomie.

She looked in her mid-fifties and was small-framed with the legacy of childhood scoliosis in the hunch of her shoulders. Her sparse hair was dyed an adamant brunette and as she heaved her case over a wrinkle in the carpet, she seemed to Sean to embody the cruelty of the ageing process as well as the vulnerability of the body. Just then a heavy file under her arm slipped and cracked open on the ground. She exclaimed in frustration and Sean went to her aid.

'Leave them.' She crouched on the ground before he could get there, protecting the papers with a crabbed hand. Then she recalled her manners and looked at him. 'But thank you, Mr Cawson.' Her eyes were deep set and black, with an intelligent, knowing expression. With a shock he thought of the bear on the glacier.

Dizzy, he went back to his seat, the tiny buzzing sensation starting up in his right fingertips. The loud distinctive croaks of crows were in the room – their black feet like runes on the dirty glass of the sky lantern. For a moment he saw another window, a cold white lozenge as he lay immobilised in a bed, his arms held in place by straps, an unbearable burning in his fingers. He touched the side of his mouth, then his nose. His fingertips were soft and whole, his skin was warm. He would have to talk about all that, very soon. Sawbridge was saying something to him, nudging him, and Sean realised the courtroom had filled.

'Please be upstanding for His Majesty's Coroner.'

A youthful middle-aged man in a grey suit strode down the aisle, followed by one in his twenties. The coroner took his seat behind the desk on the low platform, and his clerk cleared his throat. 'Please be seated.'

With a scrape of chairs, the inquest into the death of Thomas Walter Harding began.

One of the very remarkable characteristics of the West Greenland 'Husky' is the very varied appearance of different dogs. In the same district one sees animals which look like the old English sheep dog and others which resemble short-legged Alsatians, and neither can be said to be untrue to type. However the majority look more like the Chow than any other European breed. This great difference in appearance suggests that they are a collection of mongrels, like the bastard breed of natives who own them. In point of fact they are probably the purest-bred dogs in the world, being so securely segregated from the rest of the canine world.

Sledge: The British Trans-Greenland Expedition 1934 (1935)
Martin Lindsay

16

'My name is Allan Thornton and I am the King's Coroner for Canterbury and East Kent. I am charged to discover and record, through this inquest, as many facts about Tom Harding's death as is in the public interest.' He surveyed his court with a deliberate gaze and Sean felt a jolt of adrenaline.

'You are all free to come and go at will,' said the coroner, 'but I hope you will respect the process and find the appropriate moment.' Then he indicated the opposite side of his platform, where witnesses would stand to make their statements, and the chair they could use if they needed. There was a television monitor on each side.

'And now, at the request of Tom's family, and for clarity of understanding, I am going to screen footage of the actual moment of discovery of his body, taken in Svalbard in March of this year. I must warn you that at the very end, you will see the body itself. If you do not wish to see this, please leave now.'

When no one moved, officials either side of the room pulled the vertical blinds and put out the lights. The black monitors popped to bright grey readiness. Sawbridge leaned in to whisper to Sean.

'I knew nothing about this – obviously, I would have told you. Terribly bad form – are you sure you want to see?'

Sean nodded, his eyes fixed on the nearer of the two screens. He desperately feared and needed to see Tom's body. The words appeared:

Svalbard Cruise – Property of Mr and Mrs John Burke

The older couple with the silvery blond hair. They held hands, faces rapt.

The footage was slightly jerky and the time code flickered at the bottom. Then the POV lunged to the ship's rail to focus on the face of the left-hand fork of Midgardbreen where the blue ice met the water. The buffeting sound of the wind muffled the excited babble of voices in different languages, then the camera tilted and refocused higher up the glacier. The POV studied the white puffs rising into the air, before rushing down to the front wall of ice at the waterfront as it lifted and bulged before exploding out in the calving. The courtroom heard the deep rumbling sound audible beneath the shouts and exclamations of the passengers.

The camera stared at the great blue floe gliding by, then back to the waterline at the ice-foot. Sean recognised the new cave. It had grown bigger since this footage was taken.

The POV went in closer, tightening on the red shape that had appeared just below the surface of the water. Courtroom No. 1 could clearly hear a woman's voice above the wind and the rustle of clothing.

'My god, is that a body?'

The image on the screen was paused. The silhouette of the coroner spoke.

'We are now about to see the recovery of Tom's body.'

No one stirred and the film resumed. The POV on the deck was slightly different, with a new hubbub of voices. The camera focused unsteadily on the blue face of the glacier, then down to the water and a black inflatable boat with four people in orange survival suits. Small pieces of ice fell around them as the boat pilot held its position, whilst the other three pulled the red shape from the water.

It came up long and heavy like a shot seal, but unmistakeably a human body. North Face. Sean remembered Tom's red jacket. The trousers were black. The camera pushed forward over the rail, desperate to see.

The boat then turned around and headed back to the ship and the POV cut out, resuming at a different position on deck. The person filming was leaning over the rail to keep the boat in focus as it returned, the familiar sound of the Zodiac engine cutting through the voices and the wind. The crew on the landing deck below were standing ready, and the camera managed to catch a glimpse of the red shape – and the purplish frozen face Sean can still recognise.

The blinds were opened and also the windows at the top. Pressure popped in Sean's ears and the sound burst loud again. His hands and feet were freezing cold as if all the blood had rushed to his heart. Mr Thornton the coroner consulted a paper before him.

'Tom's family have asked me to explain that they wanted the entire sequence shown to emphasise his concern about the dangerous pace of climate change. That was the biggest ever recorded calving in Svalbard. They feel it's a very powerful way to bring attention to the issue he devoted the last years of his life to bringing to public awareness.'

Angela Harding clapped, others joining in. The sound mixed into something else behind it, a faint plasticky pattering like rain. Sean turned. A couple more journalists – adults at least – had joined the girl in flip-flops. He felt Ursula Osman watching him.

'OK?' Sawbridge leaned in. Sean nodded. Because that twisted horror was not Tom. That was not how he looked.

Tom was handsome in the sleepy-eyed way girls found irresistible and that Sean envied – despite attracting plenty of female attention himself. They had first met thirty years ago, when he was literally waiting on Tom at the Trinity Term dinner held by the elite Lost Explorers' Society. It was the summer term of his first year at Oxford, and the dinner was held in the private upstairs room of the Crown and Sceptre, a fusty conservative pub where he would never have chosen to drink.

He'd specifically asked to work that evening because he'd heard mention of the Lost Explorers' Society, in his obsessive polar reading. The society was several generations old and exclusive, and their focus was on the glory days of polar exploration. It was upper class, extravagant and mounted a serious annual expedition, with sponsorship and risk. He knew he would despise everyone there, but he still wanted to be in the room with them – those fortunate young men of means, whose loud entitled voices he'd heard and hated on the high street, who snapped their fingers at waiters their own age.

It was fascinating. Twelve members were in attendance, they wore black tie – something Sean simultaneously admired and mocked. He was the only waiter and ran up and down the narrow stairs with chilled champagne, then platters of pâté on tiny pieces of toast and yellow wine that smelled like honey, that he discovered were foie gras and Sauternes. When he'd cleared that, he brought up dusty bottles of vintage Pomerol – he had been told to leave them that way – and twelve heavy aromatic plates of Beef Wellington, far too rich for the hot summer evening, but delicious, as he licked his finger of gravy before coming into the room. They wolfed it fast, grenades of laughter exploding around him as he came in to clear their plates. They no longer saw him, but he saw them, how drunk they were, how they shouted over each other, struggling for dominance, and then he heard a magic word: Greenland.

They were talking about their forthcoming expedition in two months' time, in the long vac. This summer! Sean scowled at himself for even thinking of it – he ran back down with their order for another four bottles, and when he came back the leader of the group, whose name, Sean had gathered, was Redmond, stood and grabbed one from him.

He was a thickset young man with a ruddy face and wavy brown hair, and to a roar of general approval, he displayed his father's favourite 1976 Tokay, with the old bastard's compliments – and then Sean was off up and down the stairs again, bringing and clearing plates of apple crumble and cream, port and Stilton, and finally, Armagnac, coffee and truffles.

'You, waiter, stay, will you,' Redmond pointed at him, even more autocratic in his drunkenness. 'Then no one's got to break their neck on the stairs to find you.'

Sean stared back at him for a second, imagining punching him off his chair. But this was the Lost Explorers' Society, formed in the 1930s following the disappearance of Gino Watkins, legendary young polar explorer. He had pored over Gino Watkins' fate, sitting on the curling carpet tiles in his school library. Now he was in the room with the actual people who got to see the real beauty of icebergs. Yes, he would fucking stay. He stepped back into the shadows by the door, and made himself disappear.

Redmond got to his feet and in his booming pompous voice, announced a toast to Gino Watkins – Sean said it in his own mind. When they had downed their brandies – he could not believe how much they'd eaten and drunk – Redmond added that this was also the vetting of the prospective new member of the society: Thomas Walter Harding of Wickton, Kent, who would speak last.

There was a drumming of fists on the table as that young man stood up, tall and handsome, with a disarming smile. He bowed to the assembled company, including, at the end, the waiter by the door. Caught by surprise, Sean reflexively bowed back, and Redmond spotted it.

'Good man.' He turned to his cohorts. 'One anecdote, short and on a polar theme, in order of title which means I go first – yes, still me – new man last.' He looked at Tom Harding. 'Unless you have a title?'

'Mister.' Tom Harding smiled back at Redmond. 'Is that a problem?'

He sat back down too fast and Sean saw him grab the table for balance.

'We move with the times,' Redmond said magnanimously, then launched into his anecdote about his hero, Commander Peary. He was clapped – dutifully, Sean thought – and then the others took their turns, announcing themselves and emptying the bottles as they went. Most of them had some kind of title. Standing in the shadows, Sean forgot he was the waiter and revelled in hearing their stories. It was hard not to jump in and correct their frequent inaccuracies.

And then at last it was the new man's turn. Sean watched Thomas Walter Harding stand up, how he gripped the table. He saw him staring at the picture on the opposite wall, a stag brought to bay. He was clearly very drunk and for a moment it looked as if he would fall sideways, but then he started:

'And now – I shall tell you – an extraordinary story – about – the Arctic.'

Sean could see he was in a bad way. The slow-handclapping started.

'A very – unusual – story,' he gasped. 'Shit, I've drunk a bit too much.'

Before he could collapse, Sean stepped forward and pressed him back down in his seat, keeping one hand on his shoulder until he felt him steady.

'I'll speak for him. I have a story.' He was astonished at himself.

'What are you, his fag or something?'

Sean looked at Redmond sitting in his chair, fat and florid in a few years' time.

'Want to step outside for the answer?' he said. 'Or shut up and listen? Because I've got an Arctic story better than anything I've heard tonight.'

At the challenge to the leader, a frisson of delight ran around the table. Redmond grimaced a smile.

'Love your pluck, waiter. Go on then, tell it.'

Sean stepped into the light and looked around them all. Now he was going to do it, he felt different. They might be dressed up, but they were soft. He could take each and every one of them, if it came to it. They would listen.

'This is the story of Jens Lund and Aksel Søren of the 1902 Kristianborg Expedition to the Greenland ice cap,' he said, and as he did he stood straighter and taller, because whatever happened after this, for this one night he was part of the Lost Explorers' Society. 'And in 1902 there wasn't any reliable data from the ice cap in the winter, but these two men had volunteered to gather it. They knew each other a little, but there was no psychometric testing or anything like that. In October their ship anchored at Daneborg, and the supply team accompanied them to their base, where they had ample provision until the return of the sun in February, when they'd be collected with their data. Then the two men were left alone.'

He saw Thomas Harding drinking water, looking at him gratefully, admiringly. He could feel it, like they were already a team.

'The winter intensifies everything. Both men were diligent in their duties and went out in any conditions to read their instruments, but inside the hut at their evening meal, Søren liked to talk, and read, and exchange ideas. Lund was quiet, and became more taciturn every day, and Søren's cough before he spoke began to annoy him more and more. One day the cough and the questions and the talk became too much for Lund and he decided to go out with a tent alone for three days, and record from further into the ice cap. He completed his work and returned, looking forward to the hot meal he was sure Søren would be preparing.

'At first he thought the hut had vanished, because there was no light on. When he found it, there was no vapour from the ventilation pipe and no friendly smell of cooking when he came in. He got angry because he thought Søren had copied him and gone out on his own research observation, but when he lit the lamp he saw him right there, sitting at the table.'

Sean saw they were all transfixed, even Redmond. No one moved, or drank.

'So Lund decided it must be his turn to make dinner, and made up some seal soup, with some of the dried herbs Søren used. While he was cooking it, he thought of the questions that Søren had asked him, and decided he would answer them over dinner, so he did. He ate his soup, and as Søren wasn't very hungry, he ate his too. All his fears about what Søren would say or think of him were quite unfounded, and he enjoyed talking to him. Usually they took it in turns to cook or clear, but Lund was in such a good mood he said he'd do both, and Søren didn't object.

'In fact, Søren was enjoying himself so much he didn't want to go to sleep, but Lund insisted and helped him to his bunk. Søren wasn't well the next day, so Lund did both their work, but helped him up in time for the evening meal, when they carried on their conversation from the night before. Søren was such a good listener that Lund found himself remembering all sorts of things from his past, even telling jokes, and some personal things that had happened to him, but Søren never judged him. It was a shame he still didn't feel very well, but Lund had energy for two. He told Søren when he felt better, he could get back to it all.

'But after a week Søren was still not better, and Lund had noticed that at their evening meal, he was starting to look quite unwell, and letting his personal hygiene slip. Maybe it was too hot in the hut, and so he took Søren outside and made him a comfortable bunk in a snowdrift, quite near the hut. Søren was much more comfortable because when Lund brought him in for dinner the following evening, he sat up straight at the table, and their conversation continued. They went on like this all winter, and Lund grew extremely fond of his expedition partner, even though he was a bit lazy these days. But he brought out the best in him, like no one else ever had.

'One day he noticed something upsetting. A paling of the darkness. When he checked the calendar, Lund saw to his shock that it was early February, and the ship would be coming back. He told Søren about it that night when he brought him in, but Søren refused to discuss it. Lund didn't want other people invading their happy society and felt his old fearful nature coming back. When Søren refused to help with the dishes or even answer a civil question, he snapped and hit him. Søren's frozen body fell to the ground with a strange sound.

'Only then did Lund truly know what had happened, and that he could not go on bringing Søren in every night, because he was quite dead. He wept then, for the first time in his adult life – we know this because he said it later at his trial in Copenhagen. So he buried Søren outside – which was hard work, digging a grave in the frozen soil, but he did it. When it was ready, he did the thing he hated to do, that caused him all the trouble later. He took the axe and beheaded his friend, so that he could never come to dinner again. Then he buried the head and the body, piled the grave with stones, made a cross, said a prayer, and waited until the ship came.'

Sean found himself at the head of the table: they had moved their chairs back, the better to see him tell the story. He saw Tom Harding gave him a thumbs up, eyes bright with triumph.

'The ship returned with the sun and the supply team came to help pack up the cabin and support the two men. And of course when only Lund was there, they wanted to know what had happened. He explained Søren had died of his cough while he was away, and so he had buried him. That was the truth and he showed them the grave, but when they exhumed Søren to bring him back to his family in Denmark, they found his head had been cut off, and they didn't believe Lund's story. Søren was the popular one and Lund wasn't, so they put him in irons and took him to court back in Copenhagen. Only then, in fear of hanging, did he tell them the whole story, which was written down and can be read by anyone with sufficient interest to find it, and check these facts.' Sean looked around the table. 'And that is the story of the Frozen Friend, and I tell it on behalf of that man there.'

It took a few seconds for the Lost Explorers' Society to realise the tale was told. They stamped and roared and called for more, and more drink to go with it, but the proprietor came up to turn on the lights and kick them out, frowning at his waiter as he did so. Sean's tiredness was gone, he was electrified by his performance, by the story, and he was trembling with his daring. He collected plates and glasses, glad to disappear from view, retreating back into himself, collecting his wages, going back to his room where he lay in bed, smiling in the dark. The world had changed.

The following day he found a note in his pigeonhole at Hertford College. It was on headed Christ Church College notepaper and from Tom Harding, who had traced him. He wanted to thank him in person at the earliest opportunity, and would be in the King's Head pub around the corner, that night. PS He had something to ask him, involving Greenland.

The next depot is – nowhere. Gone, vanished – used for dog-feed. We have already marched as far as we thought to go today, but when we fixed the length of our day's journey we were still in paradise, and never dreamed of any serpent. But now all is changed, the empty tins grin devilishly at us out of wide gashes cut by the axe – we must get in at once, for, in our certainty of finding food here, we have made deep inroads on our stock. It was but a pound a day in all – but it was yet too much; the depot here laid waste speaks ill for what may await us at the next.

It is stern work now: a feverish race with death – the grim death of hunger, and we wonder often as we toil along which is to win in the end.

Lost in the Arctic: Being the story of the 'Alabama' Expedition, 1909–12 (1913)
Captain Ejnar Mikkelsen

17

Angela Harding was next to take the stand. She asked, on behalf of the family, for as much information as possible.

'If we know,' she said, and her voice was small but strong, 'we can stop imagining. I don't enjoy that, I'm better with facts. Don't think you're sparing us by not saying.' She went back down to her seat, and then the coroner called Inspector Pal Brovang of the Sysselmann's Office, Svalbard, in the Kingdom of Norway.

Sean twisted round as Inspector Brovang came in, a quiet-looking man in his fifties with close-cropped grey hair, the lean compact frame of a much younger man, and a light tread. He and the coroner nodded to each other as equals. Mr Thornton thanked him for making the time to attend this inquest, then Brovang took the oath in fluent English, a skill in Sean's experience shared by 100 per cent of Norwegians.

Though he had been in contact with Brovang before, in every sense, Sean had never been conscious and in the same room. This was the first time. The thought of his own hands, cold and frozen, in that man's warm armpits, was embarrassingly intimate.

'Inspector Brovang,' commenced Mr Thornton, 'you attended both the aftermath of the accident on the Midgardbreen glacier, during which Tom Harding is believed to have lost his life, and also the subsequent discovery of his body in June of this year, by the cruise ship *Vanir*.'

Brovang nodded. 'A sad coincidence, but it meant I was well placed to help.'

'If you would please summarise the events of the accident to us?'

'Certainly.' Brovang looked out across the court. 'But first may I offer my condolences, and that of my whole team, to all Tom's family. We greatly regret we were unable to recover his body for you at the time.'

'Thank you.' Sean knew the small clear voice of Granny Ruby.

'So then. Late on the twentieth March 2015, the day of the solar eclipse, the coastguard received emergency calls made from the buildings now known as Midgard Lodge, by Miss Martine Delaroche and Mr Danny Long.' Brovang's eyes searched the court before he continued. 'She reported there had been an accident at the Midgardbreen ice-caves and said that two people – Sean Cawson and Tom Harding – were still inside, and there had been an internal collapse. Three people had managed to get out because they did not want to go so deep and had stayed near the entrance. These were Miss Delaroche, Miss Young, and Mr Kingsmith. Mr Cawson and Mr Harding wanted to go in to see the feature that was known as the Great Hall.'

'Was?' asked the coroner.

'Since this accident we put warnings against exploring ice-caves everywhere on the archipelago. The stability of the permafrost is compromised in many places; houses and mines are also collapsing. In Greenland too, and in Russia.' Inspector Brovang looked out at the silent courtroom. 'In the Arctic the weather can change very fast, and this is what happened that day, all over Svalbard. We had many incidents of people in difficulty.'

'Is Miss Delaroche testifying today?' The coroner consulted notes. 'I see, Wednesday. Very well. Please go on.'

'Also at the location of the cave – not inside it, but at a vantage point higher up the glacier – Mr Long and Mr Bjornsen had been standing bear watch. But because of the rapid change in the weather they were already heading down to the cave when the three got out. Then because of the fast-approaching storm, they made the decision to get the three visitors back safely rather than further risk all their lives. Our phone records show that the storm had stopped their phones working. The best satellite technology is no match for Nature.'

Brovang poured some water from the jug on the stand and drank. Sean realised he was holding his breath. He knew this story like a fable: the solar storm that knocked out all the satellite phones, the collapsed cave, the blizzard. Then they all went back to Midgard Lodge and left him and Tom under the ice.

Brovang's eyes found his. 'You know they had to do it: they could not clear a collapsed ice-cave with their bare hands, and a storm coming in. They acted with sense, but they were very distressed when they got through on the telephone.'

Sean nodded, to show *Yes, of course. They had to abandon us.*

'We had many emergencies on Svalbard over this period, and because of the storm and the fog it was impossible to travel to Midgardbreen for four hours after we received the distress calls. Fog is the most dangerous condition if you want to render aid, because you risk also having an accident and … compounding? – compounding, the first crisis with a new one. We had to wait until it was safer to fly, then locate the entrance to the ice-cave. It was difficult because of all the new snow.'

He turned to the coroner. 'Whenever there are high numbers of visitors to Svalbard, we see a corresponding increase in the need for the emergency services. This was the case on the day of the solar eclipse. It is sadly ironic that my department had already called upon the search and rescue facilities offered to us by Midgard Lodge, for use in other incidents. It is possible that without the arrangement Mr Cawson had with the Sysselmann's office, aid would have come sooner. But it is my opinion that, because of the storm, the outcome of the situation would have been the same.'

Brovang's eyes now found Tom's family. 'It is normal for the family to want to know everything. I would be the same. So I will tell you that, by our records, from the time of the phone call from Miss Delaroche, to the time we arrived, it was nearly seven hours since the cave system collapsed. The fact that the other three members of the party survived is because Mr Long and Mr Bjornsen got them back to Midgard Lodge. Then it was night and we could not continue searching. We sent the three survivors back to Longyearbyen for medical support; we stayed on at Midgard Lodge, and in the morning by first light we resumed the search for Tom and Sean.'

Sean felt a peculiar pang at how Brovang had changed to his first name. He had a fleeting fantasy of Brovang as his older brother. He had that quality; someone you could lean on and trust, who would make the thugs think twice before taking him on.

'We called reinforcements from Longyearbyen,' Brovang continued. 'Some of the search and rescue staff from Midgard Lodge had also returned to help. But it was impossible to open up the cave without further risk of life. We had to accept the strong chance that both men were lost. Then we had news of another storm coming in, so we had a maximum thirty to forty minutes more to search. It was during this time that I discovered Sean in an old polar bear den. In the Arctic, we say you are not dead until you are warm and dead, and so I did that: I warmed him.'

Brovang stopped. In the silence everyone heard Angela Harding sobbing quietly. Another mother's son found, and hers lost. Sean didn't know it was a den. He thought he had burrowed that hole himself. Explorers did that, he knew. That was what he'd said in the interview, that was what he remembered. A polar bear den was a much better story, and it was even true.

Suddenly he didn't know what was his own experience, and what were things he'd unconsciously gathered from other sources, and wanted to believe. Like the stories he'd told about his supposed father, the lost polar explorer. Inside him he had felt that it was true. He was taking deep breaths of air, and he felt the deliberate pressure of Sawbridge's arm against his.

'Steady now,' murmured his lawyer. 'Steady.'

'It is important, I think, to say that Svalbard is an unrestricted environment,' Brovang addressed the courtroom. 'We are there on Nature's own terms, and at our own risk. Sean and Tom knew this, they were experienced travellers. Also, I believe the cave was checked by Danny Long and Terry Bjornsen two days prior to this visit, and they found no unusual risk factors – beyond of course that going into a glacier has an inherent risk.'

Brovang paused, and looked directly at Angela Harding. 'In my opinion, this is a tragic example of a true accident. The weight of the collapsed ice and the lack of oxygen would be similar to being caught in an avalanche, which is what I said in my report. When I interviewed Mr Cawson in hospital, he told me about Tom's fall to the deeper level, and it was only at that time I gave instructions to stop the search. We could not go down any further, and the time had passed to expect to find him alive.

'And now, three years later, we have more than one hundred pieces of evidence of how his body was found, from all the passengers on the *Vanir*, who were in the fjord because of a bear sighting. Otherwise no one would have known, because his body would have sunk within minutes.' Brovang looked back to Sean. 'This time Mr Cawson's men were on hand, to offer assistance, but the Coastguard was already there so we did not need them.'

The coroner sat forward with a frown. 'Mr Cawson's men? I don't understand. And how did they know?'

The courtroom became quiet. Sean felt himself very far away, under the ice.

'Mr Cawson's business, Midgard Lodge, is further down inside the fjord, almost at the boundary of the National Park. They would have picked it up on the radio, when the *Vanir* called us with the emergency.'

'Why would they do that?' asked the coroner.

'In remote places like Svalbard, your life might depend on a good neighbour. If you are a little nosy, well, OK. An emergency on the doorstep would be important to know about. I am guessing that is why they were there so soon.'

The coroner made a note on his pad.

'I'll be coming to Mr Cawson's business later, so I'll save further questions about that for him.'

Sean sensed the room shift in awareness. People moved to take a better look at him. So he had a business there did he, he was nosy, was he? He heard the tiny plastic rattling of keyboards, but he did not look. He could feel Sawbridge tapping his foot, and his own collar tight on his throat.

'There is one more thing,' said Brovang. 'At the time of the accident, I asked for photographs of both Tom and Sean, to show my team. I also took samples from their clothing, for DNA, which has been held at the Folkehelseinstituttet in Oslo. So when Tom's body was found, I could still recognise him, and his family kindly provided a DNA match also.'

Sean kept his eyes forward. All these things going on, and he hadn't even known Tom had been found.

'A question,' said the coroner. 'When you identified him, I believe you first notified Dr Ruth Mott, the tourist lecturer. Why her?'

'Ah.' Brovang took off his glasses. 'Because her name and number were in the back of Tom's passport. I had the details from before.'

The coroner looked out. 'Mrs Osman, Mr Sawbridge, any questions?'

They both nodded, but Sawbridge waved her forward.

'Ladies first.'

Mrs Osman stood crookedly, and spoke in her rasping voice.

'On behalf of Tom's family I would like to thank you, Inspector Brovang, for your diligence in all matters concerning the search for Tom, your care in assistance with his repatriation home, and your time in attending this inquest. First, I'd like to ask you a bit more about your choice to call Dr Ruth Mott, rather than Mr Cawson, whose details you also held. And who, after all, had been in the accident with him.'

'Yes.' Brovang spoke quietly. 'But he had not written Sean's details in the back of his passport.'

'Is that the only reason?'

Sawbridge half rose. 'Terribly sorry,' he called out, 'but the relevance of the question is … what, exactly?'

Mrs Osman addressed the coroner, not Sawbridge.

'I believe Tom Harding's relationship with Ruth Mott will prove to be significant in illuminating the circumstances of his death. My other question concerns the exact nature of these "search and rescue" staff at Midgard Lodge?'

'I don't know.' Brovang said it simply. 'But they are good neighbours.'

'Where is this going, please?' Sawbridge leaned forward.

'Agreed,' said the coroner. 'We have a lot to get through. Mr Sawbridge?'

'Thank you.' Sawbridge pushed his spectacles up his nose and smiled respectfully at Inspector Brovang. 'You said people visit Svalbard "on Nature's terms". Could you explain that a little more?'

'The simplest way to put it is to say, be humble. Every single time you step outside, respect her power.'

'No matter how experienced you think you are?'

'Especially then.'

'Thank you, Inspector Brovang, no further questions.'

Sean stood on the side-street with Sawbridge, his mouth and eyes burning dry. People from the courtroom ducked their eyes as they passed. Sawbridge aimed his match hard and accurate into a drain, then puffed on his cigar for a while.

'Exploitative and unfair, showing that footage. What's Osman playing at, going in so hard right at the start? That's the worst, though: seeing it. How're you doing?'

Sean felt the warm brick wall against his back. The gritty air near the ring road was refreshing after the stillness of the courtroom.

'I needed to see it.' His voice did not sound his own.

'Sean?' Brovang had followed them. He nodded to Sawbridge then shook hands with Sean, his grip warm and vigorous. 'I heard you were fully recovered,' he said. 'But it is still good to see with my own eyes. And also to say thank you for the generous donations,' he went on. 'Midgard Lodge helps Longyearbyen stay Norway's Most Generous Town every year. But you know it was our duty to help. You don't need to keep paying for it.'

'You're sure,' Sean said, 'that it was a polar bear den? Perhaps if they'd known that, people wouldn't have thought so badly of me. A polar bear sells anything.'

Brovang smiled.

'Oh yes, we are quite sure. Higher up the glacier, and we think long unused. I did tell you, afterwards when we spoke in the Sickehaus. You were very pleased – you said you were lucky, because it might have been occupied!'

'I don't remember that at all. But it would be a pleasure to see you at Midgard Lodge, I'll be there much more often now. I just couldn't face it for a while.' He felt like he was apologising to Brovang.

Brovang nodded. 'That is very easy to understand. I think many people will be glad to know you are in charge.'

'I've always been in charge. What do you mean?'

'Ah.' Brovang looked at his watch. 'I must make sure I catch that train. Good luck, Sean.' He hurried away and Sean watched him go, disturbed.

When a human being dies, the soul leaves the earth and goes to one or the other of two distinct regions. Some souls go up into heaven and become Uvdlormuit, the People of Day. Their country lies over toward the dawn. Others again go down under the sea, where there is a narrow belt of land with water on either side. These are called Qimiujarmuit, the People of the Narrow Land. But in either place they are happy and at ease, and there is always plenty to eat.

Those who pass to the Land of Day are people who have been drowned, or murdered. It is said that the Land of Day is the land of glad and happy souls. It is a great country, with many caribou, and the people there live only for pleasure. They play ball most of the time, playing at football with the skull of a walrus, and laughing and singing as they play. It is this game of souls playing at ball that we can see in the sky as the northern lights.

The greater among the angakoqs, or wizards, often go up on a visit to the People of Day, just for pleasure. Such are called Pavungnartut, which means, those who rise up to heaven. The wizard preparing to set out on such a journey is placed at the back of the bench in his hut, with a curtain of skin to hide him from view. His hands must be tied behind his back and his head lashed fast to his knees; he wears breeches, but nothing more, the upper part of his body being bare. When he is thus tied up, the men who have tied him take fire from the lamp on the point of a knife and pass it over his head, drawing rings in the air, and saying at the same time; 'Niorruarniartoq aifale' (Let him who is going on a visit now be carried away).

Across Arctic America: Narrative of the Fifth Thule Expedition (1927)
Knud Rasmussen

18

Flip-flops, as he had mentally named her, rushed up to Sean before he sat down with Sawbridge for the second session. At first he didn't recognise her – she had changed into 'the most boring clothes I could find', she told him breathlessly. 'I am so sorry to dress disrespectfully, I didn't know.' She looked down at her black shoes and skin-coloured tights. 'Sorry.'

'You weren't to know.' Sean thought of the strange outfits Rosie wore. This girl was about the same age. He looked over to the long trestle, where a couple more journalists, a man and a woman, had taken up positions a couple of seats apart. 'Who are you with?'

'With?' The girl followed his eyes. 'Oh. I'm freelance.' She gave him a card, her name handwritten in block capitals. BETH BURNHAM, ENVIRONMENTAL CORRESPONDENT. He tried not to smile.

'That's right.' She looked at him earnestly. 'You have to imagine yourself where you want to be, then it can happen. You said that in your *Sunday Times* interview.'

'Shouldn't you be in school?'

'This is more important.'

'Than your education? No, it's not.'

'It is! The Arctic is melt—'

'The Arctic, the Arctic: do you have any idea what you're talking about? It's not a theme park with indigenous dolls, you know, or some kind of fantasy game with polar bears against the oil demons. You

can't save it. You can only manage it. Understand that, first of all.'
Sean saw the alarm in her eyes, but she didn't back down.

'I know it's complicated and I know I don't understand it all. That's
why I'm here, because you are, you're really involved so I thought—'

'Here's what I think' – Sawbridge peered at the handwritten business card – 'Miss Burnham. You're doing media studies and thought
this was a good project.'

'How'd you know that?' Her indignation made Sean fond of her.

Sawbridge smiled. 'I'm also guessing you're local, you heard about
the inquest and you saw the words "interested party" and thought to
yourself, ooh yes, *I'm* interested, why don't *I* go along, and observe
other people's grief, and other people's business, and I'll put it down
to environmental awareness. Or did you not consider that part?'

The girl frowned. 'It's a public hearing. I'm allowed to be here.'

'Mm. Thing is, you're not.' Sawbridge dropped his voice so only
they could hear him. 'Unless you have a demonstrable vested interest,
or are with a recognised official press organisation, you need to leave.'

'Official press organisations,' she retorted, 'are stale, male and pale.'
She stood up straight. 'I've changed my shoes, which was a fair
comment from Mr Cawson, but in case you didn't know, things have
changed. I *am* a global citizen journalist and what happens in the
Arctic affects us all. So I would call that a very strong vested interest,
thank you.' She was breathing hard at her own defiance. 'And if people
like me don't take a stand—'

'Or a seat by the socket,' said Mrs Osman, a gleam of amusement
in her hooded eyes. 'Oh dear, too late.' They all turned to see a new
male journalist, large and slobby and vaguely familiar to Sean, sweeping her things down the table and taking her place. He ignored Beth
Burnham's glower as they were all upstanding again for the second
part of the morning. Sean recognised him, he was the coiner of the
'Dirty Davos' nickname, and was constantly trying to join one of
Sean's clubs, under false names. Sean knew he bore him nothing but
ill will, but he still felt for him. The man craved status.

*

Sean's clubs were the foundation of his fortune, started with one humble investment property in the early days of apprenticing with Kingsmith. Back then he had done whatever his mentor asked: back office admin support, proxy purchases of shares, and, occasionally, holding large amounts of money in his own name, which he scrupulously returned the instant he was asked. He had no criminal bent, wanting only wealth by the straightest route, and Kingsmith applauded him for it, and gave his protégé tips Sean was quick to act on. One developed property became a thriving and fashionable hotel, then a private club, and with an open line of credit from Kingsmith, Sean created several more outposts, ever more elite. He wished Tom had used the free membership he gave him, but in the time Sean had built his brand, Tom had embraced Greenpeace, and a militantly puritanical attitude to the finer things in life. Which was all very well, Sean had thought, if you'd had time to get bored of them in the first place.

The American cruise tourists from the *Vanir* were next on, the wife speaking for both of them. Sean listened as she described how the passengers yearned for a bear and how passenger power had got that drone up, and found that bear, that led them, like some kind of animal guide, wasn't it? to where they needed to be. Even if the captain hadn't wanted to go there and there was some sort of to-do about it. But it was the right thing, because then they found that poor man's body. She was ready to give forth their views on the warming Arctic, but the coroner glanced at the clock and thanked her.

'A moment?'

The coroner nodded to Mrs Osman.

'Do you mean, there was a disagreement about following the bear?'

'Something about going up that fjord,' the woman said. 'One fjord, another fjord – we wanted to see the thing they'd sold us on: a polar bear! Nine days of glaucous gulls and fulmars – then some walrus we weren't allowed close enough to see properly in case we upset them. There were people on board who have died natural deaths since that voyage, and seeing a polar bear was on their bucket list! So first they announced over the PA system they'd seen it and we all rushed out and some people even got a glimpse, then all of a sudden they changed their mind and we couldn't sail down that fjord where it was headed and take a look?'

She smiled. 'You can trust a bunch of oldsters to make trouble. The attorneys got up a memo for the tour operator who took it to the captain, and that's how come we went down that fjord, and then – well. The calving and all.' Her bright tone fell away as she looked at Tom's mother for a second, and bobbed her head in condolence. 'I just hope it was a good thing, in the end, that we followed that bear. We're going to light a candle in the cathedral for him.'

'Thank you.' Mrs Osman sat down.

Sean felt his heart beating harder and composed his face to show nothing but calmness. Osman must know something of the activities of Midgard Lodge, she must be curious or she wouldn't have asked about the passage of the ship into the fjord – but this process was simply about the circumstances of Tom's tragic death. Not the favour Sean was doing, for both the governments of Norway and Great Britain. He was sticking his neck out for his country, and he would be recognised for that courage. It had to be confidential, of course it did.

Sean declined Sawbridge's offer of the guilty pleasure of a cheap bacon sandwich, in favour of clearing his head with a walk. He bought some peanuts then ducked through the concealed gateway to the cathedral precincts, lifting his hand casually to the porter as his lawyer had done. With some time to spare, he decided to take a quick look in the cathedral.

He stepped out of the wind and into the vaulting stone space, where jewelled light fell down between the pillars onto the paving of ancient tombs. Traders in the temple, in the form of two gift stands, were overhung by the tattered regimental banners once held by living boys and men.

Sean moved deeper, drawn by the sound of a choir somewhere in the cool stone depths. The nose-less alabaster effigies and curlicued marble scrolls recording noble young death after death, reminded him of the legless soldier, on his new career path of medical re-enactment. He hoped his Equity card had arrived.

He went up scooped stone steps, shaped by centuries of footfall, heading towards the music. Two black-robed clerics talked intently at the top – comparing budget flights to Rome these days. The choir kept pausing and returning to one musical phrase, like a many-throated bird – and then Sean saw them, their young faces angelic in the light falling from hundreds of feet above. Their music master set them off again, and to stay and listen for longer, Sean wandered across to a small chapel within their chapel, where a large book was set on a low stand. A pen dangled from a string.

It was a prayer book, and visitors to the cathedral were invited to write their requests. Many people had already done so, and Sean looked closer as the music washed over him.

For my mother's operation, said one.

For my lost family, said another.

And then further down, in writing so hard the page was almost torn, someone had dug the words into the paper: SHOW YOURSELF GOD.

He looked around. The force of the words and the writing itself was like a challenge to anyone reading it. Whoever had written it might even be in the cathedral now, might be watching him read it. All he saw was the choir, distant tourists, a few clerics walking quietly. He picked up the pen and – a respectful distance under the great spiritual demand, added two words: *forgive me*.

He stared at what he had written. Then he put a ten-pound note into the donation box and went to light a candle, not because he was religious but because he liked the act of doing so. To his horror, John and Trudie Burke, the cruise passengers, were heading towards him. He looked back across at the book – if they read it and had seen him write it, they would get completely the wrong idea.

They were coming closer, it was definitely them, he could hear her distinctive voice. Sean lowered his head as if deep in prayer and walked in the opposite direction. It turned out to be a one-way aisle with arrowed signs pointing ahead, which led to a small landing above a flight of candlelit stone stairs, and another sign To The Crypt and Way Out. The second part was what he wanted.

Naturally there were frequent storms and intense cold, and in regard to the storms of the Arctic regions of North Greenland and Grant Land, the only word I can use to describe them is 'Terrible', in the fullest meaning it conveys. The effect of such storms of wind and snow, or rain, is abject physical terror, due to the realization of perfect helplessness. I have seen rocks a hundred and a hundred and fifty pounds in weight picked up by the storm and blown for distances of ninety or a hundred feet to the edge of a precipice, and there of their own momentum go hurtling through space to fall in crashing fragments at the base. I have been there and I have seen one of my Esquimo companions felled by a blow from a rock of eighty-four pounds in weight, which struck him fairly between the shoulder-blades, literally knocking the life out of him. I have been there, and believe me, I have been afraid.

A Negro Explorer at the North Pole: The Autobiography of Matthew Henson (1912)
Matthew Henson

19

Even after the Svalbard accident, Sean had been fine on the London Underground, but then a few months ago there had been that thing at Knightsbridge station – or more accurately, his experience in the tunnel just before. Heading down towards the crypt made him think of it, but he pushed fear away. Becoming phobic about being underground meant too many places where he would no longer be able to go.

The Piccadilly line train had just stopped for a few minutes between stations, nothing massively unusual in that. But it was the morning rush hour and, without a seat, Sean faced out into the blackness as without warning the engines and lights went off. In the crowded silence he felt the press of flesh and backpack around him, he heard people breathing. The feeling oscillated through them all: they were trapped in the dark earth in a metal tube.

Sean was already physically tensed with his effort to keep maximum headspace, and the collective body heat rose around his face. He shifted against the interconnecting doors to the next carriage and squeezed the two metal latches to drop the heavy glass window, letting in more air. The only light was from the hundreds of oblongs of phones, underlighting people's faces in a horrifying way.

The same was happening in the next carriage. He listened to the silence of the tunnel, which smelled alien and industrial and ancient all at the same time. He had the idea that they were all dead, that some disaster had taken place but his consciousness lingered in anaesthe-tised death-lag. Soon he would feel the pain of the explosion or atro-city or whatever had befallen his train. His body might already be indistinguishable from the red shreds of others, they were carbon, atomised back to stardust, the tunnel blocked for months—

—he was in the ice again – he was blinded with terror, he had to plunge and kick and force—

Commuters shouted angrily at him as with a great cry the tall man by the connecting door went crazy, shoving them all back, his eyes wild – and then the lights went on and the train resumed its motion. The driver's distorted voice apologised through loudspeakers for the delay, and Sean stared at the shocked faces of the people around him. He was on a train.

When the doors opened onto the platform of Knightsbridge station, he burst out and ran through the tunnels, up the sliding metal teeth of the escalator, he slammed his plastic card against the ticket barrier and did not stop until he was out on the roaring street.

The crypt was completely manageable, however, nothing like the closed-in darkness of the tube tunnel. There were only a few steps down to it, and it smelled of stone and incense, not soot and sweat. He walked on to where the passageway opened into a little chamber, a large pillar candle flickering in the middle of flagstones. A guide with a small respectful group told them of the murder of Thomas Becket in this spot on 29 December 1170.

Who will rid me of this turbulent priest? Thomas the troublemaker. Thomas who probably refused to understand statecraft, who saw things in black and white, like Sean's Tom.

He looked back – no one had followed him. He was spooking at everything and it was ludicrous. He ran up the exit steps and out into the bright day. A small group of grey-robed monks were gathered together, and Sean stared at their high-tech hiking boots, and cross-country walking poles. They were youthful and fit, more like young explorers than monks. He longed for another expedition. When this was all over, he would find one to join.

*

Sawbridge was waiting in the lobby when Sean arrived, and hurried him in. Straight-backed, tall and in good clear voice, Sean took the stand and the oath. Going to the cathedral had worked – he felt strengthened in some way.

'You kindly submitted a prepared statement of the events of February fifteenth,' said the coroner, 'but I will trouble you, if you can, to tell the court in your own words, what happened.'

'Of course.' Sean had worked on this statement precisely to avoid what Sawbridge had predicted could turn into a lengthy testimony.

'I appreciate that it's three years ago now,' said Mr Thornton, 'so I don't expect your memory—'

'Oh no,' said Sean. 'It's pin sharp.'

'Then if you would take us from your arrival with Mr Harding, in Svalbard, and why you were there.'

'Yes. Of course.' Sean could see Ursula Osman poised and still, like a cat in the bushes. He needed Martine here, she was the antidote to whatever charge Osman put out into the atmosphere.

'The party I took up to Midgard Lodge consisted of the five members of the consortium that bought the property – myself, Tom, my long-term backer Joe Kingsmith, another investor called Radiance Young, and my partner in business and now also in my personal life, Martine Delaroche.' Sean felt the catch of tension before the keyboards rattled again.

'I'm the director and CEO of Midgard Lodge, but everyone on that trip had a financial stake. Tom didn't contribute equity but he received a large signing-on fee, plus he would have been entitled to a salary and dividends for his directorship, and for his ongoing work: helping tailor best environmental policy for the business leaders we hosted on retreat. It was a business deal for him too. He took the money.'

Sean felt the reins now. 'The summer sea ice has gone and while some people are wringing their hands, I have chosen actively and responsibly to be at the vanguard of those changes and make sure they happen in the most positive way. If the opportunity is there, someone will seize it. Better it be us. Tom wanted to speak truth to power, and he knew he needed to be in the room to do that. You have to have a stake in the Arctic to have a voice there.'

'I've done a bit of research myself,' said Mr Thornton, 'and I'm surprised you got permission to develop at Midgardfjorden. Isn't it a national park?'

'Just outside the boundary,' Sean said. 'We've done it very sympathetically. If we weren't so discreet, the architect would have surely won awards. That was part of the reason for our trip – no one but myself had seen the completed work. Nor had we all been able to meet in person before, so it was a double celebration. Plus the solar eclipse happening, which was best viewed in Svalbard ...' He paused. 'We said the stars were in alignment.'

When a mature male appears on the scene, all the other bears pay attention. The general rule is, the more mature, heavier, and stronger the bear, the more dominant it is in any interaction. However, there is another rule that says a bear that approaches confidently and without hesitation is accepted as a potential threat by the bear that is being approached. Even a mature male may be frightened by a young bear under certain circumstances. Polar bears are powerful animals; they are also intelligent. They realize they can hurt one another, and they avoid situations in which their power might be put to the test. They also know that the outcome in any particular situation depends on a bear's personality, current motivation, and individual circumstances. Where possible, they err on the side of caution.

Polar Bears: Living with the White Bear (1996)
Nikita Ovsyanikov

20

Three years earlier

A private Boeing 747 cruised at 36,000 feet over the Greenland Sea heading in a north-easterly direction for Longyearbyen airport, Svalbard. Inside it, Joe Kingsmith napped in the larger of his two bedrooms, while out in the salon his steward attended the needs of the four other passengers, variously relaxing.

Having flown with Kingsmith before, Sean was familiar with the luxurious environment, but it was the first time for Martine, Tom, and for Radiance Young. She was currently engaged in a game of online chess with someone from her cosmonaut training programme – which she was doing privately in Moscow, 'for fun'. This joined a list of activities that included polar exploration, motor racing and collecting important estate jewellery. She frowned as she considered her next move. Sitting nearby, Tom ignored her red-nailed toes wiggling towards him, and her occasional glances.

Behind them, Sean and Martine observed with discreet amusement. He was browsing an online portfolio of interior designers for the new building in Cochin and she had laid her iPad aside and was looking over his shoulder. In the white heat of early lust, Sean had welcomed her involvement in the interior of Midgard Lodge – with spectacular results – but the process had revealed Martine's dominant personality, and he had declined to involve her in the design of his other businesses.

'Checkmate!' Radiance lifted her own iPad in triumph. 'He is senior and thinks he beats me, but he never does!' Her accent was an odd mix of English private school and native Mandarin. She turned to Tom. 'Now you.'

Tom put his book down. 'I'm hopeless. Ask Martine, she's a good strategist.'

'Martin likes to play with men better, like me. Right, Martin?'

'I'm very happy to play with you, if you'd like.' Martine forced a smile.

'No, it's OK. I see Sean eye-boss you to say yes.'

'He didn't.'

'Oh yes he did!' Radiance had evidently been to British panto-mimes. She returned to her first target. 'Tom, why are you single? No children, no ex-wife?'

Sean looked up with interest. Tom shrugged.

'There was someone, once. It didn't work out.'

'Why not? It's OK I'm asking?'

'Radiance, stop torturing him. He doesn't know how to fob you off with a lie.' Sean caught Tom's grateful look, but she was not so easily dissuaded.

'What happened?'

'We fucked it up. And then it was too late. OK?'

'Huh. Doesn't sound OK!' Radiance held up her left hand with its empty ring finger. 'Look at me: sad face: no kids. Still time though if I hurry, before I'm old and dry. Husband too. Maybe I adopt one, like Martin!' She laughed for a second. 'Martin, you want kids too? How old are you, little bit more than me? Thirty-nine? Forty? We should get busy!'

When Martine didn't answer, Radiance winked at her. 'We talk more later. You can tell me how you make Sean leave his wife. I need to learn that trick!'

'Considerably younger and it was no trick.' Martine pointedly returned to her own iPad, but Tom looked round at Sean.

'You've done it?'

'It's in progress,' Martine said immediately. 'We need to be honest.'

Radiance pointed at Sean. 'Oh! Angry smiles are dangerous! Don't be angry, Sean. Martin's right.'

'Martine.'

174

'That's what I said: Martin.'

'Radiance, lovely special, talented Radiance,' said Sean. 'Shut up.'

'Sure.' Radiance was impossible to offend.

Down the cabin, Kingsmith emerged from the bedroom, freshly showered and changed. The PA system chimed and the captain announced they were starting the descent to Longyearbyen. He took his seat.

'Everything OK? It's gone very quiet.'

'Joe, you want a baby?' Radiance leaned forward. 'Let's do this thing!'

Kingsmith patted her hand. 'I'll take that in a friendly spirit, thank you. But can we discuss it a bit later, over a drink?'

'Sure!'

Kingsmith shot the others a look of panic. Sean winked.

'Take one for the team,' he mouthed to him. Then they began the descent into Adventfjorden and conversation ceased. Sean looked out as they entered the narrow channel of the mountains, the sharp black peaks tipping the snowline. Ahead was the small runway of Longyearbyen which terminated in a headland on the south shore of Isfjord, against which the Barents Sea burst against the rocks. The approach was notorious since 1996, when a Russian Tupolev transit plane, arriving to rotate coal workers in and out of the settlement at Pyramiden, crashed with the cost of every life on board. Sean thought of it compulsively, every time he came in.

The Arctic year is made of four very long days: the midnight sun of the summer months, from late April until mid-August, when it does not set at all, then the brief season of dusk at the change of the year in autumn, when the polar night is coming and the light shrinks faster every day. By late October there are only a few hours of twilight in the middle of the day, and by mid-November total darkness has fallen, with no day at all. For three months, or about two thousand hours, there is no natural light. For some people, this is a relief compared to the high-crime season of the summer months, when the bars manufacture night inside, while on the other side of the door, the sun bleaches all sense of time. There is endless liberty to work, travel, or make any kind of mischief – there are no restrictions, except on peaceful sleep. For some, it becomes a time of madness. For others, that is the polar night. For a few, the madness can strike at any time; it quivers in the Arctic silence that can be spiritual, or demonic as it claws reason off balance. When survival is the ultimate value, many inhibitions are released.

For Sean's party, touching down on the ice-swirled tarmac of Longyearbyen in the smoky blue February twilight, it was a time of great excitement. They readied themselves to transfer to the helicopter that would be waiting to take them straight up to Midgard Lodge – but as they disembarked, Sean couldn't see it. The captain hurried up to Kingsmith with the message that it wasn't there, they had to go in. Sean shouted through the wind for everyone to get inside, and they hurried over to the small terminal building, mini-snow cyclones rushing along the ground and bursting against their ankles.

It was nothing serious, the captain told Sean and Kingsmith, at least not for them. There had been an incident with a bear and a big bunch of tourists up at Dronningsbukta, and all the helicopters on the islands had been scrambled to help. Danny Long, as an experienced Arctic pilot, had been commandeered for search and rescue by the Sysselmann's office, along with the Midgard helicopter.

The captain apologised for not having more information. He looked at his watch and asked Kingsmith what he wanted him to do.

'Passports and on your way,' Kingsmith told him. 'While you still can.'

Sean could tell by the set of his shoulders and the particular smile, that Kingsmith was displeased. They waited by the motionless luggage carousel, presided over by a medium-sized stuffed polar bear, every tourist's first picture. The captain returned with the passports.

'Mr Long has left another message, sir: he'll pick you up in the morning and he's very sorry, but you can't get to the Lodge tonight, all men are required by the Sysselmann.'

'In the *morning*?' Martine and Radiance said it together.

Sean took the message from the captain and read it.

'Nothing to worry about. We're aiding search and rescue – remember, Joe?'

Kingsmith frowned. 'Danny had his instructions.'

'Tell the Sysselmann that,' Tom said pleasantly. 'I'm sure it would make a big difference. What men, by the way?'

'Lodge staff,' Sean said, truthfully. They were. 'Fortunately, we've got rooms booked in town too. Always have a contingency plan.'

Kingsmith patted Tom's shoulder. 'You're right to rag me. I'm getting old and inflexible. Of course we should be helping out.' He turned back to his waiting crew. 'Happy returns to Benoit. Tell him to have fun.' The captain confirmed he would pass it on. The crew hurried back to the plane.

'Who's Benoit?' asked Martine.

'A pal, a mere kid turning fifty. Lending it to him for his celebrations. But they've got to stop in Riga to pick up the other guests.'

'Where's the party?' Tom said it in the casual way Sean knew meant trouble. Kingsmith too, by his smile.

'Central African Republic. Though I'm guessing they'll probably bar hop.'

'Where the beautiful pink wood comes from,' said Radiance. 'So popular now in Asia.'

'Pink mahogany? I hope you're not importing that—'

'Of course not, silly. But I've got eyes in my head, it's everywhere. Hey, Tom, come visit with me, while you're still single. I show you all the sights of outrage.' She grinned at him.

He ignored her. 'I hope those guests from Riga are of legal age.'

'Thomas! As if I'd compromise my crew like that. Everyone's a fully consenting grown-up.'

Tom didn't smile back. 'So you've started up in the CAR again?'

'Sure. Last time I looked, mining was legal, as was helping the local economy, setting up health centres after the epidemic, and bringing prosperity to a lot of people. Tom, you'll give yourself a hernia trying to police the whole world.'

'I don't want to police it, I just want—'

'Things done your way – I remember. The good way, the green way, the right way. I know, and please god, don't change – it's why we want you here. But let me tell you, you go looking under stones and you know what you'll find? Good clean dirt and the creatures that live there. It's called a financial ecosystem, and I'm just as keen on protecting that one as you are with any of yours. That's how the world works and it's prudish to deny it, any more than your own bodily functions.

Come out of denial and join the party! Your beautiful idea of everyone pulling together only happens in the movies, war, and sport. Real life, it's everyone for themselves and their families – and there is nothing more selfish than a new family.'

'Joe, you're wrong, and it's my job at Midgard to convince people exactly like you—'

'There's no one remotely like me—'

'—that it's better to think collectively than selfishly, and you'll make more money when you do.'

'You're fighting human nature.'

'People are better than you think.'

Joe Kingsmith turned to Sean. 'I love this boy.'

'Man.' Tom didn't smile. 'And we both know you don't.'

'OK. But I give you respect.' Kingsmith stopped the joking. 'So seriously, Tom, let's get you down to the CAR, the DRC, even South Sudan, if you want.'

'Are you crazy? You're in there?'

'Aha, you see – right there, that's what I'm up against. South Sudan has a lot of talented, hard-working people developing the infrastructure – come see for yourself what I'm up to, I'll set your mind at rest.' Kingsmith paused to admire his plane rolling past towards the runway.

When it had gone, a small figure was revealed in the arc lights, crossing the snow-swirled tarmac towards the terminal building. She entered in a blast of cold air and the glass slid shut behind her. She wore a long brown parka with a fur-trimmed hood and rummaged in its pockets for her ringing phone. They all watched as she unzipped the parka, trying to get to it in time – revealing it was in the pocket of a bloodstained white lab coat. She cursed as she missed the call, then realised people were watching her. Her look turned to shock as she saw Tom.

'I look that bad?' He went up to her. She was speechless. They kissed so clumsily, their past as lovers was blatant. Martine and Radiance exchanged a look.

Sean took a deep breath and went forward.

'Ruth!' he called out. 'Fancy seeing you here!' He kissed her on the cheek.

'Everyone,' Sean took control, 'this is Dr Ruth Mott, eminent biologist specialising in …'

'Ice-obligate marine mammals,' said Tom. '*Ursus maritimus* in particular.'

'No longer in the field,' she said, 'but covered in the blood of the one I've very sadly just prepared for autopsy.' She looked round them all. 'Hello. Sorry about the gore, I've just removed the head. And, um, more small talk like that.'

She looked at Martine and Radiance, then Tom. 'Well, I better …'

'No. Don't go.' Tom looked at Sean. 'We're here for the night, aren't we? So we have to eat.'

Sean knew what was coming. Get out in front.

'We are. Ruth, if you're free, would you like to join us for supper?'

'Thank you, but I wouldn't want to gatecrash your party.'

Radiance pointed to Kingsmith. 'That one's mine tonight.' She pointed to Martine, and Sean spared them all.

'Martine is with me.'

'Martine?' Something went through Ruth Mott's eyes. 'Hello.'

'Yes, the Terrible Homewrecker herself.' Martine smiled. 'Please don't hate me until you know me first-hand.'

Despite herself, Ruth smiled. 'I can't promise, but I'll try.'

'Good enough,' Martine said. 'And please do join us.'

'You must.' Tom was completely focused on Ruth, Kingsmith forgotten.

'You can tell us about the bear!' Radiance was as eager as a child for an ice-cream. 'Or maybe we could even see it now? I'm fine with blood. What happened?'

'Tourist stupidity. I'm sorry, right now I'm really upset about it all.'

'Were there many casualties?'

Ruth Mott looked at Kingsmith.

'Upset about the bear.' She turned to Tom. 'What are you doing here?'

'Going up to Midgardfjorden.'

'That's – *you*? But that's amazing! The whole world was after that.' She turned to Sean. 'Wow. You are never to be underestimated.'

'That's the truth.' Tom looked as proud as if she'd meant it for him. Sean felt a mixture of shame and gratitude, and a lot warmer towards Ruth. She'd only ever been a loyal friend to Gail. And until Rosie had involved her, she hadn't interfered.

'Guilty as charged, this is the purchasing consortium. Ruth, if you are free, please do join us tonight. It's been too long.'

Ruth smiled, and Sean noticed how Tom smiled too. 'I'm supposed to be talking to drunken eclipse tourists after dinner,' she said. 'Let me see if I can find a stand-in.'

Auks pickled in oil. *This is done by killing a seal and skinning it through its mouth without splitting the skin. Not every hunter can do this, but when it is accomplished satisfactorily it makes a magnificent poke, because most of the blubber still clings to the skin.*

The person intending to fill the hide takes it along with him to a spot where the birds are thicker than fish in any aquarium and, with a net attached to a long stick, he catches the auks as they fly past, often bagging enough in one day to fill his sealskin, which is then latched and covered with stones. The sun must not reach it or the oil will turn rancid. During the summer the blubber turns to oil and soaks the birds, which decompose slowly without interference from the air.

This makes a dish which tastes like nothing else in the world, and one loved by young and old alike. The white feathers turn pink, and may be easily plucked out. The birds are often eaten frozen, but some connoisseurs say they are better warmed up. In fact, frozen meat never tastes as strong as it does when it is thawed out. When frozen the diner must chop the birds out of the poke with an axe, but after they become soft, they may be eaten with grace and elegant manners. The gastronomist takes them by the legs and bites off the feet. Then with a deft twist of his hand he removes the feathers – or most of them. After that he skins them, from the bill backwards, and, having turned the skin inside out, sucks the most delicious fat from it. Finally he swallows the skin at one gulp, and then begins on the meat.

Arctic Adventure: My Life in the Frozen North (1936)
Peter Freuchen

21

Across the courtroom and without directly looking at her, Sean felt the force of Ruth Mott's steady stare. He wanted to be kind, but in case she did not – and the way she'd spoken to him at the funeral suggested she wouldn't – he had briefed Sawbridge about her. It had to be done.

'We all checked into our hotel,' he said, 'the Polar Dream – then we went for supper at a restaurant called Amaruq, where Dr Mott joined us. We had supper, then we came back to the hotel.'

'All of you?' asked the coroner.

'Ruth was staying somewhere else. In the morning, we met in the lobby and took a car back to the airport, where Danny Long flew us up to Midgard as planned.'

'When you say *we*—'

'Myself, Tom, Joe Kingsmith, Martine Delaroche and Radiance Young. Just the consortium partners.'

Amaruq, which the menu explained meant Wolf in the Inuktitut language, was the new restaurant just outside the town limits. Already famed for its bold interpretation of traditional gourmet Inuit dishes alongside its regular Nordic menu, its proprietors were a Danish couple who had lived in Greenland, and supported one of the last remaining traditional communities through exporting their food. They offered a literal taste of a lost world, and it was impossible to get a reservation for the whole of the summer season. Sean felt gratified that one phone call to Skadi Larssen's secretary in Oslo had sorted that out.

They'd had one round of cocktails before Ruth Mott arrived, flushed from her skidoo ride. The men all rose to greet her, and Sean enjoyed the eyes of the other diners on their glamorous table. Both Radiance and Martine, au fait with wilderness chic, were understated but had each put on a serious cocktail ring as a token to their status at this business dinner, even if was happening in the Arctic. Ruth wore jeans and a black silk shirt, which gleamed – Sean could not help noticing – where her breasts pushed against it. Her eyes had changed too. She was wearing makeup.

'Something wrong?' She smiled at him.

'You haven't changed a bit.' He thought the opposite; she was much less strident, and seemed to have softened with the years. More drinks came. Sean ordered one Inuit tasting menu to share, and the six-course Nordic set menu for each. Both Tom and Ruth asked for substitutions for the 'whale beef', which could be served either as carpaccio or seared as a steak. Sean looked forward to his, which tasted like nothing else and he ate on every ethically sourced and defensible occasion, which was the great USP of the restaurant.

Kingsmith ordered vintage champagne from the extensive wine list, and they toasted the success of Midgard Lodge. Ruth Mott was preoccupied by the bear, she said. They should not mind her. The animal was pregnant but with strange complications. And in the wrong season.

'Don't say any more.' Martine shuddered.

'I wasn't planning to.'

Radiance studied Ruth, unabashed.

'You and Tom. Exes, right?'

Ruth glanced at him before she answered. 'That's right.'

'If that's your final word.' Tom looked at her.

Radiance grabbed up a menu and fanned herself.

'Something on fire here!' She nudged Kingsmith. 'Hey: sexy old man: when do we have our special talk? Like you said, on the plane?'

Sean burst out laughing at Kingsmith's look of agitation.

'Radiance, you're too good for me. Also, you might kill me.' Then he said something in her ear that made her slap him playfully. Ruth and Tom sat side by side, not speaking, but obviously intensely aware of each other. The waitress passed among them with the bottle.

'Bad idea,' Martine said it so low Sean barely heard it, but they were both thinking the same thing: Tom must not invite Ruth up to Midgard with them.

'So, Ruth,' Sean broke them apart without knowing what he was going to say next. 'How is the world of tourism?'

'Disasters waiting to happen. Oops, they already are. The Arctic's the new Mediterranean, and Svalbard its Ibiza.'

The waitress brought the first course of the Inuit tasting menu. She set down a board of small blocks of terrine, fine strands of a dark meat, threaded with translucent lines of fat.

'This is pickled auk,' she explained. 'The little birds from the cliffs? We serve it just thawed, so it melts in the mouth like foie gras. Enjoy.'

They each took one, Radiance's eyes bulging as she tasted it. She had another. Joe Kingsmith took one, looked like he was going to throw up, and had a big gulp of his wine. Sean did the same, Ruth ate one and declined more, Martine shuddered and passed, so Tom and Radiance ate all the rest.

'You know how they make them?' he said.

'Don't,' said Sean. 'I remember.'

'He's right,' said Ruth. 'Seriously don't.'

'But what about my knowledge of the minutiae of Greenlandic culture?' Tom said to her. 'And my superior knowledge that I like to parade, even when other people might know better? Or have jobs equally valid?'

'Not me, not any more,' Ruth said. 'Now it's just you. I hope.'

'What if I've changed? Lost all my bad qualities?'

'I'd be very sorry. I haven't lost mine.'

'Good.'

'We saw them made,' Sean announced loudly. 'In Greenland – remember, Tom?'

'That's right.' Tom smiled but he didn't want to relive it, he wanted to stay connected to Ruth.

Sean turned to Martine. 'We spent some time in an Inuk village, while we were students, living with the people, eating like they did.'

'I didn't know that.' She smiled politely.

'What was the girl's name, Tom, who made us those mittens?'

'I can't remember any girls.' Tom looked at Ruth. 'Not one.'

Sean turned away from their separate dinner for two, feeling a dull wash of deprivation. He and Martine shared lust and excitement and passion, and thrilled to the deals to be done, but where was that ineffable sparkle between a man and a woman? With a stab of pain, he remembered it as love.

'Sean: don't stare.' Tom winked at him.

Sean laughed, despite himself. 'I'm not fucking Roxy.'

'Who's Roxy?' Radiance looked at Martine for a reaction. 'Cute name.'

'Their Greenland rescue dog,' Ruth said. 'Who ruled them.' She looked at Martine. 'You must have heard.'

'Oh. Many times.' Martine forced a smile. 'Forgive me,' she said, 'but being an Arctic biologist sounds so fascinating. Why did you stop?'

'I haven't,' Ruth said calmly. 'I am still a scientist or I wouldn't have been asked to carry out the post-mortem of the bear today. That's not a job for a cruise-line speaker. Hasn't Sean filled you in on why I left fieldwork?'

'He hasn't,' Martine lied. 'But please excuse me: I didn't realise it was a painful story for you.'

They were all silent for a moment. Then Radiance tinged her fork against her empty champagne glass. 'Very serious! I have the glass with the hole!'

Kingsmith agreed, and requested more champagne when the waitress returned with the whale steaks and cloudberry sauce. This, she stated with cheery defiance, was a traditional food from sustainably harvested right whale, which was plentiful in the region and whose stocks were restored. There was evidence. She strafed the table with her smile, checking for troublemakers.

'If you really want to know,' Ruth said to Martine, when the waitress had gone, 'I'll tell you. I killed a bear by accident. A sponsored bear, of viable reproductive age. We were due to take new readings and I darted her.'

Ruth paused, and Sean watched Tom take her hand under the table. 'She suffered a reaction to the tranquilliser,' she continued, 'and she died. No reason, correct dosage, it just – happened. But they said that I'd got the dosage wrong, that I was over-tired. I was forced to take a sabbatical. While I was gone, the story got twisted. Now I can't get another research job. But when you love the Arctic, you find a way to be here. And, as you saw earlier today, I can still be trusted with dead ones. If there's no one better around.'

'There never has been, there never will be.' Tom said it so directly, she looked at him in shock. To cover her feelings, Ruth took out her phone and scrolled for a picture, hiding her shining face as she searched.

'But today, look what I found.' She showed Tom her phone. 'A lip tattoo like we did in Qarrtsiluni. Imagine if she'd come all the way from there.' She put it away, her face glowing. 'Sorry. No one needs to see that. I don't need to talk about this any more.'

'Everyone makes mistakes,' Martine said. 'It's healthy you've moved on.'

'It was not a *mistake*.' Ruth looked at her fiercely.

Kingsmith replenished her glass.

'Qarrtsiluni?' he pronounced it effortlessly. 'You know that place?'

'Do you?' Ruth disengaged from Martine.

'Sure. We were considering a couple projects with the government – when I say *government*, I mean everything was clear from the Danish side, but the natives – the Greenlanders—'

'Inuit,' Ruth said. 'That's what they call themselves.'

'Sure,' Kingsmith agreed, 'the Inuit – so tricky to work with. Charming, extraordinarily talented people, but no idea of timekeeping, non-existent administrative system – long story short, things just didn't pan out.'

'Pan out,' she repeated. 'Things, meaning mining? In Qarrtsiluni?'

When he thought back to this moment, Sean knew that what was about to happen was completely his fault. He could have headed this off at the airport, he might have prevented all that followed. Instead he had succumbed to that old competitive urge with Tom where women were concerned, and got in first to invite Ruth to join them. Now here she was, facing off with Kingsmith. Two elements that should never have been mixed.

'Prism Mining.' She stared at Kingsmith. 'That was you.'

'Proud to say so.' Kingsmith could not have been more relaxed. 'Back in the day, what a great company! Sadly, long gone. Too many delays, too much bureaucracy. Leave them on the table too long, and some deals spoil like meat. Prism Greenland was one. We wanted to bring prosperity to those poor people – if you've worked there you know how desperate their lives are. All very well being nostalgic for Arctic Past, like these two boys here – but you and I know that old romance is a complete crock. Arctic Future is what they want: TVs, iPads, foreign travel, all the rest of it. You can't keep kids in the last century.' He went back to his food. 'Losing battle, but we gave it a good go.'

Ruth spoke too carefully.

'Some people there, some young people, still wanted to choose. They did not want to be resettled. They didn't want Prism's money, or to be bullied when they refused. I know that for a fact.'

'Delicious, this beef.' Kingsmith looked at her over his whale-loaded fork. 'How's that then?'

'My research guide was one of the local leaders. He told me that, before he disappeared. Tom, I'm so sorry – for all that. He wasn't—'

'I know.'

Radiance held out her glass. 'You've got a lot of stories, Bear Lady.'

'No story, Mad Lady,' Ruth said to her. 'But not everyone wanted mining.'

'Here's the thing,' Kingsmith said, and Sean heard the edge cutting through the charm. 'If you take the money, it's a done deal. Right, Sean? Right, Tom?'

'Your company tore up denning sites that were used for generations.'

'Oh, Ruth, please.' Tom put his head in his hand.

'No, she's got a point,' Kingsmith said. 'Old ways change.' Now all the other diners were listening. 'They serve whale here because the whale stocks are restored, so once again they're a food source. Like cows. Neither of them want to die and be eaten, but we've all got canine teeth in our heads, whether we use them or not. I do, because I'm not just an animal, I'm a natural predator. So be sentimental and angry about how business is developing the Arctic, or get on board to make it a positive thing.'

'You destroyed a human and an animal community, for profit! You call that a positive thing?'

'Sunny side up, please,' Radiance interrupted. 'Tell the shipping story! So much less fuel in transit across the North Pole, so much less pollution – you know how many days you save?'

'You know how many whales are hit by ships?'

'No, and you don't know either,' retorted Radiance, 'because no one does, no one can, because there aren't any statistics. You say that to make me feel bad? Go on then, open the Suez Canal again, go make the terrorists be nice – oh no, you can't. So we better send all those things another way, right? I better send them over the North Pole! Where there's no more summer sea ice and climate change has made it quicker and cheaper for everyone! It's not bad, Bear Lady, it's progress. But new shoes hurt, right?'

Ruth turned to Tom. '*These* are your partners?' She pulled a handful of notes from her pocket and put them on the table. 'Wow.'

'Ruth! Don't be so silly!' Sean called after her, but she didn't stop. Tom grabbed the money and ran out behind her. The whole restaurant remained paused, listening to their raised voices beyond the entrance curtain. Then there was the sound of a skidoo engine. Tom returned, holding the money.

'May I?' It was Osman. The coroner nodded permission. 'Thank you.' She cleared her throat with the small rasp Sean was growing to hate. He noticed a long scar just above her clavicle – surgery probably. Or an attack.

'Mr Cawson, thank you for your very brief account. You alluded to Dr Mott leaving the restaurant first – do you know why?'

'Dr Mott took offence at something my partner Joe Kingsmith said, about the future of the Arctic. They were coming to it from pretty much opposing points of view, and she stormed out before the meal was over.'

'Was Tom involved? In this ... disagreement?'

'No. But he went after Dr Mott, to try to talk sense to her.'

'She seems eminently sensible to me.'

'She very rudely threw down some money, even though it was my invitation. He wanted to give it back to her. He was embarrassed at her behaviour, she was very ungracious.' Sean left a pause. 'Some people hold their drink better than others.'

Mrs Osman shifted slightly, her crabbed shape now blocking his sight line to Ruth Mott. 'Yet I believe she is godmother to your daughter, Rosie?'

'She is.' Sean was wary. 'She's always loved her, even if she led her astray.'

Ruth Mott jumped to her feet. 'I've done no such thing! I know exactly what you're referring to and that was completely her own idea – just because you lied to her did not mean I had to.' At Mrs Osman's look, she sat down again.

'Thank you,' said the coroner. 'If you do not observe the protocol of the court, Dr Mott, you will not be permitted to remain. And let me remind you, Mrs Osman, Mr Sawbridge, that this is a Jamieson inquest, in which all we are seeking to do is understand by what means the deceased met his death. It is not an Article Two inquest, in search of all the circumstances surrounding that fact. And it is emphatically not a criminal trial, much as you would both like to show off your rhetorical abilities on such a stage. Is that clear?'

Mr Thornton waited until both Mrs Osman and Mr Sawbridge had respectfully nodded. 'Then Court is recessed for fifteen minutes, after which, if you are able, Mr Cawson, we will hear of the events of the following day and the accident.'

The event to which Ruth Mott referred was bitter to Sean to this day. At the age of fourteen, during a half-term at home, Rosie had heard a savage row. Gail knew about Martine, and pleaded with Sean to either stay or go. Not yet ready to do either, and in miserable desperation to buy time to think, Sean lied. He swore to Gail that she was wrong, she had misheard, he had been foolish in the past with silly girls, but now she was paranoid.

Gail had wanted to believe him more than the truth. She had comforted Rosie, who came down in tears and stood between them, and told her she had made a mistake. Rosie had wept in relief, and for two or three days Sean felt like a good man and loved his wife and daughter with a fierce protective passion. Then Rosie heard him answer his phone in a different tone, and speak to Martine, who had been calling repeatedly.

Rosie hid, and heard her father apologising, and promising. She noted the time, and when her father left his phone for a few minutes, she noted the number that had called. A friend hacked it to an office location, and as Sean found out later, Rosie did not go to London to meet friends, as she'd told her parents, but to Martine's work – where, dressed as a bicycle courier, she delivered an envelope to her hand. She said she needed to wait for a reply and watched as, at her desk, Martine pulled out photographs of Sean and Gail's wedding, of Sean and Gail and Rosie on their most recent holiday, and of Sean and Gail watching television, Harold the cat sprawled between them.

'Leave my family alone!' Rosie shouted in her face, before snatching back the photographs and running faster than the security guards coming to get her. Distraught, she'd gone to Ruth Mott's. Ruth had applauded her courage, let her cry it out, and kept her for two days. It was the beginning of the end for Sean and Gail, and because he could not blame his own child for his own lies, he blamed Ruth. So had Gail, for a few years, until the truth of Sean's infidelity had become impossible to ignore any longer.

It was my boy O-tah who disclosed to me that Peary was to leave me behind in the final few miles to the Pole, and with E-tig-wah he witnesses the disappointment of Commander Peary when a few miles from his camp, his observation told the lieutenant that he had overstepped and gone past the Pole, which we had reached the night before. Our camp itself was practically situated on 'the top of the earth'. For the crime of being present when the Pole was reached Commander Peary has ignored me ever since.

After twenty-two years of close companionship he refused even to say good-by when we separated in New York. And at Fort Conger, nearly ten years before, we had carried Peary nearly 200 miles with his feet frozen, traveling days and hunting nights for food to keep him and ourselves alive!

A Negro Explorer at the North Pole: The Autobiography of Matthew
    Henson (1912)
Matthew Henson

22

The press bench had filled up some more. Flip-flops was pushed further towards the end by reporters who checked emails and sent texts until the last possible moment before being upstanding. Sean saw they all had a photocopied sheet – and so did the front two rows of lawyers and family. He had one too, on the stand: a large-scale map of Midgardfjorden with an inset showing its location on a map of the whole of Svalbard. At Mr Thornton's request, he resumed his account of the eclipse trip.

'Danny Long picked us up at the Polar Dream after breakfast and then we flew to Midgard. The mood was very upbeat, everyone was excited. The Lodge was looking great and it was an extraordinary experience to watch the eclipse from there ...'

Danny Long was all contrition. Sean reassured him: always better to be owed than owing, and this was the first time the Sysselmann's office had required them, and must surely have been impressed? Danny Long admitted they'd done Midgard proud. Their twelve-man Dauphin had clocked nearly 500 kilometres ferrying the hapless British stag party out from the accident scene and back to Longyearbyen. He assured them no one else had flown it, nor noticed its many capacities. He added that they'd all been pleased to have the chance to serve.

They put on their headphones and strapped themselves in, Kingsmith insisting, despite Radiance's protest, that he ride shotgun with Danny Long. Radiance had also trained as a helicopter pilot, but everyone – even Tom – instantly protested against the suggestion of her showing them her skills.

Airborne, no one spoke much. Tom was lost in thought, gazing out at the pale blue mountains. They flew north-east from Longyearbyen over Isfjord, banking to the right as they passed the Russian settlement of Pyramiden, so that Sean and Kingsmith could look down on the new constructions. The speed and scale of the expansion was impressive. Or, if you were Mrs Larssen, disturbing.

They continued north over the great glacier of Mittag Letterbreen and then its delta into the steely water of Wijdefjorden. Martine and Radiance photographed the rippled strata of the mountainside, its layers of colour piled up and swirled like ancient stone marble cake.

'It's the only place on earth where you can see this much geological time.' Tom's voice came over the headphones again. 'Each of those stripes represents about two thousand million years.'

'Nice numbers,' came back Kingsmith. 'Keep talking. I wish I'd been a college boy.'

Sean relaxed as Tom, now with permission, released the brake on his geological passion and talked them through what they were seeing: the clasts and the tillites, the glaciofluvial moraines, the time banks of plant and dinosaur fossils where armoured fish forever swam through seas of rock, the Devonian age, the Silurian, the Ordovician, the Cambrian ...

'We've got to record him, so we can have this on every flight,' shouted Kingsmith, as Danny Long banked to show them the green glittering ribbon of rock as Tom pointed it out. 'It's like poetry – I don't understand but I love to hear.' He twisted round to see Tom. 'You and Dr Mott, you two could be a lecturing duo. She talks whales, you talk rocks—'

'Like a light entertainment double act? Joe, if that's all you wanted me for—'

'It wasn't.' Sean stepped in quickly. 'He meant, you're fascinating.'

'That's exactly right. And I have huge respect for your knowledge.'

Tom didn't answer, and Radiance put her hand on his arm.

'Tom,' she said, 'I could listen to you for strata.'

'Your English is brilliant, Radiance,' he said. 'Where did you learn?'

'Roedean,' she said. 'While English girls still went.'

Sean recognised the volcanic chimneys on the edge of the ice cap where the glacier pressed down towards the sea. It gave him an immense satisfaction to begin to recognise parts of the terrain. Then they clattered out over the middle of Wijdefjorden for the central approach between the high walls of Midgardfjord, the Dauphin a noisy mechanical insect lowering itself down onto the gravel beach.

As the rotor chop slowed, Sean listened to them exclaim as first they saw the silvered wood of the old whaling station, and how subtly the scale of the building and its artful materials revealed themselves. The blackened wood was not a pile of driftwood, it was the upper part of the wall, made of a huge shelf of granite rock-fall.

The whole edifice was an angular flow, an aesthetic paradox in Svalbard, where colossal geological actions formed cubist patterns on a massive scale, and the lack of man-made anything – buildings, signs, roads – was disorientating. Midgard Lodge met the eye as a restored old whaling station on the beach – and grew backward into the mountain from which it became indivisible.

'Ye gods.' Tom was beside him. 'What a brilliant job.'

After the bear all-clear had been radioed down to Danny, they ran up the beach to the steps, where Terry Bjornsen's wife Anne was waiting.

'Welcome to Midgard Lodge, even if you own it,' she said in her soft South African accent. 'It's thirty minutes to the eclipse, so please make yourself at home and let us look after you.'

Midgard Lodge looked as fine as Sean could wish. The reception area smelled of fresh coffee and cinnamon pastries, and was paved in under-heated stone strewn with worn sealskin rugs. The space was half-timbered with the same silvery wood used to restore the exterior: specially treated driftwood from the Russian taiga forest, washed up (actually shipped) across the Kara and Barents seas. A wide turning staircase led up to the rooms, each (a diplomatic essential) as good as the next.

Silver nitrate photographs of the early Pedersen family, heroes of polar exploration, and photographs of the whaling station at work adorned the walls, and a silver samovar stood ready with Russian tea glasses on a colourful enamelled tray. The mezzanine seating area was walled with polished, fossil-embedded stone, before wide shallow steps rose to the main salon. Here, the central freestanding fire-pit with bench-height stone surround gave the feeling of a chieftain's hall, and the great triangular window wall looking down the fjord, the aspect of a chapel. Today the water was mercury-coloured, but Sean had seen it gold.

Anne Bjornsen brought out cloudberry cocktails, crystal tubes of dill vodka, and water from icebergs thousands of years old. Then ruby-red reindeer carpaccio and pearly wafers of halibut sashimi, to eat with moist black bread and sweet Norwegian butter.

And then, Sean showed his guests the wardrobe full of furs from Sami or Greenlandic Inuit collectives.

They were irresistible. The weight of them, the sensual illicit touch … Even Tom succumbed to the childish pleasure of dressing up in the romance of the north. Kingsmith chose a polar bear parka, and Martine let Radiance grab the long blue fox coat with dramatic hood. She then debated between a wolverine jacket with a black-tipped sable pelt, or a narrow dark sealskin parka with a hood. She chose the wolverine, and was pleased to catch Tom staring. Her triumph was spoiled by Sean excitedly calling him over to show him the two old jackets he had at the back: ragged and worn sealing anoraqs, handmade, exactly like Gino Watkins wore on the British Arctic Air Expedition—

—No, like Knud Rasmussen had, Tom said, equally happy. Like Peter Freuchen had when they were in Greenland, and Sean had forgotten that, yes more like that, and they marvelled over them. The wolverine stood impotent in her beauty, then followed the blue fox out to join the polar bear on the deck, and Anne Bjornsen made sure they all had sunglasses. Two telescopes were positioned ready. Tom and Sean came out in glacier glasses with the leather eye guards and their old sealing anoraqs and their arms around each other's shoulders, posing and grinning.

'Beards,' said Tom, 'we should have thought.'

'With frost,' Sean agreed.

'Photoshop you.' Radiance shot them on her phone. 'Like brothers. With ice eyelash too, looks so hot – you're welcome.'

There was no need to time the eclipse: the birds told them it was near. At 10.40 they shrieked and wheeled across the long V of fjord sky, then disappeared. The grey mountains filled with black ink. The rippling water turned to sheet metal and the clouds stopped. All that moved was the colour of the sky. Changing faster than any dawn or dusk, from pink to violet to blue, a fast dark shadow pulled night over the mountain as Earth moved behind its moon.

One telescope was shared by the polar bear, standing between the blue fox and the wolverine. The two sealskinned explorers shared the other. Or rather, Sean did, but when he pulled back from the telescope to offer it to Tom, he saw his friend standing in the dark of day, lost in thought.

'You're missing it,' he said.

'I've got this feeling I am.' Tom looked at him in the darkness. 'But what?'

'The eclipse—' Sean stepped aside and Tom put his eye to the scope.

'We decided not to go round the headland in a boat,' Sean's underarms prickled with stress, 'but to go by skidoo – snowmobile – up to the ice-caves on the other side of the glacier tongue. It was a better use of the time we had.'

'We've found an image of the topography,' said the coroner, as behind Sean the screen glowed to rectangular life. Projected on it was a line drawing of Midgardfjorden, which changed at a click to a satellite photograph.

'Where did you get that?'

'Google Earth, I think,' said the coroner's clerk. 'Whole world's there.'

Sean stared. There was the beach and the grey oblongs of the whaling buildings. But, as they had always planned, the rest of it disappeared into the contours of the mountains and the moraine. He repressed the urge to point out the architectural brilliance.

He felt the force of eyes pushing at him like a tide. His hearing, always good, had become acute. The rattle of keyboards. The sound of clothing rustling. Someone eating – he could smell the mints.

'Mr Cawson.' The coroner leaned forward. 'Please go on.'

'Do you think you could ask the press bench not to type as I talk? It's very distracting.'

'Press bench,' said the coroner, 'please be aware of the witness's preference, at your discretion. Go on, Mr Cawson.'

'After the eclipse we went to the ice-cave on skidoos. It was on the other side of the ridge – you can see it behind me. It had been checked the day before, and passed as safe. People have gone there every season.'

'I believe that's not now possible, though, is it?' said the coroner. 'Because the demesne of your property goes to the water's edge, blocking access – if you choose?'

'It's remote and it's always been private property,' said Sean. 'But the Pedersen family pretty much abandoned it, and so there were no regulations enforced.

'Two of my experienced and trusted staff visited it the day before and went all the way down to the chamber known as the Great Hall …' He waited for the typing at the press bench to keep up. 'And these very experienced men found it safe.'

There was silence, and he knew he'd given them that already, but he was mindful of Sawbridge's advice: *The heart of your testimony is due diligence, personal responsibility of each party, and your blamelessness.*

'So we had checked it the day before. We went in good light with a good weather report. We posted bear watch overlooking access to the cave and the snowmobiles parked near the mouth. We were half a kilometre from the Lodge. We had planned to be in the cave for a maximum of thirty minutes. We could not have been more careful. No one' – and now Sean did look at the press bench, and out at the courtroom, at Angela Harding, at Ruth Mott, at Ursula Osman and her black hooded gaze – '*no one* could have predicted the collapse.'

*

Directly after the eclipse, Tom disappeared. He was not in his room nor any of the public areas. Then Sean saw him, rifle on his back – he had helped himself from the gun safe, he must have seen Terry Bjornsen key it open – walking across the beach. He should have asked Sean, he was behaving like he owned the place as well. And now – Sean and Kingsmith watched from the chapel window – he was heading to the boat hangar.

Sean ran down to the beach, calling to Danny Long – currently sitting in the Dauphin with a coffee, on bear watch – then he went down after Tom.

'Hey!' he followed him into the cavern of the boat hangar. 'You should have said – I could have showed you round.'

'No time like the present.' Tom emerged between the two stacks of Zodiacs. He wasn't smiling. 'Lot of boat here. How many people are we planning to host?'

'Varies.' Sean kicked himself for not mentally rehearsing this. 'We had the space. And search and rescue – we just proved our community credentials.' He should have told him. He knew it.

'Right. Search and rescue for the Sysselmann.' Tom looked around the hangar. 'Where's the manpower, right now?' Without asking Sean, he went up the three steps and opened the door at the top.

'That's the dorm,' Sean said, as casually as he could. He could see the room Tom was looking into: an insulated and ventilated space with stacked bunks. Tom climbed up a ladder beside one set of bunks, and received the view down the fjord. He looked back at Sean.

'A barrack lookout. Where are they right now?'

'On leave, after yesterday.' Sean followed him out.

'I thought the retreats would bring in their own people. That's what it said in the proposal.'

'We're trialling a new idea, I'll tell you about it later, or we'll miss the light—'

'What's that?' Tom pointed his powerful pencil-torch beam at the keypad on another door in the rock.

'That's the strong room.' Kingsmith stood silhouetted in the doorway.

'Strong room?'

Sean walked past Tom and tapped in the code. 'I want to tell him.'

Kingsmith shrugged. Sean pulled the big steel door open, activating the light inside a smaller cave. Tom looked at the stacked arsenal.

'Just how big have the bears got up here? Are we expecting trolls or an aquatic assault from a sea monster?' He picked up a shoulder holster. 'These are for RPGs. This is an armoury for guerrilla warfare.' He took out his phone, but before he could photograph it Sean pushed his arm down.

'Tom, don't. I'll explain it all.'

Tom shook him off. He stood in front of Kingsmith.

'What exactly are you doing here?'

They were equal height; Tom was younger, but Kingsmith far bigger. They held each other's stare. Then Kingsmith smiled.

'So serious! Tom, I'm bankrolling your conservation campaign, I'm investing in the Arctic, and I'm helping Sean boy get his boy scout badge for being neighbourly. My immediate concern? Let's not miss the window of opportunity – I want to see this Great Hall.' He turned to go. 'And, boys, do not leave me alone with Radiance: I'm not sure I can keep up the good daddy routine much longer.' Kingsmith went back out onto the beach and they heard him exchange pleasantries with Danny Long. They stood in silence as his footsteps receded towards the Lodge. Sean closed the door to the armoury. The locks whirred.

'Four RIBs,' Tom said very quietly. 'Body armour and harnesses for RPGs. Quite a lot of kit for an ethical retreat. So talk. Because my name is on this.'

'Tom, please trust me. I was asked to do this.'

'By him?'

'By Philip Stowe. You know, our Defence Secretary.'

'*Stowe?* That crook? You know he's bloodstained, don't you – he sells British arms to the highest bidder, he cares fuck-all about human rights – you're telling me you're doing something for *him*, and *I'm* involved?'

'Sean!' Martine called in to them. 'Danny says we need to go now or we'll miss it. Are you guys ready?'

'Just coming!' Sean turned back to Tom. 'Long story short, as well as everything that you do know about, we're also protecting radomes for the Norwegians. Now NATO's gone, they're really scared – Tom, think about what could happen if a hostile power—'

'Wake up! You're protecting the means of warfare for Philip fucking Stowe and his business cronies! This isn't about patriotism, it's about money—'

'And you're so up your own holy arse now you can't even see that Midgard is helping with the stability of the whole region—'

'What I see is that Midgard is being used, and so am I. By you.'

Sean couldn't bear the look in his eyes. 'I want to explain everything to you, so that you understand. I'm sure, *I'm sure*, Tom, that you'll be OK when you do. Everything you want to achieve here – you still can. Everything I said about the business and the retreats is still true. Private security isn't a crime: you of all people know how it works. How does the press stay safe? How do NGOs do their work? Peace-keeping means having a big stick.'

'What about that little thing called the Svalbard Treaty? The one that specifically prohibits any warlike purposes—'

'Everyone ignores it! It's out of date!'

'Like our agreement. It's void.'

Before Tom could go, furious with fear, Sean grabbed him by the arm and pulled him back. They stared at each other in the gloom of the strong room. Sean took his hand away. They heard the skidoos starting up, and Radiance cheerfully calling them.

'Please,' said Sean. 'Please, let's just go to the cave. And then I'll tell you everything you want to know.'

'I don't want that. I want the truth.'

'I promise.' Sean said it to Tom's back. He followed him out.

'I need to pee,' Tom yelled, heading for the Lodge. 'Wait for me.'

The bad news was brought this afternoon that 'Job' is dead, torn in pieces by the other dogs. He was found a good way from the ship, 'Old Suggen' lying watching the corpse, so that no other dog could get to it. They are wretches, these dogs; no day passes without a fight. In the day-time one of us is generally on hand to stop it, but at night they seldom fail to tear and bite one of their comrades. Poor 'Barabbas' is frightened out of his wits. He stays on board now, and dares not venture on the ice, because he knows the other monsters would set on him. There is not a trace of chivalry about these curs. When there is a fight, the whole pack rush like wild beasts on the loser. But is it not, perhaps, the law of nature that the strong, and not the weak, should be protected? Have not we human beings, perhaps, been trying to turn nature topsy-turvy by protecting and doing our best to keep life in all the weak?

Wednesday, 11 October 1893
Farthest North: The Norwegian Polar Expedition 1893–1896 (1897)
Fridtjof Nansen

23

Five skidoos went up the glacier, the roar of their engines muffled by the deep snow. Up ahead, Tom kept pace with Terry Bjornsen who led the way, then came Sean with Martine pillion, and close behind, Radiance with Kingsmith on the back. Danny Long brought up the rear. The snowmobile trails glittered pale pink and the sky glowed all shades of rose above the sharp violet peaks.

Sean had never seen Svalbard so beautiful as he guided his skidoo in Tom's tracks. Now was not the time to lose his own cool – he must stay focused on the super-objective of Midgard: an inspiring venue in which to promote the reconciliation of business and environmental ethics. And here they were, the two of them, actually living out that conflict, at this very second. He wanted to laugh – of course Tom would see it too. And the solution was to keep talking, arguing if necessary, but always in pursuit of that shared goal. Sean's heart lifted. As long as Tom did not act rashly, they'd get through it. As long as Tom and Kingsmith were not left alone – that would be a recipe for disaster. He and Tom could argue above their solid bedrock of friendship – but Tom and Kingsmith had never clicked.

At the first saddle in the ridge between the two tongues of the Midgard glacier they crossed over, leaving the Lodge behind and out of sight. They dipped down onto the other side where the snow shadow was pale blue, Terry Bjornsen leading them around a darker blue track to an easy further ascent. Two small fluorescent orange pennants fluttered ahead like candle flames, marking the entrance to the ice-cave.

They parked the skidoos in a line angled for the descent. The pennant flags were mounted on whippy plastic masts weighted deep in the snow, from which emerged a length of orange nylon rope. One end was hooked to a mast, and the other attached to the cave cover, revealed when Terry Bjornsen kicked away the snow to show them a scarred white plastic slab. Sean knew Tom was avoiding his eye, but that was better than conflict, for now. They were still together.

Radiance, ever the expert traveller, was checking all her equipment, tucking in her own loose straps and then fussing over Kingsmith. He allowed her, rolling his eyes at Sean. Martine called Sean to help with hers. When their heads were touching, she whispered, 'What's going on?'

'Nothing to worry about.'

She nodded, but her eyes went to Tom, standing alone, still as a stone cairn. Sean had a terrible fear that at any second he was going to turn and denounce him. But Tom remained looking back towards Midgard Lodge. Then Danny Long, who had already climbed to a lookout ridge, radioed the first all-clear and Sean put the unpleasant thought of their impending conversation aside. He watched Terry Bjornsen take up his pre-planned spot on the opposite side to Danny. The cave was well positioned for surveillance: this side of the glacier narrowed between the rocks and a bear would easily be spotted. The spotters had flares as well as bullets and would be in constant contact by iridium satellite phone. Sean had two, and had intended to give one to Tom. He changed his mind.

To reach the Great Hall and return would take thirty minutes, max. Beneath the plastic slab the entrance to the cave system was a neatly edged circular hole in the ice, a metre wide. A few centimetres below, a wooden ladder had been secured to the ice wall with large and reassuringly new steel clamps and screws. This fed down three metres to the first landing, where weak daylight illuminated the area called the Lobby. Black plastic grids were half-sunk into the hard ground to aid progress and along the wall, new rope fed through steel rings where the tunnel sloped away into darkness.

Sean climbed halfway up the ladder to phone Terry Bjornsen – everything looked good. His crackly laugh came back, saying it bloody should, they'd killed themselves making it pretty. Then they all switched on their head torches and Sean led the way in, followed by Tom, Radiance and Martine, with Kingsmith bringing up the rear.

The sound quality was very different inside the ice. When Sean spoke to make sure they all wanted to go on, he had to project loudly because the frozen density sucked his words away. But they all called out to show they were keen, even Tom, who the others ushered into second place in the line. Radiance went behind him, then Martine, Kingsmith last. They followed Sean down the slope away from the Lobby, along the ice corridor where their torch beams bounced and shone on white curves.

Sean called reassurance as he led the way down rough steps cut with an ice axe, and was relieved to see Tom slipping naturally into an authoritative role, helping Martine, who was grateful. Radiance didn't need him, and turned to help Kingsmith down. They all waited for him, passing through a smaller landing, then out into a wide passageway where even Tom could stand upright in the centre.

'Everyone's fine.' Tom's tone was still curt.

'Thanks.' Sean was grateful he was helping. He was more than grateful – he was happy that they were doing their favourite thing together, even if all was not well. Surely Tom was glad he hadn't sulked and missed it?

They went on.

The rope holds continued, the floor had been graded and black grip-tiles filled gaps or places where the walls were glassy either side. As the passageway continued its descent, they paused to marvel at the changing colours of the ice, from white to a fairytale pale blue. In one place a streak of sulphurous gold matter ran diagonally across the wall and into the ice, and a few metres further on, down another set of ice-axed steps, the passageway became a domed room with a natural porthole in one ice wall.

They crowded around it to look. Their torch beams showed a deep narrow chamber filled with ice stalagmites and stalactites, stretching up and down towards each other and sometimes forming delicate ice columns. Their breath came in clouds, drifting into the cavern and trailing between the frozen forms.

'Where's that air coming from?' Tom had moved closer to Sean, his voice low.

They watched the pale vapour from their lungs move around the stalagmites, then disappear.

'The air vent from the hatch.' Sean said it automatically. He watched the five halogen beams from their head torches shifting the shadows and making the ice strobe and gleam with light, as if stirred to life by their observation. Radiance exclaimed in frustration that her micro camera, guaranteed for polar conditions, did not work.

'So expensive,' she said. 'Complete rip-up.'

'It's too cold for the battery,' Tom said. 'But you don't need a camera. Use your eyes. This is truly awesome.'

Standing beside him, Sean smiled. Everything was going to be all right.

'OK, team?' Sean avoided Tom's face, but let his beam rest for a moment on Martine, who smiled, Radiance, who gave him a thumbs up, and then Kingsmith, who was looking up at the roof. He looked back at Sean and nodded.

'Tom,' Sean said, 'go first?'

'Sure.' There was no need for explanation; Tom understood Sean's concern for the others, and immediately moved a few paces into the darkness ahead, waiting.

'Don't you worry about me,' Kingsmith called. 'I'm doing just fine.'

Sean fell into second place, and was glad to feel Martine squeeze his shoulder. They went on, Tom's beam showing the way. The passageway continued to descend, its shape changing as they went – sometimes wider around the head area, sometimes narrowing, sometimes with a ledge protruding at waist height that they had to pass by, taking the ice by their mittened hands and feeling it glide as the friction melted it.

They came into a broader section, and again Sean checked their faces. They were all smiling, but he could hear their breathing was faster.

'Still OK?'

The three of them nodded, then Tom called out softly that the ice was good.

'I can make out a big arch ahead – that's got to be the Great Hall. There's this narrow bit, then a couple of big shelving steps down, it's right here.'

Sean could hear the excitement in his voice.

'We're coming!'

'No, I don't think so.' Kingsmith's voice came from further back in the tunnel. 'I'll see you guys back up top.'

'Hold up, Tom,' Sean called ahead. 'Joe's not OK.'

'I'm fine,' Kingsmith called back irritably, but Radiance and Martine were already with him, and he did not look at all OK. He was leaning against the ice wall and smiling, but it was more of a grimace. He deflected Sean's torch beam from his face and started back along the passageway.

'You take care of things down here, I'll see you up top.'

'Hey, old man,' Radiance said. 'You need me. Admit it.'

Kingsmith laughed weakly. 'Radiance, you kill me.'

'What are you talking about? I save you! I make your life so fun!' She grinned back at Sean and Martine, her teeth white in the darkness. 'Martin, come on. I save you too, no fee.'

Martine did not reply, but Sean saw her tense expression.

'Go,' he said. 'Tom and I will just have a quick look.'

'Or we can take them back.' Tom had returned to Sean's side.

'We'll be fine!' Radiance winked at them. 'I'm their leader now.'

Martine rolled her eyes at Sean. 'Don't be too long.'

'Ten minutes,' Sean said.

'Fifteen, realistically,' said Tom.

'I'm the leader,' Radiance called back. 'Fifteen is OK.' She herded Martine and Kingsmith back up the passageway. Sean grinned at the thought of what Martine would say later.

'Might as well take a quick look,' Tom said. 'We've come all this way.'

'We have.' Sean looked at him, and this time Tom met his gaze for a second. They went down the passage together, towards the ice-cave known as the Great Hall.

'We went inside,' Sean told the court. He felt like the ice was taking his breath again, he almost expected it to come out in clouds. 'Tom went in first.' His lungs worked fast and shallow at the thought of it all.

*

They were so excited neither could speak, but they turned to each other to confirm they really were seeing this marvel. They were in a huge cavern, some ice giant's baronial hall. By unspoken instinct, they moved their two torch beams together, like a single pair of eyes.

Parts of the structure glowed to life under their double gaze. Slowly, amazed, grinning at each other, they went a few steps deeper, nudging each other to point out the blue ribs and rafters of ice above them, a cathedral crossed with the inside of a whale. They gazed on a massive slab resting on smaller blocks, a chieftain's table. Below it, softer-shaped extrusions formed huge sleeping dogs. Here and there were stalactites spreading like candelabra, and other strange forms twisted into ropes hung with ice tassels.

Sean saw gargoyles and effigies, and then one eye of the double beam shifted, and Tom was looking at him.

'Tell me now,' Tom said. 'While the cat's away.'

It took a few seconds for Sean to remember what he meant. Kingsmith. That whole mess above the ice. Tom had broken the spell and now they stood looking at one another in the Great Hall, each face pinned by the other's beam.

'Fine,' Sean said. 'You have to understand though, no one's doing anything wrong.' But as he said it, he didn't sound convincing even to himself. 'We're just protecting the place we both love.'

'With a private military.'

'Tom, I told you – it's standing security for guests.'

'You let Kingsmith do this, didn't you? Of course you did.'

'Yes, I left that side of it to him, but, Tom, if your own government asks you to do something …'

'You're delusional.' Tom's breath came in bigger clouds.

'You know something, Tom?' Sean's breath billowed out as well, they were like dragons facing each other. 'There are lots of ways to protect the Arctic, but you think you've got the only answer, you want a vital new trade route just taken off the table – you think the world really will put ice and whales and—'

'Climate change first? Yes! I'm hoping—'

Tom stopped suddenly. He turned away, his beam flashing over the blue-and-white ice walls. Then back to one spot, where the blue ice gleamed more vividly.

'Shit. Look—'

Sean's torch beam picked it out too. A narrow thread of water trickling from high above, following the curve of the vaulted wall, down into the cavern floor, through the crack they both saw, running beyond the range of their light.

They stopped arguing, hearing the tearing sound. Only a second, then it stopped. Then came another sound – the high-pitched moan of ice squeezing ice.

Sean held on to the lectern. The eyes of the courtroom were on him like ants, he wanted to scrape them from his skin. The carpet tiles smelled dirty, someone was wearing too much hairspray. He was close to it. He wanted to push his fingers under his jacket, into his shirt and the warmth of his sticky armpit – they were burning like they had when he was recovering. He put his fingers into the glass of water on the stand, and heard the tapping of keyboards, no doubt recording this strange gesture. Sawbridge was looking at him with an urgent expression.

'Your Honour,' he called out, 'a break for my client, I think?'

'Do you need that, Mr Cawson?'

Sean heard the metallic scrape of the louvre windows being opened. A trail of air moved through the room and over his face.

'No. I'll go on.' His voice felt deadened, as if still in the ice. 'A massive blow hit us under our feet then we were – we lifted up as the ice shifted and I fell sideways, there was nothing to hold on to, there was this rumbling noise and even as I was slipping I knew the cave was collapsing.'

He put his hands back on the lectern. 'I tried to push my feet against something so I could get upright – I was still on my side – but I couldn't find any purchase because everything was slippery and my torch had got knocked sideways so I couldn't see. Then the rumbling stopped.'

Sean closed his eyes. No one moved in the courtroom, not a finger on a keyboard or a hand in a pocket. He could hear his breath, loud and shallow, and he didn't know if he was at the lectern or in the ice.

'I called for Tom. I called out – and then I heard him, his voice was coming from somewhere below me. He was alive but he'd fallen. I called to him to hold on – I got my boot against something and I pushed up so I could secure my torch – and all I could see was a jumble of huge ice fragments. I called out again and when he answered I saw the hole it came from.'

The sound of Angela and Ruby Harding's weeping brought Sean back to the courtroom for a moment. He spoke directly to them.

'I said hold on. I said the others will be out by now, they'll raise the alarm. I kept saying, "I won't leave you, just hold on, Tom, hold on."'

Sean braced himself against the ice, his belly against a freezing slab of it, the hard edge of his boot soles scraped in behind him to get a hold. With one hand he felt for his torch and secured it, then shone it down into the black chasm.

'Tom!' He waited. '*TOM!*'

There was no reply. All he could hear was the great bloody gulp of his own heart. He was completely alone in the ice, deep below the surface. Tom was gone.

Sean stared into blackness for a moment. Then the court came back into focus. The staring faces. The sound of the traffic.

'I don't remember much after that.' He did not wait for the coroner to release him, he left the stand and walked back down to his seat. Sawbridge stared at him with grave concern and patted him on the arm. No one spoke. The coroner cleared his throat.

'We'll adjourn for today. Mr Cawson, thank you, but I'm afraid I'll need to ask you back to the stand tomorrow morning for questions.'

Sean nodded, then did not move until all the motion in the room was over, the scraping chairs, the stares, the chiming of phones released from silence. When he finally looked up, Sawbridge was waiting at the end of the row.

The traffic of Canterbury's ring road looked like a film, as unreal and alien as the jerky Inuit of *Nanuq of the North*.

'A drink, that's what we need.' Sawbridge steered him in the other direction, around the corner into the back streets where kebab shops jostled medieval walls and an old pub stood waiting.

They went into its gloomy womb of beery carpet and ugly dark-wood furniture, the only people except for the barman, his belly prominent under a sports shirt. He looked at them disapprovingly as he sloshed a pint of water down in front of Sean – the only thing he wanted – and a tomato juice for Sawbridge. Somewhere in the background a fruit machine whirred and pinged. Sean stared through the darkness that still clotted his vision.

'You did splendidly.'

'I failed.'

'Rubbish! If it were water off a duck's back, if you just sang your song all well-rehearsed, it would be a disaster. You went through hell to survive.'

'I failed Tom.'

Sawbridge held up his hands appeasingly, as if to show he understood. He opened the peanuts and ate them in meditative silence for a while, then hailed the barman. 'Don't suppose there's anywhere I might fire up a very small cigar?'

'The street.' The barman was unimpressed. 'You from the inquest?'

'Ah, you know about it.' Sawbridge pepped up his charm, just in case.

'Know the family. I knew Tom.'

Sean looked up. 'A friend?'

'Village cricket, when he was around.'

Sean stared at him.

'You were one of the pall-bearers.'

'That's right.' The barman looked at him. 'I remember you, too.'

Sean held out his hand. 'Sean Cawson.'

'Yeah. I know.' The barman hesitated fractionally then shook. 'John Burnham.'

Sawbridge stood: 'A great tragedy.' Sean ignored the signal.

'I couldn't save him.'

'I'm not asking. Mate, you look in a bad way.'

'He's doing extremely well and we are almost at the finish line.' Sawbridge tapped Sean on the arm and went to the door. 'Very best to you,' he called to the barman. 'I'm sure we'll stop by again.' Out on the street a safe distance away, he stopped. 'Important you hear this: discretion is most certainly the better part of valour. Quite serious now. Absolutely no vino veritas-ing with anyone, please, and I include myself in that.'

'I wasn't planning to.'

'Who ever does?'

They walked back to the White Bear in silence. Sean changed his clothes, did not check his phone or email, went down to the restaurant and ate before Sawbridge arrived. They were both relieved to miss each other for dinner and, back in his room, Sean stared at whatever was on the television and drank vodka, until he was able to pass out.

Now we are in the very midst of what the prophets would have had us dread so much. The ice is pressing and packing round us with a noise like thunder. It is piling itself up into long walls, and heaps high enough to reach a good way up the Fram's rigging; in fact, it is trying its very utmost to grind the Fram into powder. But here we sit quite tranquil, not even going up to look at all the hurly-burly, but just chatting and laughing, as usual.

Such an ice conflict is undeniably a stupendous spectacle. One feels one's self to be in the presence of Titanic forces, and it is easy to understand how timid souls may be overawed and feel as if nothing could stand before it. For when the packing begins in earnest, it seems as though there could be no spot on the earth's surface left unshaken. First you hear a sound like the thundering rumble of an earthquake far away on the great waste; then you hear it in several places, always coming nearer and nearer. The silent ice world re-echoes with thunders; nature's giants are awakening to the battle.

Friday, 13 October 1893
Farthest North: The Norwegian Polar Expedition 1893–1896 (1897)
Fridtjof Nansen

24

Summer, 1988

The first time Sean stood on Arctic ice in Greenland, sponsored by Kingsmith and with Tom Harding by his side, he wanted to shout in triumph. He was here, he had made it. There were no green-tinted icebergs or radiant pink light, as in the painting, but the cold on his face, the sunny glitter of the air, the bluest sky and the sound of excited sled dogs howling at their approach, filled him with real joy.

It didn't matter that Redmond was a tosser, that the whole thing still smacked of elitist privilege – he was here and that was all he cared about. Taking part in the Lost Explorers' Society point-to-point dog-sled race, on a section of the route of the 1935 Oxford University West Greenland Expedition.

They would be in six two-man teams, with no backup save each other. They could wear modern base layers, but the aesthetic was strictly 1935, and Redmond looked forward to his photographs being displayed at the Royal Geographical Society. He enjoyed documenting Sean and Tom's fumbling attempts at harnessing their team. They could not help noticing they had been given the smallest dogs.

'It's like he wants us to die on the ice,' Sean muttered.

'Fuck him,' Tom agreed, as they were the last to set off.

Redmond was pleased to humiliate them but not quite to the point of death, so he sent a couple of teams to escort them safely to the first base camp.

Inside an alarmed perimeter fence, to protect them against bear attacks, and with the thirty-six Greenland sled dogs, they all felt quite safe. The twelve young men fed their dogs, pitched their tents, gathered to share a communal meal of rehydrated chicken curry, followed by rehydrated apple crumble with custard – then they retired to try to sleep. Each pair had a rifle, just in case.

Sean was excited beyond being able to rest, but Tom insisted they try. They lay in their glowing orange tent, talking in low voices.

'Thank you,' Tom said after so long a pause that Sean thought he was asleep.

'What for?'

'Coming with me. Partnering up on this.'

Sean lay silent for a while, absorbing this. 'This is my dream, to do this. If you hadn't asked me …'

'You'd have found another way. You're resourceful.' Tom wriggled around in his sleeping bag so that they were facing each other. 'I really admire you, Sean. I've had everything given to me, and I know you wish you hadn't told me, but you—'

'Shh—' Sean heard a dog's short whuff outside.

'No let me say it – you've done it all yourself—'

As the dogs began baying they were both on their knees scrabbling for the rifle. Sean was out first with it, loaded and cocked, Tom right behind him – and there, two hundred feet away from their encampment, was a huge female bear with a yearling cub, coming to investigate.

'Flare!' Sean shouted, and Tom grabbed one and released it into the air. It arced towards the animals, almost invisible in the sun. All the dogs were baying now, everyone was scrambling from their tents. The female stood straight ahead, curious and unafraid. Her deep pelt was cream against the blue-hued snow but her cub was pearly fluff. As she stood up on her hind legs, she looked so human, so intrigued, that Sean would not have been surprised if she had called out to know who they were. She was the most beautiful, most thrilling creature he had ever seen.

Tom fired two more flares and at their screech, the cub ran behind its mother. That seemed to decide her, she gave them one last look and turned to leave, but Redmond was taking aim with his rifle.

'Mine!' he called out.

'Don't shoot! she's leaving!' Tom yelled, as Redmond fired. He missed and when the mother and cub began to run, he took aim again. People were shouting to release the dogs, hold the dogs, the dogs were howling and barking—

Before Redmond could fire again, Tom hurled himself at him, knocking his rifle skywards and wrestling it from him. Redmond struggled for it but Tom threw it away into the snow, before catching a furious punch on the jaw. As Redmond landed it, Sean was on him, slugging him back then kneeling on his chest and holding him down in the snow, one arm across his throat like he'd learned as a kid, putting his face close and telling him to be calm, be calm—

Sean knew how fights went, and this one was his. No one was coming to Redmond's aid. He pressed down a little harder, and Redmond stopped struggling. Sean got off and offered his hand to help him up. Redmond spat at him, murder in his eyes.

'You fucking oik.'

'I think what Redmond is saying,' said Tom, rubbing his chin, 'is that he won't shoot the fucking bears unless he fucking needs to – is that right?'

'We could have died!' Redmond screamed at the rest of them.

'Anyone can panic,' Sean winked at him, 'don't feel bad.'

'You fucking morons! Never touch my gun again!' Everyone stared at him, even the dogs. He turned on Sean and Tom. 'You're off this expedition, do you hear!' He glared at Tom. 'You and your fucking oik servant—'

Tom grabbed him by his jacket. 'Don't talk about my friend like that.' He shoved Redmond back so hard he fell over his feet, and the others laughed.

Sean turned to the rest of them. It was a surreal sight, the bright orange tents glowing in the midnight sun, the dogs, Redmond holding his nose, the red seeping through his fingers, dripping on the snow. 'I've paid my way,' Sean said, with all the confidence he could muster. 'I've got a right to be here. Anyone who disagrees, say now.'

'I do! This is my expedition.' Redmond was staggering to his feet, still murderous. 'Shut those fucking dogs up!' He looked around for support. 'Who's with me?' No one answered.

'*Fram*,' Tom said to Sean.

'Fucking right, *Fram*,' Sean agreed.

They walked back to their tent, not daring to look at each other, half expecting to feel a blow from behind – but all they could hear was Redmond's furious hissing at the others, and the yelp of one of their dogs.

They settled their own team, they checked for bears – they caught each other's eye with a glint of triumph – but only when they were back in the orange glow of their tent, the rifle safely stowed by the flap, did they turn to each other and high five, then lie on their backs and kick their legs in the air, laughing until they cried.

They did sleep, but a couple of hours later they woke to the sound of barking again. Looking out, they were astonished to see the other five teams had packed up and were harnessing their dogs. They were being left behind. They watched in amazement as, led by Redmond's sled, their fellow explorers abandoned them, although they did leave them the tripwire fence.

'Bastards.' Tom scratched the head of Roxy, their lead dog. 'Like we care.'

'We don't need them.' Sean looked at him. 'From now on, we can do our own expeditions. I bet Kingsmith'll fund us.'

'Fine. But let's come back alive from this one first.'

They decided to make a circular route of their own, and as they sledged and switched over, and as Sean ran with the sled and leapt on, and the pure clean wind rushed over his face, and the jingle of the dogs' traces made music, he thanked Joe Kingsmith with all his heart for this chance.

And then finally we were back on our own glacier, *and far below lay our own fjord and the dots that were Thule and home – the spot we had been longing for during the endless, tedious months.*

We called a halt and waited for Uvdloriark to explore the crevasses between us and home, and while I sat there Knud walked over to me and gave me his hand.

'Many times during the summer,' he said, 'I didn't believe we could go on. But now that we have completed such an expedition together, we ought never to be apart again. Wherever we go in the whole world, we must always stick together.'

I have heard many speeches in my life, most of them stupid libels on friendship and loyalty at banquets or meetings, but there on the glacier Knud dared put into a simple declaration exactly what he felt. I replied in kind. It is seldom men have the courage to do what they want to do and say what they really think, especially to other men. But Knud said these things, and I never forgot those words while he lived, and I shall never forget them so long as I live.

Arctic Adventure: My Life in the Frozen North (1936)
Peter Freuchen

25

On Tuesday morning, like a general achieving the ridge before the opposition mustered below, Sean was the first in court. He'd slipped out of the White Bear early and walked the city walls, then gone to a chain café in the town. Its soothing weekday hustle calmed his racing mind. Tuesday, Wednesday, Thursday: Over.

He felt the brisk heavy tread on the floorboards and caught the aroma of a cigar before his lawyer was upon him, thumping down into his seat with a cheerful grin. Then came Mrs Osman, looking as if she might have slept in her black suit, and today allowing her two young aides to pull the document cases for her. They had the air of monks from some martial sect. She returned her counterpart's greeting pleasantly enough.

'So showy,' Sawbridge murmured after they had passed. 'But makes the family feel cared for. Done it myself.' And then he allowed Sean quiet reflection, before the ordeal to come.

Sean kept his eyes from any one face, and his testimony simple.

They were in the cave. The cave had collapsed. Tom was on one side, he was on the other. Tom tried to get back across but slipped and fell into a crevasse.

'It was completely black, except for my head torch. I crawled to the edge, and there was nothing. My beam went about twenty feet, and I could see the sides where the ice had broken apart. It was very deep, and then my beam wouldn't reach any further. I couldn't see Tom's head torch. It was just black. I called out, I called to him. But there was nothing. I was frightened. I thought I was going to die too. But I pulled myself back and I felt my way along, trying to get up to where I thought the opening was. I was terrified I would slip into the crevasse as well. I didn't know how long the torch would last. I couldn't hear anything and I didn't know if the others had got out in time. Everything had fallen and crashed, the whole cave had collapsed, there were bars and huge chunks of ice everywhere and I had to crawl. I just kept trying to move up and find the tunnel. I can't remember clearly after that.'

Sean is on his belly, he can hardly breathe but he knows oxygen is vital so he forces himself to control his gasping. The beam of his head torch picks up a jumbled plane of surfaces, matt and shiny, white, grey, blue, transparent. His mind and body are throbbing, he can't tell if he's injured, if he's bleeding and that's the pumping feeling – but he knows he has to move or die.

He hauls himself forward on his elbows, a huge weight of ice dragging on his right leg. He hauls through and keeps going. Too much vapour – overspending – slow the breath or suffocate. Slower ... can't call to Tom because no shouting, no disturbing vibration, he remembers that too – burning feeling on his face – takes his forehead off the ice, do not stop! Keep moving up, keep forcing forward – get help – buried alive if he stops, then they're both dead. In training: under an hour to survive before hypothermia or asphyxiation or both set in. The torch beam is still steady, but batteries don't last forever. Find a gap, keep moving, stay calm.

There: a black triangle in the jumbled plane of ice. He might be imagining it or there might be air movement, he closes his eyes to feel it better.

Tom.

He calls it, but in his mind not with his voice and lungs. It's death if he stays and it might be death to try, but he worms forward on his elbows into the black hole until his helmet jars and stops him, so he has to try to take it off, fumble the strap and clip – he uses his teeth to pull off his glove – and push the helmet aside. It drags hard and painful on his ear and scalp, but he pushes on, feeling it scrape deep into his back as he forces forward into that hole where there is different air—

—like an animal, he can taste it, taste air, because his rational brain has gone. In his panic, he forgot his torch was on his helmet and now there is only dark and cold and the pressure of the ice around him, death touching him on all sides, but like a blind worm he does not stop, he uses his bare head as a ram when he has to because pain is a sharp tool and even a parasite has the will to live and this is what he now is, some ancient ice parasite working its way through the ice-giant's gut—

That thought fires him with rage and powers his boots against the great bastard's intestinal wall; he will get himself out through the mouth or the eye or the arse or the skin – he makes himself a great pulsing worm for the rhythm to keep moving, writhing, the friction melting just enough space to give him passage—

Sean's will powers him on, hauling and forcing this length of meat and bone and cartilage through the tight hard spaces, even though the ungainly weight is too much and he only wants to rest – but thought of failure whips him on and gets that sack of meat thrashing its legs and almost vomiting with the effort—

He shoots forward into black air – and a wall of ice slams him from underneath.

TOM – the name does not stir his lungs or tongue but drops down instead into a hole in his mind and vanishes.

In the blackness, Sean's mind moves, then his body. He is not dead. He feels space around him. He fell.

'Tom!' This time the sound comes out. He hears the acoustic bounce. He calls again in different directions. In the blackness, one side is solid, but the sound quality changes to the other. He crawls forward, blind but sensitised—

Tom, Tom, Tom—

In the blackness like a drum beat, reaching forward using Tom's name for echo-location, he feels a drift of air ahead. The ice beneath is starting to dip down. He slips and grabs but there's nothing to hang on to, steeper and faster – then a gasp as something blocks his hurtling force. Impact but not pain. His mouth full of soft snow. He struggles out into a howling black snowstorm.

Sean turned to the coroner.

'I was lucky. Somehow I got into another part of the cave system and was able to get out. The rest of it is all in the *Sunday Times* interview I did afterwards, that Mr Sawbridge submitted.' He felt ashamed now. He had let them make a hero of him.

'I know, Mr Cawson, and thank you. But as I am not a *Sunday Times* reader, I missed it three years ago, so what you say is fresh to me. I did see you had included it, but I chose to wait to hear your own account live, rather than an edited version. Though of course we all edit our memories, it is unavoidable.'

Sawbridge did his push-up move on the chair in front. 'Your Honour, it sounds as if you're suggesting—'

'That memories are subjective; indeed I am, Mr Sawbridge. Mr Cawson, can you continue?'

Sean nodded. To his surprise, he saw Martine's face, a pale beacon in the spot beside Sawbridge. He had not registered her arrival.

'I knew we'd gone in at midday, an hour after the eclipse. At that time of year, the light's almost gone by about three, and when I – when I came out into the drift, it was dark. So it could have been three, or ten – I had no idea. I couldn't see any lights, I couldn't hear anything over the wind. The weather had totally changed. All I could think was that I couldn't be on the ice cap because I'd fallen, but I couldn't see the mountains. I didn't know what to do except get back into the tunnel, because at least that would provide shelter, but I couldn't find it.'

The wind is a devil screaming in his ears, trying to kill him with the sound. With numb hands, Sean struggles to tighten all his toggles: jacket hem, sleeves, hood, trousers. No Tom. No skidoo, no survival suit. He is going to freeze to death on the Midgard glacier, or a bear will get him – that thought sparks his vision fractionally keener, searching for a different movement in the snow. The pumping fist of muscle in his chest goads him on. Shelter or death.

A wind of a thousand fists knocks him off his feet and he's face down again, pummelled back every time he tries to stand. A tiny part of his brain understands he's facing down the slope – the blows spin him but most seem to come from behind – it's coming down the mountain. His brain clings to that information, it's important – yes! Because katabatic wind comes off the land towards the sea. The wind will drive him down to the fjord, to take his chances with the bears.

The wind has another idea. It lifts him up and hurls him about like a ragdoll thrown in a tantrum. Sean stumbles and falls until he can't get up any more. The wind shrieks in triumph and he knows exactly what is happening, but it's really not so bad at all. Because he's stopped struggling, he feels as safe and comfortable as if he were in an igloo, like the Inuit made so cleverly.

Knud Rasmussen and Peter Freuchen learned the skill. The best of friends, like him and Tom. Rasmussen and Freuchen, Cawson and Harding, the four of them in sealskin anoraqs, they would build one in no time.

We don't need to make it big, not everything has to be big to be good, Sean, we'll just do what we can – get up, you lazy bugger.

Sean turns his face to Tom's voice, the effort coming from a thousand miles away. Tom is right there beside him in the snow, showing off how he can dig with his bare hands. He grins as Sean copies him, but much, much slower. They keep going, they're getting there, they've made a hole in the snow – or rather uncovered one, and Sean gets into its smooth curved sides and curls into the foetal position, out of the howling wind and punching fists. And somewhere on the slopes of Midgardbreen, beneath the ice cap of Midgardfonna in the archipelago of Svalbard, two men lie lost beneath the ice, one deep, one shallow.

'It was a miracle I survived. I don't remember being found, just waking in the Sickehaus the next day. I only know I gave statements because I was told. But I don't remember.' Sean clamped his right hand under his armpit and felt it moisten. He became aware of his shirt sticking to his back, and the adrenal sweat smell that rose from him.

'All I know is that cave fell in on us and Tom slipped down. Somehow I got out. Inspector Brovang found me.'

'Thank you, Mr Cawson.' Mrs Osman adjusted her ill-fitting jacket. 'Thank you for revisiting that … ordeal … for us. My questions are less to do with the fact of your survival, and more to do with how Tom was not so … lucky.'

Sean nodded respectfully. Here it came.

'We will later be hearing from an expert witness … a glaciologist … that the structures of ice-caves, wherever they are found, can never be relied upon for stability. But that you had every reason to think that this one … on Midgardbreen … was safe enough to venture with your partners.'

'I did. Yes. And so did Danny Long and Terry Bjornsen, both of whom have masses of polar experience and live there year-round.'

'Yes. I did note that. So a gap opened up in the … floor? Of the cave known as the Great Hall. Is that correct? How wide was it? Could you describe it? I am trying to get a sense of the danger.'

Sean stared at her a moment. So was he.

'It was very hard to see. Everything under our feet had shifted. There was water, it made everything slippery, or Tom could have jumped it.'

'It sounds very frightening.' Mrs Osman frowned down at her open file. She shook her head and used both hands to lift the mass of papers, bristling with Post-it notes. 'I'm sorry, a moment …'

Sawbridge's deep audible sigh signalled his opinion of her competence. The coroner tapped his pencil.

'Yes. I'm sorry, here we are …' Mrs Osman looked up again. 'How would you characterise your relationship with Mr Harding?'

'We were friends from college. From 1988 to Tom's death. Three decades.'

Mrs Osman inclined her head encouragingly.

'Would you say it was a stable and constant friendship?'

'Very much so.' Sean felt a tremor as he said it.

'Though it was not without its … gaps. Was it?' She looked down and turned a page. 'Because when I looked at your written statement delivered to my chambers, and also to the coroner … apart from finding it very helpful – for which I thank you and Mr Sawbridge for the foresight – I did wonder … If there was a time when you might not have been … so close. A gap of maybe seven or eight years, during which time you had no contact with Mr Harding.' She studied her file again. 'Until you resumed contact, and shortly afterwards, Mr Harding came on board with your consortium, the – Fairlight Group. That you used to make your purchase bid, for Midgard Lodge. Registered in Jersey.'

'Might I ask my learned colleague where exactly she's going with this?' Sawbridge tipped his head to the side and smiled. Mrs Osman ignored him.

'I ask because it looked to me as if a … gap … might indeed have opened up between you. And I wondered why.'

Sean interlaced his fingers and took a deep breath, the way he had read could work as a stress management technique. He wanted to yell at Osman to say what she wanted, not lay traps – but that would alienate the room.

'You're right,' he said. 'We didn't exactly fall out, but there was a serious difference of opinion. Political not personal, but there was fallout.'

It was a Sunday in February. Tom had come for lunch and to discuss his latest breakup with Ruth Mott. Sean was of the opinion he was better off without her, but Gail thought he should propose and be done with it, then they would both know where they stood, and commitment could carry them through the difficult bits.

Somehow the conversation had strayed into the minefield of what shape that could take, between a man and a woman, and having recently regretted and strenuously denied his latest philandering, Sean felt increasingly under attack. Thinking to save him, and simultaneously drawing a picture with Rosie, Tom had changed the subject to next Saturday's march in London, to protest the imminent invasion of Iraq.

'I can't,' was Sean's immediate reaction. 'I've got a meeting.'

'On a Saturday?'

'Sean's a workaholic now.'

Sean heard the sadness in his wife's voice, and the guilt made him defensive.

'Yes, on a Saturday. It's the only day Joe can do.'

Tom added a shark to Rosie's picture, and she nodded seriously, approving it.

'Sean, you've got a profile. People would take notice if you joined in. There is absolutely no evidence of weapons of mass destruction, this will be an illegal invasion.'

'But if there are—'

'IF! But so far, there aren't! Tell me one good reason we should go ahead.'

'I'll tell you a reason it *will* happen,' Sean said. 'I'm not saying it's a good one, but it's the truth. This invasion is going to happen whether you march or not, because it is in the interest of the global economy to end the uncertainty.'

Tom and Gail stared at him. Then Tom laughed. 'I'm sorry; for a moment there I thought you said—'

'Yeah I did.' Sean felt suddenly quite drunk. 'It's very simple. The banks want war. So that's what's going to happen.' He looked at Rosie's picture. 'That's brilliant.'

'It's completely immoral!' Gail cried.

'It's a *shark*.' Rosie was upset by the atmosphere.

'I didn't say it was *right*, I said it was what was going to happen.' Sean felt the cat rubbing his ankle, as it did when it detected stress in the family. He took the picture from Rosie. 'A very scary shark! But listen to me, marching will not make a blind bit of difference. The money's decided. That's how it goes.' He gave the picture back to Rosie, hating how Tom was looking at him.

'I cannot believe I'm hearing you talk like him.'

'It's economic realpolitik. It's not just Joe saying it.'

'Sean, it's disgusting, it can't be true—' Gail looked like she was going to cry, and Rosie actually started.

'For god's sake I'm not saying *I* want war' – Sean took a huge slug of wine to control his own anxiety – 'but the banks hate uncertainty, everything is on slow, people's livelihoods are going to suffer it if goes on much longer.'

'More people are going to die very soon if it doesn't! You're going to sit back and do nothing?' Tom covered his glass against a refill, and Sean thumped the bottle down.

'Tom, don't talk to me like I'm responsible for all this and you're trying to save everyone – you've been a bit too sanctimonious a bit too long.'

Tom got up. He folded his napkin, kissed Gail, and turned to Sean.

'Thank you for your hospitality.' He bent down and kissed Rosie. 'Oh please don't tear it up, it's such a good drawing.'

'See how you've upset everyone?' Sean stood up. 'You can't go, you can't bloody well drive! I'm just telling it like it is!'

'Mr Coroner!' Sawbridge did his half push-up on the seat in front. 'Long friendship has its ups and downs, and I believe Mrs Osman is diverting our attention away from our common interest.'

'Agreed, Mr Sawbridge. Mrs Osman, in view of the limited time and availability of all parties, please confine your questions to our remit: how and in what manner, did Tom Harding meet his death. We do not seek existential causes that may extend back several years to wars illegal or otherwise, nor to plumb the psyches of our witnesses.'

'Hear hear!' called Sawbridge, and clapped his hands slowly.

'Your Honour, with respect.' Mrs Osman turned to him. 'Is it not also the function of any inquest to fearlessly investigate all causes and seek out and record as many of those facts concerning the death as the public interest requires—'

'Mrs Osman, I am quite up to date with Lord Lane's pronouncements, and the requirements of my own office.' Mr Thornton laced his fingers and bumped his hands down on the table with each word. 'Can we go on?'

'Certainly. No further questions, thank you, Mr Cawson.' Mrs Osman sat.

Sean had sweated throughout his testimony and wanted a shower at the White Bear, but there was no time. Concerned for him, Martine had come down earlier than he expected, and had researched a small bistro a short walk from the court. They repaired with Sawbridge, who primed her for her own testimony.

'Smile, but not too much. I say that because if beautiful women don't smile, they're perceived as aloof and threatening. But if they smile too much—'

'Everyone gets the wrong idea,' Martine said. 'Believe me, I know.'

'Try not to finish anyone's sentence either.' Sawbridge tucked into his veal. 'So clever of you to find this place.'

'Maybe you should give me some performance notes.'

'I hoped I might.' Sawbridge grinned. '*You* are the brilliant, soignée femme-fatale who is responsible for the breakup of this poor chap's marriage – best you get over it now, because that's what they'll say about you.'

'It could be worse.'

'Ha. It might well be. But regardless, you did everything you could to save Tom, and Sean here has been distraught ever since.'

'I have.' Sean had barely spoken since they got there. He felt hyper-sensitised – he saw a trace of makeup on Martine's face, and then he saw it everywhere. All over her skin, on her eyelashes – even some clever paint that gave her hand a pale shimmer. He took her hand and looked at it. Tiny little flecks of mica, suspended in lotion. Misinterpreting the gesture, she smiled and squeezed his.

'Darling. It'll be OK.'

'Of course it will,' said Sawbridge. 'Tell him to eat or he'll keel over.'

'He can't, when he's agitated. I'm the same.' Martine took a mouthful of food. 'Tonight he'll be hungry.'

'I do hope so. He needs his strength.' Sawbridge winked at him. 'Join in whenever you feel like it, or not. Anyway, this afternoon should be OK. We've got a video postcard, I believe they call them, from Miss Radiance Young. Then it's Martine. And the glaciologist, Professor Roger Kelly. Ocean Physics at Cambridge. Controversial with the oil lot, adored by the green lot, so we'll have to watch out for him.'

Martine leaned forward, her hand on Sean's thigh.

'You're the hero of this story, don't you worry.'

Sawbridge grimaced.

'What?' she asked.

'The survivor is rarely the hero,' Sawbridge said. 'We must go carefully.'

Gangrene, as it develops in a frozen limb, *is not so painful as it is odorous. It stinks fearfully and one cannot get away from it. The nurse had a special cure. She captured small lemmings – the Arctic mice that multiply faster than guinea-pigs – killed them beside me and laid the warm skins on the open wounds, bloody side down. After some hours, during which she caught more, she peeled off the skins, the decayed flesh adhering to them, and replaced them with new ones. She also muttered magic formulas over the foot and sang pain-killing songs.*

Nevertheless, the flesh fell away until the bones protruded. I could endure no blankets touching them, and the sight of them sent my nerves jangling. If the room was warm the stench was unendurable; if it was cold, I froze. I went through a living hell, and each night felt that the old man with the scythe was close after me.

When a man is sick and cold and lonely he gets strange ideas, and one day I told the nurse that I wanted to have those toes off. She thought that might be the best thing to do, and she knew just how to do it – bite them off at the joints and prevent the ghosts from occupying my body – her mouth would close the wounds immediately. I thanked her very much, but took no stock in her method; instead, I fitted a nail puller over each toe and banged it off with a hammer.

I cannot attempt to describe the physical pain – but there was a spiritual pain, too – in discarding a portion of my own body, even a part that would never be of any use to me again.

Arctic Adventure: My Life in the Frozen North (1936)
Peter Freuchen

26

The courtroom absorbed Martine's business glamour as she took the oath in her accent of cosmopolitan privilege. The coroner's clerk stared at her slightly too long. Mr Thornton, unsmitten, asked for her account of the events at the ice-cave.

Martine channelled demure respect. She told Mr Thornton how thrilled she had been to work on such an important venture. How delighted to bring such exciting value to her green-minded investors, all hungry for rare ethical vehicles such as Midgard Lodge. She was herself excited to go to Svalbard for the first time and believed in the power of spending real time with one's partners, as people, not just financial co-investors. She expressed her deepest condolences to Tom's family, and told them how Tom believed Midgard Lodge would be a place where great things might be accomplished, to the benefit of the whole world.

'Confine yourself to the facts and avoid speculation, Miss Delaroche.'

'Yes, sir.'

Sean knew Mr Thornton's neutrality would have offended Martine on other occasions, but she understood her role. He had seen her protean ability before, matching herself to the taste of the dominant force, before gradually moulding it to her agenda.

She described how they prepared with every precaution to go to the cave, how Sean could not have done more for their safety. Everyone travelled at their own risk, she was herself intrepid when it came to skiing and diving and driving – she'd been allowed to drive her father's collection of sports cars from a young age – so it was a great surprise to her when she did not like the cave experience. When Joe and Radiance decided to go back, she did too. Only when all three were in the last part of the tunnel with the ladder in sight did they hear the sound of the collapse behind.

When they got out, Mr Long and Mr Bjornsen – Danny and Terry – were already on their way down because they'd seen the sudden change in the weather. As soon as they realised they couldn't break through what had fallen, they hurried back to the Lodge to raise the alarm. Despite insisting that she must stay to try to save Sean and Tom, she'd had to submit to being taken back to the Lodge.

And then the most terrible sleepless night of the storm, not knowing if they were alive or dead but fearing the worst, and in the morning came the Sysselmann's team and then thank god – and here Martine shamelessly crossed herself like the good Catholic she was not – they found Sean, out in the snow. Miraculously alive. Martine looked out at Sean, tears in her eyes. Then to the coroner, lest he miss the full benefit of her emotion. That was all she had to say.

'Not quite all, Miss Delaroche, I believe both counsel have questions. Mr Sawbridge, please go first this time.'

Sawbridge would rather have mopped up any damage Mrs Osman might have tried to inflict, but could only agree. He spoke gently, to signal Martine's fragility.

'Miss Delaroche, what do you think this project represented to Mr Harding?'

'The chance to influence the environmental conscience of the business community, from a position of soft power.'

'Soft power?'

She allowed herself a small smile. Sean found her performance disturbingly good.

'When people are sharing important experiences, when the stress of the deal is put to one side and they are enjoying themselves, it is so much easier to come to agreement. That is one of the most important things about the Lodge; how the environment itself speaks every language. The spiritual quality is stronger there, it touches people inside. It's truly humbling.'

'Quite.' Sawbridge looked genuinely impressed. 'How would you characterise the mood of the participants on this expedition, to see the eclipse at Midgard Lodge? We have heard about the unavoidable delay, and you were all very busy people. What was the mood like, on the day of travel?'

'Very upbeat. Like an amusing, wonderful, school trip.' Her smile faded. 'But with a tragic outcome. At least we have resolution now.'

No, don't say that, shouted Sean in his head. Resolution of what? Osman will go there.

'I understand.' Sawbridge was aware of the danger. 'The pain of not knowing where Tom was lost.'

'That's right.' Martine wiped her eyes again. Sawbridge held a look of deep compassion for several seconds. 'No more questions. Many thanks, Miss Delaroche.'

'May I?' Osman was up before Sawbridge was back beside Sean. 'Miss Delaroche, you work in a so-called "clean-tech" equity firm, is that correct? Raising capital for environmentally friendly businesses?'

'I'm very proud of that,' Martine was considerably less charming to women than men. 'It's something I strongly believe in.'

'I notice your company stresses its business ethics, and the ethics of all its partners, of which you are one. Is that also correct?'

'Why would anyone trust us otherwise?'

Mrs Osman considered this.

'Do you think personal ethics have anything to do with business? Or, to put it another way, do you think a moral code is important?'

'Of course.' Her eyes went to Sean for the briefest moment. Mrs Osman turned to follow Martine's look. Other heads did the same.

'Yes. I would have thought it was,' Osman went on smoothly. 'So, for instance, someone with a … flexible attitude … to morality in their personal life, might also carry that over … into business dealings.'

'Are you accusing me of something?' Martine became poised and still.

'Is it not a fact,' pursued Mrs Osman, 'that you were accused of stealing jewellery – a necklace, I think? – from the wife of a man with whom you were having an affair? While you were living in Geneva? I do have the dates, somewhere.'

'That was a vile accusation, and withdrawn!' Martine flushed, the first time Sean had ever seen her do it. 'It was a gift, I had no idea it belonged to her. I returned it.'

'But only after being threatened with court proceedings.'

Martine made a sound of contempt and exasperation. 'She was old and jealous and she wanted revenge.'

'Not very sisterly of you, Mrs Osman,' called out Sawbridge. 'Aren't you supposed to be a feminist?'

'Justice is my interest,' Mrs Osman continued in the same calm tone. 'And my professional experience shows that people in the habit of having affairs are also in the habit of frequent … economies … with the truth. Miss Delaroche, I have reason to doubt the trip to Svalbard was as harmonious as you present it. I believe that, despite your shared endeavour, there was no love lost between yourself and Tom Harding, because he was a friend of Mr Cawson's ex-wife and, rightly or wrongly, held you responsible for their divorce. I believe you disliked Mr Harding.'

'I'm still sorry about the accident! And you blame the woman because the man falls in love with her?' Martine dropped her eyes. 'Sean pursued me and I couldn't resist. I didn't know he was married at first. I'm not proud of that.'

Sean sat forward in shock. Martine in the sauna of the Kempinski hotel in Berlin, asking him if he liked her tan lines. He was trying to keep his word to Gail, no more dalliances. Martine naked, tanned dark and pale, telling him she knew he was married, it suited her better. Getting up to stand above him, his weakness plain to see.

'I wanted Tom to like me,' she told Osman. 'I knew how much his friendship meant to the man I love. And yes, I wanted him to respect what I had brought to the deal, not to behave as if he was the single thing that made it happen, and I was just one more corrupt piece of the business.'

Mrs Osman spun the silence before she spoke, very quietly. 'There was corruption?'

'I didn't say that! I meant his attitude was that we were all corrupt capitalists and he was the holy one coming in to set us all straight. So no, I didn't like his attitude. And no, he didn't like me. But that had nothing to do with the accident or how hard we tried to find them both, or how sorry I am that he died! I don't know what you're trying to say to me, or make of me, or why you're questioning my integrity. It's insulting!'

Sean removed his hand from his mouth. Unmasked by Osman, Martine could not have projected a worse image. Sophisticated, defiant, aloof. He heard Sawbridge's low intake of breath beside him and knew he felt the same. Mrs Osman nodded gently.

'I'm simply searching for the truth about—'

'I'll *tell* you the truth,' Martine broke in. 'The ice-cave collapsed, Tom fell and died. It was a terrible accident and I had *nothing* to do with it. I would never have come here if I'd known it was going to be so' – she looked directly at Osman – '*ugly*.'

'As the truth so often is. Thank you, Miss Delaroche.' Mrs Osman sat down. Sean looked at his hands as Martine stalked back to them, furious. A PR disaster. How on earth could Osman possibly have known about Tom blaming Martine? Then he understood. From that reliable troublemaker, Ruth.

Stunned by Martine's misrepresentation of the start of their affair, he did not trust himself to speak to her until they were in private. She had twisted it completely. When the break was called, he made an excuse and went to the lavatory, leaving Sawbridge to cajole her out onto the fire escape to keep him company while he had a quick puff – and, Sean knew, deliver a cautionary briefing. He returned to his seat and busied himself with his email as they came back. She knew he was angry, and he knew she did not care.

The next testimony was 'a video postcard', the coroner announced, from Miss Radiance Young, a partner in Midgard Lodge. She could not attend in person, as she was literally in space this time. She had, however, sent the answers to his questions.

The screen behind him brightened and Radiance's face smiled out at them. She was wearing a white zip-up sports top with stripes down the arms, and sat against a blue tessellated background with a Cyrillic logo. Her hair was pulled back in a ponytail revealing small but sparkly diamond earrings.

'Hi, Sean,' she said to the camera. 'Hi, all court officials. Hi, Joe, you naughty man, if you're there too. Hi, Ruth Mott – Bear Lady.' She dropped the smile. 'Hi, Martin.' Then she leaned forward.

'First I want to say please tell Tom's family sorry we couldn't find him. Very sorry. Thank you for passing on this message.' She looked down at something in her lap. 'I'm going to answer all the questions one time, right? OK. We all had a good time together, no argy-bargy except stressy Bear Lady and Joe at the restaurant. But everyone loved Tom, no arguments, everything was great! Joe's plane was very nice, Midgard Lodge is very beautiful, so well done Martin for that. Good taste bad person – no joke!'

The coroner paused it. 'When Ms Young says "Martin", I take it she refers to Miss Delaroche – is that correct, Mr Cawson?'

'I believe so,' said Sean. He felt Martine tense beside him. Sawbridge had clearly failed to pour oil on troubled water.

'Joe rode with me to the cave,' Radiance said from the back wall. 'Very strong man but an old man too, right? No good in tight spot, I said to him, when we got out. Breathing like this' – Radiance closed her eyes in a grimace and demonstrated rapid, panicky breathing. 'I thought he was dying of heart attack. But it got worse! The bad sound inside – then Martin starts shouting all weak and screamy, and the bad weather comes from nowhere. Nowhere, like it happens there.' Radiance shook her head sagely.

'We got back to the first place under the ladder, but you can feel the shaking in the walls – like this' – Radiance shuddered her whole face and body, raising a few titters. Granny Ruby looked around indignantly. On the film, Radiance seemed to remember the camera.

'Storm cut out phones, right? Solar blasts. So interesting but bad news here. Long and Bjornsen treat us like kids, made us go back to the Lodge to call for help. Martin useless, Joe no good. Even me. We thought: Sean dead, Tom dead. For sure.' She shook her head. 'So sorry, to Tom's family. Very beautiful man. I liked him a lot.' She looked down, then back up with a big smile. 'OK – and by the way, Martin, if you're there: "I must tell you friendly in your ear, sell when you can, you are not for all markets."' She blinked innocently. '*As You Like It*. Just popped into my mind when I thought of you.'

The screen went black, and the clerks opened the blinds. People whispered, and Sean could hear a few muffled laughs, then the room quieted for the coroner.

'Perhaps some of you are familiar with the physics of glaciers, with their caves and calvings. I'm not, so I'm pleased to have the benefit of an expert witness in Professor Roger Kelly, chair of Ocean Physics at the University of Cambridge, who has kindly made time for us.'

Sean watched him take the stand, and the secular oath. He was a kindly-looking donnish type who gave the impression he'd be more at home in a country pub than roaming the oceans of the world, as was his preferred habit when not teaching. Professor Kelly looked out.

'Go ahead,' he said. 'I know the Midgardbreen glacier, I've been in that cave system. What can I tell you?'

'How it might have collapsed,' said the coroner. 'How Mr Harding's body might have emerged. And how, out of interest, Mr Cawson managed to get out.'

'Isn't that last part interesting?' said Professor Kelly. 'Suggests a hidden structure of tunnels, made accessible by the shifting of the glacier. That's probably what caused the collapse of the caves. They've been on record since the end of the nineteenth century, then the Oxford Air Arctic Expedition mentioned them in 1929. At least, the Great Hall was mentioned, named after college hall, I believe. Sounds to me like that chamber collapsed unevenly, part of it dropping into a chasm and part of its structure falling to block that drop.

'Looking at the footage, I think it's possible that after the initial collapse the whole inner structure of the chamber called the Great Hall slipped down a very long way within the interior of the glacier – and was eventually forced out as an underwater shooter during that calving event witnessed by the cruise ship. Fascinating, but diabolic in meaning.'

He looked over at the press bench.

'The most likely cause of this cave collapsing is climate change. We know for a fact that the warming seas are increasing rain over the Arctic, creating lakes of meltwater all over the ice caps. They look very beautiful as you fly over, but it's one of the worst sights in the world, because now it's not snow collecting and compressing any more, it's just water. So it seeps through into the glacier, weakening its structure. Caves collapse. Calvings increase in magnitude and frequency. The summer sea ice has gone twenty years ahead of predictions. People who want to get at the minerals unlocked by the thaw, or to exploit new sea routes, want us to believe this is a good thing. Accelerated warming, rising sea levels, increased disruptions of global weather patterns – how is this a good thing?'

'Professor Kelly, if you could confine yourself to the singular matter of this particular cave system.'

'Sorry, but I absolutely cannot, any more than we would sit here feeling safe if there was a fire raging in the next room. I have shifted everything to be here this afternoon – and the press bench need to report my testimony, not least so that Mr Harding's very valuable life's work might also be supported by his death.'

'Professor Kelly, this is not a political forum—'

'I'm sorry, Your Honour, but we're in a burning building! The world is going crazy, the president of the United States called climate change a hoax invented by the Chinese – the world is governed by lunatics and we just sit quiet? Tom Harding died in an ice-cave accident – and it is my expert and considered opinion that the destabilisation of the ice-caves was a direct consequence of climate change.' He looked to the press bench: 'Those exact words please. I believe that the seeping of the meltwater down from the Midgard ice cap compromised the structural integrity of the caves. I believe this is why they collapsed, and also that Mr Cawson escaped with his life because in the collapse a hitherto unknown section of these same caves was opened up, with a shallower lateral exit. Tom Harding's body probably emerged through that same action, the water taking him out into the fjord. We're seeing this in Greenland at an unprecedented rate and at glaciers all over the polar ice cap.'

Professor Kelly noticed the stewards at the doors and came off the platform before he could be ejected. 'Wake up!' he called out. '*Wake – up!*'

They broke for the day, Professor Kelly at the centre of Tom's family group, Ruth Mott part of it. The journalists vanished. Sensitive to their tension, Sawbridge left Sean and Martine to walk back together.

The late afternoon was balmy for October, the cathedral bells were ringing. Martine had lied in court, and Sean did not know what to say to her. She talked brightly about the benefit – and again he had to force himself to acknowledge that it was still going ahead, and he was an integral part. A grand black-tie dinner, in forty-eight hours' time, at the Carrington. He had to make a speech; Martine assumed he had it all ready and it was easier to agree. The main thing was to get through the inquest.

The restaurant was full when they arrived and she was pleased at her acumen in finding out about it and booking it, despite how busy she was. Sean listened to her talking about stress, and agreed with her advice of what to order, and what wine. He listened until the wine made the lights seem softer and beautiful Martine sat there with him, her skin gleaming gold over her bones. It was relaxing just to listen, after the intensity of the courtroom. He didn't argue when she told him he was exhausted, and they should both go away after this was over, maybe on Kingsmith's yacht, as he had suggested.

Sean thought of *Brisingamen*, the nearest thing Kingsmith had to home. It was an exquisitely converted Canadian frigate whose muscular capacities lay hidden beneath the best taste in ocean-going luxury. He had been on her a long time ago during his stint as Kingsmith's assistant – but things were different now. There would be no admin to keep at the forefront of his mind, Kingsmith liable to ask him about anything at any time. With Midgard under his belt and Martine in a bikini, he would feel distinctly equal to his mentor. Life was going to improve, unlike the steak, which was overdone – he'd ordered rare. He raised his hand for the waiter, who turned from a nearby table and came over.

'How can I help you?' Tom asked through his crushed and purpled face.

Sean leapt up, overturning his chair and wineglass. He stared at Tom in horror.

'Sean!' Martine scanned around. 'What is it?'

'I know.' Tom winked gruesomely at him. 'I look all washed out.' He offered the menu.

'Get away from me.' Sean backed into another table.

'Sean!' Martine grabbed him. 'Look at me.'

He saw her. Then he saw the waiter standing there in confusion, a young man in a black apron, a frightened stranger. Sean looked around the restaurant. Diners stared in astonishment. He bent to pick up the bottle of wine that had spilled all over the pale boards and took a napkin to blot it with. He enjoyed how the red soaked into the white. In the distance he could hear Martine's voice, paying, apologising, lying.

They walked back, her arm through his like a mother shepherding a child after a tantrum. He was not at all OK, she told him, he needed a break, the coroner must adjourn, Sawbridge would want that too – and he must share with her what just happened in there and not treat her like a stranger.

They reached the White Bear. Martine's voice was percussion against his head. Sean still could not speak and to stop her talking he turned her to him and kissed her. He needed air, he would be up soon. When she left him, he sat on the flint wall in great relief. For the first time since morning, he was alone. He stared into the darkness. He had seen Tom and although the sight was shocking, there had also been something perversely cheering about the encounter. Sean remembered the feeling of true friendship, a feeling he had missed for so long.

In Svalbard, in Midgard Lodge where the October wind slammed and screamed at the windows, Danny Long sipped his coffee and checked his screens. He went wide, checking on the number of vessels in line, slowly making their way over the North Pole. He clicked on them for their vital statistics, port of origin, flag of registration – and found the one he was looking for. The *Zheng He*, coming from Dalian. Making steady progress, in very sporty conditions. He wondered what sort of bonus the captain would be getting when he exchanged cargoes in West Africa. Then he put it from his mind, and rang down to Anna Bjornsen to see what she was cooking.

The Great Bear

A woman whose child had died left her home and walked away. Then she came to an igloo and went inside. She found the skins of bears, left like coats. The people who lived there were bears in human form, and she stayed with them.

The big bear would put on its skin and go out to hunt. It might stay away a long time but it always came back with food.

The woman had stayed away from her people a long time and felt homesick. She wanted to see them again. So the bear spoke to her:

'Do not speak of us when you return to men,' it said. It was afraid lest its two cubs should be killed by the men.

The woman returned to visit her people, and the need to tell burst inside her. One day she said to her husband,

'I have seen bears.'

And now many sledges drove out, and when the bear saw them coming towards its house, it felt so sorry for its cubs that it bit them to death, to spare them falling into the hands of men.

Then the bear hunted down the woman who had betrayed it, and broke into her house and killed her. But when it tried to return home the dogs closed round it and fell upon it. The bear struck out at them then all at once they rose up in brightness to the sky, and became the stars called Qilugtussat, which look like a bear beset by dogs.

Since then, men speak carefully of bears, for bears hear what men say.

Inuit legend, as told to Knud Rasmussen, 1921
Across Arctic America: Narrative of the Fifth Thule Expedition (1927)
Knud Rasmussen

27

Dr Ruth Frances Mott took the secular oath, the picture of academic respectability in her black linen suit and white blouse, her thick hair neat in a ponytail. Sean studied her. Still those bright eyes and air of focus he'd found so alarming when they were all young, still that don't-care style, a provocation to this day. That beautiful girl in the pub with Tom had the same quality, but at a lower strength.

Martine glanced at him, then back at Ruth Mott, now answering the coroner's questions.

'I am a marine biologist specialising in ice-obligate mammals of the Arctic. Over twenty-five years I've gone from being a generalist on different species of whales, to studying the walrus, the population dynamics of different seals – bladdernose, ringed, harp – then specifically, the polar bear, focused on the reproductive cycle of the female. My most recent peer-reviewed work is on the denning behaviour of the East Greenland population, the least studied of the twenty-two known population groups.' She looked out at the court. 'At least, that's what I was doing until the area I was studying was destroyed by mining activity.' She cleared her throat. 'Now I work in the tourist sector, in my capacity as a biologist. Lecturing. That was the reason I was in Svalbard for the weekend of the eclipse, and met Tom again.'

'Thank you, Dr Mott.' The coroner made a note. 'Would you please describe your relationship with Mr Harding?'

'We were mates.'

'As in, friends?'

'As in, the primal bond.'

Mr Thornton paused.

'I'm not sure I know what that is. Would you give me a context in time?'

When Ruth smiled, Sean saw that, unconsciously, people mirrored it. Except Sawbridge, still and watchful.

'First at college,' Ruth said. 'Then we lived together in London, before our careers started pushing us apart. Tom finished law school and went straight into activism and journalism, so he was off the whole time. I was getting positions on different field studies in the Arctic, but we'd find different places to meet. We were together in Alaska when the Parrish oil pipeline failed, which was when he joined Greenpeace full-time. I was taking part in a field study in Nunavut for the season.'

She paused. 'That was the beginning of our end. It was too painful to go on trying. We kept hurting each other. So we let it go.'

Sean counted the brass studs on the chair-back in front of him. He could smell the mints someone was eating, and the tired air in the room. He wanted to be outside.

'Except,' he heard the coroner say, 'when you met in Svalbard, the day before the eclipse. But that was not planned.'

'Not unless that bear planned it.' Ruth's smile faded. 'I followed up on the autopsy results, and it came from East Greenland, from the very population I'd been studying when my project was cancelled.' She looked out across the court. 'Is Joe Kingsmith here?'

'He's coming later, Dr Mott. Please confine yourself to answering my questions, not asking them.' The coroner held her eyes. 'But why do you ask?'

'I think Tom found something out he didn't like. I think something happened at Midgard that led to his death. I don't think it was an accident.'

It was not her words so much as the complete silence that followed them.

'You know, Dr Mott, that there is no doubt the ice-cave on Midgardbreen collapsed, trapping Mr Cawson and Mr Harding.' The coroner leaned forward and spoke clearly. 'You are making a serious allegation, so please explain it.'

She nodded. 'You know how we met at the airport because I was performing the autopsy on the bear that was shot in the tourist incident. Tom invited me to join them for dinner at Amaruq, and I did. They all invited me, or I wouldn't have gone. I should say that Sean and I had sort of fallen out sometime before, so I was pleased he did that.' She looked at him. 'I really was.'

Everyone in the courtroom turned to look at Sean, and his skin burned.

'Is that falling out with Mr Cawson significant, Dr Mott?'

'I interfered in a marriage. I was wrong. I'm sorry, Sean.'

He shook his head – it no longer mattered.

Sawbridge leaned closer to Sean.

'No more of that please.'

The coroner observed the silent exchange with a raised eyebrow.

'Dr Mott. Regarding your opinion that Mr Harding's death was not an accident: I would like to know more about that.'

'I was really shocked Tom was involved in Midgard Lodge. Like a lot of people, all I knew was that some British group had bought the property and developed it, and it was all top secret. The rumour was that it had nothing to do with environmental concerns and everything to do with protecting the satellite company over the ridge, or something like that. Why else would they be allowed to fly in and out with helicopters? No one else on Svalbard had those privileges. It seemed crazy that Tom was involved – even after he explained about the retreats.'

'When did he do that?'

'At dinner. They all gave me sound bites about what a great thing it was and how global rapers and pillagers of the environment would come on Arctic jollies and do deals and some of the fee would go to Tom to fund climate change education, or something like that. I told Tom he was a lackey – and then there was another row.'

'Another one?'

Ruth nodded and pushed her hair back in the way Sean remembered, her tell before steaming into some ethical brawl and ruining a nice evening. Tom was the only person who could ever rein her in.

'If I'd known that Joe was Joe Kingsmith, I'm not sure I'd have gone. He was the owner of the mining company that closed down my survey in East Greenland.'

'Objection, Your Honour, this really can't be allowed.' Sawbridge stood up, smiling. 'My client does *not* recall the events as Dr Mott relates them. Additionally Dr Mott has no evidence for her irrelevant accusations against Mr Kingsmith. After she left the restaurant she took part in no further conversation.'

'I did,' she called to Sawbridge. 'Tom spent the night with me after leaving the restaurant.' Sawbridge looked quickly to Sean, and she almost smiled at their shock. 'You didn't know?'

Sean did not. His mind raced. Ruth nodded slowly.

'At the airport, I thought whatever god there was that I didn't believe in, had brought Tom back to me. Then at the restaurant, I thought he'd sold out, and I was so upset I had to get back to my shitty broom cupboard of a room where I could cry.' She paused, and when she spoke again, everything about her was softer. 'But he followed me. He tracked me and found me.'

'And … you talked?' The coroner sounded almost embarrassed.

'Talk? Oh yes … we talked … all night. And we planned that when he came back from Midgard Lodge we would be together. We'd both been long enough in the wilderness but we'd found each other again. Suddenly it was easy.' She looked at Sean. 'We just had to hold on, this time.' He sat very still.

'But you said you thought his death was not an accident,' said the coroner.

'That's right. We talked about what Sean was really doing up there. About Kingsmith. I don't know about the other two. Radiance was into shipping and hotels. Tell me how that's a good thing for the Arctic. The other one, Sean's current whatever, she's just into the money, as far as I could make out.'

Sean felt Martine glitter in anger beside him. Part of him wanted to applaud Ruth for being as combative and difficult as he had ever thought her. Another part of him was on his knees.

'In the morning, Tom left me and went to the hotel very early to meet them and go on to Midgard Lodge. We thought it was better to be discreet, for him not to say anything. That was the last time I saw him. We joked about bailing on everything and staying in bed – but he wanted to see Midgard. He completely believed in Sean again.' She took a deep breath. 'He loved him. But Sean had apparently told him not to bring me – "for confidentiality". I knew

252

it was because I'd upset his billionaire friend.' She looked at Sean. 'I did, didn't I?'

The press bench turned its hydra head to observe Sean for reaction.

'Dr Mott.' Mr Thornton was impatient. 'This is not a platform for debating matters that do not concern my inquiries. Did you discuss the matter of Midgard Lodge and its affairs with Tom?'

Ruth hesitated. 'No. He'd signed a confidentiality clause. And he was honourable.'

Mr Thornton had no more questions for Dr Mott, and he allowed Sawbridge the first opportunity to question her. Sawbridge gave her his eyebrow-flash smile as he rose.

'Thank you, Dr Mott. Given your relationship with Tom, this must be an extremely sensitive process for you.'

'I want the truth.'

'Very good.' Sawbridge narrowed his eyes. 'We're talking here about the tragedy of Tom's death, and your belief that it was "no accident". This raises very serious questions. First of all, the matter of your judgement.'

'Ah, the ambush.' She looked levelly at Sawbridge. 'Would that be about the reason my survey in East Greenland was shut down?'

'I did wonder if we might touch on that—'

'No, please, let me, I was actually there. Mr Thornton, the court, reporters, everyone: I believe my survey in Qarrtsiluni was discredited in order to close me down, so that Sean's partner Joe Kingsmith could push ahead with his mining assay. They used the fact that I was in a relationship with my Inuit guide to press for me to leave.' She was breathing hard. 'Does that touch on it enough for you?'

'Oh, and the drinking,' said Sawbridge.

Sean felt ashamed.

'Sure,' she said. 'Plenty of it, at the time. But I still know that Joe Kingsmith of Midgard Lodge is the same Joe Kingsmith of Prism Exploration in East Greenland, and the same Joe Kingsmith of Prism Mining in the Central African Republic – before Ebola closed him down there. That was one of the things Tom and I talked about, over-night. The last time I saw him.'

'Mmm.' Sawbridge rubbed his chin. 'Thing is, that's neither here nor there, is it? Because Tom died when the ice-cave collapsed, very possibly because of a lake of meltwater on the ice cap feeding through and destabilising the glacier, as we have heard. The cause of this tragedy is not because of what happened to you, a long time ago, in another country. Or who does what in which developing nation, filling you with moral outrage. Though I can understand why, at some level, you might want to connect it all together.' Sawbridge looked around the courtroom. 'Perhaps you need to damage my client Mr Cawson's good reputation, because you need to make someone, *any*one, responsible for your loss. But you are misguided and your reasoning is specious.'

He looked back at Ruth Mott with a pained compassionate smile.

'So there we are, a few bugbears unearthed – but for now, can we go back to your autopsy of the actual bear, in the hangar at the airfield at Longyearbyen? Am I right in thinking that, were it not for that random accident, of a polar bear being killed on that particular day, and requiring someone – anyone – with the credentials to do it, to perform the autopsy, you would not have met Mr Harding that day? Because neither of you were aware of the presence of the other.'

'Longyearbyen is still small.' She was white-faced. 'There was every chance we would have seen each other.'

'But you were not staying at the Polar Dream, were you? Where Mr Cawson's party had rooms? You were far downhill at the Radisson, where you were booked to have dinner with holiday guests and afterwards to talk to them about the Arctic and polar bears and eclipses and so on. Those hotels being some distance apart, you were not intending to eat at Amaruq that night – which was not only fully booked, but extremely expensive and an unlikely venue for a single diner on a modest lecturing fee, let's put it like that. Not to diminish the importance of highly qualified after-dinner speakers – it sounds like a very good tour company! And Mr Cawson's party certainly had no plans to go out bar-hopping later, so it's fair to say the odds were slim, of a chance meeting with Mr Harding.'

Sean watched her face as Sawbridge let the black powder burn towards her. The room knew the explosion was coming. Go on, Ruth. Let rip. You're really upset, no one will hold it against you, and I will publicly forgive you. But she listened calmly and Sawbridge pressed on.

'The dead polar bear was the random agent that brought you into contact with Mr Harding again.'

'I told you: the bear was from East Greenland. Its lip tattoo proved it. What could be less random?' Ruth Mott made sure the press bench was paying attention. 'It travelled about eight hundred miles. So it either swam, which would be extraordinary, or it went the whole way around the North Pole clockwise, *or* the polar currents are already so disrupted by climate change that it came counter-clockwise. All sorts of marine species are found where they've never been known before; it's like all the ocean currents are scrambling, invasive species travelling in ship bilge water—'

'Bravo! Bravo!' Professor Kelly stood up at the back of the court, clapping. 'Exactly what I've been saying! When are people going to listen? Does no one understand England has a monsoon season now? Oh, another rainy June – NO! Wake *up*!' He sat down quickly before the clerk could get to him, and vigorously gestured to Ruth Mott to go on.

'So yes,' she said, her voice stronger now, 'yes, it might be random that a bear comes from East Greenland to Svalbard. It might be random that Joe Kingsmith wrecks his way around the world but I end up opposite him at dinner. And it *might* be random that before I got sacked in East Greenland I was studying reproductive anomalies in female bears, which is exactly what the eclipse bear in Svalbard was full of. Undeveloped blastocysts with evidence of pollution at the deepest cellular level. So, Mr Thornton, before you pull me off this witness stand because a dead bear has nothing to do with why Tom died, let me say that I believe she did, at a causal level. And another bear led the way to the ship finding his body.'

The journalists pattered away. Sawbridge waited for quiet again.

'Thank you, Dr Mott – a fascinating perspective on the facts. You've said to ask you anything, so I will. It's clear you and Mr Harding shared the kind of passionate feelings that, frankly, make me rather envious. A great love. A – primal bond?'

'Yes.'

'But turbulent, in the past?'

'Yes.'

'Did you and Mr Harding arrange that he would visit you, after the dinner?'

'Absolutely not. He persuaded a colleague to tell him my room. I'd talked to her about him. So she knew what he meant to me.'

Sawbridge sighed in sympathy.

'You said you, um, *talked* all night. Did Mr Harding get *any* sleep? I won't insult your intelligence, you'll know what is at the root of my question. Was he – perhaps – in a state of emotional exaltation but physical fatigue that next day, due to lack of sleep? We of course have no way of knowing, but you do.'

'To a man like Tom, a sleepless night would make no difference. He had great endurance, he was very strong.'

'Yes. I can completely understand why you would want to believe it made no difference – because it would be unbearable, would it not?' Here Sawbridge gathered up Angela Harding and Granny Ruby in his compassionate glance. 'Quite *unbearable* to think that a night of passion had cost Tom vital energy when it came to the physical ordeal he was unwittingly about to face. To be just that crucial bit below par. To be … tired.'

Ruth stared at him in shock. So did Sean. To blame Ruth? Sawbridge shook his head gently, as if he, too, could hardly bear to think it. 'No further questions.' As he sat, she spoke again, but her voice was weak.

'He didn't trust Kingsmith.'

Sawbridge half-rose, as if to be polite to a lady. 'If I might respectfully suggest, Dr Mott, it was *you* who did not like Mr Kingsmith, but in your grief, to protect yourself from the possibility of culpability, no matter how innocently, in his death – you now project that fear posthumously onto Mr Harding. Who was, I remind you, quite happy to be in business with Mr Cawson, Mr Kingsmith—'

'He wasn't! He was full of doubt! And I believe something happened inside the glacier or before, I don't know what—'

'Dr Mott, you've led research teams in the Arctic on a number of occasions, been a senior scientist in your field – yes? Have you never doubted yourself? Never had a moment of wondering if you're doing the right thing, right time, right team? Never made a decision, then gone over your reasoning again before implementing it? A sort of safety routine?'

'I think things through very carefully, so that I trust myself. You can't lead a team if you're indecisive.'

'Or if you've lost your job.'

'No. Don't use that.' Sean said it impulsively, and the court turned to stare. Sawbridge held up his hand and nodded soothingly.

'My client is a very generous man to feel protective towards you, Dr Mott, but I'm afraid for his own sake I must persist with this line of questioning—'

'Nicholas, don't, you've said enough.' Sean was on his feet now, but Sawbridge refused to look, keeping his palm up as if stopping traffic, his eyes trained on Ruth Mott.

'Nothing you could say would be any worse.' She looked as if she were mortally wounded, but still standing.

'Isn't the reason you're now an after-dinner speaker,' continued Sawbridge, 'rather than a respected working scientist, because you made a fatal error of judgement in your last position? Isn't it because of that business about the fatality with the sponsored bear? I didn't want to bring it up, but wasn't it to do with your responsibility for administering the wrong dosage of the tranquilliser? A case of being over-confident in your decisions, rather than having the humility to check, to question yourself, to *doubt*, on occasion?'

'Someone sabotaged me. I know I loaded the right amount.'

'Ah,' said Sawbridge. 'The mysterious *Someone*. But not a shred of evidence.'

'Someone on my team. Prism paid them, I was the only one fighting to protect the denning site, the rest of them had already taken the money!'

'So you blamed Mr Kingsmith's company for the closure of your study?'

'Rightly!'

'And then when you met him with my client, Mr Cawson, quite by happenstance, in Svalbard, you perhaps felt every wrong could be righted in one go, if you could only separate Tom from his purpose with them. You'd lost the man and the job you loved, but here was a second chance. No wonder you wanted to hang on to him for every minute you could.'

Sawbridge reverted to compassion.

'I think the coroner will take into account that – in Mr Harding's likely fatigued state due to lack of sleep following a highly intense reunion – we have found a strong contributory factor to his inability to save himself in this tragic accident. I thank you, Dr Mott. No further questions.'

I once met a woman who saved her own life by eating her husband and her children.

My husband and I were on a journey from Igdlulik to Ponds Inlet. On the way he had a dream in which it seemed that a friend of his was being eaten by his own kin. Two days after, we came to a spot where strange sounds hovered in the air. At first we could not make out what it was, but coming nearer it was like the ghost of words; as it were one trying to speak without a voice. And at last it said:

'I am one who can no longer live among human kind, for I have eaten my own kin.'

We could hear now that it was a woman. And we looked at each other, and spoke in a whisper, fearing what might happen to us now. Then searching round, we found a little shelter built of snow and a fragment of caribou skin. Close by was a thing standing up; we thought at first it was a human being, but saw it was only a rifle stuck in the snow. But all this time the voice was muttering. And going nearer again we found a human head, with the flesh gnawed away. And at last, entering into the shelter, we found the woman seated on the floor. Her face was turned towards us and we saw that blood was trickling from the corners of her eyes; so greatly had she wept.

'Kikaq (a gnawed bone),' she said, 'I have eaten my husband and my children!'

She was but skin and bone herself, and seemed to have no life in her. And she was almost naked, having eaten most of her clothing. My husband bent down over her, and she said:

'I have eaten him who was your comrade when he lived.'

And my husband answered: 'You had the will to live, and so you are still alive.'

Then we put up our tent close by, cutting off a piece of the forecurtain to make a shelter for the woman; for she was unclean and might not be in the same tent with us. And we gave her frozen caribou meat to eat, but when she had eaten a mouthful or so, she fell to trembling all over, and could eat no more.

She is still alive to this day and married to a great hunter, named Igtussarssua, and she is his favorite wife, though he had one before. But that is the most terrible thing I have known in all my life.

Across Arctic America: Narrative of the Fifth Thule Expedition (1927)
Knud Rasmussen

28

Sean bluntly refused Sawbridge's offer to have lunch. Ruth would now believe that *she* might be culpable for Tom's death. It would blight the rest of her life.

'You underestimate the lady,' Sawbridge was ever affable. 'She strikes me as very resilient. And when it comes to reputations in a courtroom, it's a zero-sum game. Ours or theirs, never both. You're paying me to know this and act accordingly. So hear this: squeamishness in a client comes from one of two things. One, he's innocent but to prove it, he's forced to hurt someone. Or two, he's a coward who'll let someone hang in his place but please don't make him watch. Obviously, you're the former.' Sawbridge looked at his watch. 'You're confident he'll come?'

'Already landed.' Sean had received a text message from a new number, a Kingsmith move on arrival. Too many calls, otherwise.

Sean let Sawbridge peel off, then got himself a coffee and a ham-and-mustard sandwich and found a bench by a weir. Birdsong threaded through the sound of an open-air market and the water rushed fast and bubbling. As Sean ate, his mouth filled with wheaten mulch and long-dead meat. It sickened him. The coffee was bitter and cloying. Could it be stress? Jenny Flanders came to mind. He didn't want to see her again but he knew he would.

Young people walked past him – pretty girls. For once he did not look carnally at their taut hips and flinging hair, but instead saw them as only just past childhood. Boys followed, young men unmarked by life. Early twenties, Sean guessed. For a moment he saw himself and Tom, and Gail and Ruth, laughing by the river all those years ago, just before they had become two couples. Before all the mistakes.

Since Sean had saved Tom's bacon at the Lost Explorers' Society dinner, Tom Harding made a point of getting to know this stroppy waiter whose Arctic obsession outstripped even his own. Sean had gone to meet him at the King's Head that first time, and was amazed and touched, that this young man of similar age but in every other way from a different planet really and emphatically did want him to go to Greenland as his expedition partner. Sean could spot those who were privileged from birth – the Abbott's School and Oxford had taught him that – but there was nothing snobbish about Tom, and he was wildly impressed with Sean.

When Sean was finally forced to admit that he couldn't afford to go to Greenland, Tom immediately offered to pay. He refused.

'No charity. But thanks.' Sean got up to go, but stopped at the sight of two lovely girls heading their way. One of them grabbed Tom and amorously embraced him, and Sean and the girl's friend looked away as Tom reciprocated enthusiastically. With their friends absorbed in each other, they smiled at one another awkwardly.

'Clearly they're back on again.' The girl rolled her eyes. 'I can't keep up.' She touched her face. 'What? Is it pasta sauce? Ruth cooked it in her room. It was horrible.'

'It was delicious. And cheaper than going out.' The girl called Ruth looked around, aglow with happiness. She was sitting on Tom's lap, his arm was around her waist and he was grinning stupidly. He looked up at Sean.

'You're going?'

'Oh,' said the other girl, 'are you?'

Sean suddenly decided he wasn't going anywhere. He pulled out a chair for her, and found out her name was Gail. Before he'd come back from the bar with the round he'd bought with his week's food money, he was in love. She was studying art, her parents lived in the country, she was unfashionable and didn't care, she followed Ruth around so that she could meet interesting people – like Sean …

Ruth and Tom were wrapped up in each other so Gail and Sean talked, and ate crisps, and drank beer and he spent far more than he should because he refused to let her pay for anything, and it occurred to him that if he was going to be friends with Tom Harding – and this girl had sealed it for him – then he had better find a way to make more money, quickly.

A businessman with a reputation for supporting young people was coming to speak at the Oxford Union. He told Tom they must go, and ask him for sponsorship.

The businessman was Joe Kingsmith, and the Union was packed with students eager to see this exotic American animal, the maverick entrepreneur who preached something called globalisation, and avoided paying tax by living in the air or out at sea on a yacht – or so rumour had it. Sitting at the back, Sean craned to see him.

Tall and heavy in the shoulders, his ridged bronze dome of a head giving him a gladiatorial look, Kingsmith offset his air of danger with an easy manner and elegant low-key clothes. Shunning the small platform at the front, he welcomed the audience from the floor of the Union, as if it were his own space, then spoke of the need to remove all trade borders and regulations and release the energy of free enterprise. He mused on the family fortunes built on colonial exploitation, and how expansion and investment must now happen in a more just way, as he practised it. Security was essential, but so was a genuine profit for the less technologically sophisticated partner: it was only good business.

Kingsmith had no qualms about enumerating his own achievements – his work in Chad, his mines near N'Djamena, how he was bringing health and prosperity to the whole country. He told the audience not to be timidly nationalistic but think boldly and globally, to mistrust terms like government, and coup, belligerent or insurgent. Take Burkina Faso, for instance, where the most recent coup had been celebrated by the people.

The chamber was silent in astonishment. Kingsmith smiled. 'Oh, it's quite true,' he told them. Power was security, and security was power. They shouldn't feel squeamish to hear it said, or guilty for wanting it. Just for a second he caught Sean's eye – and Sean nodded back.

Kingsmith moved on, talking about catastrophe bonds and how they were going to be the big financial news of the future, but Sean was more interested in his dominance of the space, how people at the ends of the rows moved their legs out of his way as he strode towards them, the avid expressions on their faces as they looked at him. He felt chosen, he felt understood.

And then suddenly Kingsmith was thanking them for the invitation, they were lucky kids to be here, he hoped they knew that – and he must leave for a meeting. The pink-cheeked president of the Union stood up, astonished. Awkwardly he explained that they'd booked him to speak for an hour and he was sure the audience had many questions to put to him, but it had only been fifteen minutes. Kingsmith looked at him kindly.

'Kid, you've misunderstood. I was curious to see this place. A lot of friends of mine have spoken here. I've said what I wanted, so good evening to you.' He walked out, raising his hand to salute the few timid boos that grew louder when he was safely out of the chamber.

Sean was on his feet at once, pulling Tom with him. They ran out in time to see Kingsmith fold himself into a cab, which they chased on foot as far as the Randolph Hotel, where he got out. Panting, they followed him into the lobby and begged him for five more minutes, they had a question. He laughed and told them to wait in the bar.

Sean and Tom collapsed at a table. A waiter arrived to tell them Mr Kingsmith invited them to order whatever they would like. Daringly, they ordered bottled foreign lager, the taste of adventure and sophistication. Sean looked around the Randolph Hotel. There were people who lived like this always. He wanted to be one of them.

'He must be a multi-millionaire.' He tried not to sound too admiring.

'At least.' Tom was excited as well. They had scooped a meeting with a big beast, and now they mustn't blow it. They practised what they were going to say when Kingsmith returned – which was sooner than they expected. Sean felt his heart pounding as Kingsmith came in and spotted them. They both stood up in automatic respect, and he grinned and motioned them back down.

'Nice of you to run so fast,' he said. 'You don't look like assassins, but I could still be wrong. What do you want?'

'Sponsorship to go to Greenland,' Sean said straight away. 'Not charity.'

Kingsmith laughed. He waved away their compliments and they got to the point: the Lost Explorers' Society, and the fees. He looked at Tom, then at Sean.

'But only you need it. Right?'

'How do you know?'

'You're wearing your best clothes.'

Sean felt humiliated. It was true. 'How can you tell?'

'You were dressed smarter than everyone else in your row, and you paid attention to everything I said. Don't worry, kid, I read a room fast. A lot can depend on it. And I like it when someone shows respect.' He looked at Tom, in jeans. 'Right?'

'I always wear jeans.' Tom looked confused. 'Unless it says black tie.'

Kingsmith turned back to Sean. 'You got black tie? They love it here.'

'I've never needed it.' Sean heard himself, defiant and upset.

Kingsmith smiled. 'I'm betting you will, and soon. Go on then, your Greenland vacation. What's in it for me?'

This, they were ready for. They told him about all the minerals hidden under the ice, the copper and rubies and diamonds and gold, the lithium, the uranium – the centuries-old attempts to find the fabled sea route from Europe, the ancient Chinese beads found on Inuit spears, how Pytheas the fourth-century Greek trader was the first to tell of the frozen seas to the north, how it wasn't Peary who first set foot on the North Pole but his Negro manservant Matthew Henson—

Kingsmith held up his hand to stop them. He looked at Tom. 'Why don't you lend him the money? Or give it? Isn't that easier than running after a stranger?'

'He won't take it.' Tom shook his head. 'Sean, come on, he's just playing with us. Let's go.'

'If he was going to say no he wouldn't still be talking to us.' Sean looked Kingsmith in the eye. 'Will you or will you not sponsor us to go on the Lost Explorers' Expedition to Greenland? We'll give you something in return, but you have to tell us what you want.'

Kingsmith burst out laughing. '*He's* making the deal!'

'I'm not a joke and I don't want charity.' Sean didn't smile. 'I'm reading Economics, I'm hard-working, I don't mind getting my hands dirty and I don't get tired.'

'What's the most important thing you've learned so far?'

'Seize your chances.'

'What's your name?'

'Sean Cawson.'

'What's your problem? Lack of money's only the symptom.'

Sean suddenly choked up. 'I just – need – to go to the Arctic.'

'You *need* to …' Kingsmith looked at him with deeper interest. 'Why?'

For a second Sean was on that landing, looking across the void of stairwell where the light caught the peeling wall, gazing at the painting of the icebergs.

'Why not take charity?' Kingsmith held him in his gaze, and Sean felt the back of his eyes burning. He pushed the feeling down.

'I've had enough of it. I spent time in care. There was a painting of the Arctic there. It was where I went. When I needed to.' He looked at Kingsmith, defiant again. 'All right?'

'Good on you,' Kingsmith said. 'And good instinct to stay.' He looked at Tom. 'You're worrying about your friend but you don't need to. He'll be fine. And I can tell you're thinking, this guy doesn't know either of us from Adam, how can he say that—'

'That's right,' Tom said. 'I was.'

'Your friend reminds me of me.' Kingsmith turned back to Sean. 'Plus, you got me on a good night, I just had some nice news. So here's the deal: I don't know much about your fancy society, but I like how you two operate, so I'll take a chance. You boys go to Greenland for me, you have a good time, you tell me about it.'

Sean frowned.

'What's in it for you? That's no kind of deal.'

'Ah, he's sharp. OK, not much at first. But if what you say's remotely interesting, I might send you somewhere else you want to go. You love the Arctic? I'm pretty interested too. So go have a trip on me, and we'll take it from there.'

'Is this the give before the take?' Sean stared at him, and Kingsmith laughed. 'For sure! Come on, it's easy: I like to have scouts on a new frontier.' By some signal, a waiter came to his elbow and Kingsmith glanced up and signed the bill. He turned back to them. 'One-time offer: take it or leave it.'

'Take it.' Sean put out his hand. 'We'll take it, thank you.'

'Yes,' said Tom, a moment later. 'Thank you.'

Kingsmith shook hands with Sean, then Tom, and gave him a business card. 'Lawyer,' he said. 'Call him tomorrow afternoon, he'll advise.'

'On what?' Tom looked at the card suspiciously.

Kingsmith winked at Sean. 'Where to send the money.'

At the half-landing on the way up to Court No. 1, Sean passed Mrs Osman, motionless by the window. Over her asymmetric shoulders he saw a black Vauxhall saloon swing into a narrow space in the court car park. Then the welcome shape of Kingsmith unfolded from the driver's door, dusting imaginary specks off his jacket. He slammed it and looked up, as if he knew he was observed. Sean raised his hand in greeting and went down to him. Mrs Osman continued to the court.

Kingsmith gave him his familiar heavy clap on the shoulder. He was as well dressed as ever, a dark linen suit for the hot October weather, light leather brogues and an olive cashmere sweater over one arm. His head was tanned and smoothly shaved. 'Bearing up?'

'Sure. Thanks for coming.' Sean smiled the truth away. Kingsmith didn't like sickness or weakness, never succumbing himself. 'That's not the car I thought you'd drive.'

'Now I just drive what my PA books, it's easier. Come on. Let's get you through this so we can go have some fun tomorrow.'

Sean had to think for a moment what he meant. Tomorrow was the benefit dinner, for Tom. Fun was the last thing it would be, but it was good that Joe was upbeat.

In the courtroom, after a brief introduction to Sawbridge, Kingsmith made straight for Angela Harding and respectfully introduced himself. Sean and Sawbridge watched him take her hand in his two big ones and speak in a low sincere voice. Then he came back to Mrs Osman, who was speaking with her two aides sitting by the aisle. Fascinated, Sawbridge dropped all pretence of not listening.

'Mrs Osman?' Kingsmith had done some research. 'It's an honour to meet the lawyer who ensured justice for the Waterby girls. We heard about that case in the States. Beyond words. But at least you brought peace for their families.'

Mrs Osman's eyes were so dark, and the sockets so deep, that if she turned her head a certain way as she now did, she resembled some ancient blind seer.

'Peace? No. Justice, maybe. But it's poor coin for murder.'

Sean was surprised, first that Kingsmith knew anything about it, and then that Mrs Osman had anything to do with those young abductees, missing for two agonising years and then unearthed. He watched her move away to talk to Ruth Mott, who sat hunched and had clearly been crying. The lawyer murmured to her, they heard the word 'bathroom'. She walked out, painfully slow. Her back must hurt, Sean thought. Years of black document cases, and their darker contents. Kingsmith sat down heavily beside him.

'You've met Osman.' Sawbridge leaned forward with a grim smile.

'I heard she also arranged the killer's cellmate.' Kingsmith glanced around, but Osman had gone. 'And that justice was protracted.'

Sawbridge grimaced. 'Yes. We do hear that.'

Kingsmith took in Ruth Mott. 'And our good biologist?'

'Quite docile now, I think.' Sawbridge answered before Sean could.

As the chairs scraped and the afternoon session began, he looked over at Ruth, no longer fierce and bright, but bowed by her broken heart.

Kingsmith took the Christian oath in his deep and pleasant baritone. He would have made an excellent actor, broad-shouldered and deep-chested, and now in that ageless state that money brings a man who keeps his fitness, dresses well, and whose tan will never fade. The court stared at this exotic animal with his powerful face.

Kingsmith gave his home address as being in Zurich – Sean recognised the street as the same as one of the banks he used. Perhaps, like so much in Switzerland, the lie was part of a larger and absolving arrangement. He watched his mentor in skilful deferential mode, the coroner at ease at once. Sean felt reassured. The cavalry had arrived. He would take Ruth out for lunch when this was behind them. It was a shared loss, and he would find a way to support her in rebuilding her life.

Mr Thornton seemed rather charmed that Mr Kingsmith had made a very long journey to attend his court, and invited him to simply give his account of everything he felt was relevant to the tragic outcome of their trip to the ice-cave. He himself would interject as required, and counsel would please signal – and here Mr Thornton looked severely at Mrs Osman's late return from her bathroom break – if they wished to ask a pertinent question.

Kingsmith began. He described in glowing terms his long relation-ship with both Tom and Sean boy – and went on to sketch out their shared love of the Arctic, placing himself in a line of worthy hard-working miners going back to his father's humble beginnings. He stressed his own hard-scrabble entrepreneurial journey and glossed the global empire part, before returning to Sean and Tom's pursuit of him when he spoke at Oxford, back in the Jurassic age.

Kingsmith's smile was genuine. To everyone who didn't know, he wanted to say that those young men, with their dreams of discovery and heroism, were just irresistible. Before he knew it, he'd agreed to underwrite their Lost Explorers' Society, and that was how he knew them both. Over time, Sean better, Tom, less so.

Mrs Osman put her hand up.

'Why was that? Why did you know Tom … less well?'

Kingsmith nodded thoughtfully, as if grateful for the question.

'Sean liked how I did things, he knew he could learn from me. And he has. Tom had his own ideas – but that's good too. I'm a maverick myself, so I value independence. But we had philosophical differences. On a grand scale! Everything on the grand scale with Tom. But I'm the same.'

Sean noted Kingsmith didn't try his coroner-style charm on Mrs Osman. 'I sent them on a few trips, in return for building up my knowledge. I funded their passion, in return for information. Mostly just background colour. Sean stayed close. That's all.'

'Where did they go for you?'

'Greenland.' Kingsmith made sure people saw him look over to Ruth Mott, and nod to her. Sean knew he was signalling that he was ready for whatever she might try. Ruth looked away.

'A remote place of great interest,' observed Mrs Osman. 'At that time. When was that exactly? 1988? 1989?'

'I guess round then. Not remote any more though: it's open for business. But still dangerous.' Kingsmith looked out. 'The people who set up the infrastructure take the biggest risks. The pioneers. That's me, that's Sean over there, that was Tom. And that's what happened at Midgard – the pioneers, taking the risks for everyone else, suffered a terrible loss. It could have been any of us, or all of us, or none of us. It was Tom. And I am so, so sorry.'

Sean was completely caught up in the performance. Once again, Kingsmith had the room in the palm of his hand. Like Tom had in Claridge's. What a force he and Kingsmith would have made, on the same side.

'Let me make something very clear,' Kingsmith went on. 'And this might be unpopular but I tell it like it is. I don't care how many movie stars and popsicles you get pushing a stuffed polar bear round the streets of whichever capital chanting Save the Arctic. It's. Too. *Late*.

'Business is already there, making money and doing it safely. It's not the story that sells, but it's the truth. Change is part of life, and Tom knew this one was unstoppable. But what he also knew was that it's all about the *how*. *How* you ship, to bring down the price of goods. How you extract the commodities that the world needs. How you fish, to feed more people. How you set up your comtech.'

'Comtech.' Mr Thornton peered at Kingsmith. 'Satellite technology.'

'Right. And while we're on it, ask why it's business gets the beating in the Arctic, not the military or tourism. Naval war games everywhere, cruise ships in the gaps. The place is heaving! So dry your tears, because the new Arctic has just unblocked a load of congestion on our crowded planet.'

'What mendacious and utter bollocks!' Professor Kelly stood up, turned to the press bench and pointed at Kingsmith. 'He is a dangerous man and we are sheep to the slaughter if we believe him!'

'Professor Kelly, I regret my decision to allow you to stay,' called out the coroner.

'Do not believe a word he says! Get your hands off me!' Professor Kelly beat away the clerk attempting to usher him out. A couple of journalists took the opportunity to photograph the exchange, and Mr Thornton also pointed them out to the clerks.

Sean saw Ruth, pale-faced with fury, Osman keeping a light finger on her arm to hold her back. Professor Kelly could still be heard shouting as he was escorted down the stairs. Then there was silence, and Kingsmith took it.

'But about what happened in the ice-cave. I have a confession.' He gathered the room in his pause.

'I'm not proud to say it, but I was very frightened. I thought I'd be OK, until the ice walls started to get closer together the further in we went. When Sean and Tom went on ahead, I realised I was hanging back with the girls. Then I wasn't feeling good and, bless her, Radiance got the sense of it and she said we should go back. I'm not used to feeling scared, but that's what was happening. Some kind of panic attack, if you believe in those. She and I started back for the entrance then Martine came right behind us, calling on us to wait. She said Sean and Tom were having a quick look in at the Great Hall and then they'd be right after us. The three of us had just gotten back to near the ladder when we heard this rumbling, like heavy furniture falling in the next room.'

Kingsmith rubbed his head with both hands.

'When we tried to go back, the passage was blocked. There was no room to move and the three of us were all shouting and treading on each other in there, trying to yell to them through the ice – and then we all felt it give again under our feet and after that we ran for the ladder, because you can't help people if you're trapped too.' He looked at the coroner. 'Danny and Terry were already at the top to get us out because the storm was coming. They didn't even know about the collapse. They were very good, they checked inside the entrance, then they got us back down to the Lodge just before the blizzard hit.'

Kingsmith looked for Angela Harding in the silent courtroom. 'That was the safety protocol, no matter what. If it had been me down there, trapped in the ice, they'd have done the exact same thing. As soon as the phones came on again, we raised the alarm, but that wasn't until the storm passed. I can only offer my most sincere condolences to all Tom's family.' He turned back to the coroner.

Mrs Osman put her hand up and rose. 'Mr Kingsmith,' she said in her hoarse voice. 'Can I go back to when you met Tom and Mr Cawson, when they were students at Oxford and you were already a very successful ... entrepreneur.' Kingsmith nodded.

'You took Mr Cawson on as your ... protégé. Is that right?'

'I mentored him. Still do, if he wants.'

'You mentioned differences, with Tom. Did you fall out, at any time?'

Kingsmith frowned. 'As in, ever have a disagreement? Or a fight? With Tom?'

'Either,' Osman said mildly. 'At any time, right up until ... I suppose ... the incident in the ice-cave.'

'I do wish you wouldn't call it that.' Sawbridge stood up fully. 'Your Honour, don't you think it gives a very unpleasant slant to things? Mrs Osman is no stranger to correct terminology, so I fail to understand why she doesn't use it. It was an *accident*.'

'Mr Sawbridge, I will tell you what I think in my summing up and not before. Mrs Osman, I am in no doubt there *was* an accident: please use that term.'

'Thank you,' Sawbridge directed it to Mrs Osman.

'*Accident*,' she drawled, making it sound far worse. 'The *ac-cident* ... in the ice-cave. Were there any ... arguments? Before you went in?'

'Arguments?' Kingsmith looked bemused.

'Yes. Arguments.' Mrs Osman looked through her file, laboriously. Everyone waited. She looked up. 'Because Dr Mott received a call from Tom on the morning of the eclipse, from Midgard Lodge itself. Before his phone was cut off.'

Sean's eyes went to Ruth – she was right there waiting for him. She nodded. He looked away, his heart pounding. Tom had told her.

He leaned into Sawbridge and whispered. Sawbridge nodded vigorously and popped up again.

'Objection! My client insists that no phones were "cut off" by human action, and that it is a most pejorative claim we dispute in the strongest terms. My client reiterates that it is a feature of the location that regular cell phones will not work, and the signal for the iridium phones provided by Mr Cawson to the whole party, and with which Mr Harding was also personally familiar from other remote travel, were also being affected over the whole of the archipelago, by the solar eclipse. It's well documented. Mr Harding's phone was certainly not "cut off", but might well have been functioning erratically.' He stared at Mrs Osman. 'I hope that is quite clear.'

'But they did have a few seconds to speak ...' Mrs Osman pulled out a sheet from her file. 'Here is Dr Mott's phone record for that day, which shows it as 10.58 a.m., registering one minute. Dr Mott says it was less, but one minute is the basic unit of record by the phone company. She says Tom was agitated about something.'

'Mrs Osman, why did you not give this to me sooner?' Mr Thornton was losing patience.

'I apologise. I must have mis-filed it.' She handed the page to one of her aides, who took it to the front. As the coroner studied it, Sean felt his spine prickle.

'In Dr Mott's words—'

'Dr Mott is sitting in my courtroom, so if she does not mind, I will ask her to come back to the witness stand and tell me herself. Dr Mott? Are you willing?'

Ruth Mott nodded. 'Mr Kingsmith, would you mind? You don't need to leave the platform.'

'Of course.' Kingsmith stepped aside, his eyes fixed on her as she came up the aisle. She looked back defiantly, puffed up like a small threatened cat against the dog that could kill her. The coroner directed her where to stand. Now she ignored Kingsmith completely.

'I'll consider you remaining as sworn in. Please tell me what Tom said, in this very short phone call.'

'He said there was a cave full of guns. He said it was unbelievable.'

'Dr Mott, why have you not mentioned this before?'

'I asked her not to,' Mrs Osman interrupted. Sawbridge made a loud sound of exasperation and looked around for support.

'Because?' Mr Thornton was now visibly annoyed.

Mrs Osman remained calm. 'Because I believed, had Mr Kingsmith known of this detail, there was a chance he might have found himself busy today. And I thought it useful for him to be here, as scheduled.'

The courtroom was silent, all eyes now on Kingsmith. He stared at Mrs Osman, and licked his lips once. Sean was suddenly put in mind of a Komodo dragon, tasting the air. Then Kingsmith smiled.

'Well, I'm delighted to meet you too, Mrs Osman. But let me tell you, the décor at Midgard Lodge is truly impressive. There's this majestic window, double storey, looking straight down Midgardfjorden. Stone fireplace on the back, same height. And then my collection of antique firearms on the walls.'

'No,' Ruth said loudly. 'He said it was a cave. A cave full of weapons.'

Kingsmith looked at her sympathetically. 'That's absolutely the feeling of that part of the room. But the way you describe it makes me think it does strike the wrong note. It might feel threatening. Sean, maybe you want to look at that.' Kingsmith spoke as if he were happy to talk about interior design all day. 'Anything else?'

'Yes. Dr Mott, can you tell me anything more about this phone call?'

'He said they were about to leave. He didn't say where. Then his phone cut out.' She looked at Sean. 'For whatever reason.'

Sean remembered. Immediately after their confrontation in the boathouse, and before leaving on the skidoos, Tom had gone back into the Lodge. He'd said he needed to pee. But he hadn't. Sean closed his eyes. As soon as he'd seen Tom heading for the boat hangar, he sensed trouble and told Terry Bjornsen to block the Wi-Fi. But he hadn't done it in time.

'OK?' Sawbridge murmured it. Sean nodded, his eyes on Ruth Mott.

'Your Honour?' Mrs Osman spoke. 'I do have a few questions more for Mr Kingsmith.'

He bowed. 'Please.'

'Thank you. A point of curiosity really, but perhaps ... of relevance. Why are you driving an armoured car?'

'A *what*?' Kingsmith laughed.

'Your Vauxhall Insignia. It's armour-plated.'

'What an extraordinary thing to suggest!'

'Not really,' she replied. 'When you're familiar with them, the sound of the heavy door closing is quite distinctive. Then, when I walked around it, I noted it does indeed feature inch-thick bullet-proof glass. I merely wondered.'

'Ma'am, with the greatest respect, you're mistaken.' Kingsmith smiled. 'But I'd be very happy to let you inspect it at your leisure, if you fancied a spin.'

'I don't, thank you. What I really want to ask is how you would characterise your role in the affairs of Midgard Lodge.'

'Surely.' Kingsmith switched tactics, as relaxed as if they were flirting in a bar. 'I'm valued as a very amiable sleeping partner. For a long time, Sean and I have been involved in business ventures together. It started with me inviting him in, but in recent years he's done a lot more hosting – by which I mean he's thrown the party and I've brought the bottle and sometimes some of the guests, if you follow me.'

'I'm afraid I don't.'

'OK. If there's an interesting financial opportunity, we like to help each other out. That's how you grow. One way or another, I've been investing for him since his student days, and it's no secret he's done pretty well for himself on the gains. And for some time now, I'm pleased to say the pupil's returned the favour and brought the old man in on a few deals.'

'So Midgard Lodge was a financial opportunity, in which Mr Cawson invited you to participate? Yes or no would be the most helpful answer.'

'Ah, Mrs Osman – you know how they so often limit our understanding.'

'Or seek to obfuscate it.'

'Business is always about relationships. They're delicate living things, way past the yes and no binary. Relationships are about politics, and politics is always about needs, resources and access. And before you pull me up for being evasive, I *am* answering the question fully – if you'll just stay with me a minute. When Midgard Lodge came up for sale in Svalbard, Sean saw a great business opportunity – but he's made plenty of money. This time he wanted more. Sorry, Sean boy, but let's be honest and help this inquest along. Plain and simple, he wanted glory. Anyone thinks he's a playboy in a suit, hasn't got him. In his heart, he's an explorer, and they're the world's greatest romantics. No amount of money makes up for a lack of adventure in life. Not for men like us.'

Sean felt a surge of pride. *Men like us.*

'And then this chance of a lifetime comes up – it fits perfectly with his brand, and it's the part of the world that's closest to his heart. And now he's mature enough to want to give, not just get.'

Kingsmith came out from behind the witness stand, the better to connect, and the clerk moved out of his way. Sean thought of Kingsmith the first time he'd seen him at the Oxford Union, how people had physically reacted to him, instinctively drawing away. As though they were afraid.

'Protecting the Arctic is a job that needs doing and it goes hand in hand with trying to steward best business practice there. Sean's trying to do both – he knew he needed Tom's help.'

'Mr Kingsmith.' The coroner was less enamoured. 'You're not running for office. Please simply answer my questions. Do you think Mr Harding shared your view on development in the Arctic Ocean?'

'Yes, as his vision became more sophisticated.'

'That is a lie!' Ruth Mott said it to Kingsmith, then turned to Sean. 'What did you *say* to him? What lies did you tell him, to get him in? He knew, didn't he? He found something out – I *know* he did!'

'Dr Mott, please, if you have some evidence – other than your wishful thinking—' Sawbridge was also standing, 'you've had ample opportunity to bring it to the coroner's attention. We understand you're very upset, but while we sympathise—'

'Being upset does not make me a fool! Making mistakes in the past does not mean I'm going to miss this chance to do the right thing!' Ruth also came out to the front of the stand, looking ready to punch the next person who spoke.

'Everyone sit down!' The coroner banged his palm on the table. He pointed at Mrs Osman: 'Not you.' And at Kingsmith, who was unperturbed: 'Or you.'

'There's a cover-up!' Ruth turned to the coroner. 'I know it!'

Sean wanted to grab her by the shoulders and shake her, and yell in her face to shut up, none of this will bring Tom back so just let it go, we all have to move on without him, we all have to live with our mistakes. Tom is dead and it didn't have to happen!

Ruth looked right back at him as surely if he had actually yelled it out loud instead of in his head. Then, trembling and white-faced, she walked off the platform and between the staring rows of people.

'Dr Mott!' called the coroner, but she did not stop, and as she went to push the double doors it looked as though they were opened from the outside. Sean caught a flash of a tall figure in a red jacket.

'Let her go.' Sawbridge put a restraining arm on Sean's, but he broke free.

'Mr Cawson!' called the coroner. 'Mr Cawson!'

Outside Court No. 1 the lobby was empty. Then Sean saw her, huddled in the seat on the first-floor landing, her face turned away. Sean looked around for whoever had opened the door for her, but they were alone. There was no one in a red jacket, and the only movement was Ruth Mott's shoulders, shaking. She knew he was there.

'Something else happened.' She did not look up. 'I absolutely know it.'

Sean could not help himself, he went to her.

'Ruth. We both lost him.'

To his surprise, instead of shoving him away, she held out her hand. He crouched down beside her, then he put his arms around her. Her grief went through him like a shock wave.

'Ruth,' he heard himself say, in a tender tone he'd not used in so long. She heard it and turned and clung to him, and through her sobs he felt the heat of her wet face against his neck, and held her closer. He felt her breasts pressing against him, and the curve of her ribs under one hand. He let go abruptly.

'Sean, you're freaking me out.' Ruth stood up and wiped her eyes on her sleeve. 'I can't breathe in here. I have to get out.' She ran down the stairs.

Sean stayed where he was until her footsteps were gone. He wanted air too. A thread of freshness was coming from somewhere and he turned to find the source. It came from a door on the staircase landing, opening onto the black iron fire escape. It was slightly ajar. He became aware of someone repeating his name.

'Sean!' Sawbridge stood higher up, outside the double doors of the court. 'Thornton's about to lose it. Are we bailing for the day?'

'No I'm there.' Sean went back in, but as he did, suddenly he understood. The fire escape led down to the car park. Mrs Osman's dark hooded eyes had a new brightness as she met his gaze. Her bathroom break had been her chance to go out onto the fire escape, and down to the car park. That was the only way she could have examined Kingsmith's car. Smiling faintly, she turned away.

If we only had a little pemmican to eat when the tent is pitched, we should not mind being fatigued, for pemmican is easily cooked, and then one can lie down and rest. But dog's flesh must be boiled for a long time to make it eatable at all, and it is hard to keep awake until it is done. We let it stew for about an hour and a quarter – we cannot wait any longer, and for the last five or ten minutes we are wakeful enough, digging and poking at the meat with a sail needle, to see if it is tender. As soon as we think it is cooked, soup and meat are divided as fairly as possible; the soup is what we value most, for there is not much meat, and what there is, is tough as leather. I have considerable difficulty in eating it, for my teeth are still loose from the scurvy, and to my great annoyance I cannot even pick the bones clean.

Lost in the Arctic: Being the story of the 'Alabama' Expedition 1909–12 (1913)
Captain Ejnar Mikkelsen

29

At the end of Kingsmith's cross-examination at 16.30 on the Wednesday afternoon, Mr Thornton announced that, in the light of the new evidence – the phone record and subsequent testimonies – he needed more time to consider all factors. He knew an event connected with Tom's legacy was being held the following evening, so he had *hoped* (and here a look specifically to Mrs Osman) to deliver his conclusion before that time. Instead it would be Friday morning.

'Better, actually,' Sawbridge said, packing his papers as the court-room dispersed. 'Gives you a chance to recover before your big night. Chin up. Might be very therapeutic for you.'

Sean nodded and smiled, but he was dreading it. After these three days, his starring role would be a very particular form of torture. Smiling, pressing the flesh, raked over by five hundred pairs of eyes as he eulogised Tom. For once, he loathed the thought of the spotlight. At least in black tie he would blend in and disappear. And at least Angela and the Harding family had declined his invitation.

'You'll have Martine by your side,' Sawbridge said wistfully. 'She's rather wonderful.'

Sean smiled, but if Martine had suddenly needed to go away on business, he would have been glad. He wanted telly and wine and to bury himself in comfort. He wanted to disappear.

'Told you this was a bugger,' Sawbridge said, 'but you've done very well. Always tell my clients, book yourself a really good holiday afterwards. Push the boat out. These things are like throwing a bloody great rock in a pond – ripples long after the whole thing's past. Got to physically get away, mental and physical space. Move on.'

'Good idea.' Sean thought of the blazing chandeliers of the Carrington, the colossal floral arrangements, the swarms of dull people he would have to charm and connect and fan to life. 'Are you sure you won't come tomorrow? We can easily find you a place.'

'Good grief no, completely wrong signal, having me along. Make you look nervous! Never travel with your KC – unless you did it.' Sawbridge glanced up and his chortle died in his throat. He switched to sober respect incarnate. 'Mrs Harding.' He withdrew.

'Excuse me, Sean,' Angela touched his arm. 'You're probably very busy, but at six o'clock we're going to light candles in the cathedral for Tom, if you'd like to come?' She lowered her voice. 'I asked Ruth and a few other people. I – I just thought I'd ask you too.' She walked away quickly, before he could answer.

Relieved to have a reason not to go back to London straight away, Sean said goodbye to Kingsmith in the lobby – he would see him at the Carrington tomorrow evening. Sawbridge was visiting friends in Kent, and staying in Canterbury until the inquest was over. Back in his room in the White Bear, Sean checked his mail and messages. It was mercifully quiet, all his managers were good. Danny Long had nothing to report from Midgard, and Rupert Parch sent a cheery line confirming he would see him tomorrow evening, and that his master also sent his best wishes. He added an emoticon: a smiley face version of Munch's *Scream*.

Martine had left a voice message: everything was perfect and in place for tomorrow, it was going to be a triumph. She knew things must be OK or he would have called her, so she was out at a dinner tonight if he was still away, or cancelling it to be by his side if he needed her. Something in her tone hoped he wouldn't.

Sean texted back all was well but he had to stay another night. He'd call her tomorrow. He clicked on the x key. It looked strange. He made it a capital, and sent it. He emailed Jenny Flanders to ask if she had any time tomorrow before five. Then he put on his last clean shirt and went to the cathedral.

Angela Harding hadn't said where in the vast structure they would be. It was almost dark outside so the stained glass was subdued, but now the stone contours were alive in the candlelight. Once again, he followed the sound of singing deeper into the nave. The chapel where he had signed the book was dark and quiet, and the singing came from below. He found them in the chapel of Thomas Becket.

Tom's mother gladdened at the sight of him. 'Oh you came.' She embraced him as she had done all those years ago, when he used to wolf food at her table, and Granny Ruby rapped Tom's knuckles for dropping scraps for Roxy. She was there too, holding hands with Ruth Mott, who looked surprised to see him.

'Sean! I'm – it's good you came.'

'Thank you.' He kept his distance this time, standing with people he didn't recognise. But one knew him.

'All right?' It was John Burnham, the publican from the Feathers. They nodded awkwardly to each other. Sean was embarrassed at the thought of Sawbridge's superior attitude to the man.

'Here.' Angela Harding gave them each an unlit candle and moved on. They stood in silence, until Sean remembered Flip-flops.

'Do – do you have a daughter called Beth?'

'Oh, I know, she's been in there, hasn't she? I said, don't you make trouble—'

'She hasn't. She's extremely bright. I've got one too, a bit older.'

John Burnham's forbidding expression disappeared, and the trials of teenage daughters transformed them from wary mourners to commiserating fathers. Sean found himself speaking of Rosie as if she were still his loving daughter, until the deacon interrupted with her lit taper. She arranged them in a semi-circle, then in a high singsong voice asked for blessing on the friends and family of Tom Harding at this difficult time, before leading them in the Lord's Prayer.

Wanting to do the right thing, Sean murmured a few words, but it felt hypocritical so he tailed off into silence. Surreptitiously, he looked up to see what other people were doing, and caught Ruth doing the same. For a second they shared a complicit look, intercepted by the disapproving deacon. Ruth snorted with a giggle, which Angela Harding interpreted as tears, and reached out to hug her. This toppled Ruth into real grief, and they wept together.

Sean's eyes stayed dry. He could smell beer on John Burnham's clothes and it was a friendly smell. Tom's spirit wasn't in some cold crypt, solemn and spiritual as this was – it was in the diamond whirl of sunny Arctic air, or the clink of pints. It was rammed next to Sean at a gig, roaring along with the crowd, Ruth and Gail on their shoulders. It was racing on a sled in Greenland, and making the dogs howl in song when they bellowed their way through Bowie's 'Heroes'. *That* was the hymn he wanted to sing for Tom, he wanted to hear it blasting through the cathedral, and howl like a dog for the friend he'd lost.

He would never see Tom again. It hit him.

He felt Ruth looking at him again, and then the strange sensation in his face: his mouth was shaking, his eyes were burning, tears running down his cheeks. Ruth left Angela and came to him. Without a word she put her arms around Sean and held him. He went rigid for a moment and then a great gasp came out of his mouth, and sobs began to tear out of his very core. He didn't know if the deacon was still speaking but he felt hands touching him, patting his back, rubbing his arm; he didn't know who it was and he was too ashamed to look. When he regained control, he apologised to whoever was there but he couldn't look up. He pulled away and hurried out of the crypt, back to the White Bear and went straight up to his room. He wasn't hungry, he didn't want a drink. He kicked off his shoes and crawled into bed. He curled himself into a ball, shaking.

Only in the morning, waking fully clothed under the covers he didn't remember pulling over himself, did he realise he'd slept the whole night through.

It is impossible to go through all the challenges faced by or *limitations placed on the freedom of movement of ships. What makes the ensuing limitations or attempted restrictions on the freedom of movement so problematic is that they are undertaken multilaterally, by involving competent international organisations, as well as unilaterally or bilaterally. Such limitations are not easy to harmonise since they have different legal bases.*

Furthermore, it is their cumulative impact on the freedom of navigation/right of innocent passage/transit passage which should be cause for concern as regards the legal framework established by the United Nations Convention on the Law of the Sea.

The legal situation in respect of international straits raises particular problems, given the enhanced status of international navigation.

Whether ships carrying weapons of mass destruction which are not targeted against a particular State may be interdicted on the high seas by warships of another State without the consent of the flag State concerned is a matter of controversy. The exclusive jurisdictional relationship between a flag State and one of its vessels on the high seas is well-rooted in customary international law.

Judge Rüdiger Wolfrum
President of the International Tribunal for the Law of the Sea
8 January 2008

30

'I've been seeing Tom,' Sean said to Jenny Flanders, before he'd even sat down. After his full night's sleep, he had considered cancelling, but it felt right to keep the appointment. The end was in sight and this was part of the process of closure. She'd done some tidying since his last visit – the windows were sparkling clean and he could actually see the Victoria and Albert Museum in the distance. She was all in beige again and he wondered if she had several copies of the outfit.

'No flowers today?' Some indistinct jade thing sat where the vase of tulips had sprawled. 'I bought some afterwards, the same kind.'

She looked. 'Oh, the parrot tulips. They're seasonal,' she said. 'Very brief.'

'You've got a good memory.'

She smiled but did not speak. Suddenly he was anxious again. He'd come prepared to talk, but now he changed his mind. He kept his eyes on the jade thing. Bad feelings fluttered inside him like moths.

'You're not my friend. I'm just paying you to listen to me.'

'That's right. But I still want to help you.'

'Then help me.' Sean felt himself slipping again, he heard himself talking, he hadn't even realised he had begun, but Jenny Flanders sat there with her pale eyes on him, nodding as he told her about the walrus wife in a film he'd seen who stayed to watch her mate be butchered on the ice, and how he would never have this kind of love with Martine, how he wasn't sure he even *liked* Martine, how Midgard

Lodge was a dangerous place, with a maelstrom in the fjord now, new since the calving that brought out Tom's body, and how it wasn't true he was all crushed and purple, Tom still felt alive, he still couldn't quite believe he was dead, he didn't know what it was going to take if the funeral hadn't done it—

Sean had the sense of tipping out a great bag of rubbish on her sitting room floor. A great huge mess for her to sift through with her pals Jung or Freud or whoever she thought made sense of things. But Jenny Flanders just sat quietly. The rumble of traffic drifted in from the Cromwell Road. His fingers started burning. Soon it would be time to go to the Carrington.

'Why do you say Midgard Lodge is dangerous?'

'The Arctic is dangerous.' He went to the window. Outside, the plane tree leaves were still green, and people wore shirtsleeves and light dresses. 'It's all wrong. It's nearly Halloween but it's like summer. Any second we'll start hearing "White Christmas". We're never going to see another one of those at this latitude.' He came away from the window. 'No one wants to face the truth.'

'You said you've been seeing Tom.' There was a stillness to her.

'Do other people with PTSD ... have what I have? Do they ... see things?'

'Sometimes.'

'And how do you treat them?'

'We start like this. Talking. It's a painful process.'

Sean stared out. He knew Ruth Mott was a friend again, despite what he had told Sawbridge about her. In the crypt, she had held him as only a true friend could. He must, he vowed that he would, make some reparation to her. He would ask her – humbly, not as a rich patron – if he could fund her to start her research again.

'You're smiling.' Her face reflected it.

'I was just thinking ... maybe I've got some things wrong.' Sean felt slightly dizzy at the thought. 'Midgard was supposed to be a good thing, but Tom died there. And it feels like ... it's getting out of my control – but I'm the CEO.' He felt his heart thumping, like it had when he saw the bear. 'Can you give me something to take, for anxiety?'

'You would have to see a medical doctor. I'm just a PhD, but I can refer.'

Sean felt the kayak swinging in the current. He put both hands down on the armchair to steady himself. He did not remember coming back from the window. He felt the bear's eyes on him, intelligent and intimate, pulling him closer.

'I saw this bear. On the glacier. He was calculating how he could get to me, he wanted to eat me.' He put his hand on his chest and felt his heartbeat under his ribs. 'I imagine it. And at night I hear my blood in my ears. When Sawbridge first told me about you and suggested I might have it, PTSD, I thought he was joking. Do other people get that pumping sound? It's like bass coming through the wall. The vibration makes you feel sick.'

'Do you feel sick now?'

'Not physically. But what happened with Tom did something bad to me too.' The words fly round the room on their own. *What happened with Tom.*

Jenny Flanders re-crossed her legs, and he saw her inner thighs, pale and plump. He looked away. 'Nothing can bring him back. It's all over tomorrow morning. It's either climate change that made the cave fall in, in which case the whole world's to blame, or it was Ruth Mott keeping him up all night so that he was too tired to save himself. I got a full night's sleep and I survived. That's what it can come down to, a night's sleep. I was able to hang on and get out. But Tom slipped. He couldn't hang on.'

Jenny Flanders looked at him with the same kind expression. Sean realised his right hand was clamped in his left armpit, and his fingers were burning. He pulled it out. His eyes fell on the jade Buddha.

'You're not a Buddhist, are you?' he said again. 'It's just decoration.'

'That seems rather important to you.'

'It's like you're pretending to be someone you're not.'

'Me?'

Sean stared at the jade. The beautiful blue-green colour of the melt-water lakes, on the Midgard glacier. The seeping water, undermining everything. The colour of danger.

He got up. Jenny Flanders glanced at her watch.

'We still have some time.'

'No. We don't.'

'May I ask why you suddenly feel you have to go?'

He looked at her. 'Instinct.'

Only when he had pulled the big black front door shut behind him, did he breathe more deeply. One more day and it was over, and he and Martine – he winced at what he'd said about her in there – they could go somewhere, into nature, far from people. He wasn't sure if he meant it, that he didn't like her – or that it was even necessary to like the person you were with, all the time. He was exhausted, that was what it was, he needed to rest, and they could do that together, and then see.

Standing at her first-floor window, Jenny Flanders watched him go, then dialled a number. Two miles away in a small, unfavoured Whitehall office, Rupert Parch answered, and listened with interest.

In Svalbard on Christmas Day in 1921, trapper Georg Nilsen went out to visit the German research station at Kvadehuken. When he failed to arrive, two of the station members went out searching for him, but they too disappeared, their bodies not found until June 1922. Later that summer the German station master took his own life.

In 1965, the remains of a skeleton and a rifle were found – a cartridge jammed in its chamber. People believe that it was Georg Nilsen and his gun, and that he probably died when he met a polar bear, took aim and fired, but the bullet stuck. They speculate how he must have felt, as the bear came toward him, and killed him instead. They are careful to keep their weapons in full working order, but accidents still occur.

The jammed rifle is now in the Svalbard Museum.

As told to the author, Svalbard 2013

31

Sean's taxi pulled up under the illuminated portico of the Carrington. The smell of the flowers grew thicker as he went to find Martine in the ballroom. Everything was black and white with accents of gold, conservative elegance to reassure the donors. He looked at the big board of placement on the easel by the door, then decided he did not care who sat where. He felt in his pocket for the speech cards and then remembered he had left them on the dresser. It didn't matter, he didn't need notes. His deepest feelings about Tom were not a performance for this crowd, or the coroner. He'd present the award, say something truthful. Long, short, awkward, eloquent – it didn't bloody matter. Tom was dead.

Sean looked about him irritably. Martine was supposed to be here to meet him, or he would not have come this early. He checked his phone – still switched off after his troubling appointment with Jenny Flanders. He turned it back on, that electronic nipple he constantly sucked from.

'Sean – there's a problem with Midgard. Kingsmith's in a state.' Martine was at his side, her face strained. She was in a dress he hadn't seen before, a column of heavy lime-green silk which draped her small high breasts and dropped in a low V back, showing off her toned musculature and – he admired it dispassionately – boyish arse.

'What's the problem?'

'I don't know, but he's got no respect for you if he talks to me like that. One minute we're having mint tea and planning a diving trip on *Brisingamen*, the next he gets a call from Danny Long and kicks me out.'

'Out of where?'

'His suite. I texted you to say I'd be there; it's huge, much better to get ready in. You're not jealous, are you? Are you calling him?'

Sean didn't answer, because his phone was on now and he scrolled down the list of calls – nothing from Danny Long, or Midgard, or Terry Bjornsen. Or Kingsmith.

'Shit.' Martine smoothed her dress, then waved across the room. 'Darius! I'm so glad you're first!' She touched Sean's arm before she left him. 'My investors have a stake in Midgard too, so whatever's going on, I need to know. But no drama.' Then she clicked into gear, a lithe green flame moving across the room to warm the wallets of the early birds.

Sean waited for the lift to the tenth-floor suites. He looked at the man in the copper-burnished mirror as he ascended. Good-looking, calm, entitled. Kingsmith did not have crises. He occasionally assisted in them and took his profit. But no one made money constantly, there had to be some reversals. Even for Kingsmith. More than likely, Martine's hostess stress had made her melodramatic. But Danny Long's phone went straight to message again.

He paused outside the door of Kingsmith's suite. At first there was silence, then he heard the muffled rise and fall of his voice. Sean knew at once by its timbre: Kingsmith was agitated. Not wanting to be caught eavesdropping, he squared his shoulders and pressed the buzzer. Immediately there was silence within. Kingsmith would be padding to the door to look through the spyhole. Then he opened the door, almost completely dressed but for the tie and shoes. He smiled broadly.

'Hey! Sean boy, you're through the fire. Come in, have a drink. How's it looking down there?'

'Battle-ready. They've started arriving.'

'What'll it be?' As Kingsmith went to the bar, Sean saw the laptop open on the console table. Kingsmith pushed the cover down, but not before Sean glimpsed the flashing green dots of the AIS shipping location screen.

Kingsmith held up a heavy crystal tumbler with a finger of topaz liquid. 'You don't like Scotch, but this is beyond that description. I bought some tweed from the island it comes from – that's all they do. Tweed and whisky.'

'Just water,' Sean said.

'Martine said you got a call from Danny and there's a problem at Midgard. His phone's going straight to voicemail. So is Terry's. And the main office.'

'It's their weekend off. The weekend they only get every ten days – you want them there twenty-four seven, three-six-five?' Kingsmith grinned. 'Lucky they'll never have a union.' He stretched. 'Sometimes it's good for them all to kick back together. It's bonding; no visitors, nothing to do – so a whale breaches or a bear stops by; one time they miss it.'

'Joe. Tell me.'

'OK, OK. You know Danny, conscientious to a fault. He picked up a signal that he thought meant trouble, so he let me know.'

'You? But I've already told him—'

'Yes, me, Sean, because you know fuck-all about sailing, but I live on the ocean, remember? And by the way, have you made sure your pal in Oslo tips us off when something's going on up there, because the Sysselmann's office always forgets. It's like they don't trust us or something. Keep on that, OK?' Kingsmith was talking a lot, as genial as if he were with a stranger.

'Who were you talking to before I buzzed? You sounded agitated.'

Kingsmith took another sip of his Scotch.

'Sean, I know women are your thing, or at least they were, but you are sounding like a jealous lover. Excuse my French, but I'm going to put it down to stress from that fucking inquest. Midgard might be the centre of your world, but believe me, it's not mine. So cut it out.' He smiled. 'Come on. Take the edge off with something.'

'Just water.' Sean rubbed his forehead. Then he took out his phone and pressed the key for Danny Long. It went straight to voicemail again. 'Danny: it's Sean Cawson, your CEO. Call me immediately.' He hit the red button and looked at Kingsmith, ignoring the annoyance in his eyes. 'Joe, we both know he's always supposed to answer. His phone is never supposed to be off. You just spoke to him.'

'That wasn't him! And I am telling you, Sean, so listen to me: everything is cool. You really do need that vacation, so I've let Martine bully me into lending you *Brisingamen* in the Seychelles. Fully crewed. How does that sound?'

'It sounds like you've told them not to talk to me.'

Kingsmith broke their stare.

'You'll give yourself a nervous breakdown, which is what I'm trying to spare you after the week you've had. It's not a big deal, and we do not want to make it one, but there's a cargo ship with engine trouble. I didn't tell you straight off because I knew you'd freak. But if you insist, here, have it. It's no big deal.'

Sean forced himself to speak calmly. 'If a cargo ship is in trouble near Midgard Lodge then we have to render aid. It's part of our deal with Oslo.'

'*Our* deal? Way back when, right here in this room, you told me you were the only person to set it up and handle it, remember? Critically important it all went through you, and you alone. But don't worry: the vessel is not so near, and she hasn't requested assistance. She's doing OK.'

'Engine trouble in the Arctic, in October, how can that be OK?'

'See? I knew this would be too much for you right now, that's why I tried to shield you from it. You've had so much stress you've lost all perspective. For everyone's sake, step back and let me handle it.'

Kingsmith passed his hand over his bald head, and Sean heard the faint rasp. It was the one tell of Kingsmith's that he'd ever picked up on. He'd been too busy to shave – which meant an emergency. Out of the corner of his eye, Sean glimpsed another laptop on the bathroom counter.

'Excuse me.' He went in and clicked the lock before Kingsmith could stop him. He touched the mouse pad and the AIS screen popped to life, the green dots of ships bright on the black, but the central one unmoving. He enlarged the view of the Barents Sea – the irregular yellow line showed the contour of Wijdefjorden. Before he could further zoom in the screen was turned off at source.

Sean flushed anyway.

Kingsmith tapped on the door. 'OK. I've cut you some slack, but now it's getting boring.' He paused. 'Come on out.'

The instant he unlocked the door Kingsmith slammed it into him and took the laptop. He looked at Sean in the mirror.

'Don't do that again.' He went back out into the suite. 'And get out here. We are going to talk about what's been happening and I am going to tell you what you are going to do.'

Sean sat down, winded. Terry Bjornsen, Danny Long, all of them, were taking their instructions directly from Kingsmith. He'd never been their boss.

Kingsmith snapped his fingers in front of his face. 'More importantly,' he said, and Sean smelled the Scotch on his breath, 'you are not going to panic. You're going to stay calm and you're going to trust me, because if you don't, if you let your ego ride you any more – oh, we will come to that too – you will bring down more trouble than you knew one man could wreak in this world.' He clicked the laptop back on and turned it to face Sean. 'What do you see?'

'Wijdefjorden, just outside it. And right there, a ship, not moving.'

'She is, very slowly. She's only got a bit of engine trouble and they're fixing it as we speak, but if they haven't sorted it by the time she's into Icelandic waters and if she still needs it – then she'll get all the help she needs.'

'Why Iceland, when we could render aid now?'

Kingsmith smiled. 'Along with setting up that generous endowment in her name, for the Sino-Icelandic poetry translation prize, Radiance also bought a port. So your ship can go there.'

'*My* ship?'

Kingsmith smiled. 'Have I taught you nothing? First rule of business is good housekeeping. But you just see the dividends; you stopped looking at the delivery vehicles a long time ago. What was it you said? That's right: "*You understand them, so I don't have to.*"' He chuckled. 'Out of the mouths of babes.'

Sean stared. It was completely true. Kingsmith had been investing for him for twenty years. He'd grown his entire business from seed capital created in this way. He was financially grafted to Kingsmith's root stock.

'What have you put me into?'

'You don't want to know. Or rather, why start caring now, at this late hour?' Kingsmith's smile had faded. 'Don't feel too bad, most people are the same. Give them enough profit, and they'll skip the details. Unless they're very strategic players.'

An image of Radiance came to Sean, on the plane, three years ago. Her red toes wiggling as she trounced her online chess partner. The realisation clubbed him.

'That was you she was playing chess with, on the plane. While you were in the bedroom. I didn't introduce you at all.'

'To Radiance? Of course you didn't. But you just assumed you did, and it was funny. We were going to tell you, but somehow we missed the moment. And it made life easier, you know? Plus everyone under-estimates her. She's a very clever girl. Speaks perfect English, good French and Russian, gets by in Arabic – but she puts on the bad gram-mar to let people feel superior.'

Sean got up. 'I don't own any ships. I've never signed anything.' But as he said it, he could not be sure.

'No, not wholly – but you share an interest with one of my other protégés. You've even had a private meeting with him, earlier this year, at Midgard. I'm sure Danny has some photographs of you two shak-ing hands.' Kingsmith watched him. 'I did try to stop you going, but you insisted ...'

'Benoit.'

'Benny boy, another eager protégé. You see? You are into Africa after all.'

Sean could barely breathe.

'You've used me. You're using Midgard – what are you using it for?'

'Now, now, don't be like Tom, going off half-cocked with half the facts. You of all people know how dangerous that can be.' Kingsmith looked him deep in the eye. 'Which is why you're not going to bother Danny or Terry or the Sysselmann because the—' Kingsmith stopped himself. 'Because the ship herself hasn't yet done that. And I don't think she's going to. I think she's going to be OK.'

'What's her name?'

'The Doesn't Fucking Matter.'

'What's she carrying?'

'Useful things.' He winked. 'So we want her to get where she's going.'

'You're supplying Radiance's businesses in Africa.'

'Sean boy! I'm starting to believe there's hope. Yes, *we* are. And can you guess what's the on-board treat?'

Sean could hardly bear to say it. 'You're taking arms across the Arctic and my name's on it.'

'Of course not; that would be illegal. Just home improvement supplies. Biodegradable 3D printers, 4D, if they can afford it; changes use over time – means elegant and ecologically approved deniability. Robotics are so impressive. Plus supplies, of course: raw materials, chemicals for all the full effects – no half-measures with Radiance and her pals.'

'Does Martine—' He couldn't bear to think of that.

'As if I'd do that to you! Anyway, she's a short-range thinker; she'd slip up as soon as it stopped being about her. Look at the glass half-full, Sean boy, see how our clever Radiance and her friends are investing to raise the standard of living for a whole country, once all the chaos, panic and disorder is cleared up. Even your secret friend Mrs Larssen needs a helping hand sometimes, and haven't you been a helpful errand boy to her?'

Kingsmith poured a Scotch and left it by him, then topped up his water from a carafe.

'And since we're having a frank chat, watch out for Philip Stowe – I find him slippery. Though I admit that having you as our go-between has made everyone's life a bit easier these last three years. So I'd say you'll be getting your Safety in the Home medal.' He went to the mirror and began to do his tie.

'Ah come on, lighten up. We're just clearing the air – and long overdue it is, too. Once you get over the shock, you'll see the funny side. You've been a great boy scout – without you, I'd have missed out on the TransPolar Route. I'm grateful!'

Sean sat rigid, trying to believe it. His money, his Midgard, tied into Kingsmith's arms trafficking. And it was true, he had brought Kingsmith into the very heart of the Arctic, he'd begged for his help in setting up Midgard's security. Or so he thought. In reality, he'd created an Arctic base for Kingsmith's mercenaries, tacitly approved by Philip Stowe. It could not be.

At ease, he'd said when Danny Long had introduced him to those men in the dorm room. The barracks – the standing force

LALINE PAULL

of men in Midgard's name – *his* name – and all the while he had refused to see it. It was like saying Defence Expo instead of Arms Fair, or alt-right instead of fascist. Kingsmith nodded to him in the mirror.

'Let's get you down off of that meat hook. You've done a good thing, you'll come to see that. You've created a service station on the newest trade route on the planet! International waters too, so no political shackles. Tom was all about the whales and the Inuit and the climate, but who knows what's going to happen? We won't be alive to see it.'

'My daughter will.'

'She'll be fine.' Kingsmith turned. 'How's that? Taken me years to get it right. I think I look pretty damn handsome. By the way, your British defence universities are the best in the world. But with all our business investment, so they should be.' He watched Sean sympathetically. 'How else do you think I know Philip Stowe? Tennis parties?' He sighed. 'Sean boy, stop with the suffering. Midgard is still a truly special place on earth, just not what you think. It's more; the reality is *better*. Don't lose heart – it's a foot in the Arctic door for British business. Follow Uncle Joe's advice and don't worry about one little ship in the night. Think about your knighthood.'

'Fuck the knighthood!' Sean stared at Kingsmith. It wasn't possible he'd misplaced his trust so badly. 'Did you – did you never believe in anything we were trying to do?'

'Hmm. How to say this nicely? It. Didn't. Matter. The world doesn't understand carrot, only stick. Midgard Lodge is a beautiful, organic, fairly traded exquisitely cooked, fucking carrot.' Kingsmith tied his shoes and finished his drink.

'But what is also true, is that you and Tom really did have this big romantic thing going on for the Arctic, and I loved that. You were so right to bring him in, you totally seduced the Pedersens. They even took less money, because you two so utterly believed in what you were selling. Midgard Lodge meets so many needs for so many people; I take my hat off to you.'

'What's happening with that ship. Pull it up again.'

Kingsmith smacked himself on the forehead.

'Sean, you've not understood a word I've said. You know how elegantly you dealt with that problem in the cave? I thought you might

300

be a rightful successor, one day. Poor Tom, falling like that. Nothing you could have done.'

'What do you mean?' Sean stood up. 'What problem in the cave?'

Kingsmith shrugged. 'Your skilful leverage of force majeure. No need to tremble, come on, it's over. Back to the situation in hand – this is just another opportunity to practise. Life isn't black or white, it's in the grey, and if you weren't so fucking overwrought, I'd kick you up a grade and let you handle this one yourself. But as you *are* … I'm telling you to stand down. Better to lose that ship than make a mess of the scale you'll create.'

They both became aware of someone knocking on the door. Kingsmith strode over – and then as he looked through the spyhole, his back relaxed, no longer gathered to strike. He beamed as he opened it.

'Martine! You look criminally gorgeous. Was I a bit short earlier? Forget about it, it's all sorted now. And may I say, Sean is one lucky man.'

She smiled thinly, then looked past him.

'Sean, you have to come! I cannot do this without you there. It's heaving, everyone wants to talk to you.'

Kingsmith stepped aside, making sure Martine saw him admire her. He gripped Sean's shoulder as he went out to join her, and smiled.

'Front of house. Very important.'

I was trapped. The hole was too small to let me get through, my beard would not let me retire into my grave again. I could see no way out. But what a way to die – my body twisted in an unnatural position, my beard frozen to the sled above, and the storm beating my face without mercy. My eyes and nose were soon filled with snow and I had no way of getting my hands out to wipe my face. The intense cold was penetrating my head, my face was beginning to freeze and would soon lose all feeling.

With all my strength I pulled my head back. At first the beard would not come free, but I went on pulling and my whiskers and some of my skin were torn off, and finally I got loose. I withdrew into my hole and stretched out once more. For a moment I was insanely grateful to be back in my grave, away from the cold and the tortuous position. But after a few seconds I was ready to laugh at my own stupidity. I was even worse off than before! While I had moved about more snow had made its way into the hole and I could hardly move, and the bear skin had settled under my back where I could not possibly get at it.

I gave up once more and let the hours pass without making another move. But I recovered some of my strength while I rested and my morale improved. I was alive after all. I had not eaten for hours, but my digestion felt all right. I got a new idea!

I had often seen dog's dung in the sled track and had noticed that it would freeze solid as a rock. Would not the cold have the same effect on human discharge? Repulsive as the thought was, I decided to try the experiment. I moved my bowels and from the excrement I managed to form a chisel-like instrument which I left to freeze. This time I was patient, I did not want to risk breaking my new tool by using it too soon. While I waited, the hole I had made filled up with fresh snow. It was soft and easy to remove, but I had to pull it down into my grave which was slowly filling up. At last I decided to try my chisel and it worked! Very gently and slowly I worked at the hole. As I dug I could feel the blood trickling down my face from scars where the beard had been torn away. Finally I thought the hole was large enough.

Vagrant Viking: My Life and Adventures (1953)
Peter Freuchen

32

Pre-dinner cocktails were in the mirrored and filigreed Chinese Room. Sean's plan was to flash a smile with Martine then disappear somewhere he could check on the Svalbard shipping situation, but he found himself the target of pension chiefs, insurance barons and private bankers all wishing to offer their condolences about Tom – and reimprint their faces as they did so.

He went to stand by the big photograph of Tom, hoisted on a gold easel by the bar as if at auction. The magnitude of what had just happened up there on the tenth floor was too great to take in. Part of him desperately wanted to believe Kingsmith, that maybe the ship had a bit of mechanical trouble, trouble that could be fixed enough to get it into Icelandic waters. That kind of thing happened all the time at sea. There were maritime insurance bosses in the room right now who wouldn't be remotely surprised to hear of losses or accidents unreported – it kept the prices down.

And how could he check what was really happening, when he didn't even know the ship's name? But of course that was not true. Sean put himself onto smile-and-nod autopilot, splitting his mind off to rack up his options. If the ship had not turned off its AIS locator then it could be found – there were not so many vessels in that area that it would take very long. Then, he could call the coastguard and raise the alarm by saying … What? There's a ship in trouble in Svalbard waters, I believe it's trafficking arms across the TransPolar

Route and by the way I'm a part-owner. That's right, Sean Cawson of Midgard Lodge. Yes, the one your Assistant Defence Minister Mrs Larssen thinks of as a friend. Would I rather go to prison in the UK or Norway?

He exchanged small talk without hearing a word, his shirt sticking to his back. Soon they would all have to go in to dinner. If he disappeared now, Martine would definitely come looking for him. He was making the speech and presenting the award. Perhaps it was a grim joke Kingsmith was playing on him, telling him he was involved, simply to frighten him off raising the alarm. Or … perhaps by the time he'd investigated which ship it was, the problem would be fixed, and he'd only make trouble. Jeopardise everything he'd worked for.

It was certainly true he was exhausted by the inquest. Maybe he should just focus on the dinner, and look into it afterwards. He'd trusted Kingsmith for years, what was one more night? And hadn't he just been to see Jenny Flanders this afternoon – it felt like years ago – to tell her he'd been hallucinating? Before he'd run out without knowing why. He looked up at Tom's handsome face, smiling back down at him.

'Is that him in Nepal? He climbed Everest and Annapurna, didn't he? Wow!'

Sean turned to see a pretty young waitress beside him, a glass of juice on a tray. She cleared her throat. 'Sorry to ramble! I was told to look after you.'

Across the room Sean saw Martine, the centre of attention of a grinning group, each member soon to be several thousand pounds lighter. Grateful for her thoughtfulness, he drank it. He watched her shine brighter with every man's attention. He turned to flirt with the waitress, but she'd already gone.

The juice was refreshing and primed him for a vodka tonic, which he drank in three pulls, to steady his nerves. *The world works in the now.* And here he was, in the thick of a buzzing social event, the Chinese Room full to capacity with smiling faces and laughing voices. Martine's green flame burned in another part of the room. Jenny Flanders was right: he did not trust himself. The week had shot his judgement – no wonder he'd had a run-in with Kingsmith. If the ship was really in danger, the crew would raise the alarm. But still, he had to know.

Sean slipped out into the great lobby and tried all the numbers again: Danny Long, Terry Bjornsen, Lodge reception. All went to voicemail. He tried getting onto the AIS system online from his phone but he needed a laptop. A false alarm would make trouble, but if there really was a terrible situation and he did nothing … He pulled up the Sysselmann's emergency number on his phone, but did not press the call button. Suddenly his vision was blurry as a snow dome. He shook his head to clear it.

He wouldn't raise the alarm until he had spoken to Radiance. They had their own relationship independent of Kingsmith. They clicked – he got her, he liked her – he would just come out with it all, and she would laugh and put him straight – Kingsmith was a bad joker, right! That's what he needed to hear her say. Sean blinked away the black flashes in front of his eyes, trying to focus on the scroll of names. Then the phone was taken out of his hand and Kingsmith sat down heavily beside him. 'Don't even worry.' He laid his heavy arm over Sean's shoulder as he pocketed the phone. 'I was looking for you to tell you it's all sorted. Relax already.'

Sean wanted to push him off, but his body wouldn't do it.

'You're lying.' His voice was thick in his ears.

'A lie down? Good idea. You're probably feeling a bit strange. But first, look at all the people who want to meet you!'

Sean saw the lime green flash of Martine's dress and tried to get up.

'Easy now.' Kingsmith kept him down and she approached, trailing a group of young men in old-fashioned black tie, with short side-parted combed-back hair. A few wore tweed Alpine plus-four trousers and roll-neck sweaters. They were in their early and mid-twenties. They all smiled at Sean.

'The Lost Explorers' Society bought a table and they can't wait to meet you.'

Sean stared as one by one the young men came forward and introduced themselves to him, effusive in support of the event, of Tom, of finding Arctic careers now it was all opening up. They surrounded him, eager and loud. Their features blurred and a tumble of noises came out of their mouths. His brain felt like some heavy cold weight was sliding around inside.

'Sir? Are you all right?' one of them asked.

307

'Boys,' Martine stepped in, 'it's been a tough week. Go have a drink. We'll see you later.'

All Sean could feel was the burning in his fingers. Kingsmith leaned in.

'PTSD,' he said in Sean's ear. 'Hallucinations, delusions. The stress of an inquest could definitely trigger it.' He dropped his voice even more. 'So can guilt. That's what Jenny Flanders says.'

At that name Sean twisted round and slipped. Kingsmith hoisted him up. 'Martine,' he said, 'our boy's had one too many – and I don't blame him. You better do the Tom eulogy. It's too much for him.'

Martine crouched down in front of him. Sean saw the concern – and irritation – in her eyes. She slid a golden arm around him. 'Oh, darling.'

Sean's mind clung to consciousness. Joe had his phone. Martine must not go. He reached for her hand and grabbed her dress instead. She pulled back and he felt it rip.

'You're right,' she said to Kingsmith. 'Take him. I'm really sorry.'

'Don't you worry about a thing,' he said. 'It's been tough on you too, princess, and it won't be the first time he's crashed with me. I'll take care of him.'

The green shimmer disappeared, then Sean felt himself hoisted up.

'When you're so tired,' Kingsmith said in Sean's ear as he hauled him towards the lifts, 'sometimes even a juice can put you over the edge. Lucky I'm here.'

The impeccable staff took care not to notice the over-refreshed guest, being assisted by his older and very solicitous pal. Sean felt the rising motion and shut his eyes against the gold and mirrors. The doors opened with a long hiss and he staggered along the deep mossy carpet, one wrist tight in Kingsmith's grip, the older man's sinewy arm around his torso. Whatever he had been given was coming on even stronger now.

'You just sleep it off, Sean boy,' Kingsmith gritted in his ear, 'where I can keep an eye on you and make sure you don't do anything stupid and dangerous – like touch the fucking phone when I told you not to.'

He held him against the wall while he used his key card. 'And I thought Tom was the problem.' He opened the door, quickly checked up and down the empty corridor, then flung Sean in with great force. The door clicked shut behind them.

The carpet slammed into Sean's face and body but did not hurt. He saw Kingsmith's black patent dress shoes very close to his face, then one of them lifted up.

He felt the blow in his stomach and heard the gasp – but still there was no pain. He heard the order to get up, he was struggling to do that anyway—

From his knees to the floor again, then the blows – he kept his brain awake counting them – one two three—

Instinct rolled Sean into a ball, coughing. His shirt was tearing – he was being hauled to his feet, he still couldn't feel his legs but somehow he was flying backwards, landing on something soft—

Kingsmith was in his face, he bent over Sean as he half sat, half sprawled on the sofa. He punched him twice in the face, and the picture of the icebergs filled Sean's mind. Great big icebergs, the glassy green foot—

He felt his body jerking under the blows, he kept his imagination on the icebergs, the pink light on the strange shapes—

'Tired – and emotional.' Kingsmith stopped and stood back, breathing hard.

Sean returned to consciousness with the shock of water flung in his face. He coughed. He felt himself grabbed up, his hands flailed for something to hold on to. He smelled the Scotch, heard the familiar voice.

'You know what happened, Sean boy?' Kingsmith held him by his lapels so that he could punch him again. 'You needed some air. You got in a fight outside, some poor fucking taxi driver I had to pay off not to make a scandal. You – were very – *stupid*! Lucky for you I was *there*.'

A ping came from the laptop, and Kingsmith paused his assault and went to check. He sipped his Scotch, then brought the rest of the glass back and forced it into Sean's mouth. 'What a fucking waste, but you just couldn't stop, could you?' He slapped Sean around the face. 'You're a lazy – greedy – little – fucker, and that's why I'm having to do this, you hear me? Everything I've done for you, but you've got – no – fucking – *loyalty*.'

Sean felt his body jerk with different impacts, but the drug muffled the pain.

They were all as children, yet they had served us well. They had, at times, tried our tempers and taxed our patience; but after all they had been faithful and efficient. Moreover, it must not be forgotten that I had known every member of the tribe for nearly a quarter of a century, until I had come to regard them with a kindly and personal interest, which any man must feel with regard to the members of any inferior race who had been accustomed to respect and depend upon him during the greater part of his adult life. We left them all supplied with the simple necessities of Arctic life better than they had ever been before, while those who had participated in the sledge journey and the winter and spring work on the northern shore of Grant Land were really so enriched by our gifts that they assumed the importance and standing of Arctic millionaires.

The North Pole (1910)
Robert E. Peary

33

Half an hour before the sun rose over London, long after the Grand Ballroom of the Carrington had been restored to cleanliness and order and Tom Harding's photograph taken home by an ardent waitress, Sean woke breathless with pain. He rolled over to touch Martine – who was not there – and he gasped as his face pressed against some cold hard thing. He could hear a strange ragged rumbling sound, and he realised he was lying on the floor. Very slowly he opened his swollen eyes.

He was on the carpet in the gap between a sofa and a coffee table. So many parts of his body hurt as he slowly turned his head, but instinct told him not to make a sound. A furlong of carpet led to the dark cave of a room, the source of the rumbling sound. A man's snore. He deciphered heavy gold drapes. Rugs. Huge vases of flowers. The silver oblong of a laptop on the table. This was Kingsmith's suite, and something bad had happened.

His tongue explored slippery clots on the inside of his sore cheeks – he let one fall out onto the carpet. Dark bloody jelly, from where his own teeth had cut into his mouth. He couldn't think why he was lying here and the pounding in his brain made him lay his head back down. Nausea swirled in his guts. Through the glass of the coffee table he could see the crystal hobnails of a tumbler of water. As he moved slowly to try to reach it, he saw something else. Attached to the underside of the table frame was a round silver button. A circle of matt

313

metal with a shiny central depression. Swallowing the gasp of pain, Sean twisted his head to check that Kingsmith was not stirring. Then he reached up and pulled the button off the frame.

Held on by ineffective double-sided tape, it dropped to the carpet. Sean lunged to retrieve it and lie still, just as he felt the shift in the floor as, from the bedroom beyond, a heavy form got out of bed and padded into another room. He heard Kingsmith urinating, but not flushing. He clicked the silver button repeatedly then closed his hand over it and lay motionless as the footsteps came closer. The red of his eyelids turned black and he knew Kingsmith was standing over him. Then he felt the sofa being pulled back, exposing him. The door buzzer rang, and Kingsmith muttered. Sean felt his footsteps move away, then Kingsmith called out he didn't need anything.

Sean clicked the silver button again and again before he felt Kingsmith's tread returning. He still didn't know what had happened but he kept his eyes shut.

'Sean, I know you're awake. So stupid: you did this to yourself.'

The door buzzer rang again, and this time Kingsmith swore. As Sean felt him move away he staggered to his feet, ignoring the pain.

'Help me!' he shouted hoarsely as the door opened. 'Don't go!'

Kingsmith spun around, but the butler had seen him. Sean caught his shocked expression in the moment before Kingsmith tried to close the door.

'We're fine.'

'Are you sure, sir?' The butler was young and slight, but he put his foot in the door against Kingsmith's pressure, long enough for Sean to crash the older man aside and break out.

Sean lunged into the corridor, where mirrors reflected a bloodied man in black tie. Other butlers hurried down the corridor towards the room, panic in their averted eyes. Behind him he could hear Kingsmith calling to him to come back – *Sean boy!* – but he stumbled on, his vision still blurry and his head splitting. He hit his fist at every door buzzer, he knew he needed witnesses – but no one came out and no one stopped him. A frightened-looking maid jumped back as she came out of the staff staircase and Sean barged through and grabbed hold of the brass rail, the only thing he could focus on, and started running down the black and white stairs until there were no more and he found himself in a lobby that smelled of disinfectant and food, where more faces stared at him.

He was on the service floor, doors in all directions. Through one pair he could hear noise and bustle, he went in and it was the kitchen, bustling with the breakfast orders. Nobody stopped him; instead, they opened doors for him, passing him through their space as fast as they could, until Sean found himself out in the cold air by the huge waste bins. Someone was gripping his arm then a gate was opening and hands were pushing him through it – and he was on his knees on the grey and grimy Mayfair pavement, at dawn.

Automatically he reached for his phone that was not there. He got to his feet and managed to walk to the kerb, to the corner. His head felt like an axe was jammed through his skull, every pulse of his blood hurt the back of his eyes – he went to the corner and stared out.

Kingsmith sitting down beside him. Taking his phone.

He heard the surge of Park Lane. A cab went by with its yellow light on, but when he stuck out his hand it accelerated past him. The next cab switched its light off, and the next. He put his hand up to his face, and his fingers came away with blood on them. The corner of his mouth was bleeding again. He looked down and saw the blood on his shirt front. Why had Kingsmith taken his phone? Why was he frightened of him?

The corridor, the stream of butlers – Sean started walking towards Park Lane, just because he knew the route. The way home. He had to go home, he knew that, and if he got into the park he could walk.

Horns blared as he stepped into the traffic, he held up his arm and crossed over to the central grass reservation of Park Lane, and then stared up towards Marble Arch, where the red buses loomed. He waited until two of them went past, then stumbled across the south-bound lane, with more screeching horns. The green of the park was ahead, he could feel the cool of it. He stared at the trees. He walked unsteadily along the black metal railings until he found a gate. He was just about to go into the park when he saw them, in the distance. The cavalry horses, being exercised.

Even now, bleeding and blurry, the horses held him. He hung on to the railing, focusing on the animals gathering on the curve. He was in time, they were starting to trot – he felt pain in his face as he smiled, they were going to canter and he was right there—

He felt them in his feet, he heard one of the riders shouting at him to stay back, and then they were upon him, he felt the rhythm of their feet in his body, he saw the light on their necks and the darker sweat patches, the flowing black manes and tails – their sweet warm animal smell cut through whatever was in his head—

Sean, are you at home? I've got bad news—

The horses passed by and then there was just the vast expanse of Hyde Park before him, and the roar of morning traffic behind him.

Sean boy, they've found Tom—

Tom's inquest. Tom's inquest, the last day in Canterbury, starting this morning. And there, across Park Lane, the Carrington hotel, and Joe Kingsmith – and the ship, the ship he remembered it now—

He spat in his hands and pushed back his hair, pulled his lapels up to hide the worst of the blood stains, and drew himself up straight. Then he ran back to Park Lane and in the most autocratic way he could, raised his arm at the next taxi with its light on, and jumped in before the driver could object.

'Canterbury,' he said into the intercom.

'Canterbury? You need a hospital, mate.' The driver frowned at him in the mirror. 'I'll take you.'

'No. I have to get to Canterbury for the summing up.' Sean fumbled at his wrist and took off his watch. He wiped some blood off it and passed it through the window. 'I have to get there. You can have this if you take me.' Horns blared as the driver pulled across into the slip road at the top of the park, and stopped to examine it. He looked back at Sean in the mirror.

'It's a Cosmograph. My son's dream.' The cabbie held it up so the light caught on the ice-blue face. 'Sure now? Can't change your mind halfway.'

'Don't let me.'

Sean sat back and closed his eyes. He thought his nose might be broken, but he didn't want to check in case he started bleeding. He worked backwards, to take his mind off the lurching and bumping of the ride. The white twisting stairs with the shiny handrails, the staring staff, the open door out to big wheelie bins – the Carrington hotel. Kingsmith's carpet. The laptop on the table. *The ship.* He clicked the intercom.

'I need the news. I have to hear the news, Radio Four—'

The cabbie muttered something but changed the channel. Sean listened. Voices arguing, but nothing about any ship. He sat back, paralysed by the fear of what he was about to do.

At 8 a.m. the driver turned the news up without being asked.

'Just in case I'm an accessory, mate,' he called back. He held up the watch. 'Still got a deal, though.' In the back, Sean listened equally attentively. He was rewarded, or punished, with the last item, an as yet unconfirmed report of a capsized cargo ship off the coast of Svalbard, travelling late in the season on the still-contentious TransPolar Route. Reports just coming in suggested fuel oil was already leaking into the water, threatening the pristine Arctic archipelago of Svalbard. The presenter hesitated, then with great excitement told of the latest report, that there had been a firefight between rival rescue teams. They would of course bring more details when they had them. They moved on to the environmental threat, the risks of shipping, and three, two, one, segued to the stagnant situation in Suez, before the sports news.

Sean stared out unseeing. A firefight between rival rescue teams. One would surely be Midgard. The other – probably Russian. Kingsmith left the Russians alone, even he knew his limitations. But if he was trafficking arms through Russian-contested territory – and the TransPolar Route ran right across the Lomonosov Ridge – then he might well prefer to lose the cargo than face that music. No wonder he wanted to get the ship to Icelandic waters. Or – Sean felt sick at the possibility – let it go down, rather than be exposed.

He wanted to weep at his own stupidity. But it wasn't just his: he was the trusting go-between, but Philip Stowe and Mrs Larssen imagined they'd bought themselves a guard-dog at Midgard – they were duped too. At least the Midgard clients were simply greedy and vain, delighted to feel they were worth a standing security detail of presidential calibre.

All he'd seen was the money multiplying from everything he did with Kingsmith, more than he could keep track of – and so he didn't. If Kingsmith told him something was good, it invariably was – financially. He'd had the freedom to do whatever he wanted with it, and what had he chosen?

Any and everything to claim his place at the top table, to feel secure. It was not enough to be married to a woman he had loved and whose background gave him status, not enough to be able to dishonourably indulge himself with the stream of beautiful women passing through his clubs. Not enough to be rich, to break bread with and profit massively from the appetites of the 1 per cent he catered to. Because nothing was ever enough.

You always were a greedy little bastard—

Kingsmith was right. And so was Tom, who had never really trusted Kingsmith, even that first night at the Randolph Hotel. His own frozen friend, ever ready to take on injustice and cruelty whenever he found it. But Sean had valued money and position more highly.

He caught the cabbie's eye in the mirror. They were now in the slow approach to Canterbury, where a state school gate was crowded with parents depositing their children, and the traffic crawled. Men and women were kissing their children goodbye. His vision was less blurry now, and he saw the pictures on the cabbie's dashboard – a young couple with two small children. Son and grandkids, he guessed. They were on the ring road outside the old city walls. Almost there. He braced himself for what was coming.

'*Svarten,*' alias '*Johansen's Friend,*' looked bad in the lantern-light. *Flesh and skin and entrails were gone; there was nothing to be seen but a bare breast and backbone, with some stumps of ribs. It was a pity that such a fine strong dog should come to such an end. He had just one fault: he was rather bad-tempered. He had a special dislike to Johansen; barked and showed his teeth whenever he came on deck, or even opened a door, and when he sat whistling in the top, or in the crow's nest these dark winter days, the 'Friend' would answer with a howl of rage from far out on the ice. Johansen bent down with the lantern to look at the remains.*

'Are you glad, Johansen, that your enemy is done for?'

'No, I am sorry.'

'Why?'

'Because we did not make it up before he died.'

And we went on to look for more bear-tracks, but found none; so we took the dead dogs on our backs and turned homewards.

Tuesday, 12 December 1893
Farthest North: The Norwegian Polar Expedition 1893–1896 (1897)
Fridtjof Nansen

34

The cabbie switched on the intercom.

'Say where.'

Sean looked out as they passed the street the court was on, and saw the white outside broadcast vans and a small crowd. 'Two more blocks.'

The cabbie went on, then pulled over. He had the watch on his wrist now.

'Can't change your mind.'

'I haven't.' Sean looked at the photograph on the dashboard. 'Is that your son? The one who loves watches?'

'Yeah.' A world of pride in that one syllable.

'Tell him to get a better dream.'

Sean got out and the cab pulled away almost as he slammed the door. He stood on the street, stunned by the sudden pain. The interior of the cab was limbo, it was unreal, but now he was here, the court was two blocks away. He didn't have to go, he could go to hospital instead. He felt the bruising and rawness and pulsing of what he was sure was his broken nose. He doubled over and was sick, traffic hooting at the debauched sight, at this decent family hour.

He didn't have to go through with it, he could call Martine – now he thought of her, in her green dress – the benefit – but he had never memorised her mobile number. He could go into any police station, any hospital – he found himself walking down the street to the grim-looking pub, the Feathers, where he and Sawbridge had gone a thousand years ago. He could stop here, for a moment.

The front door was shut but there was a side gate for deliveries, and before he could lose his nerve he stepped through into the brick court-yard. A radio was playing inside the building. He went closer. He could see into the kitchen. John Burnham was at the stove and his daughter Beth was at the yellow table eating cereal and checking her phone.

'What the—' John Burnham spun round, fists ready as Sean came in. Then he recognised him. 'Who did this?' Before Sean could answer, he went outside and looked around. Then he locked the gate to the street and came back.

'There's a ship sinking off the coast of Svalbard,' Beth said. 'It's on the news. Is that to do with you?'

'You wait a minute, miss,' said her father. He turned to Sean. 'What the fuck's going on? Why are you here?'

'You were a friend of Tom's. And I'm testifying again. I don't want to make trouble for you ...'

John Burnham stared at him. He sighed as he sat down. 'A friend of Tom's is a friend of mine.'

Sean felt his lip and saw the blood on his fingers. 'Do you need to warn anyone I'm here? I'm not too pretty.'

'Don't worry.' His daughter put a mug in front of Sean. 'It's a pub. We've seen worse. Milk?' She added it anyway.

Sean wanted to smile, but it would split his lip again. 'You're lucky,' he said to Burnham.

'When she's not gurning, or kicking off.' But there was love in his eyes. 'What's yours again? Rosie?'

'Yes. Did I tell you?'

'In the crypt.'

Now Sean remembered. The hands on his shoulders, the people around him. Talking to John about their daughters. That feeling that tore out of his chest, in great gasps.

'If you want to get there, I'll go with you.'

'And can I take your photograph? Can I write about it? Dad you know this is far more important than school, so don't even try.' Beth looked at Sean. 'It's the summing up now, isn't it?'

'Conclusion,' he said. 'Be accurate.'

'Conclusion. Thank you.' She took his picture with her phone. 'Seize your chances, that's what you said in your interview. Do you want to clean up? Or is it better all bloodstained? Bloodstained. Can I interview you?'

'Afterwards.' Sean closed his eyes.

At first the journalists and waiting crowd just saw the stocky figure of John Burnham striding down the street in his white trainers and jeans, beefy arms loose, Spurs supporter shirt tight over his barrel chest and belly. His slip of a daughter hurried alongside. It was only when they passed the first of the outside broadcast vans that anyone noticed the state of the man behind them, and who it was. First they stared, then they shouted.

'Mr Cawson! Sean! Sean, what happened? Sean, do you know anything about this ship? Sean, over here – can we have a word?'

John Burnham shoved their cameras and microphones back at them and Beth blocked their lenses with her schoolbag. A small crowd of young people clustered together in the street. Some had placards saying *Save the Arctic*. When they saw Sean, they ran towards him, their faces distorted with anger.

'Arctic poisoner!' shouted a girl, and someone else screamed 'Save the Arctic!' but John Burnham was well practised in crowd control. He opened his big arms wide and took up position on the steps, holding them back so that Sean could get into the court, but one girl darted through and grabbed Sean's arm.

'Dad, what have you done?' cried Rosie – and then she saw the state of him.

Sean threw his arm round her and John Burnham understood. He blocked the rest and Sean pulled his daughter into the lobby. They stared at each other.

'Dad.' Rosie's eyes were full of tears. 'You said you loved the Arctic.'

'I do. I'm going to make it right.'

'You can't!' she cried. 'There's no way—'

'There is.'

'Of course there is,' Sawbridge came forward, 'and I must say we're all very glad to see you. My god, London's getting so rough, I hope you reported it. Quite the panic, everyone looking for you.' He flashed a quick smile. 'You must be Rosie.'

'I want to speak to my father.' She was trembling.

'Of course, but we have a rather urgent matter in hand – Sean, a private word?'

'A ship is going down in the Arctic!' cried Rosie. 'What's more urgent than that!' Then she saw Martine running forward and her face hardened. Dressed for work and with evidence of crying, Martine pulled Sean from Rosie.

'Darling! I've been going crazy wondering where you are! Joe said you ran away – no one knew where you were – why didn't you call me?'

'No phone,' Sean said. 'That hurts where you're holding me.'

'Joe's been trying to find you – even Rupert's been calling the whole time.'

'Parch? Did he know about the ship?' Sean drew back. 'Do you?'

'Me? Of course not! I heard on the news, but it's got nothing to do with us. Has it?'

'Absolutely nothing.' Sawbridge stepped between Sean and Martine, and included Rosie in his caring authoritative look. He lowered his voice. 'Were they migrants, do you think?'

'*Migrants?* What are you talking about?'

'Chaps who attacked you. Or was it only one? Very brave to tackle you, but of course drugs do that. I've heard they hang around the best hotels, picking off the wealthy and well-refreshed. We really must give the police greater power—'

'Dad! Talk to me!'

'Your father's got a crisis to deal with.' Martine tried to be kind. 'You can see him later, I promise.'

'Don't tell me when I can see my father!'

'Ah, splendid, it's free.' Sawbridge threw open the door to the small meeting room they had used before, but before he could guide Sean in, Mr Thornton appeared.

The coroner stopped at the sight of him. 'Good grief, Mr Cawson. What on earth happened?'

'I have to testify again.' Sean felt the blood seep from his lip.

'He can't, Your Honour,' put in Sawbridge, 'you can see he's not fit to—'

'He needs to go to hospital at once,' Martine agreed.

'Shut up!' Rosie looked as if she were about to punch her. 'If that's what my dad wants—'

Sawbridge blocked Sean's way. 'It's PTSD, this poor man—'

'Mr Cawson will testify,' the coroner told his clerk. 'Any more? No? Good.' They went on.

'Please, dear chap,' Sawbridge implored Sean. 'It's been beyond abominable for you, but I beg you, don't waste it all now. We are so close. It's so nearly all over. Think of Tom's family, and what's kindest for them.'

'I am.' But Sean stepped inside. Martine followed, her phone in her hand.

'It's Rupert, he won't stop ringing me until I let him speak to you to prove you're alive.' She gave him her phone.

Sean took it. 'What.'

'Man alive, am I glad to hear you!' Parch sounded like he was outside somewhere windy. 'What the fuck happened? Martine says you were mugged outside the Carrington? London's like Mogadishu these days. Are you OK?' His voice seemed to move inside. 'Course you're not. Matey, you're beyond heroic, getting yourself back there, but it just proves you're off the scale. No one expects you to say another word, you need the best TLC money can buy. A car's on its way—'

'No.' Sean turned away from Sawbridge and Martine's intent gaze. He felt Rosie take his hand, and he squeezed it gently.

'*Yes*, matey,' said Parch. 'Because you've got PTSD, which rhymes with, get out of jail free. Do you understand what I'm saying?'

Sean glanced at Sawbridge, his debonair expression forgotten. He felt his daughter's hand in his. He kissed it.

'Tell me,' he said into the phone, 'so I do.'

'OK, listen: all the goodwill you have so brilliantly earned, truly you have, and all the rewards for which you are so truly deserving, are still yours if you'll only—'

'I won't. Goodbye.' Sean pressed the red button and returned Martine her phone. She stared at him in horror.

'Dear me.' Sawbridge shook his head. 'Sean, even if you senselessly throw yourself on Tom's publicity pyre, nothing will bring him back. It's not heroic, it's pure self-indulgence. You're deeply unwell, you're injured – you need help.'

'What's happened with that ship?' Sean slammed his hand down on the table so hard Sawbridge and Rosie jumped. Martine's eyes filled with angry tears.

'No one knows! I don't know, Nicholas doesn't know, it's only just been on the news! The *Zheng He* has nothing to do with us, and if it does then I've got fifteen per cent equity in a disaster and what are my investors going to say?'

'The *Zheng He*. You knew its name.' He almost laughed. 'Was it sabotage? Look how upset Joe got with me, when I suggested going public.'

'They said the name on the bloody radio! Sean, you're crazy. Surely you're not saying Joe did this to you? OK, you're done – I'm calling an ambulance—'

'Leave him alone!' Rosie stepped in front of her father.

'Security!' called Martine. 'We need help in here!'

'Rosie, stop it,' Sean said to her, as two stewards arrived.

'She needs to leave,' Martine told them.

'Don't touch my child.' Sean turned to Rosie. 'Now you can sit in court or—'

'Don't tell *me* what to do,' she cried. 'You've made this fucking mess.'

The stewards stood back to let her pass.

Just under two thousand miles away to the north, the stricken *Zheng He* lay on her side in the Barents Sea, off the coast of Svalbard. Helicopters from Longyearbyen, Barentsburg, Midgard Lodge threshed the freezing air above and harnessed news cameramen zoomed in as close as possible on the black seep spreading out across the water.

The closest vessel was the Sysselmann's new coastguard boat, and others bearing the Norwegian flag blocked the Russian tug and the two RIBs from Midgard Lodge, one of which was now disabled and roped to the other. A high wind stopped the sound of the conflicting tannoy shouts being intelligible to the news crews in the air, but it was clear that it was not a united rescue effort. The *Zheng He* reared up as if she would right herself – and then, very slowly, tipped up on her stern and began pointing her bow to the sky.

*

Outside, in the street directly below the windows of Court No. 1, a roar went up – and it was clear that the crowd of demonstrators had swelled. 'She's sinking! She's sinking!' And the boos started.

'There's nothing I can do about the noise,' Mr Thornton told his courtroom. 'And may I remind you all, that in this room we are strictly concerned with the events concerning the tragic death of Mr Thomas Walter Harding in Svalbard three years ago – and not this morning's news. As of 9 a.m. I was ready to deliver my conclusion, but between then and now, we have had an extraordinary request which I must grant. Mr Cawson has asked to make additional testimony, so thank you for your patience.'

'Dear chap,' murmured Sawbridge, 'I *implore* you. Let me handle it, it will all be all right. You're about to cross the finish line, it's all over—'

Sean stood. 'I'm ready.'

In the time it took for Sean Cawson to walk up the aisle and take the secular oath, the Sysselmann's vessels moved back, the Midgard boats and the Russian tug pushed even further away, guarded by every boat the coastguard had. Helicopters hung overhead, pulverising the air. Slowly, the bow of the *Zheng He* began to rise, so that at first it appeared that her 400-metre length was rising up out of the sea like a metal iceberg, the water cascading like skirts from her sides. She balanced upright on her stern for one long moment, and then as gracefully as she had risen, with news cameras her witnesses, she sank into the frigid deep of the Barents Sea.

And now from the far-away western horizon a fiery serpent writhed itself up over the sky, shining brighter and brighter as it came. It split into three, all brilliantly glittering. Then the colours changed. The serpent to the south turned almost ruby-red, with spots of yellow; the one in the middle, yellow; and the one to the north, greenish-white. Sheafs of rays swept along the sides of the serpents, driven through the ether-like waves before a storm-wind. They sway backwards and forward, now strong, now fainter again. The serpents reached and passed the zenith. Though I was thinly dressed and shivering with cold, I could not tear myself away till the spectacle was over, and only a faintly-glowing fiery serpent near the western horizon showed where it had begun.

Tuesday, 28 November 1893
Farthest North: The Norwegian Polar Expedition 1893–1896 (1897)
Fridtjof Nansen

35

In Court No. 1, Mr Allan Thornton studied the man on the stand.

'I'm very concerned by your physical state. Are you both mentally and physically fit enough to testify?'

'Of course he's not, look at him!' Sawbridge called out.

'I am.' Sean stood firm.

Ruth nodded, her eyes never leaving him. Beside her, Angela Harding and the family were like stone. On the press bench, the keys pattered. And then moments later, a great boo rose up from the street.

'Ignore it,' said the coroner. 'Go on.'

'Everything happened as I said,' Sean continued. 'But I left certain things out. When we went up for the eclipse, Tom discovered that we – my other partners and I – had a wider agenda for Midgard Lodge than he knew about. Ruth was right, he did find weapons.'

'*Yes!*' she said, and he saw in her eyes she was willing him on.

'I tried to explain they were for the good – because I was allowing Midgard to be used as a base to help Norway gather intelligence on Russia—'

'Intelligence gathering?' The coroner leaned forward.

'Not personally. But I enabled it.' Sean avoided Martine's burning glare. Sawbridge had his hand over his mouth. Mrs Osman sat calmly as her two aides made rapid notes. The only person in the room he felt connected to was Ruth. Her clear gaze steadied his freefall. *Don't stop now.* He nodded to her.

'I agreed to use the cover of our in-house security to host a small private militia, which I arranged through Joe Kingsmith and which would be available to the Norwegian government should they need it. Tom was furious. He was going to publicly denounce it and withdraw his name.'

He saw Martine whisper in Sawbridge's ear and Sawbridge push her back, intently focused on his client's self-destruction. Mrs Osman put up her hand.

'Absolutely not – Mr Cawson, please go on.'

'Ruth Mott met Joe Kingsmith when we all went to the restaurant in Longyearbyen. Greenland came up, and his business interests – his mining, and they got in an argument. Next day, Tom saw the strong room and he thought the worst.'

'Meaning?'

'He thought I'd deceived him. But we didn't get to that because we never got to talk properly. We went to the ice-cave and ...' Sean stopped and wiped a hand over his forehead.

'Mr Cawson, your face is bleeding. You need medical—'

'Afterwards.' Sean touched his lip where it had opened again. The clerk passed him a few tissues and he took them. 'I found out last night about the *Zheng He* being in trouble near Midgard Lodge.' He stopped on the brink.

You always were a greedy little bastard.

'I believe it's carrying arms.'

'Darling, stop! You're not well!' Martine stared at him in disbelief.

'Shut up.' Ruth Mott looked at her with such fury that Martine sat back out of her eyeline. Mrs Osman put her hand up again and the coroner allowed her to stand.

'Mr Cawson, this is very courageous of you. But are you telling us that the ship ... the *Zheng He* ...' and Mrs Osman looked at her phone, 'which has just been confirmed ... as sunk, was connected with Midgard Lodge?'

'I believe my backer Joe Kingsmith was using it to transport weapons to the Central African Republic and South Sudan, via the port of Bissau.'

'PTSD, you know,' Sawbridge said, to anyone who'd listen. 'Terrible cross.'

'I believe it loads in the Chinese port of Dalian.' Sean looked over to the press bench. He felt a grim satisfaction at meeting their eyes.

'Which is where our other partner, Radiance Young, owns a wharf. I believe Joe Kingsmith uses it in the supply of weapons and their components, including 3D printers, to several end users. One is Radiance and I believe another is a man from the Central African Republic called Benoit. I believe Joe Kingsmith's main business is private militias, supporting Chinese corporations as they expand in certain African countries where he has interests. The Central African Republic for one, South Sudan another. I believe he might have been involved in Guinea Bissau when I first met him, in 1988. Because of my own greed and stupidity, I've been his unwitting assistant since that time.' Sean forced himself on. 'I think *Zheng He* was carrying chemical weapons.'

The press bench was so stunned that for several seconds they did nothing – and then their fingers clattered and raced. Some got their phones out and started making calls. One journalist – Sean's old enemy – raised his hands and clapped slowly.

'I haven't finished.' Sean gripped the stand, rushing with adrenaline. 'I thought Tom was naïve and he thought I was corrupt. We were both right, but now I realise I was naïve as well. We were so angry with each other that we missed the signs in the cave. I said I helped him, but it was the other way round. It always was.'

Sean and Tom hear the groan and creak in the ice before they feel the sliding planes around them. With one long ripping sound the floor of ice splits apart, the two sides peel away from each other, and from above stalactites plummet and shatter against the sides of the chasm as they fall. Sean is on one side, Tom the other. A great chunk of ice drops, wedging across the top of the break.

'Quickly,' Tom whispers, shining his head torch on it. 'Crawl over now, while you still can.' Sean stares as the bridging block slowly begins to slip.

'Don't look down, look at me,' Tom calls to him. 'Over here—' He reaches out and they grab each other in the hand-to-forearm boat grip. Tom pulls Sean across. They haul themselves back towards the passageway – but everything has changed.

'You're still a lying shit,' Tom pants to him as they go, 'don't think you're not. Nothing's changed when we get out.'

Sean stopped speaking. His hands were freezing. His legs shook and he could feel the surge of the drug breaking down in his brain. Then he saw a face at the back of the courtroom, Gail was there, looking at him steadily, as if she had come to his execution and would not look away. He would die properly then.

'We started to go back,' he said, 'and we knew we had to be quick because there was water coming in from somewhere, it was flowing, and I couldn't believe it because Tom started asking me about the Lodge again, and what else I was hiding, and what was Kingsmith hiding, he wasn't letting go of it even when we might both die – that was what he was like.'

The odd sound was Ruth clapping, standing up, her face wet with tears, nodding at him. *Keep going.*

'We were both so angry with each other, even in this situation, but we kept going on, Tom kept saying "*Fram*" like we used to, *Forward*, like he wasn't frightened at all. He said we were going to get out, *he* was going to get out because he wanted to get back to Ruth.'

He saw her put her arms around herself and close her eyes.

'We felt one of the plastic grip tiles and we knew we were closer to getting out and then everything goes sideways, the whole thing collapses again and Tom's shouting where he's wedged so he doesn't drop, and I've found a rope in the wall, I grab hold of it with my left hand and I reach for him with the other.'

'Here, Tom.' Sean reaches out his right hand, but not quite far enough. His wavering head-torch beam is on Tom's face. 'But first promise not to say anything. Give me your word. When I explain it to you—'

'Give me your fucking hand!'

'I will, just promise me—'

Tom falls. Sean's beam arcs down into blackness. He calls out. Again, again, louder. There is no reply.

Sean fixed his gaze on the back wall of the courtroom, unable to meet a single pair of eyes. His right hand was tingling. Not from frostbite, he knew that now. From what he had not done. He felt about to burst into flames. 'I killed Tom. Not deliberately. But I did.'

In the silence in the courtroom Granny Ruby slowly got to her feet. 'Shame on you,' she said, and her voice was small but as piercing as her eyes. Outside, the booing started again. A mob sound.

'Silence! Everyone!' The coroner stood and addressed Sean. 'Mr Cawson, you are telling the court, you are telling me, that you delayed rendering aid to Mr Harding, in order to attempt to elicit his promise not to say what he had witnessed at Midgard Lodge?'

'Yes.' Sean closed his eyes a moment. 'Tom would not have got involved if he'd known the true scope of what we were doing. And had I known the extent of Joe Kingsmith's other activities, I would not have accepted his investment.'

'Irrelevant, irrelevant, irrelevant!' Sawbridge had had enough and was on his feet as well. 'Your Honour, I move that it is impossible to know if my client could or could not have saved Mr Harding's life, despite his desire to throw himself on his sword, and that because of my client's post-traumatic stress disorder—'

'Mr Sawbridge, sit down—'

'—he is incapable of distinguishing truth from paranoia and is completely delusional. He is suffering from a psychotic disturbance!'

'Must I have you removed?' Mr Thornton shouted it, and Sawbridge sat down. Mrs Osman raised her hand and the coroner permitted her to stand.

'Mr Cawson,' she said quietly. 'I admire your courage. And I am legally bound to tell you that, if you answer my questions, those answers might cause this inquest to be moved, in the public interest, to a criminal trial.'

'I understand. I accept.'

'Are you financially involved with the ship the *Zheng He*, now sunk off the coast of Svalbard, and which you believe is carrying chemical weapons across the TransPolar Route?'

'Yes.'

'You also said you are complicit in allowing Midgard Lodge to be used for intelligence gathering by Norway on Russian activity in the Svalbard archipelago. Are you willing to expand on this?'

'Yes. It was with the approval of Philip Stowe, the British Defence Secretary, and Skadi Larssen, Assistant Minister for Defence, in Oslo. She said Norway was very concerned about Russian expansionism, she said many countries were. We met at the arms fair in London in November, three or four years ago. I brought Kingsmith in on it, but he and Stowe also know each other. I believe I was the go-between.'

He wondered how he could still be standing there, alive. Mrs Osman held his eyes, and he felt her support.

'Do you also have a theory about the cause of this shipping disaster?'

Mr Thornton appeared to have forgotten what was relevant and what was not, and leaned forward for the answer. Sean nodded.

'I believe it ran into trouble in a storm, but, Joe preferred to let it sink rather than report it in distress and have the cargo exposed. He wanted me to think it would cause a massive diplomatic incident. But it was to protect himself.'

The tapping of the press bench went out almost live, online. Outside on the street a hundred smart phones picked it up and the chant rose, loud and angry in the courtroom.

Eco-cide! Eco-cide!

Sean felt the liberation of self-destruction. There was nothing more to hide.

'My meeting with Philip Stowe was arranged by Rupert Parch, his private secretary. He implied I'd get a knighthood for my trouble. At one time, I wanted it.' He found Gail's eyes. 'I wanted stupid, empty things.'

'Sean!' called Martine. 'You're delirious!' She twisted round to see what he was looking at, and saw Gail. 'Did you ask her to come?'

'No.' Sean looked at Martine as if seeing her for the first time.

'You've got no business here,' she called out to Gail.

'Miss Delaroche, you will please leave the court,' said Mr Thornton. 'Now.'

'Fine. But there's something I need to do first.' Martine stood up and turned to Osman. 'You wanted this to happen. You're evil.' She flung the contents of her water glass in the barrister's face and strode towards Gail. 'And you did too, didn't you? You've always wanted to destroy us.' Martine's face tightened. 'Answer me!'

Gail didn't look at her, but nodded to the stewards. As they took a step forward, Martine's eyes burned hatred at Gail – then she stormed out.

Everyone's eyes returned to the extraordinary spectacle of Mrs Osman carefully slicking down her wet hair and standing up straight. The hunch was gone, and her face, though still unusual in its stark bone-structure, was rather beautiful. Nor was she as old as Sean first thought. Meeting her eyes, he saw the amusement in them, before she turned back to the coroner.

'Your Honour, I believe we have heard enough to request a verdict of unlawful killing, and that it is without question in the wider public interest that this inquest be moved to a criminal court.' She looked around. 'I don't expect Mr Kingsmith is available today? No, I rather thought not.'

Sawbridge, slightly recovered, did a half push-up.

'Your Honour, might I cross-examine my own client? As everything is so highly irregular?'

'Please.'

Sawbridge waited until Mrs Osman sat.

'Now, Sean,' he said gently, 'you've been having psychiatric treatment for PTSD, haven't you? You've suffered hallucinations. Remember? In that restaurant? And panic attacks on the Underground—'

'I never told you that.' But he had told Jenny Flanders.

'Memory lapses, confusion – fact is, you're *not* a competent witness. I think His Honour and even my learned friend Mrs Osman can see that. Survivor's guilt is one of the most pernicious burdens facing our returning armed forces. Who here hasn't put a note in the bucket for Help for Heroes? In his own way, Sean Cawson has served his country and paid the price. Shouldn't we respect his sacrifice? Let's remember both Sean and Tom shared a lifetime's obsession for the Arctic and both knew the risks. That was part of the appeal! Yes, they had political differences; yes, they argued, but at the end of the day even heroes can die, and that's what's so hard for Sean to accept. That's why he's trying to make himself responsible for everything that ever went wrong. Survivor's guilt.'

Sean looked to Mrs Osman.

'I stand by everything I said.'

In the silence, the coroner drew a deep breath.

'The court will recess for fifteen minutes.' As he walked out, the courtroom burst into noise.

Sean couldn't hear anything as he walked down the aisle; he felt half dead but it was not unpleasant. The stares no longer bothered him. Gail stood up as he reached her. They regarded each other in silence. He saw the delicate lines around her eyes, her mouth, he saw her neck, her breasts, the small knots of gold in her earlobes – the girl inside the woman.

'You haven't changed.'

'You have. Well done, Sean.' Her smile broke his heart. Before he could answer, Sawbridge took him by the arm.

'Terribly sorry, but the moment is critical – Sean, you must come now.'

'Wait,' he said. She nodded.

He stood with Sawbridge in the small room. The angry chanting floated up. *Eco-cide! Save the Arctic!* He forced open the window, peering down into the street where police had arrived to manage the situation.

'Something far more urgent here, old chap.' Sawbridge held up his phone. 'Let's see: don't believe anything until it's been officially denied twice – we're way past that. Denials flying in all directions, official rebuttal of all your "specious claims" from Stowe's office – already online so you know it's serious. Yep, google-translated in every country in which you've got us into the deepest diplomatic excrement. Ah, here we are, British trade talks with the Sino-Arctic Alliance suspended – aren't you clever? Just from one stupid, undisciplined outburst. All this fuss. I'm your counsel, did you even think how it would reflect on me?'

Sawbridge wound up with a quick, pained grin. 'Never mind, worse things happen at sea, don't they just.' He glanced at his phone screen, flashing with incoming emails. 'And completely par for the course, the Sysselmann's office in Svalbard has questioned the legality of your ownership. Midgard personnel in altercation with Russian search and rescue from the Arktik Dacha – all Greek to me, but maybe means something to you? – yes, and here we go, links to more outrage – you're trending, Sean! All the fame you can handle. Nobody's cared for years about the flouting of the Svalbard Treaty until you show them up as a bunch of hypocrites. You didn't mean to, I know; you were just playing geopolitics with your Lego, and now you're in all this trouble.' Sawbridge squinted at the screen. 'Aha. Someone I think you know.'

He turned his phone to Sean, where a YouTube clip played: a furious Skadi Larssen denying everything in Norwegian, with English subtitles. He winked. 'Honey trap, was it? Must say, I'd probably fall for it too—'

Sean knocked the phone from his hand. A tiny angry Skadi spun on the floor. Sawbridge picked his phone up and examined it sadly.

'I'll add it to the bill. Be a good chap and pay me before the deluge of all your other costs comes in, won't you? Much obliged.' He peered into the crazed screen. 'More emails, oh dear, so many from our mutual friend Rupert Parch – you seem to have greatly upset him. But he really shouldn't cc me.' Sawbridge brushed a few invisible specks from his jacket. 'Shall we agree that I'm not the best representation for you going forward? Excellent.' He looked at his watch. 'Tell you what, we'll stop the clock yesterday. Do excuse me, and the very best of luck with everything.'

Sean sat alone in the small cell of a room, with the flat-pack furniture and the damp-curled carpet tiles, and the blue upholstered chairs. His face and body hurt, but it was nothing compared to the pain in his heart. Outside, the chants were louder – the crowd had grown. He looked at the blank space on his wrist. He hoped the cabbie's son would be happy. He felt grateful to John Burnham and his fiery daughter.

And to Rosie – he felt a flush of love at the thought of his daughter who had come back to him, violently angry though she still was. He burst out of the room in search of her, straight into Mr Thornton, Mrs Osman, Ruth and the Harding family, heading back in for the summing up. He halted, waiting for the abuse to fall on him – but instead Ruth put her hand on his arm. Angela Harding looked him in the eye. 'Thank you, Sean,' she said quietly, and walked on with her mother-in-law. Sean followed behind, with Ruth.

'It's not true, you know,' she said. 'You did help Tom. When you spoke for him, when he was too drunk, when you stopped Redmond from hurting him more in Greenland. When you told him not to care what people thought, to do what he wanted with his life. He told me those stories so many times. Sean, he loved you.'

Granny Ruby turned. 'And you loved him. We saw that.'

They went in. Mr Thornton entered a silent courtroom full of standing people. The Harding group went to one side, but Sean, now alone, walked to his empty row. No Martine, no Sawbridge. Gail remained at the back, Rosie by her side.

Mr Thornton was brief. Despite Mr Cawson's astonishing and, he agreed, most courageous testimony, he had not changed his opinion.

If there were evidence that Mr Cawson had wilfully let Mr Harding die, there would be a case for unlawful killing. But it was his belief that, although Mr Cawson made a morally unwise attempt to coerce Mr Harding into a promise under extreme circumstances, he had neither wished his death nor sought it in any way.

It was also Mr Thornton's belief that Mr Harding, whilst he might not have become involved in the Midgard Lodge purchase bid had he been in possession of all the facts, was nevertheless experienced in Arctic travel, and knew its risks. He had entered the ice-cave of his own volition.

He was therefore of the considered opinion that Tom Harding lost his life due to the proven collapse of the Midgardbreen ice-cave system, most probably due to the pervasive action of meltwater on the ice cap above. This was arguably an effect of climate change but even if so, and he believed it was, that was not in itself a direct cause of Mr Harding's death.

He also stated for the record that Mr Harding's body was believed irretrievably lost in the ice-cave on the date of the accident, until it was revealed by further action of the glacier, in the calving witnessed by the passengers of the cruise ship *Vanir* – at which point it was recovered.

But – and Mr Thornton looked at Sean as he said this – given Mr Cawson's new testimony, and the wider events in the world, namely today's sinking of the cargo ship the *Zheng He* off the coast of Svalbard, he believed a further investigation into the activities and partners of Midgard Lodge was warranted.

He waited until the sound of cheering and applause from the street died down and then looked to the press bench.

'Are you transmitting this live?'

They all nodded. At the back, Beth Burnham also raised her hand to be counted.

'Whilst I therefore return a narrative conclusion to this inquest, that the cause of death of Mr Thomas Walter Harding be recorded as Nature Unknown, I also recommend that the entire body of evidence I have collected in this process be moved on to criminal investigation, as requested by Mrs Ursula Osman, KC.'

Ruby Harding rose to her feet applauding, joined by a number of people in the court, the sound drowned out by the roar from the crowd in the street below.

Mr Thornton and his clerk left in a sweep of robes, the courtroom burst with noise and movement, but Sean stood where he was. Someone came up to take his photograph with a phone but Gail pushed the phone aside.

'Leave my husband alone.'

That phrase brought Sean back. He looked at her.

'Slip of the tongue,' she said. 'Need a lift? I've got my car at the back.'

He felt as slow as a dream, the Rohypnol spiking again. 'Where's Rosie gone?'

'Outside. She knows some of those people.'

'Gail ...' He saw the lines around her eyes, he wanted to touch them. 'Would you bring the car round there? I have to do something first.'

When she'd gone, the clerks and security guards allowed Sean a moment alone in the courtroom to collect himself. He stood in the empty space, the mints spilled on the floor, the disordered chairs, his own toxic sweat. He sat down and put his face in hands that no longer burned. It was over.

The crowd were chanting for him. The ugly sound swelled as they saw him coming through the lobby but Sean stepped straight out onto the steps.

An egg broke against his shoulder, then another one. People jeered and booed and he wondered why the police weren't there – but they were. There were just so many protestors – hundreds more had arrived, some with placards and masks, others whose fresh young faces opened and closed in angry shouts he couldn't quite hear. For a moment it all swam in brightness and he felt the drug still in his system. Even the young could look ugly, if they were angry enough. He picked out the word Arctic in their chants and screams.

'Arctic,' he repeated, trying to bring himself back from the dangerous haze on the edge of everything. 'The Arctic,' he said. He heard another word. 'Ecocide.'

Arc-tic! Eco-cide! A heavy paper cup hit him, and the coffee smelled good.

He recognised a red jacket and a friendly face in the crowd – of course it was Tom, Sean was pleased to see him. He waved. Young and handsome, Tom waved back, holding something up. Something brown and pointed. Sean recognised it. The shit chisel. He held up his own imaginary one, and thinking he was addressing them, the crowd shouted louder.

'Let him speak!' Armed with a megaphone, Rosie furiously elbowed her way out of the crowd and joined her father on the steps. 'Just shut the fuck up for a minute,' she said through it, his warrior daughter and human shield. Sean gazed at her in wonder as she handed him the megaphone. 'Quick,' she said under her breath, 'if you're going to.'

'You're right to be angry,' Sean called out to them. 'I've been stupid and greedy and blind, I've betrayed and lost my best friend, and I've destroyed everything I've touched. And the *Zheng He* has sunk—'

He waited for the noise to die down, 'But I am going to cooperate in every way I can to make sure this cannot happen again, and I'm going to do it in a criminal court. And I want as many of you there as will fit in, I want you in the room because Tom can't be there. And I don't want there to be a conservation bequest in his name. I want there to be no need for one.'

To his surprise, there was a smattering of applause. He looked at the crowd of young people holding up their phones recording his shame. But standing there with his daughter who had returned to him, and his wife – she still was – coming for him, he felt the opposite. As if some burden he hadn't known he carried was lifting.

A mineral white BMW drove up the street, slowly parting the crowd. It took a moment to recognise the woman at the wheel as Gail. He went down the steps, Rosie by his side, flashes going off in his face. He climbed in.

'I'm staying.' Rosie had tears in her eyes as she smiled. 'You did good, Dad.' Quickly, she leaned in and kissed his cheek, then slammed the door. Gail clicked the locks as photographers tried to block them for more pictures. She drove slowly into them and they jumped back, cursing. Sean looked at her in amazement. She shrugged.

He moved around in the seat and fiddled with the controls. Something occurred to him. Some tall bastard had sat here, with long legs. Gail's lips twitched, as she understood what he was processing. She had had a lover. Maybe she still did. Sean was harpooned by jealousy.

She pulled out onto the ring road and they drove in busy silence for a while.

'Rosie called me Dad again.'

'I heard.'

Neither was aware of the black Vauxhall Insignia following two cars behind.

'Where shall I take you?'

'Home.'

'I'm not going to bloody London—'

'Nor am I.'

She looked at him a moment. 'Sean – you can't just come back like that.'

'No. I know.' He waited a moment. 'Is the tall bastard still around?'

Gail did laugh now, but she didn't answer. They drove on in silence for several miles. He recognised the roads. He looked at his watch, or the space where it had been.

'Do you mind if we have the news?'

She turned it on. The environmental disaster of the *Zheng He* was now the top story and the Ministry of Defence had issued a denial of the shocking allegations at the inquest of respected environmentalist Tom Harding—

Sean looked out at the familiar fields, the hedges, the fences, as the news presenter explained about the environmental integrity of Svalbard, the suspension of British businessman Sean Cawson's troubled Arctic venture ...

There was the Acorn, the beautiful country pub where they hadn't been in years, he would like to go there again—

... *investigations to be carried out over a suspected breach of the Svalbard Treaty ... trade relations ... historic allies ...*

Sean didn't care that the Russian ambassador had already made a formal complaint in London, he didn't care if he never walked into a smart party again, if all the grand doors in grand houses owned by grand people slammed in his face – because what mattered was that his daughter had grown up while he wasn't looking but that now she had come back to him. What mattered was that he was with Gail again and the band around his chest, that he hadn't even known was there, was gone and he could breathe again. He recognised the roads, and the trees, and the fields as they sped home in her new car. And he was going to make her happy again, and come back from the ice and finally deserve her love.

In another, chauffeur-driven car, Martine and Sawbridge sped back to London in silence, listening to the same news, caring very much about the formal complaint by the Russian ambassador, and the mention of Midgard Lodge. In an office overlooking Whitehall, whilst checking three other screens and writing an email on a fourth, so did Rupert Parch, his eyes not remotely merry, and his disposition far from playful.

*

344

Cruising at 36,000 feet, Joe Kingsmith cut into a blue steak, three phones and two laptops open beside his plate. Occasionally he swept them all with a glance. Nothing.

In Canterbury, the Feathers pub was doing uncharacteristically brisk business for the hour, as activists and journalists crammed in, and John Burnham had put the football flat-screen on to watch the breaking news about the ship. In the hubbub, Ruth Mott and Rosie Cawson sat together, both tearstained, and drinking pints. Ruth had her arm around Rosie, and Rosie had her phone out, listening and nodding while Ruth spoke.

Sean sat back as Gail drove. In his wing-mirror he saw a black saloon approaching fast, indicating to overtake. Gail glanced up in the rear-view mirror and saw it too. How extraordinary that he felt no pain about Martine. She had abandoned him in court, but he felt nothing, not even anger. Yet to leave Gail had been agony only trumped by lust. Sean saw as the black car overtook that it was a Vauxhall Insignia. Its brake lights glared red, it suddenly skewed to the side and Gail hauled on the wheel – but it skewed again, forcing them the other way – their speed too fast and the road too narrow to miss the long drystone wall. The impact hurled the BMW into the air.

Ah, sighed Anaralunguaq, *and we used to think Nature was the greatest and most wonderful of all! Yet here we are among mountains and great gulfs and precipices, all made by the work of human hands.*

*

The BMW crashed down on its roof, activating its on-board emergency satellite communication. Two hundred miles above the road accident it reported, that information was beamed back down to earth, and the relevant civic authorities.

Nature is great; Sila, as we call it at home; nature, the world, the universe, all that is Sila; which our wise men declared they could hold in poise. And I could never believe it, but I see it now. Nature is great, but are not men greater?

Four hundred metres down the road, where the drystone wall ended and the road curved around, the driver of a Dutch-registered eighteen-wheeler had stopped for a break in a layby. As the oncoming Vauxhall flashed its lights, two men inside opened the rear doors and dropped the hinged ramp. The Vauxhall drove in and braked hard. They pulled up the ramp and closed the doors. The lorry drove away.

The wheels of the BMW spun slowly to a halt. Nothing moved but the wind.

One of Kingsmith's phones flashed. Still chewing, he slid it towards him. A blank text from a UK number. He deleted it then signalled the steward for more wine.

In the press, on social media, in Chatham House, in bars, in cafés, even in Highgrove House (where the King was hosting an interdisciplinary debate on the role of monarchy and the wilderness) speculation raged over the connection between the sinking of the *Zheng He* and the death of environmentalist Tom Harding.

Those tiny beings we can see down there far below, hurrying this way and that. They live among these stone walls; on a great plain of stone made with hands. Stone and stone and stone – there is no game to be seen anywhere, and yet they manage to live and find their daily food.

On the floor of the Barents Sea, the steel hull of the *Zheng He* settled into the swirling sediment. Her oil, and other substances lighter than water, continued to leak out into the darkness, towards the troubled gyres of the seven seas.

Have they then learned of the animals, since they can dig down under the earth like marmots, hang in the air like spiders, fly like birds and dive under water like the fishes; seemingly masters of all that struggled against ourselves?

Inside the inverted vehicle, a human voice speaks from the onboard computer, assuring the driver that BMW have been informed of the collision and location, and that assistance is on its way. A rap ringtone interrupts, coming through the car's digital system.

Gail manages to reach up and press the button on the steering wheel.

'Hi.' She's hoarse, and gasping. The remote voice coming from somewhere in the car continues to reassure the passengers.

'Mum?' says Rosie's voice. 'Dad, can you hear me? What's that noise? I've got major anxiety about my dysfunctional parents – but I just want you to know I love you both.'

Sean reaches out to hold Gail's shoulder. The blown airbags make it difficult. He clenches back a gasp of pain. 'We love you too.'

'Rosie,' Gail calls out. 'Remember, deep breaths.'

I see more things than my mind can grasp; and the only way to save oneself from madness is to suppose that we have all died suddenly before we knew, and that this is part of another life.

The mineral white BMW blocks the road, emergency lights flashing. Motorists have stopped to help, traffic is starting to back up. Inside it, Sean and Gail have found each other's hand. Sirens wail. They hold on.

AUTHOR'S NOTE

Since the fourteenth century, men have sought a northern maritime trade route between Europe and what was once known as Cathay; the Far East. Countless sums and lives have been spent in its pursuit.

The end of the Arctic summer sea ice means that finally, the long-sought TransPolar trade route directly over the North Pole is now open; through the 1.1 million square miles of the international waters of the Arctic Ocean – covered with permanent ice for all of human history, until now.

Distance savings compared with traditional trade routes using the Suez or Panama canals, can be as high as 35 per cent. And with possible closures to both these historic routes due to political instability, traffic across the TransPolar Route increases every day.

A VERY PARTIAL BIBLIOGRAPHY

Bones, Stian and Petia Mankova (eds.), *Norway and Russia in the Arctic: conference proceedings from the international conference 'Norway and Russia in the Arctic', Longyearbyen, 25–28 August 2009* (University of Tromsø, 2010)

Byock, Jesse L. (tr.), *The Saga of the Volsungs: The Norse Epic of Sigurd the Dragon Slayer* (Penguin, 1990)

Chapman, F. Spencer, *Northern Lights: The Official Account of the British Arctic Air-Route Expedition 1930–1931* (Chatto & Windus, 1932)

Davis, Wade, *The Wayfinders: Why Ancient Wisdom Matters in the Modern World* (House of Anansi Press, 2009)

Gearheard, Shari Fox *et al.*, *The Meaning of Ice: People and Sea Ice in Three Arctic Communities* (International Polar Institute Press; University Press of New England, 2013)

Emmerson, Charles, *The Future History of the Arctic* (PublicAffairs, 2010)

Freuchen, Peter, *Arctic Adventure: My Life in the Frozen North* (William Heinemann Ltd, 1936)

Freuchen, Peter (tr. Johan Hambro), *Vagrant Viking: My Life and Adventures* (J. Messner, 1953)

Henson, Matthew, *A Negro Explorer at the North Pole: The Autobiography of Matthew Henson* (F. Stokes, 1912)

Horwitz, Joshua, *War of the Whales: A True Story* (Simon & Schuster, 2014)

Klein, Naomi, *This Changes Everything: Capitalism vs. the Climate* (Penguin, 2014)

Lindsay, Martin, *Sledge: The British Trans-Greenland Expedition 1934* (Cassell & Co., 1935)

Lopez, Barry Holstun, *Arctic Dreams: Imagination and Desire in a Northern Landscape* (Scribner, 1986)

Malaurie, Jean (tr. Gwendolen Freeman), *The Last Kings of Thule: A Year Among the Polar Eskimos of Greenland* (George Allen & Unwin Ltd, 1956)

McFate, Sean, *The Modern Mercenary: Private Armies and What They Mean for World Order* (Oxford University Press, 2014)

McGhee, Robert, *The Last Imaginary Place: A Human History of the Arctic World* (University of Chicago Press, 2007)

Mikkelsen, Captain Ejnar, *Lost in the Arctic: Being the story of the 'Alabama' Expedition 1909–12* (William Heinemann Ltd, 1913)

Nansen, Dr. Fridtjof, *Farthest North: The Norwegian Polar Expedition 1893–1896* (Archibald Constable & Co., 1897)

Ovsyanikov, Nikita, *Polar Bears: Living with the White Bear* (Swan Hill Press, 1996)

Peary, Robert E., *The North Pole* (Hodder & Stoughton, 1910)

Rasmussen, Knud, *Across Arctic America: Narrative of the Fifth Thule Expedition* (G. P. Putnam's Sons, 1927)

Scoresby, William, *An Account of the Arctic Regions: With a History and Description of the Northern Whale-Fishery* (Archibald Constable & Co., 1820)

Scott, Jeremy, *Dancing on Ice: A 1930s Arctic Adventure* (Old Street Publishing, 2008)

Singer, P. W., *Corporate Warriors: The Rise of the Privatized Military Industry* (Cornell University Press, 2003)

Smiley, Jane (ed.), *The Sagas of the Icelanders* (Penguin, 2001)

Stirling, Ian, *Polar Bears: The Natural History of a Threatened Species* (Bloomsbury, 2012)

Wadhams, Peter, *A Farewell to Ice: A Report from the Arctic* (Allen Lane, 2016)

Wheeler, Sara, *The Magnetic North: Notes from the Arctic Circle* (North Point Press, 2009)

Wormdal, Bård, *The Satellite War* (CreateSpace Independent Publishing Platform, 2011)

Worsley, Frank Arthur and Grettir Algarsson, *Under Sail in the Frozen North: The Log of the 1926 British Arctic Expedition* (Stanley Paul & Co., 1927)

ACKNOWLEDGEMENTS

This book was written with the support of a great many people. It is now my pleasure to thank: At 4th Estate Books, David Roth-Ey and Helen Garnons-Williams; Michelle Kane, Matt Clacher and Paul Erdpresser; Lottie Fyfe, Anne O'Brien and Tom Killingbeck; Jo Walker for the beautiful cover, and Chris Wormell for the woodcuts inside.

Thank you to my agents Simon Trewin and Dorian Karchmar, and to the Royal Society of Literature for the Brookleaze Grant, which I used towards research travel to Svalbard. When I got there Frigg and Frank Jorgensen showed me generous hospitality, gave me connections and rifle training; Arild Lyssand gave me invaluable research information throughout my process; my warmest thanks to all of them. Thanks in Svalbard also to Jason Roberts, Tom Foreman and Mark Sabbatini for Arctic guidance in many forms, and to Captain Daniel Rizzotti, Mikael Arman, Dima Litvinov and Arne Sorensen for hospitality aboard the Greenpeace ship *Esperanza*.

This book has benefited from the collected wisdom of the following authorities in their fields, and all errors and omissions in the text are mine alone. It is my pleasure to thank: Dr Peter Wadhams and the Scott Polar Research Institute in Cambridge; Rear Admiral John Kingwell and Mrs Alison Kingwell; Mr Michael Kingston, insurance representative at the International Maritime Organisation on the finalisation of the Polar Code; Mr Alan Kessel, Canadian Deputy High Commissioner in London; Mr Charles Emmerson, Senior

Research Fellow, Chatham House; Professor Klaus Dodds, Professor of Geopolitics at Royal Holloway College, University of London; Judge Rüdiger Wolfrum, member of the International Tribunal for the Law of the Sea; Mr Robin Hepburn; Mr Rod Downie of the World Wildlife Fund and Mr Geoff York of Polar Bears International; and my thanks again to polar scientists Dr Tom Smith, Dr Jon Aars, Dr Lily Peacock, Dr Christian Sonne and Dr Kristin Lairdre. I must also thank those individuals who, on condition of anonymity, confirmed the plausibility of one story element; also that truth is indeed stranger than fiction.

For permission to use her real performance as a cameo in this novel, I thank Polaris and Mercury prize-winner Tanya Tagaq, and for further insight into Inuit culture of Nunavut, I thank Mataalii Okalik. I also thank Peter Freuchen's grandson Peter Ittinuar, and his great-grand-daughter, Natalie Ittinuar, for their support.

Though he will not now read this book as he hoped, I owe thanks to Peter Cawson, one of the unsung heroes of the Polarati. In return for tea and fruitcake on Thursday afternoons in his funny little shop in St Leonards-on-Sea, he dug out rare old Arctic books and told me stories. Thank you to Beannie Nicholson for baking the best, and thank you too, Natascha Lampert, and Nick Foulkes.

For inspiration and support, I thank Clare Reihill, Jay Griffiths, Cal Moriarty, Clare Carlin, Anna Orenstein, Paul Dornan, Isabelle Grey, Liz Jensen, Ruth Gravelle, Natasha Bishopp, Maggie Doherty, Tessa Boase and Hattie Ellis. For patience and love during the writing process I thank all my family but particularly my mother and my daughter India Rose.

Lastly, I thank my husband Adrian Peacock, who ran base-camp and dangerous rescue missions like a true hero.